ARDLEA WRITERS' GROUP BIOGRAPHIES

William Rocke: Editor, on whose original idea 'Last Tango In Ibiza' is based. Journalist, author and playwright. He was Deputy News Editor, Chief Sub-Editor and Reporter with the Sunday Press until its closure in 1995. He formed the Ardlea Writers' Group in Artane in 1998 Whence 'Last Tango....originated. Recently completed his second novel 'All To Play For' set in the world of big-time golf.

Joan Barrett: A native of Drumlish, Co. Longford, Joan is a widow and mother of seven grown up children. She has had a varied career from teaching in Ireland and England to owning and managing a bar in Florida. Joan has had numerous articles published both in Ireland and the U.S. She lives with her son in Artane on Dublin's northside.

Val Fitzpatrick: Val has been a comic writer for two decades. In the 1980s she helped the nation chuckle with her regular contributions to the Mike Murphy Show on RTE Radio. She has written for a number of publications, usually on the bewildering subject known as the domestic condition. Married to Martin, a journalist, she has three grown-up children. She works for a child care agency.

Monica Heavey: Monica was educated in the Dominican Convent in her home town of Wicklow. She has lived in Dublin for the past 30 years. Married with a grown up son and daughter Monica was always interested in writing and is thrilled to be part of Ardlea Writers' Group. She feels the group has given her confidence to seek publication of some of her work.

Mary Kenna: Mary is recognised among her family and friends as an interesting letter writer for the past 50 years. A member of the Medical Missionaries of Mary, she served in Kenya and Uganda for many years. When she read in the parish newsletter of the local creative writing class she joined to develop her writing skills. Mary enjoys the challenge of writing and the fun among the group. She is a tutor in the Coolock/Darndale Adult Literacy Service in Colaiste Dhulaigh.

Geraldine O'Connor: Geraldine's only claim to literary fame are her letters to the editors of newspapers and magazines. Her talents lie in computer creativity, producing cards and poems to the delight of family and friends. She works as a cashier in Tesco in Artaine Castle where her interest in people is well catered for. Dublin-born, she resides in Artane with husband Pat. They have five grown-up children.

Mary Whyms: Born in Galway, mother of five and granny of seven – an unlikely candidate for a project like this one might think! 'I joined the writers' group with my late husband Maurice, he to write a play, me to write an altogether different story. The novel evolved amid much fun and laughter. I now hope that my occasional article in the school magazine and the ten shillings prize for best story were forerunners of fame and fortune to come!!!'

The members of the Ardlea Writers' Group would like to thank the following for supporting this project, financially and otherwise: The Rt.Hon. The Lord Mayor of Dublin, Cllr Michael Mulcahy; Dublin Corporation Community Development Section; Coolock/Artane Credit Union; St. John Vianney Resource Centre; Ivor Callely T.D; Helen Quinn of HQ Publicity.

CHAPTER ONE

Caroline O'Hara gazed out of the misted car window into the late evening light. She could just about make out the lights of Dublin Airport as they approached it at a slow steady crawl.

'Nice, safe, sensible speed' as her mother and father always referred to it. Caroline had always felt her life was a bit like that. Nice, safe and sensible. Twenty four years of age and even the career she had chosen had kept her safely sheltered. Until a few months ago that is!

'Almost there now dear,' sighed Caroline's mother, leaning over to pat her daughter's knee. Caroline knew that her mother was fighting to hold back the tears. After all her one and only beloved child was going on her very first holiday all by herself. What terrible things lurked out there in those foreign places, just waiting to get hold of young unaccompanied girls? Mrs. O'Hara had heard all about those unscrupulous men waiting to use and abuse innocent girls. She knew a thing or two, but her Caroline didn't. She was so naive and she had very little experience around men. She would nearly accompany Caroline herself, only how would Daddy cope? Who would cook Daddy's dinner and make sure he changed his clothes, poor thing?

'I'll be fine,' Caroline assured her mother, 'and don't worry, I haven't forgotten your instructions. I won't go to discos or talk to strangers. And I promise to stay close to the hotel as much as possible.'

'My God, mother did you see that?' Caroline's father shouted. 'These Dublin drivers are complete lunatics. They're all flashing their lights when they're overtaking me. Don't they know they can't overtake on the inside like that. And they're all driving too fast! They should be driving at a...a...'

'Nice, safe , sensible speed,' Caroline completed his sentence for him with a chuckle.

'Don't be sarcastic to your father dear, it doesn't become you,' admonished her mother.

Caroline sighed. Her parents still treated her as a child. It could be highly embarrassing at the best of times, but she had to accept it. Her heart was full of love for these two endearing ageing parents of hers. They were almost as much out of place here in Dublin as she would be on holiday in Ibiza.. Caroline had been an adopted child from birth, but had been shown enough love, caring and kindness by her mother and father as would last her a lifetime.

Having circled the airport roundabout twice, and finally found a car park space large enough for her father to park in his usual haphazard fashion, they had finally reached the check-in desk. Caroline's modest amount of luggage consisted of one medium-sized suitcase and one small bag which she would carry on board with her as hand luggage.

Caroline checked in and said a tearful goodbye to her parents before passing through customs. Her last vision of them was of her now openly weeping mother clinging on desperately to her father with one hand and waving goodbye frantically with the other.

Caroline could have cried too - with embarrassment! It wasn't as if she was going to the other end of the world. She was only going to Ibiza for two weeks for God's sake! Already the thought of it was sending waves of excitement and anticipation coursing through her veins.

When she heard her mother shouting 'Make sure you wear a decent swimsuit now, Caroline. Not one of those bikini things - they attract too much attention!' she marched on determinedly without looking back, ignoring the smiling faces of the people who had overheard her mother's remark. She found the departure lounge and collapsed into an empty seat.

Ibiza, here I come! she thought to herself. She hadn't really planned on going on any holiday, and certainly not to the well known Spanish island. Caroline was thankful for that last minute cancellation that had come her way at just the right time.

She had needed some space to think about the awkward position in which she had found herself, without her mother and father asking questions galore. After all they only knew half the story. She dreaded to imagine their reaction if they knew everything. She knew she would eventually have their full support. Ballymahon was a small place, and Caroline knew how much her parents would hate to be the centre of attrention in it.

She sat alone in the departure lounge, observing her fellow passengers. A mixed crowd really. There were young couples, some older couples, and apparently, thank God, she was not the only one to be travelling alone.. She could see at least two other unaccompanied passengers. One was a rather distinguished looking gentleman, who Caroline surmised to be about fifty or so years of age. He obviously took great pride in his appearance, he was neatly dressed and had an athletic build for a man his age. His gaze was fixed on something, or someone, not far away......

Caroline followed his line of vision and found herself looking at a second solitary traveller. She was a tall, slim lady, quite conservative in manner of dress, and who Caroline guessed to be of quite a conservative manner also. The woman was in her mid-forties, Caroline thought, and appeared to be engrossed in the book she was reading.

She had absolutely no idea that she had made a favourable impression on one of her fellow travellers.

Caroline was feeling nervous. She had never been abroad before and was viewing the forthcoming flight with apprehension. She could really do with a drink to give herself a bit of Dutch courage. But alcohol was another thing she was not too familiar with. This was no time to start hitting the bottle. Maybe in Ibiza she would let herself go a little......

After a short while, Caroline's nerves got the better of her. She got up, paced up and down for a while, coming to a stop at one of the large windows to view the hive of activity that was taking place on the tarmac below her. She wondered which of the planes was hers and whispered a little prayer to herself that everything would run smoothly.

Just then, she felt something brush against her leg. Startled, she looked down. It was an empty cigarette carton. It had been thrown towards a waste paper basket by the young man who was now smiling apologetically at her. 'I'm so sorry. Did I startle you?' Caroline had a feeling she was about to be chatted up by this good-looking stranger......

'I just can't understand why we didn't bring the car to the airport,' fumed Evelyn as the taxi man helped Des to offload the bags onto the pavement. 'We've always brought it - you said yourself it was safer in the car park than outside our door in Templeogue.'

She watched as Des gave the taxi man two ten pound notes. 'How much did that fella charge you?' she said.

'He asked for seventeen pounds and that was without a tip,' replied Des.

'The rip-off is starting' he heard his wife say as he went to fetch a trolley on which to load their luggage.

Evelyn was right Des thought to himself as he wheeled the trolley back. He would have loved to have travelled in his own car to the airport - he would have been able to have a smoke and all. He had smoked a lot since he got the news. His stomach churned when he thought of the bombshell imparted at the company sales meeting three weeks ago. The American parent company of Digitor Drug Corporation had decided to close down the operation in Ireland due to high manufacturing costs. Thirty people were to be let go. This number included the three reps. of which he was the senior. The other two lads were in their thirties and Des knew they would get fixed up fairly quickly. He wasn't too optimistic - who would want an overweight, balding man two years off fifty years of age?

He had surrendered the keys of the car to the sales manager yesterday, his final day in Digitor. The car would be collected from his driveway while he was away on holiday.

The man on security was asking Evelyn to put her handbag on the table. He ran the scanner over it, 'Grand, madam, off you go. Enjoy yourself and have a nice holiday.'

Des decided to take this advice despite the bad news he had yet to impart. 'Come on pet, let's check in.' There would be time enough for recriminations when they arrived back. But these two weeks would be special, what Evelyn didn't know wouldn't trouble her.

Evelyn positioned herself in the queue for check-in and took stock of her fellow travellers. 'Thank God,' she thought looking down the line - there weren't too many children. There were a good few young people and by the sound of them some of them were the worse for drink. And it was only 8.30 in the evening. They must have started early. Des and herself liked a drink but you needed your wits about you at this stage of the proceedings, what with the jostling crowds and trolleys bashing into your ankles, not to mention keeping track of your passport, money and bags.

Evelyn hoped their hotel room would have a sea view and a balcony - after all they booked the holiday five months ago. The travel agent had assured herself and Des that the Hotel Orlando in the resort of Figueretas was four star and that they would not be troubled by insects. Last year's holiday in Lanzarote had been ruined by ants – they were even in the bed! Evelyn had spent most nights on that holiday out on the balcony wrapped in a blanket.

She looked again at her fellow travellers - those three girls, one with a very short skirt and another in skin-tight pants didn't appear Hotel Orlando material - they looked like people who would be more at home in an apartment. According to the travel brochure there were five blocks of apartments in the same complex as the hotel. As Evelyn looked anxiously around she noticed a young girl standing directly behind her in the queue. The girl was slim, dark-haired, in her mid-20's. She seemed to be on her own. Maybe she is joining someone, Evelyn thought, or perhaps she is going to Ibiza to take up a summer job. She didn't look like the sort who would serve you in a bar or restaurant - she looked more like a civil servant.

Evelyn smiled at the girl. The girl gave her a little smile and turned away quickly. No joy there. She turned her attention to Des. He was scowling. Des scowled a lot lately; Evelyn couldn't put her finger on it, but he seemed different in the past couple of weeks. Maybe it was the thought of going on holiday, or maybe the pressure of being a sales rep. was getting to him; The job meant a lot to him, but selling was very stressful.

Evelyn pushed these thoughts to the back of her mind, remembered her visit the day before to her slimming club; she had managed to lose her final four pounds and had even been nominated 'Woman of the Week.' Her fellow slimmers had given her a round of applause. That was the icing on the cake for Evelyn - not that any cake, iced or uniced, would pass her lips on this holiday. Too much work had gone into losing the flab.

She couldn't wait to wear the size 12 shorts and T-shirts - the only snag was the presence of the varicose veins which ruined the look of her legs. She had invested in a concealing cream recommended by the local pharmacist. She had tried it and it worked really well. The only drawback was that it washed off. Evelyn sighed - you couldn't have everything, and maybe people would think she was applying sun lotion to her legs when she got out of the swimming pool. She had made a start on her own suntan with five sunbed sessions in the gym in Walkinstown.

This holiday had all the makings of being a good one ; things were on the up. Samantha and Gary were both in good jobs and had found their own apartments and moved out. Des and herself would now be very comfortable. Maybe she would give the dining room a makeover when they got back; sideboards were gone out of fashion now. She had spotted a really fabulous mahogany suite in Arnotts, the chairs were modern and the table was an oval shape. It cost a packet but now that Des was senior rep. with Digitor they were climbing the ladder - they might even have the Sales Director and his wife over for dinner some night. That settled it, she would definitely get rid of the old dining room suite. God, this check-in queue was moving very slowly!

Des was in conversation with a man just ahead of them in the queue for check-in. They were talking about football. Evelyn took stock of Des's companion. He was middle-aged, very dapper, dressed in a dark brown herringbone tweed jacket and beige slacks. He looked very fit and healthy with brushed back hair just turning grey. Attractive looking but not her type. They were discussing soccer - the recent form of Shelbourne. She didn't like football and she had a mild panic attack when she heard the man say that the Hotel Orlando had Sky Sports in the lounge. Glory be to God she wasn't going to sit in a smoky lounge with lager louts in team jerseys watching football! - not with her case containing flimsy evening dresses with matching shoes suitable for candlelit dinners in beachside restaurants.

The man in front was checking in. 'Des, don't draw him on us - he's on his own and looking for someone to latch on to,' she hissed.

Des laughed. 'Will you stop worrying.' he whispered, 'I'm only being polite. He's just taken early retirement from Guinness brewery. He seems like a decent sort.'

'I can tell he supports the product,' Evelyn replied through clenched teeth as they made their way towards the departure lounge.

Bernice Reynolds arrived home in mid-afternoon from the Spar Supermarket in Finglas where she worked, thankful to find the house empty of family members. It meant she would be able finish the rest of her packing without interruption. After packing she would have a quick bath, wash her hair, dress and put on her make-up.

Her two friends, Georgia Fitzgerald and Alison Morris, were calling for her in a taxi shortly. Alison worked on the meat counter in the same supermarket as Bernice but had today off. Georgia worked in a boutique and had started her three week holiday the previous evening.

Bernice felt quite excited. She checked her luggage label - Ms Bernice Reynolds, Hotel Orlando and Apts, Figueretas, Ibiza. Within an hour she was ready, standing in front of the full length mirror, looking and wishing she wasn't quite so fat and small.

If only she was six inches taller and two stone lighter. Her new light blue shift dress covered a lot but she could not help thinking that she was a perfect candidate for liposuction and bust reduction.

Bernice grimaced as she turned to get a side and back view. God, she had a very big backside. Still she couldn't do anything about it now. If only... two small but important words...If only she had cut out Mars Bars and cream buns, fish and chips and the Budweiser. Okay, so there were pluses. She had lovely dark, shoulder length, hair that fell into soft natural curls. She also had soft brown velvet eyes that glinted like specks of amber.

Aloud she said, 'Bernice love, you are as you are, so get on with it!'

A few minutes before eight o'clock she looked out of the window, saw the taxi drawing up outside, her two friends alighting. Georgia looked stunning, dressed in a short straight moss green mini dress with a scooped out neckline. Her long legs looked as if they went on forever. She had a tiny waist and her full rounded bust was moulded into the tight dress. Her red hair was pulled back from her small perfect face into a pony tail.

Alison was also tall. She had nice blonde hair and a good figure which right now positively stretched her tight slacks to the limit. She had a blue denim shirt tucked into the slacks and looked real cool.

Bernice opened the front door. 'Ready Bernice?' Georgia shouted.

'As ready as I'll ever be,' replied Bernice.. 'Let's go.'

The three of them giggled their way into the taxi, Bernice trailing her suitcase behind her and the other two carrying her hand luggage. The driver had opened the car boot and as he lifted up Bernice's case he said, 'What have you in it? I'm sure it weighs a ton!'

Georgia fluttered her eyelashes. 'With muscles like yours, I'm sure you could lift a lot more than that suitcase,' she said.

Bernice gave her friend a thump and whispered, 'Stop flirting or we'll never get to the airport!'

'You've got long legs,' the taxi man said to Georgia. 'You'd be better sitting in the front seat beside me. More comfortable like. Know what I mean...' He opened the back seat door for Bernice and Alison, then skipped around the front, got in behind the wheel, leaned over and opened the door for Georgia. She slid onto the seat, conscious that her tight dress seemed to be shrinking by the minute, and that the driver was getting a view that he would probably be describing to his mates in lurid detail for the rest of the week.

He eased the vehicle out into the traffic on the Ballymun Road. 'Are you in showbusiness?' he asked Georgia after a while. 'Your face looks familiar.'

'I didn't think it was my face you were admiring!' Georgia replied tartly. Bernice and Alison giggled in the back.

The taxi man grinned. 'Look, I'm probably old enough to be your granddad - but I can still admire a good pair of legs when I see them!'

'Thanks for the compliment. But for the record, I'm not in showbusiness, I'm in the fashion business.'

'With a figure like that I knew you'd be into something.' He reckoned he had better not elaborate.'

'Well girls, we're on our way!' Alison cut in. She didn't like Georgia getting all the attention.

'Spain - here we come! For the next two weeks we're going to enjoy sun, sand, sea and sex - and not necessarily in that order!,' laughed Georgia.

'And don't forget the sangria,' Alison said. 'I love stirring it in the jug with the big spoon.'

'You love drinking it too. How many nights did Bernice and I have to carry you home from the disco last year! And you singing Ole! Ole! Ole! Ole! at the top of your voice.' The taxi driver smiled. He had heard it all before.

'I think it's a pity we're not going to Santa Ponsa again,' said Bernice. 'I loved that place.'

'Which part of Spain are you going to, girls?' the driver asked as they hit the motorway to the airport.

'Ibiza,' answered Georgia.

'Ibiza!' the cab driver echoed. 'It's certainly all happening out there. You'll want to be careful of yourselves in that place. Have you seen the goings-on on the telly lately?'

'Of course we have. Isn't that why we're going!' shouted Alison. The three of them roared laughing.

'We love that programme Ibiza Uncovered on Sky One - all the fellas and girls dancing around in the foam - we can't wait to get there,' Bernice said.

'And what about Ibiza Unzipped!' shrieked Georgia. 'It's just fab.'

These three ones are nearly unzipped as it is, the driver thought to himself - and they haven't even left Dublin Airport! Imagine the carry on of them when they get to Ibiza!

'An awful lot of the young crowd are going to Ibiza this year,' the cab driver said. 'I drove three girls like yourselves to the airport the other day. And guess what?' he paused.

'What ?' they all asked in unison.

'The three of them struck a bet in this cab before they got there.'

'A bet?' said Georgia, eager but puzzled. 'What sort of bet?'

'They made a bet - a thousand pesetas I think it was - on who would be first to get off with a fella. Any fella.... Spanish, English, Irish - it didn't matter.' The driver paused again.

There was a silence. The lights of the airport were showing ahead. 'What do you mean, get off with a fella?' Bernice asked. 'Did they mean....' she paused, left the question hanging in the air.

'Of course that's what they meant,' the driver snorted. 'What do you think they were talking about - playing tiddlywinks!'

Another pause. The trio looked at each other. Then Georgia exclaimed, 'What a great idea! Girls, we'll have the same bet. One thousand pesetas! How about it?'

'I'm on,' said Alison enthusiastically.

'What about you, Bernice?' Georgia asked. The cab driver was so caught up with the drama he nearly hit the car in front!

'I'm not,' replied Bernice.

'Why not?' asked Georgia.

'Because,' said Bernice. She was under no illusions. The other two had good figures. She was short and overweight, but it was more than that. Georgia and Alison made no secret of the fact that they lost their virginity in their teens. But there was a part of Bernice that was old fashioned. She felt that sex between two people should be special and she intended to cling to her own values. That bet was throwing pesetas down the drain as far as she was concerned.

'Come on, you've got nothing to lose except a thousand pesetas. That's roughly a fiver.' Georgia said. Just what I thought, the driver smiled to himself. These three have been around the block a few times!

'Tell you what, Bernice,' Georgia said, 'Alison and I will bet one thousand pesetas, you need only bet five hundred. How's that?' She could see that Bernice didn't want to be a spoilsport. 'Better make up your mind we're nearly there....'

'Alright,' Bernice said, 'I'm in.'

'Good.' They were driving up the ramp towards departures.

'Wait a minute,' said Alison. 'Is the bet on from here, or do we have to wait until we get to Ibiza?'

'What do you mean?' asked Bernice.

'I hope you don't think you're going to get off with someone in departures – or on the aeroplane itself?' Georgia said. That Alison really fancied herself.

'Why not,' Alison laughed, as they all piled out of the taxi. 'Have you ever heard of the Mile High Club!'

The cab driver stared after the trio as they pushed their trolleys laden with luggage into the airport concourse. If only he were thirty years younger! He grinned. Girls going on holiday enjoyed that story about the bet. He told it to every female who got into his cab heading off on holidays.

It was a good story. Pity it wasn't true!

As they approached the check-in desk Georgia said: 'What did you think of that lecher of a taxi driver?' she asked.

'You have to admit he gave us a great idea for a bet!' Alison laughed.

Bernice made no comment. She just wanted to check-in and head to the bar for a few drinks before take-off. Between working a full shift in Spar and rushing home to finish packing it had been a long day. She was glad when their luggage disappeared and they were given boarding passes and told to head for Gate B25.

They glanced around the departure lounge before heading for the bar. Alison and Georgia sat at a table when Bernice went for the drinks.

'See anything interesting?' Alison asked.

'Don't look now,' Georgia replied, 'but there's a couple of handsome hunks swanning around. They're sizing us up at the minute. I bet they'll be over before we get on the plane....'

'For God's sake watch it Mark! You'll destroy me with that chocolate bar. Bad enough us being on the end of this long queue without you rubbing chocolate all over my new jacket.'

'Sorry mate,' Mark said. 'But I hate waiting around airports. And Ibiza seems the most popular destination for the masses today.'

'I just hope it's as wild as it is on television,' Wayne said. Having watched some of the crazy carry-on in Ibiza on tv, Wayne and Mark had decided that was the place for them.

Wayne was looking up and down the queue at the check-in desk. Mark knew what his friend was up to. 'See much talent?' he asked.

'Not a lot. Nothing I'd be willing to swim the Liffey for!'

'Excuse me young man,' Wayne felt a tip on his shoulder. He turned to see a - to him!- oldish but rather striking looking lady in a well-cut summer dress behind him. 'Is this the check-in for Ibiza?'

'It is ma'am,' Wayne answered. His mother had always told him to be polite to older women. 'See, there's the sign.'

'Good, then perhaps you might lift that luggage case off the trolley for me. I'm afraid it's rather heavy!'

'Of course, ma'am.' Wayne swung the suitcase off the trolley. 'There you are ma'am. No problem.'

'You're so kind. Now perhaps you'd keep an eye on it while I return the trolley. Thank you.'

They watched her wheeling the trolley away, moving up her luggage as they inched towards the check-in desk. 'Hey Wayne, you've got off your mark there!' Mark couldn't contain his laughter. 'You know I think she fancies you!'

'Just my luck. Here we are heading off to Ibiza for what we hope will be a non-stop fortnight of you-know-what and I get chatted up at the airport by a matron - although not a bad looking one at that!' They speculated that the lady was a school teacher, or a nurse.

'Not to worry. Judging by what we've seen on telly the place is crawling with fine looking birds - all on the lookout for randy guys like ourselves,' Mark replied. 'And don't look now, but three fine looking things have just joined the queue. We could be in business, mate!'

Their new found friend had returned. 'You're going to Ibiza, then?' said Mark conversationally. She didn't seem the type to be going to the Island of Sin.

'Oh yes, my first foreign holiday, although I did work abroad when I was younger. I'm going to a resort called Figueretas.'

Wayne and Mark looked at each other. 'So are we. What apartments?' Mark asked, with a premonition of what the answer was going to be.

'The Hotel Orlando,' the matron smiled.

They looked at each other again. 'That's where we're going. The apartments.'

'Oh that's a pity, I'm in the hotel. But I hope we'll see a lot of each other,' the lady smiled. 'By the way my name is Maureen Duff. I'm from Tipperary.' She failed to notice the look of shock on both their faces.

See a lot of each other - not if we can help it was the thought running through the minds of both Wayne and Mark!

Half-an-hour later they reached the check-in. Wayne and Mark had got themselves sorted out and were turning away when the lady asked if they would be so kind as to lift her case up to be weighed. Wayne again obliged and they both quickly made their way to the departure lounge. A few minutes later they saw Maureen Duff enter, find a seat and begin reading a book. 'Probably the Karma Sutra,' Wayne said, grinning.

'Benjamin, will you push in and don't let that pair get in front of you. Wouldn't you think that in this day and age everyone would know how to form a queue. It's worse it's getting. Yesterday the problem was at the bus stop, now it has spread to Dublin Airport!'

Irene O'Rourke was very cross indeed as she glared at the couple beside her. Her husband Ben looked embarrassed.

Alo and Mamie Riordan mumbled their apologies. It was their first holiday abroad and they were excited. It was a bad start if someone felt annoyed with them.

'I swear I never saw you, Missus. With everything happening at the last minute we forgot to put the labels on the cases, and anyway I think we brought too much luggage. God! Isn't it a great day to be off on a holiday to the sun!'

Irene looked at her husband aghast. The big man certainly had a cheek! 'I wouldn't be surprised if they never saw the inside of an airport before.' She whispered, 'wouldn't it be just our luck if they were sitting near us on the plane.'

'Calm down, Irene,' Ben also whispered. 'No good getting yourself upset. There, you're next now. Have you the passports ready? And the tickets?' Of course she had. Irene was super efficient, always one step ahead of everyone else.

The pleasant, girl at the desk checked everything through, wished them a nice journey to Ibiza - boarding would be at Gate B25 in half an hour.

Ben O'Rourke had been through all this before. Taking his wife's arm he led her away through the crowd and into the departure lounge. He knew if he could get her to those two seats in the corner - and God grant nobody got to them first - half the battle would be won.

'Benjamin, I don't know why you put up with people like that.'

'Irene, I hate when you call me Benjamin in public. Everyone else knows me as Ben.' Patience, patience, he thought. Another hour and she'll be fine. By then they would be well on their way to Ibiza, the sunshine island where they had spent their honeymoon. Funny, he didn't remember Irene being so bossy then. She was more relaxed, romantic and fun to be with. But then Ibiza had changed too! It was only in the last five years or so that Irene had lost her sparkle. Maybe on this anniversary trip they could recapture some of the old magic.......

Irene and Ben had been married now for 25 years. Their silver wedding anniversary was next week. 'Do you remember our honeymoon in Figueretas - and the baggage handlers' strike in Playa d'en Bossa?' Irene was reminiscing again. 'We waited two whole days for our clothes but we didn't mind. We hadn't a care in the world...' She sighed. 'We didn't need many clothes anyway!'

'Who knows, on this trip history might repeat itself,' Ben replied, as they made their way towards the departure area.

Irene was a good wife and mother. No doubt about that. But she always wanted that little bit extra. A cut-above-the-rest syndrome, he called it. Things had worked out well enough for them over the years. They had reared a family of five - three boys and two girls. Ben and Irene were very proud of their achievements. His garage business had improved in recent times, the economic boom impacting on sales. Profits had increased dramatically. Now it was time for him to slow down, delegate some of the work, relax and enjoy life.

Ben O'Rourke breathed a sigh of relief. Ibiza beckoned.....two whole weeks to relax in the sun with not a care in the world. He would not have been so happy had he had a foretaste of what lay ahead of him on that beautiful Balearic island.

'Okay then, Doc. We'll be off.' Jimmy Best knocked back the last of his drink. 'Have a good time in Ibiza!,' he winked at the others across the table, 'and be careful of those Spanish senoritas!'

They all laughed, Jimmy, his wife Tessa, Mick Browne and his wife Pauline. 'Are you sure you don't want a hand with your luggage over to the check-in?' Mick asked.

'No thanks,' Alec Holliday, known to all his friends in the Ringsend Sports and Social Club as Doc, brushed aside the offer. 'I can handle it from here, no problem. Thanks for the lift out to the airport and the going away party....'

The four of them waved goodbye, the two wives giving him a peck on the cheek. He watched as they exited from the bar and disappeared into the airport crowds. Doc was glad to see them go. They were good company but he had had four pints of Guinness and now he wanted to check-in and be on his way.

Flight EI 503 to Ibiza. Figueretas to be exact. Two glorious weeks in the sun, swims in the Med, jogs along the sea front, a few pints every night - if he could find a pub where they knew how to pull a decent pint. It sounded great. And who knows, he just might meet one of those Spanish senoritas Jimmy Best had joked about. A mature senorita, of course, although not too mature.

After all he was 53 years of age now. Fit and healthy, thank God, a man of some considerable means. Distinguished looking with a certain style, if you were to believe what some of the ladies in the social club said about him. Still, middle-aged all the same.

His friends from the club had insisted on driving him to the airport to see him off, even though he had a brand new Renault Clio parked outside his place in Ringsend. Any excuse for a party. Mick, Jimmy and their wives had called around to his house in St. Patrick's Villas at seven p.m., although the flight wasn't due off until 11.30. Now he was four pints of Guinness the worse off.

There was a long queue at the two check-in desks. Doc put down his heavy case and the hold-all he'd take on board as hand luggage. He let his gaze wander over the passengers for Ibiza. There seemed to be an awful lot of young people on the flight. Mid-20's, young by his standards, but thank heavens also a lot of couples, middle-aged like himself.

He wondered how many like himself were bound for the Hotel Orlando apartments in Figueretas. Was he crazy to have embarked on a sunshine holiday like this on his own, at this stage in his life? Sure why wouldn't he? Six months ago he had walked out of Dublin's famous Guinness Brewery, where he had worked in the maintenance Department since he was sixteen, having taken early retirement and with a small fortune in his pocket. That lump sum was now safely invested and earning good money for him.

And he was unattached - a not very confirmed bachelor if one was to judge by his two long-term and sadly failed relationships, now buried in the past. He had inherited the family house in the centre of Ringsend, he had plenty of friends and enjoyed a good social life. He liked the company of women, but those two painful encounters so far had made him wary.

Why should he not embark on a holiday in the sun? He was footloose and fancy free. Despite the past, Doc hoped there would be some ladies of his own vintage on this trip!

It was then that he saw her. She had arrived at the end of the check-in queue pushing a trolley with a large and small suitcase on it. She was tall, slim and she had that certain air about her, although right now she was looking just a little flustered. Early to mid forties, Doc reckoned, noting the absence of a wedding ring on the finger of her left hand. Who did she remind him of? Yes, of course, that fine actress Deborah Kerr in the film The King and I! A schoolmarmish-type.

He saw her tap a young fellow on the shoulder and say something to him and his companion. The two lads looked amused - Doc had noticed them earlier eyeing up three girls one of them a stunning redhead - in the adjoining queue. Those two would not be interested in middle-aged women. Pity she had not asked him for help, it would have given him the opportunity to chat her up. He'd keep an eye out for a chance later on. He hoped she was also bound for the Hotel Orlando.

Having completed the check-in procedure he headed for the departure lounge. Once there he again noticed the redheaded girl and her two companions. Now they were heading for the bar. They were going to be good fun in Ibiza!

Doc sat down, lit a cigarette. He was feeling tired; must be excitement, or the four pints he'd had earlier. He would sleep on the plane, ignore the dreadful dinner they always served. He saw the lady he had noticed earlier come into departures. She found a seat, took a book out of her shoulder bag, and began to read. Yes, definitely a touch of class there. He wondered what she did for a living. A school teacher, or a nurse, perhaps. Even better, matron of a hospital, or secretary to a top businessman.

He tried to catch her eye but she was engrossed in her book. Supposing she wasn't going to the Hotel Orlando? He'd keep an eye out when they landed, see what coach she made for at the airport.

— ☽ —

Maureen Duff pinched herself in case she was dreaming. Could she really be at Dublin Airport waiting to board flight EI503 to Ibiza, the sunshine island off the coast of Spain? But it was no dream. She would soon be on her way to a holiday in the sun and was about to break a promise which she made to herself almost 20 years ago that she would never fly again.

This morning she had left her home in Tipperary in good time to catch the Bus Eireann coach which would take her as far as Dublin city centre. From there she had taken the No.41 bus directly to the airport. By the time she had reached the airport however, she was exhausted. The bus journey had given her an opportunity to reflect on her remarkable change of fortune.

She had taken over the running of the household on the small family farm after her mother had died suddenly. At the time she had just completed the Leaving Cert. and had planned for college, but as the eldest of six, three boys and three girls, she had offered to stay and look after the home, to the delight of her father and all the family.

That was over twenty years ago now. Amazing how the years slipped by. One by one her brothers and sisters left home for training or jobs in Dublin or further afield. During all that time Maureen had enjoyed a good social life and made many good friends. She liked all forms of dancing, especially ceili and old-time and she was a member of the local choral group. There was a swimming pool in the town and she was a regular visitor there. She even did the lifesaving course - who knows, she thought, it might come in useful someday as she spent a week each year at a seaside resort. She had swum in the Atlantic and the Irish Sea even in the Indian Ocean, and very soon would be able to add the Mediterranean to her conquests.

Maureen liked people and loved to speculate about the background of complete strangers. It was only natural then that her eyes wandered around the departure area and had a good look at some of her fellow passengers. How many of them would be going to the same resort as herself, she wondered?

Those three girls at the bar a bit loud voiced and were getting giggly. They had now got chatting to the two young men who had helped with her suitcase at the check-in. Her attention was also drawn to a lovely young dark-haired girl sitting alone She was in her mid-20's wide-eyed and anxious looking and was dressed very conservatively. It appeared as if she was travelling alone also. Very unusual, Maureen thought. One would think an attractive looking girl like that would have a boyfriend hanging onto her.

She wondered what the Hotel Orlando in Ibiza would be like. And to think - it was all due to her gambling! Maureen smiled to herself. She loved a little flutter on the horses and attended the bingo sessions in the parish hall every week. Well why not, she didn't smoke and rarely touched alcohol. Just a glass of wine now and then. Wasn't it only to be expected then that she would indulge herself and buy two tickets every week for the new Telly Bingo game on R.T.E.

That Tuesday night she was home alone as usual when the game started. Suddenly she was crossing off numbers to beat the band! Eventually it was announced that the Snowball had been won and that the ticket had been bought in the local mini-market, the very place she had bought her ticket. The prize that night was £20,000! She could scarcely believe it and surprised herself even more by promising herself a holiday in the sun.

There was little sleep for Maureen that night and she had telephoned her friends Joan, Cathleen and Sheila immediately. They had already booked a holiday in Ibiza and suggested she join them. She had been disappointed the following morning to learn that the very holiday she sought was booked out, but fortunately there was one place available the following week and would she take it? Maureen had jumped at the offer.

In the departure lounge Maureen glanced up from her book and noticed a rather handsome looking man, perhaps in his early fifties, very well dressed and sitting all alone. Interesting....what would her friends say if she arrived home with him on her arm? Unlikely. After Donal she had never really bothered....

When flight EI503 was called Maureen joined the queue. On the aircraft she was seated by the window beside the two young men that had helped her early on. Maureen smiled at them. Even before they were airborne she had told them about her big money win on Telly Bingo. They seemed only mildly interested.

— ☽ —

'Flight EI 503, that's ours,' said Mamie Riordan. 'Don't forget the hand luggage Alo.'

'And what about the big cases,' Alo asked, 'Will they be safe?'

Mamie sighed, 'Oh God give me patience Alo Riordan - if ever a woman suffered. Now that we've checked them in they will be looked after for us.'

'But supposing, just for the sake of argument, Mamie, that your nightie ends up in Rome or Paris instead of Figueretas. Won't you be in a right fix then.'

'Ah, give over Alo, I don't know if you are serious or joking, but whichever it is give over. I have to concentrate on what I am doing. You carry the cool bag Alo. I have it loaded with sausages and black and white pudding!'

'Black and white pudding!,' Alo gasped. 'What are you thinking of, woman, bringing a load of black and white pudding all the way to Spain!'

'I'm thinking of you, Alo, and that big appetite of yours. We'll let these people see we in Co.Clare know how to eat.'

Alo Riordan at that point in time was as comfortable as an antelope with a cheetah five or six paces behind him. Two main factors militated against his peace of mind. Firstly, his fear of flying, and secondly, he had a blinding headache and a rumbling stomach, brought about by the large number of pints which he had consumed last night in Murphy's Bar back home in Miltown Malbay, at a send off party with the locals.

If Mamie had any discomfort it was of a mental nature. 'Have I taken on too much,' she mused, 'taking a big hulk like Alo on a holiday like this?' Her husband was a hard worker and a wealthy man, but a sophisticated traveller he wasn't.

Mamie was a neat, well preserved woman, just turned fifty and three years junior to her husband. She looked after their light hardware shop while Alo attended to their farm machine hire service. Both ends of the business were thriving, but, due to pressure of work, Alo and Mamie could never set aside time for a decent holiday. However, over a period of six months or so Mamie had worked continuously on her towering husband until finally he had caved in. Now they were on their way to Ibiza, leaving their six adult daughters behind to look after the business.

She wished Alo and herself were seated on the aeroplane so that they might have a little snooze. Mamie prayed Alo wouldn't snore all the way to Ibiza.......

— ☽ —

Wayne's eyes were scanning the departure lounge, searching out the talent. 'See anything you fancy?' he asked Mark.

His friend gestured. Look over there.....that's a nice bit of talent, and it looks like she's on her own.....'

Wayne followed his friend's gaze The girl was standing looking out of the window at the aeroplanes on the tarmac, her profile mirrored in the glass through which she was gazing. She was above average height, dressed simply in a printed cotton dress, her dark hair cut short, framing a rather pallid but stunningly beautiful face. Wayne let his gaze travel slowly over her long, slim figure and tried to imagine what she would look like in a bikini.

'Hey, she's some beauty,' he remarked enthusiastically.

'Yeah,' Mark replied. 'That's what I call real class.'

'Where's the boyfriend?' Wayne asked. 'There has to be a boyfriend. A stunner like that couldn't be alone.....'

'How do we find out?' Mark invariably looked to Wayne for solutions.

'Simple,' Wayne answered. 'Watch me....'

Wayne strolled casually over to the window overlooking the tarmac, stood a few feet from the girl who was looking the other way and had not noticed him. Mark watched as Wayne took out a packet of cigarettes, lit one, then flicked the empty packet towards the refuse bin standing between himself and the girl. Only the empty packet didn't land in it's intended target, instead it overshot the bin and hit the girl on the leg. She turned her head to see what the object was.

'Oh, I'm sorry. Did I startle you?' Mark heard Wayne say, all apologies. He had made it look like it was an accident - and he was speaking in his upmarket voice!

The girl smiled, a shy smile. 'That's all right.' She turned back to admiring the aeroplanes again.

After a few minutes Wayne said, 'Just think, we'll be soon heading up in one of those things ourselves. Makes you nervous thinking about it.'

She turned to him. 'I thought I was the only one who is nervous.'

'This your first time?' She nodded, said 'Yes' again. 'Not to worry. There's nothing to it,' Wayne drew casually on his cigarette, exhaled. 'Just do what a lot of people do, close your eyes and relax.'

Mark nearly burst out laughing. The chancer's making it sound like he goes up in an aeroplane every day of the week!

'I think I'll say a prayer.....' the girl laughed.

'A prayer – now that's an idea,' Wayne, who hadn't uttered a prayer for ages, agreed. 'Although a drink before you take off might be better. A large gin and tonic. That would settle the nerves. Fancy one?'

'I'd love to. But I'm not used to alcohol.'

'No kidding.' Wayne was fancying her more and more by the minute. He'd never yet met a girl who didn't knock them back. This beautiful creature with the rather sad, dark eyes was unique. Probably never did the other thing either! 'You need someone to hold your hand,' he said. 'Maybe you have a boyfriend….'

She didn't answer immediately. Then she said, 'I'm travelling alone.' If her mother and father heard her now, Caroline thought, chatting about boyfriends and being offered a drink by a complete stranger - and a handsome looking one at that!

'I don't believe it……. a beautiful girl like you? Over on the seat Mark nearly freaked. Why couldn't he chat girls up like that? Wayne made it look so natural. 'You're going to Ibiza, I hope?'

When the girl nodded, Wayne asked 'Orlando Apartments?'

'That's right. For two weeks.'

'Fantastic! So are we. Me and my friend, Mark Smith over there. We're Dubs, as if you haven't already guessed.' The girl looked over at Mark, managed a smile.

'Incidentally, my name is Wayne Nolan. What's yours?'

'Caroline O'Hara. I'm from the Shannon area.' She didn't know why she volunteered the information, she was always very careful. Maybe it came with her new found freedom. And she hadn't even left the airport yet!

Wayne was dying to ask her how come she was going to Ibiza on her own without even a girlfriend. Peculiar that, he thought. She didn't offer any further information.

'I hope we'll be sitting near each other on the aeroplane,' Wayne went on.

Oh God, Caroline thought, this conversation is getting a bit heavy. 'It's unlikely,' she said, looking around. 'There's such a huge crowd.'

'Seeing as how you're so nervous I thought maybe I could hold your hand - just in case anything happened…..' He laughed, making it sound like he wasn't really serious.

Better not let him see she was a bit frightened. 'I don't think I'll be that nervous!' Caroline said coolly. 'Now if you'll excuse me, I must go to the ladies....' With that she picked up her hand luggage.

'See you in the Orlando Apartments then,' Wayne called out after her, admiring her rear view as she departed. He strolled back towards Mark.

'Congrats. You've made the breakthrough,' Mark said, 'but don't forget I saw her first.'

Ten minutes later the metallic tones coming across the P.A. informed them that their flight was now boarding. As they queued with the other passengers to hand up their boarding passes Wayne's eyes were on Caroline O'Hara as she exited. There was something about her that intrigued him, and it hadn't all to do with her looks. He sensed she was a girl with an interesting past. He had two whole weeks to find out more about her........

Gerry Murphy paced the check-in area of Dublin Airport in an agitated manner. He stopped for a moment to look at his watch for the umpteenth time, then continued with his pacing.

'If the lady doesn't arrive within the next few minutes, sir' the Aer Lingus girl said, 'I'm afraid we can't wait any longer. The plane should have taken off ten minutes ago.'

What on earth could be keeping Fiona? Gerry fretted. Their flight was due to take off any moment and still there was no sign of her. He had already tried to make contact with his mobile to see if any problem had arisen, but she must have had hers switched off. Maybe she didn't want any calls right now....

Gerry's eyes roamed frantically round the bustling airport. People were rushing about and everyone seemed to be in a hurry. He had almost given up hope when he spotted her. Yes! It was Fiona. He could tell by her mass of shiny, black hair bobbing above the crowd. Fiona was a very striking young woman, and even now, pushing a trolley with matching suitcases on board, she seemed to glide effortlessly across the concourse towards him.

'For heaven's sake, Fiona, you're dead late. I was getting really worried.' Gerry couldn't contain his anger. 'What the hell kept you?'

'Relax darling,' soothed Fiona, attempting to smooth out the worry lines on his forehead with her long elegant fingers. 'Don't look so worried. The taxi that I ordered just didn't turn up, that's all, Sean ended up driving me here.'

'Sean?' Spluttered Gerry, heaving their suitcases on the scales as the Aer Lingus girl glared. 'Why did you let HIM take you?' He looked around as if expecting to see Sean forcing his way through the crowd in hot pursuit.

'It's alright, I didn't let him come in with me. He dropped me off at the main doors. And don't worry , he doesn't suspect a thing,' assured Fiona. Her attractive face broke into a vivacious smile as she teased, 'Anyway, you don't think I'd let you go to sunny Ibiza without me, do you?'

'You know you're all I want Fiona,' protested Gerry. Although right now all he wanted was for her to check in and get on that aeroplane.

'And you know the same goes for me too sweetheart,' Fiona replied. She pulled him gently closer to her by tugging his tie, and planting a slow sensual kiss on his very receptive lips.

The Aer Lingus girl 'tut-tutted,' and pushed their tickets and passports at them. Fiona gave her a sweet smile and resisted the temptation to follow it with a two finger salute.

Thirty seconds later, the lovebirds were scurrying through the departure gate and running frantically to make their flight. As they stepped into the packed aeroplane, a sea of faces, many of them angry, confronted them. They were greeted by a slow handclap and sarcastic remarks like 'thanks for joining us,' 'nice to have you on board,' and 'take your time, we've all night to get to Ibiza!'

Gerry and Fiona squeezed into their seats in the middle of the aircraft. 'Holy God,' he hissed, 'we try to sneak away for two weeks together and half of Ireland knows about it!'

CHAPTER TWO

Alec Holliday had requested a window seat on the aeroplane. He put his hold-all in the overhead locker, with his herring-bone tweed jacket and hat. He wondered who would occupy the two seats beside him. He had a protracted wait before he found out. Everyone was now on board and still the two seats remained vacant. Passengers were becoming impatient and one of the hostesses made an announcement stating that they were waiting for a couple who unfortunately had arrived late at check-in. However, they were now in the airport and on their way.

It was another five minutes before the duo appeared; a handsome looking couple in their early thirties, Doc reckoned. He was tall, dark-haired , trendily dressed, looked like a guy out of a tv ad; she had a figure to die for, her catsuit-type outfit hugging every contour and unzipped to dangerous limits. When she stretched up to put some hand luggage in the overhead locker she had the eye of every male in the aeroplane. Her partner had the good grace to look embarrassed at their late arrival, she looked like she was doing them all a favour by travelling with them.

When she finally sat down in the aisle seat, she did so without a smile or a 'hello' to Doc. As soon as the aeroplane took off the latecomers began whispering to each other.

Doc had turned his face towards the window and closed his eyes. His friends Jimmy, Mick and their wives would be on their last drinks in the social club in Ringsend right now, after enjoying the usual Saturday night dance and the sing-along.

He would miss their companionship over the next two weeks. Still, he had a few things to look forward to on this holiday. Doc began to doze off. The last thing he remembered was the young woman in the aisle seat giggling and whispering. 'for heaven's sake stop worrying, Gerry darling, he's asleep. He won't hear a thing....'

Fiona glanced at the man in the window seat who seemed oblivious to what was going on around him. His eyes were closed and he appeared to be sleeping. She leaned close to Gerry, rubbed her leg against his. If only they were in bed right now!

'Isn't this wonderful darling? Two whole weeks in Ibiza, just the two of us.' She squeezed Gerry's hand. 'Swimming, drinking, exploring......' She broke off, 'Mind you,' she added dreamily, 'the only exploring I intend doing on this holiday will be in our hotel bedroom!'

Gerry put his finger to his lips, nodded his head in the direction of the window seat passenger and whispered, 'shush, your man will hear us!' They had already drawn too much attention to themselves by delaying take-off.

'Oh Gerry, you can be such a child sometimes. What does it matter if anyone hears. We're honeymooners, remember? People expect to hear that kind of thing from people in love.'

'And we are so in love, aren't we Fiona? I can't wait to get to Ibiza.' He leaned over, and gave her a kiss.

They were interrupted by the sound of raucous laughter. Fiona nudged Gerry and nodded towards two girls, a redhead and her blond companion sitting just one row in front of them on the opposite side. 'I hope they're not staying in the same resort as us, never mind the same hotel,' she remarked disdainfully. 'I think they had a couple of drinks too many before they came on board,' Listening to their Dublin accents she made a mental note to avoid those girls if they were in the same apartments.

Shortly after the plane had taken off, Fiona made her way to the toilet, and Gerry took the opportunity to survey his fellow passengers. He wondered about the tall man at the window seat. He seemed to be alone. He had nodded off and was starting to snore gently. Gerry laughed quietly to himself. That would please Fiona no end!

Gerry studied the two girls across from him, which was a infinitely more attractive alternative. They were nice looking even if they were a bit loud. He had been afraid to look too closely earlier in case Fiona had got the wrong idea. She did have a tendency to get jealous rather easily. Mind you, he quite liked that, because he felt it showed how much she loved him. He still couldn't believe his luck that he had made it with Fiona. But then she had made her intentions clear that first time they were introduced.

She was married to Sean, his boss, a powerful businessman, able to offer Fiona everything she could ever want. Everything that is, except the very thing she craved....

Okay, so Sean was a lot older than her, twenty years older to be exact, and more interested in his business than his sexy young wife. Gerry reckoned that was why Fiona had sought action elsewhere. They had been attracted from the first time they had set eyes on each other. A sexual attraction pure and simple. He and Sandra had just been going through the motions, after eight years of marriage and two kids, he supposed it was inevitable he would stray. He had promised himself that they wouldn't think about home at all. But how can you totally banish from your mind the fact that you are embarking upon an illicit affair with your boss's wife, and you're leaving behind two adorable children, and Sandra, a wife who loves you, but you're not sure that you love her anymore.

He was brought out of his reverie abruptly by Fiona returning to her seat. 'They should be serving dinner soon. I suppose it'll be the same crap airline food,' she observed.

'I don't care, I'm starving,' Gerry replied

'Make sure you eat it all,' whispered Fiona suggestively, 'you're going to need all the strength you've got for this holiday!'

Moments later, one of the air hostesses appeared in the aisle and spoke sharply to the two girls in the opposite row. Fiona made sure to listen in.

'I'm afraid ladies, there's been a complaint about your conduct. I must ask you to keep the noise level down, and to refrain from using bad language during the flight, as it can be offensive to some passengers.' The two girls looked far from repentant, but agreed to behave in a suitable manner that the other passengers would find acceptable,

Gerry turned to look at Fiona, and was surprised to find a look of smug satisfaction on her face. 'It wasn't you who complained, was it Fiona?' he asked suspiciously.

'Of course not,' she smiled. 'What do you take me for?' But as she turned towards the window, Gerry could see her reflection through the glass. Fiona's face bore a smile of triumph.

— ☾ —

When Georgia, Alison and Bernice finally found their seats on the airplane they discovered they had a problem. 'We're not sitting together,' wailed Georgia. 'Two of us are on this side and the other is across the aisle.'

Georgia had had a couple of drinks too many before boarding and was rather aggressive. 'Wouldn't you think that stupid bitch at the check-in could have given us three seats together,' she said at the top of her voice.

'We're holding everybody up,' Bernice hissed, 'just sit down. There's no problem. You and Alison sit together and I'll sit over the other side.'

The plane had no sooner taken off when, much to Bernice's embarrassment, Georgia and Alison began to giggle and laugh loudly as the hostesses demonstrated the emergency procedures. Not long after they tried to order drinks, but were told curtly by the air hostess that the drinks trolley would not be in service for some time yet. They showed their annoyance at this and other passengers began to glare at them. After that Georgia and Alison quietened down.

It was close to 1 a.m. when the announcement was made to fasten seat beats for landing. A wave of excitement began to ripple through the aircraft. Spain at last! After reaching the terminal building there was time to view one's fellow passengers.

Georgia, Alison and Bernice had a good look at everyone at luggage reclaim. They concluded that the male talent was a bit thin on the ground.

Georgia was in a bad mood. She had not enjoyed the flight, what with that bossy hostess insisting they could have only one round of drinks during the flight. Now she whispered to her two friends. 'Do you see that attractive girl with the short dark hair, the one on her own. What on earth would bring her to a place like Ibiza? She looks like a Frigid Brigid to me.'

Alison giggled, 'I don't think she is here for the same reason as us!'

Georgia was looking at her fellow passengers with a look of disdain on her face and observed rather loudly, 'Some of these people look as if a night of passion would kill them.'

'For God's sake be quiet Georgia, people aren't deaf. Someone will hear you.' Bernice sometimes wished that her two friends weren't so outspoken. Was it an inferiority complex, she wondered? She herself was always careful not to have too much to drink. She felt that everyone at baggage reclaim was looking at them.

The coaches for the various resorts were well signed. The Spanish coach driver's eyes lit up when he saw the trio of glamour girls from Dublin. After seeing their suitcases stored in the luggage compartment, Georgia, Bernice and Alison sat together on the long seat at the top of the bus.

The couple who had delayed the flight from Dublin were making their way up the bus. Alison winked at her two friends. 'Honeymooners! I can spot them a mile away. I heard her calling him Gerry darling as they got off the plane and he called her Fiona pet when they were reclaiming their luggage. They'll have great fun in their apartment tonight!'

After arriving at the Hotel Orlando and getting the key of their apartment at reception the girls were given directions how to find it. They went out into the semi-darkness, struggling with their luggage along the leafy walkways. Georgia's eyes lit up when she saw the swimming pool glinting through the trees.

'Anyone fancy an early morning swim?' she asked gaily. 'What do you say to us flinging off all our clothes and getting in for a nude swim?'

'Good idea,' Alison said enthusiastically. 'It's warm enough. I'm all for it.'

'Look, there are these two handsome hunks.' Georgia pointed. 'Maybe they'd like to join us for a swim.'

'Oh, for God's sake,' hissed Bernice, 'you two are drunk. Let's go to bed before you make a show of yourselves on the first night.'

Alison and Georgia looked at her. Georgia yawned. 'You know, Bernice, I think you're right. Bed sounds better than a swim just now.'

'Yes, on second thought, I agree with that,' Alison replied.

Eventually, after stumbling around in the dark up and down the pathways, they located their apartment. They quickly sorted out who was sleeping where, undressed swiftly, flinging clothes everywhere, and flopped into their single beds. Plenty of time for a rave-up later Georgia reasoned as she slipped into a deep sleep.

— ☾ —

At baggage reclaim Doc spotted the lady who had reminded him of film star Deborah Kerr. She had her suitcase placed on a trolley by one of the young men who had helped her in Dublin. Another chance to get talking to her lost! He had tracked her out to where the coaches were lined up, hoping she would make for the one with the Hotel Orlando sign. She did!

Doc eased his trolley in behind hers. The coach driver was loading the suitcases on the other side. 'Would you like me to put your suitcase on board?' he asked politely.

'Yes, thank you.'

'No problem.' He hoisted it up, slid it in between his. 'Hotel Orlando, is it?'

'That's right,' she smiled a lovely smile.

'Good, I'm there too, the apartments.'

'I expect we'll be seeing a lot of each other then.'

'I hope so,' Doc replied. 'Oh, by the way, my name is Alec Holliday. I'm from Ringsend in Dublin. My friends call me Doc.'

'Oh, are you a doctor?'

He laughed at her naivety. 'No, it's a nickname. Ever heard of the famous Doc Holliday who was in the Gunfight At The O K Corral? They made a film of it – '

She looked puzzled. 'I'm afraid not. Anyway I don't like nicknames. I prefer to call people by the name by which they were baptised.'

'No problem then. You can call me Alec.'

'I'm Maureen Duff. I'm from Tipperary.'

'How do you do, Maureen.'

They shook hands. He's very friendly, Maureen thought to herself. He was very athletic looking, with his tall slim figure and tightly cropped grey hair. Fiftyish, she supposed.

'Better get on board the coach,' he advised. 'I'll wait here until the driver closes this luggage compartment.'

A couple of minutes later Doc climbed on board. Two rows of tired faces stared up at him. He looked for Maureen Duff, hoped there was a vacant seat beside her. Alas it had been taken by the attractive young girl whom he had noticed was on her own. Maureen gave him a nice smile as he made his way towards the back of the coach.

When they arrived at the Hotel Orlando, Doc saw Maureen collect her room key and make her way towards the lifts. He surmised that she was staying in the hotel proper. By the time he had signed the register and collected his key the lady who reminded him of Deborah Kerr had long disappeared. Oh well, he had two whole weeks to get to know her better.

For Caroline the flight to Ibiza was pleasant enough. There were two minor incidents however, a delay at take-off waiting for two tardy passengers - a beautiful dark-haired young woman and an embarrassed looking man whom Caroline took to be her husband. Then during the flight there was a sort of argument near the front of the plane with the air hostess and a couple of the Dublin girls. The girls quietened down, however, and the flight passed without further incident.

The flight passed fairly quickly and just over two hours later they had landed in Playa de'n Bossa. At baggage reclaim she noticed the two young men who had chatted her up earlier at Dublin Airport glancing in her direction a few times. She felt flattered and also a little embarrassed. She was glad when her baggage came through and she followed the other passengers towards the exit where the coaches to the various resorts were parked.

Revelling in the balmy tropical heat that enveloped her, even at this time of night, Caroline secured a seat halfway down the coach, smoothed down her now crumpled dress and took stock of the people around her. Beside her was the lady who she had noticed being chatted up back in the terminal building by the tall athletic-looking man with a Dublin accent The woman felt Caroline's gaze and smiled. Caroline smiled shyly back. They had just swapped first names, the lady's name being Maureen, when a sudden screech of laughter turned Caroline's attention from the lady to the three girls from Dublin who appeared to be sharing a hilarious joke of some sort among themselves.

Caroline wondered if they were staying at the Hotel Orlando apartments. They weren't exactly her type but at least they were in the same age bracket and they might be company for her. She could see Wayne Nolan talking to his friend further up the coach. Wayne had mentioned his friend's name earlier on. Mark something or other. She'd forgotten his second name now. He appeared to be a lot more reserved than Wayne. Suddenly she realised he reminded her of someone she knew...... No, better not think of Joe, or why she was on this holiday alone. The wounds were still too fresh, too raw. She didn't want to think about him right now. He was off limits. That was the phrase that had been used. Time would tell whether or not they would ever see each other again.

Having reached the hotel and signed the register she found her studio apartment with some difficulty in the darkness. Before she unpacked Caroline went out onto the balcony, leaned forward and surveyed the scene below. Through the semi-darkness she could make out the water of the heart-shaped swimming pool, shimmering in the overhead lights. There were lovely plant-lined pathways leading from the swimming pool to the various areas of the complex. Caroline could detect the faintly intoxicating tropical fragrances flowing gently in the temperate night air. She felt as though she had stepped into a whole new world.

Intent on rising early the next morning, she dragged herself back reluctantly into her apartment and slipped into bed. It was quite a long time before she finally managed to fall asleep.

— ☽ —

Irene had dozed off on the coach bringing them to the hotel and Ben let her sleep. She had been irritable all during the flight to Ibiza, even when he had ordered a double gin and tonic for her and a whiskey for himself 'to start our wedding anniversary celebrations.'

At the baggage reclaim in Playa d'en Bossa she had begun to get hyper when their luggage had not been first out on the carousel. Ben had tried to joke her out of her bad mood. 'You know when I was a young lad my mother collected me from school every day - and she used to say that if ever I was first out through the gates that she would light a blessed candle in thanksgiving. She never did have to light that candle!'

Irene had not been amused. Now they were on the coach. Thank God she had fallen off to sleep again - he wouldn't have to listen to her moaning! He hoped Irene wouldn't get hyper too often on the holiday.

She was suitably impressed when they arrived at the Hotel Orlando with its imposing front and spacious reception area. But Irene's bad mood returned when they opened Room 405 and she entered the bedroom.

'Benjamin, come in here. Just look at that!'

Ben did as he was bid. He could hardly believe what he saw. The double bed had not been made up. Instead the sheets and pillows were neatly piled on it. 'They must have forgotten to make our bed,' Ben said rather lamely. He sensed trouble. Big trouble!

'I can see that,' his wife fumed. 'We're not having this Benjamin. Go down to reception immediately. Tell them to send someone up here at once!'

Ben looked at his watch. 'Irene, it's almost 3 a.m. They won't have anyone making beds at this time. Couldn't we do it ourselves? Anyway it's so warm we'll hardly need any bed covers at all....'

He was lucky. Irene was so tired she agreed - albeit reluctantly. 'Alright,' she said resignedly. 'But I'll go down first thing in the morning to complain. Someone is going to have to answer for this!'

Fiona had looked around the coach bringing them from the airport to the hotel, studying her fellow passengers and ticking off the ones she and Gerry would avoid during the next two weeks. She was intrigued by the rather striking looking girl, seated further down the bus, who appeared to be on her own, although right now she was sitting beside a neatly dressed middle-aged woman who also appeared to be unaccompanied.

Maybe she would get talking to the girl, find out why she was alone. Not that Fiona had to worry about mixing with anybody on this holiday. Gerry and herself would be far too busy enjoying each other. She could hardly believe she would have Gerry to herself for two whole weeks.....

The coach trip passed quickly enough and after dropping groups of people off at various hotels, the coach then pulled up outside the Hotel Orlando. Before they went inside, Alice the tour rep. reminded everyone not to forget the briefing that would take place the following day at 4 p.m. in the hotel bar. Fiona yawned. She reckoned herself and Gerry might be otherwise engaged!

It was now past 2 a.m. and the total chaos reigned at reception as the tired and bedraggled group milled around trying to ascertain where their allocated rooms were from a harassed male receptionist who spoke hardly any English.

Eventually Fiona and Gerry made their way, with there suitcases, along the lighted pathways around the swimming pool to their apartment.

'Should we unpack?' asked Gerry, closing the door.

'You must be joking..... I'd rather undress,' Fiona replied seductively, advancing on him slowly. 'Isn't that what a honeymoon couple like us are supposed to do?'

She slid her arms around Gerry's neck and pulled him close, kissing and teasing him. Then they flung off their clothes in a frenzy, made mad passionate love, and not surprisingly didn't wake up until the burning Spanish sun filtered through the curtains and fell across their naked bodies on the bed.

CHAPTER THREE

Doc Holliday's bedside alarm went off at 8am. The sun shining in through the balcony windows was a welcoming sight. Doc always got up early at home; however late he might have come in from the social club the night before he always enjoyed an early morning run around nearby Ringsend Park. Doc liked to keep fit, a throwback to his soccer days with Shelbourne.

He rose, slipped on a vest and a pair of shorts, laced up his trainers and went outside. The beach was only two minutes away. Already he could see some sun worshippers claiming sunbeds and umbrellas on the golden sand. It looked like the day was going to be a scorcher. He jogged along the beautifully paved promenade, fifteen minutes up, fifteen minutes on the return journey. Back in the apartment he had a quick shower. Yes, this was the life...

He bought an English newspaper, enjoyed a leisurely breakfast at the poolside snack bar. No way was he going to spend much time over the cooker in his apartment. He did enough of that at home. He could well afford to have all his meals out during the next fortnight, live like a lord.

After breakfast he had a read of his newspaper, then decided on a swim. He would try the pool first, although it looked a little crowded. Personally he preferred swimming in the sea, but Maureen Duff was in the pool and it would give him an opportunity to say hello. He noticed she was a good swimmer. He would invite her for a swim and lunch on the beach some day.

Doc dived into the deep end, surfaced near Maureen and said hello. She smiled in return. They exchanged a few words and she got out a short while later. Doc did a few lengths, although it was no fun dodging between the screaming kids and their adoring parents in the shallow end. He got out of the pool a short while later and found an empty sunbed. He was relaxing when he noticed Maureen and the dark-haired girl leaving the pool area. Probably going for a stroll around the town, he reckoned.

He spent the next few hours reading and relaxing. Looking around he recognised some of the people who had been on the flight over last night. It was getting on towards midday when the handsome couple who had been sitting beside him on the aeroplane showed up. Doc watched as they moved two sunbeds onto the grass margin away from the masses at the pool. She was wearing a bikini of miniscule proportions. She lay on her stomach on the lounger, the straps of her top undone, while he rubbed suntan oil over her back and down her shapely legs. All the while they were laughing and giggling. Doc tried not to stare.

There was something about those two that made him suspicious. Truth to tell their carry-on aroused more than his suspicions but that was another matter altogether! He'd put a bet on it that they weren't husband and wife.

Snatches of their conversation on the aeroplane last night had filtered into his semi-comatose brain before sleep had overtaken him and some of their whisperings had been very interesting indeed – enough to make him want to fight off sleep! Oh well, Doc smiled to himself as he passed them on his way to the poolside bar for a cooling mid-day drink, it takes all kinds to make the world go around!

Later he slipped on a t-shirt, strolled into Figueretas and had lunch in one of the town's many restaurants. Being a Sunday, the bar next door was showing an English premiership game on Sky Sports. Doc went in, found a seat at the counter, and decided to try a pint of Guinness. Not bad, he thought, but not quite as good as the Oarsman's in Ringsend. Still, it didn't prevent him from having several more of the same!

— ☾ —

Gerry and Fiona had wakened late. Not surprising, considering their late arrival at the hotel and the strenuous activities they had engaged in as soon as the door of their apartment was locked behind them! Now they slipped into the shower together, laughing unselfconsciously as they slowly soaped each other's bodies under the hot water. They broke apart reluctantly when they finally decided to go out and have brunch.

'After that we'll go to the supermarket, buy some food for light snacks.' Gerry was glad they planned on having romantic meals out most nights. He reckoned that Fiona wouldn't be one for cooking over a hot stove.

They had both decided that they would not do anything mad on the first day, just relax by the pool maybe and in general take it easy. But it didn't quite work out like that. They had waited for an opportunity to be alone like this and now they couldn't keep away from each other. God, but he was mad about her! Last night had been brilliant. It had exceeded his expectations and more. They had done it before and it had been great, but here in Ibiza it was different. They'd known a sense of complete abandonment. Really let themselves go. No fear of being caught out so to speak. As they finished brunch in the poolside snack bar, he looked across the table at Fiona, and as though reading her mind, she was looking suggestively at him, rubbing her foot sensually up and down his leg.

They acted more like a pair of teenagers than thirty-something as they made their way giggling and carrying on back to their room. As soon as they were inside Gerry locked the door and they feverishly began to pull each others clothes off. Their lips sought each others hungrily, and their hands roamed frantically over each other's yielding, aching body.

'I'm really crazy about you Fiona,' Gerry whispered hoarsely, 'you're so beautiful.' He lifted her into his arms, and carried her now practically naked body over to the bed. He stood at the end of the bed, and gazed at her long slim brown body. He slowly began to remove her black silk panties, ever so slowly ......

Afterwards they lay together completely spent and exhausted in each other's arms. An hour later they were strolling down the colourful tree and plant-lined walkways which led to the centralised heart-shaped pool of the hotel complex. They made a very attractive couple, Gerry with his tanned skin and healthy physique in a pair of snugly-fitting swimming trunks that showed off his best attributes, Fiona with her incredible body, and sunbed tan, which she had acquired at her local beauty salon. She swayed her way confidently to their sun-loungers wearing a dazzling white skimpy bikini and a dazzling smile to match.

Gerry didn't know whether to feel jealous or proud as every head at the poolside turned to stare as they passed by. When they were settled into their loungers, he decided to give the watching males a thrill by rubbing tanning oil over Fiona's soft, supple body. He was carefully pouring a little more liquid into the palm of his hand, when suddenly the bottle was knocked flying and landed on Fiona's back. They both jumped with fright.

'Sorry about that mister!, can we have our ball back please?' a young voice called out.

'Sure thing,' laughed Gerry, and threw a beach ball back into the pool where some youngsters were playing.

'Gerry darling, I thought we left all that sort of thing back in Ireland,' fumed Fiona.

Gerry, however, wasn't listening. He was staring at the young boy and girl in the pool who owned the beach ball, remembering two children he had said goodbye to yesterday evening. Was it only yesterday evening,? he thought to himself. There was no way he could forget creeping into their room, pulling up their blankets which they had kicked off, and gently kissing their little cherub cheeks, whilst tears rolled down his own. Two beautiful kids, Jake who was six and full of energy and kept Sandra busy from the word go. A great kid with lots of love to give. Then there was Rosie, a little creature that would melt your heart. She was five, small for her age, but bright as a button. The two children had been the only bright spot in his and Sandra's life lately. The children were the only thing that they had in common any more.

And what of Sandra? She had changed over the years. She didn't seem to be the same happy-go-lucky person she used to be. She was very wrapped up in the children, house-proud, never wanted to go out to party, or mix with other people. Gerry remembered how it was her eyes and her out-going manner that had attracted him in the first place.

Two big brown smiling eyes and a bubbly personality to match. When had things started going downhill? She was probably too caught up in the home and the kids to even suspect he might be having an affair....

'Gerry, are you listening to me?' came Fiona's petulant voice. 'We'll have to find a better spot by the pool tomorrow, I don't fancy being harassed by somebody's screaming kids for the rest of the holiday!'

'For crying out loud Fiona, it was only a beach ball,' Gerry chided her. 'You'd swear it was a cannon ball or something the way you're carrying on. They're just kids, let them have a bit of fun for God's sake.' He turned around on the sun lounger and closed his eyes, brooking no further conversation.

What the hell brought that on? Fiona wondered, studying Gerry's back through her Raybans. Not to worry, she would soon have him crawling again, begging her forgiveness and wanting to make it up to her. It was always the same. Until then however, she would read a chapter or two of the new Patricia Scanlan novel she had bought.

True to form, she had barely read four pages when Gerry was once more by her side, apologising for having been so disagreeable with her and offering to get her a long cool drink from the poolside bar.

Pleased that they had made up, and reluctant to suggest they go up to the apartment in case it lead to another sex session, Gerry suggested that they hang around the pool and not go to the courier's meeting. They could maybe pick up the details later.

The sound of her large husband clumping around the room woke Mamie Riordan. As she opened her eyes the present came flooding back. They were in Ibiza.

Something was bothering Alo.

'What are you looking for?' Mamie asked.

'I can't find my pants, did you put them away?'

'Why would I do that?'

'I don't know, but the question is, what am I going to do without them?'

'Put on these,' said Mamie, she had got out of bed and had rummaged in Alo's suitcase. Now she was holding up a pair of bright blue and red shorts. 'Wear them? Never!' said Alo vehemently. 'I'd go home first.'

'Put them on,' insisted Mamie, 'remember you're in Ibiza now, not Miltown Malbay.'

Alo put on the shorts. Mamie also put on a pair of shorts. 'Now give me your honest opinion, how do I look?'

Alo was reluctant to dampen her ardour but he could not resist the temptation. She was dressed in blue shorts, saffron blouse and flip-flop sandals. He was still convinced that she had hidden his pants in order to get him into shorts.

My God, he thought to himself, she looks gorgeous. Aloud he said, 'well your legs look great.'

'I wasn't thinking about my legs. How about my shorts?'

'Smashin! Beautiful! Exquisite! Except.....'

'Except what?' Mamie asked sharply.

'Ah, nothing.'

'Come on now, you were going to say something about my shorts. What was it?'

'Oh they're lovely in front, but behind they're sort of, er, stretched.'

'What do you mean, stretched?' Mamie asked anxiously.

'Now Mamie, you know what stretched means. It's like when something has too large an area to cover and it might burst. But I wouldn't worry about it, it's all right, you don't look too bad. Just be careful not to bend down too suddenly.'

'I'll kill you Alo Riordan,' joked Mamie, as she delivered a thump, which would have earned her a red card in a premiership encounter.

'Well Mamie, you asked me for my honest opinion and the truth is you're gorgeous,' said Alo as his huge arms encircled her waist.

'I'm starving,' Mamie said when he released her. 'I'll head down and scout around outside for a few minutes. I'll meet you below in the dining area.'

Compared to Mamie's shorts, Alo's should never have left the shop. The colour clash was fierce and this, coupled with the very pronounced bagginess of the garment evoked some ill concealed smirks from the other residents as he made his way towards ground floor level.

Alo was aware of the unwanted attention but, taking his usual, philosophical view of the situation, he muttered to himself, 'Ah! What the heck, it's only for a fortnight!' After that he reckoned the shorts would come in handy for wiping the dipstick of the J.C.B. He waved an hello to the three Dublin girls, who seemed to find his attire very amusing, and he also stopped for a chat with Ben's wife.

Mamie was waiting in the dining room buffet. 'What's it like outside? Did you meet anyone?'

'It's lovely out there. And yes, I met Ben's wife. We had a bit of a chat I don't think she liked me calling her Irene. Probably thought I was getting too familiar. Anyhow she gave me the up and down look. I think I'd prefer Ben.'

'Well now you know Alo where not to hang your hat. But first things first, what are you having for breakfast?'

The rashers and eggs which Alo selected were no substitute for what he was accustomed to at home. So he relished the comforting thought that Mamie had seen fit to take along the cool-bag crammed with black and white pudding. They were now safely tucked away in the room fridge. He planned to make short work of them in the not too distant future.

'If you want to scout around the shops I'll lie out here for a while longer' Alo said as they lounged at the pool later. He wanted to admire the views, especially the females in their skimpy bikinis, and more especially the ones who had taken their tops off. They didn't do that in Miltown Malbay!

'Alright,' said Mamie, 'but I'm warning you not to go asleep under that sun. Keep under the umbrella and don't let your eyes and thoughts stray too much. Just think of combine harvesters, mowers and bailers. I'll be back in an hour or so.'

Despite Mamie's much emphasised warning, Alo did nod off and paid the penalty. When Mamie returned Alo was red all over and already sunburned. At 4pm he retired to his room while his wife went to the courier's meeting alone. She hoped he would be able to go to the Sinatra Club a venue she had seen advertised on a poster in the hotel lobby, later that night. If he did make it to the club,

Mamie doubted that Alo, with his sunburned back, would be in any mood for dancing!

— ☾ —

'Hey Wayne, are you awake yet? Come over here and get an eyeful of this!'

Mark had crawled out of bed a few moments earlier and had opened the shutters that lead out onto the patio outside their apartment which overlooked the pool. The whole area was packed with half naked bodies sprawled on sunbeds, some sheltering from the early afternoon sun under large umbrellas, others lying on towels on the lush grassy margins which were further away from the noise from the screaming children and adults in the pool.

Wayne stirred. It had been so warm during the night he had kicked off the lone sheet and was sprawled on the bed in a pair of shorts. 'What time is it?' he muttered.

'Just after two o'clock. I told you we shouldn't have gone to that disco after we checked in last night.'

Wayne sat up, rubbed his eyes. 'Now you tell me,' he grinned, 'I don't feel so good, too many San Miguels at that bar.'

'Come over here and enjoy the view. This will open your eyes! Look at the talent. Some of them are topless!'

'What do you expect when you go on a sunshine holiday.'

'This is what we came to Ibiza for. Look, there's your friend Georgia with her two pals....'

'Is she topless?' Wayne asked, showing interest at last.

'No, but I wouldn't bank on it not happening before the day is out,' Mark observed, squinting into the sun. 'You should see their outfits. Talk about skimpy bikinis, I've seen bigger postage stamps!'

Wayne rose and joined Mark on the patio. He put on a pair of Raybans against the glare of the sun. He leaned on the balcony rail, taking in the view. 'Where are our girls?'

he asked. Mark pointed them out. Georgia, Bernice and Alison had commandeered three sunbeds on which they were lazing. Georgia was in the shade under an umbrella. The three of them were wearing various coloured bikinis, each of which left little to the imagination. They were wearing sunglasses and Bernice was in the process of applying more suntan lotion to her face and body.

'Hello girls!' Wayne shouted and waved. He seemed to have forgotten his hangover. The girls looked up, smiled and waved back. 'Why don't we have a quick shower and go out and join them?' he said to Mark.

'We'll have to have something to eat first,' Mark replied. 'I'm starving, and remember Alice the courier wants us along to her meeting at four o'clock.'

'A courier telling you where to eat and selling trips. Who needs that? We've heard it all before. That's for the birds.'

'It'll give us an opportunity to view the talent. That girl Caroline will probably be there. I think I'll go anyway.'

'Alright, I'll go too,' Wayne said. Suddenly he began to grin. 'Look, isn't that the couple you were chatting to when we arrived last night?' Alo and Mamie Riordan were making their entrance into the pool area. He was carrying a large beach bag and Mamie had a couple of books in her hand. They looked all set for a session in the sun. Mamie wore a pair of light blue fashionable shorts and a saffron top. Alo was wearing a T-shirt and shorts. Both of them had wide brimmed straw hats on their heads and were wearing sunglasses.

'Yeah, that's Alo and Mamie. They're from Clare.'

'Will you look at the shorts Alo is wearing?' Wayne remarked, 'not exactly top of the range are they?'

'There's enough material in them to make a small tent,' Mark said. They were both laughing loudly as they went back inside.

— ☾ —

It takes a few minutes to get one's bearings on wakening up in new surroundings, Irene always found. The strong light pouring in through the half - open shutters and the strange bedroom brought it all back to her. Of course - they were on holiday - in Ibiza. It all came back to her now, herself and Benjamin arriving in the early hours - and the bed not made up!

She glanced sideways at her husband. He was still asleep and looked like he wouldn't stir for another hour at least. Then she glanced at the bedside clock. Almost 8 am. It looked like it was going to be a lovely morning. Pity to waste it, Irene thought. She would dress, go on a walkabout, scout out the best place before the crowds came down to the pool. And she would complain at reception about that unmade bed.......

Irene slipped into her calf length slacks and matching top, studied herself in the mirror, liked what she saw. Thank God she had always looked after herself, her slim figure proved that. She hoped Benjamin appreciated the effort she had made over the years.

Downstairs the cleaners had almost finished their early morning chores, polishing ashtrays and putting fresh flowers in the foyer and the spacious lounge. As she approached the reception desk one of the young men looked up and smiled.

'Good morning. May I help you?'

'You certainly can.' Irene came straight to the point. 'I have a complaint to make.' The young man's welcoming smile froze on his face.

'I see. What is it please?' He listened as Irene, not attempting to hide her annoyance, told of the shock herself and her husband had received when, after arriving tired in the middle of the night, they had entered their room and found their bed unmade. 'I ended up having to do it myself,' she finished sternly. 'It's simply not good enough.'

'Of course. That was a mistake,' the young man said soothingly. 'Please accept our apologies. Give me your name and room number please and I will report it immediately to our Hotel Services Manager.' His smile was back again. 'You'll be very happy to know that like yourself she is Irish. She will be in touch.'

Irene sniffed. 'I hope so. The least my husband and I should get is an apology.' An Irish Services Manager, she thought, as she exited to the sunlight by the pool. That explains everything!

The air was fresh and there was a beautiful smell of flowers and freshly dug earth as Irene strolled along the shady pathways of the complex. The workmen had hosed down the whole area and there was a delightful sense of dampness which no doubt would disappear later in the broiling heat of the day.

But Irene was content; she and Benjamin had arrived safe and well and she had let the hotel management know that they were not dealing with muck and that she expected certain standards to be maintained. An unmade bed indeed!

'Well hello there! Up bright and early, a woman after my own heart.' It was Alo Riordan, a big cheery smile on his face and wearing an outrageous outfit that only he would have the gall to appear in.

'You startled me,' Irene said. 'I didn't expect any of our party to be up so early.'

'Sorry 'bout that. We met at the airport yesterday, and I'm afraid we got off to a bad start. You're Irene, Ben's wife. We're in room 407 in the hotel, across from Ben and yourself.'

'Really ? How nice.' It wasn't actually, but on holiday one couldn't legislate for who one would end up beside. 'How do you know my name?'

'Ben told me when I was battling with the electrical system in the hotel in the early hours. Imagine switching on the lights by plastic card! He was a great help. Is he up yet?'

'No, he's not -'

'Maybe Mamie and I will see you and Ben at breakfast. Bye for now!' Alo Riordan disappeared along the walkway.

Not if I see you first! Irene vowed to herself. Her stroll was spoiled, the magic gone. She would return to the hotel, fearful of meeting up with the multi-hued Alo again.

Ben was in the shower when she returned to their room. Strains of 'Oh What A Beautiful Morning' greeted her 'Benjamin O'Rourke, come out of there. I have something to say to you.'

Ben recognised the tone. Irene was annoyed about something. 'What's the problem, love?' he asked as he exited with the towel around his waist. 'Did you get any satisfaction when you made that complaint?'

'Of course I did. Now listen, I met that Alo Riordan, the fellow who tried to crash the queue at the airport yesterday. I think he and that wife of his, Mamie, are trying to get pally with us -'

'So what?'

'They're not my type. So let them go find some other couple to talk to. Next thing you know they'll be inviting themselves along to our anniversary dinner!'

'Don't get yourself all upset. Last night Alo was in trouble. He was stumbling around in the dark looking for a light switch in his room. I showed him how to work it with his plastic card. We didn't know much about it ourselves the first time we came up against the same gadget.'

'I don't mind you doing the Good Samaritan - only don't get too close to Alo and Mamie Riordan. Wait until you see the pair of shorts he's parading around in!'

Ben sighed. Irene was getting too uppity. He wished she would relax more, be more friendly. 'Come on,' he said, 'let's go down to breakfast.'

Irene was relieved when they entered the dining-room that Alo and Mamie were nowhere in sight. She was very pleased at the splendid lay-out of the restaurant and the excellent buffet breakfast that was on offer. As she ate she studied the other couples. Some of the ladies smiled a greeting and she smiled back. She was glad that Benjamin and herself were not staying in the apartments.

'Incidentally, when I complained about our unmade bed I discovered that the lady responsible for that area is Irish. Imagine that.......'

Ben was hardly listening to what his wife was saying. He was anticipating the leisurely day ahead. They would wander down to the pool or stroll around the grounds, no driving through rush hour traffic to get to work, no phone calls and no faxes. Bliss!

'By the way Benjamin, what have you planned for our anniversary on Thursday of next week?' Ben came out of his reverie and focused on Irene.

'You won't settle for the local chipper, I suppose?' Ben laughed. The crisis had passed. 'What's the name of the place we stayed in when we were here on our honeymoon? We could go there for old time sake - '

'I want to go somewhere nice for our anniversary dinner Benjamin. We couldn't afford much twenty five years ago. Let's make up for it now.'

'Top of the range this time, Irene my love. Top of the range.'

A smile lit up her face and she stretched across the table and covered his hand in hers. She did love him really.

'Let's get going, no point in sitting here all day. We'll have to look around and see what's on offer.' He looked sideways at Irene. She looked happy at last. Ben was pleased

Paula Sheridan rose early as was her custom most mornings, particularly on days when a fresh contingent of holidaymakers had arrived into the Hotel Orlando. When the arrivals were from Ireland there was an added interest on her part. As the Supervisor of Services at the hotel she liked to be on hand in case there were any complaints from new arrivals - and when it came to complaints the Irish seemed to top the list!

In the apartment not far from the hotel which she shared with her daughter Vicki, Paula made herself a light breakfast of coffee and rolls before reporting for work. Vicki, who worked part-time serving drinks in the Sinatra Club, had been on late duty last night and was still sleeping.

New arrivals to the Orlando invariably expressed surprise when they discovered that the slim, blonde-haired lady they were dealing with was Irish. She had to admit it was rather unusual, but then Paula Sheridan's life thus far had not moved along conventional lines.

'Buenos dias, Senora,' one of the staff on the early morning shift greeted her as she stepped into the foyer. There were not many residents around at 8 a.m, only staff cleaning up from the revelries of the night before, and a group of Germans departing with suitcases at the ready and waiting for the coach to collect them and take them to the airport. The handsome young man behind the reception desk handed her the list with the names and room numbers of the new arrivals who had checked-in during the early hours. Paula barely gave it a second glance; she had been holding down the job in the Hotel Orlando now for nearly five years and one holiday list looked the same as the next. Only if someone had a complaint would she need to check in detail.

She exited through the glass doors, stood on the steps overlooking the pool area, and breathed in some early morning air. Already several people had arrived down and were placing towels on sunbeds, Germans or Scandinavians probably, Paula surmised. She deplored the practice and would ban it if she had the power. She had noticed over the years that few Irish rose early enough to claim sunbeds. Little wonder, they were usually the last ones to leave the open -air bar by the pool in the early hours. It was not unknown for early morning revellers coming back from the discos in Ibiza to sleep by the pool until the early morning bustle woke them.

Paula loved this time of the morning. The sprinklers were going full blast and two gardeners were cutting the grass of the green area bordering the pool and there was a freshness in the air. It reminded her of when she had first come to Dublin as a young girl, cutting the grass in the front garden of the house that she and a few girls who worked in the civil service rented in Malahide, on Dublin's north coastline.

It seemed so long ago now. What would have happened if she hadn't had that brief affair with a married man? Would she be married, or would she be still holding down that boring job in the Department of Social Welfare back home? At least she had Vicki and they were both happy in Ibiza, making a new life for themselves working in the sun rather than dreary old Dublin.

After a leisurely stroll in the fresh air, Paula went inside again, crossed the foyer, conscious of the admiring glance of the young man behind the reception desk. Her supervisor's outfit showed off her slim 38 year-old figure to perfection. Later she and Vicki might have a swim in the pool before dinner, or maybe go to the beach. It would depend on whether or nor it was a complaints-free day.

She went down below to the huge room that housed the launderette where all the hotel's bed and table linen was cleaned and pressed. Part of Paula's job was to check that there was an abundance of clean linen on hand every day for the guests.

She was inspecting the piles of white cloth and checking them against her list when her in-house mobile phone rang. Paula unclipped it from her blouse.

'Hola?' She had a facility for languages and had picked up Spanish quickly. Indeed at present herself and Vicki were attending evening classes twice a week to learn French and German. Paula had ambitions to go far in the hotel and tourism business. She didn't aim to be a supervisor of clean bedrooms all her life.

'Senora Sheridan?' She recognised the voice of her young female assistant.

'Si?'

A slight pause. Then, 'tenemos una problema.'

Paula groaned. It was too much to expect that someone from Ireland wouldn't have a problem. 'What is it ?', she asked in Spanish.

'A couple who arrived early this morning from Dublin, Room number 405. There was fresh linen in their room but someone had forgotten to make the bed. The lady herself had to do it. She was very tired and she is now very angry.'

Silly woman, Paula thought to herself, she has little to be angry about. Has she never made a couple of beds up in her life? It only takes a few minutes. Still....

'What's is the couple's name?'.

A rustle of paper, then..... 'Some of your Irish names are very difficult to pronounce -'

Paula sighed again. 'Spell it out, please.' She took out the list she had been given earlier.

Her assistant's voice came hesitantly over the phone. 'Mr and Mrs O -r-o-u-r-k-e '

Paula caught her breath. 'It's pronounced O'Rourke,' she heard herself saying the name. The sound of it made her voice quiver slightly. What was she worried about? It was a common enough name. There were lots of couples named O'Rourke living in Dublin. She studied her guest list. It did not give the couple's first names.

'Did the lady, or her husband, give their first names?' she asked.

'No. Only their room number.'

'Never mind. It's not important,' Paula lied. 'I'll be in touch with the lady shortly. 'Goodbye.' She clicked off her mobile. Of course she had no intention of meeting the lady face to face, especially if her husband's name was Ben and they lived in Dublin.

She would check the register at reception. Paula said a silent prayer and hoped that her past was not catching up with her.

— ☽ —

Des Murtagh woke and crept over to the window, opening one of the shutters a fraction so as not to disturb Evelyn. The sun was just rising over the rich blue of the Mediterranean. To the side of the window was a sliding door leading onto the balcony. They had been too tired to inspect things when they had booked in a few hours earlier. Des was sure Evelyn would be happy with the set up. It was quite a tiny balcony but big enough to fit two chairs and a little table. He was pleased to see that there was one of those metal clothes dryer things against the wall. Evelyn would find this very useful, he thought.

His stomach rumbled and he remembered he hadn't eaten since the rubbery offering they'd had on the flight coming over. He looked over the edge of the balcony to see if there was anyone about. He was about to come in to wake Evelyn, when he noticed a lady on the balcony of the adjoining room. She had her elbows on the rail as she gazed out to sea. Des remembered her from the coach, Maureen was her name, an attractive middle-aged lady. His football friend Doc, had chatted her up at reception. Sound man. There might be a romance blooming there.

'Hurry up Evelyn, I'm famished,' Des said a short time later as he watched his wife preening herself in front of the mirror of the built-in wardrobe. She was in shorts and a top and was applying her make-up. He had to admit his wife looked very well for a woman of her age - not a grey hair thanks to their daughter Samantha, who was in the hairdressing business and made sure her mother's roots were touched up regularly.

He had put on the beige shorts Evelyn had bought for him in Marks and Spencers. He glanced into the mirror, reckoned he needed to take off a few pounds. He sighed, closed the door and followed Evelyn down the corridor. He was glad they had not booked into the apartments. They looked nice, but they were for the young crowd. Evelyn liked a bit of style. The holiday had been booked before he had received the bad news about the redundancies.

After breakfast Des and Evelyn went outside to take a look around. The sun was warm on their faces as they stepped outside of the air-conditioned foyer of the hotel.

A young man in blue overalls was setting out the sunbeds around the pool area and already they were being snapped up by couples and family groups. On the far side was a beautiful garden with palm trees and amazing flowers that looked like orchids.

Evelyn gave Des the camera and posed by the pool. This place was just as beautiful as it seemed in the brochure. This one was for the neighbours, she thought.

They relaxed by the pool for the rest of the day, only venturing down to the shops to buy some milk and fresh rolls for lunch. Evelyn had brought a jar of coffee and a box of tea-bags with her. Home was one place Des Murtagh didn't want to think about just now.

'I don't see why we should go to the courier's meeting,' Des moaned later that afternoon. 'That Alice will only want to sell us expensive trips. After she has poured a couple of sangrias into everyone we'll be putty in her hands. She'll try to get us to book trips to God-forsaken places with unpronounceable names.'

'We're going to the meeting and that's that.' Evelyn replied firmly. She wanted to observe her fellow-holidaymakers close-up. She wanted nothing to do with any 'how are ya' crowd. After all Des was upwardly mobile in his job and one had to be careful with whom one mixed. Just before four p.m. herself and Des entered the bar. At the far end a few chairs had been set out. Evelyn selected two a distance away from that boisterous man, Alo and his wife.

The seats began to fill up. When the three Dublin girls came in, drinks in their hands, sarong-style wraps over their bikinis, Evelyn prayed that they would not sit near herself and Des and start up a conversation. Thankfully the girls found seats a few rows away from Evelyn. She let Des collect any leaflets that were handed out by the courier lady. They would study them later and decide what trips, if any, they were interested in.

It was only when the Sinatra Nights in the Hotel Casablanca were mentioned that Evelyn came alive. Des was a useful dancer and it seemed like an ideal occasion for dressing up. She could show off some of her nice dresses. Alice the courier said that the nights attracted an international gathering and that the style on show was only superb.

'We'll go along to that tonight,' Evelyn said to Des. 'It sounds like a good night out.' From the way some of the other couples were making enquiries she suspected quite a few people would be going along to the Hotel Casablanca later.

Des was only too happy to go along with anything Evelyn suggested. She would be dead keen to enter the dance contest tonight and qualify for the final of the competition next Saturday. Nothing like a few dances and a few drinks to keep his mind off the problems that awaited him when they got back to Dublin.

When Maureen Duff woke and saw the sun streaming in through the window she decided she would have a quick swim before breakfast. Remembering that this was Sunday she wanted to go to Mass. She made a mental note to make enquiries about the whereabouts of the local church.

After her swim she had returned to her room and got dressed in double quick time. Her floral trousers and crisp white blouse and slip-on canvas shoes would be just right, she thought as she made her way to the dining room. There were very few people there, but in one corner she noticed one of the middle-aged couples whom she had seen at the check-in at Dublin Airport. She knew their names were Des and Evelyn; she had heard them address each other as such when they were getting on the airport bus in the early hours.

The man smiled at her and said, 'It's self-service. Everything is laid out over there.' Maureen smiled her thanks for the information. His wife barely lifted her head to say hello.

Pity Alec Holliday was in the apartments and would not be using the dining room for breakfast, Maureen thought. Earlier in the pool he had made a point of saying hello to her and he seemed very friendly. Maureen felt flattered; it would have been nice to have had him for a companion at breakfast every morning.

She helped herself to some of the fresh tropical fruits and croissants with marmalade. The aroma of the fresh coffee was irresistible. She chose a seat at the window looking out on a delightful garden. I must take a closer look at that later on, she thought. She loved cultivating flowers and shrubs. This was the life! By the time she had finished breakfast a few more of the group she had travelled with last night had come in.

On her way back out to the pool, Maureen called to the reception desk to enquire about Joan and her friends. She discovered that their hotel had been overbooked when they arrived and that they had been accommodated in the Hotel Nevada. Maureen phoned there only to discover that a group had gone on a boat to a nearby island the previous day, that the launch had broken down and they all had to stay overnight. They were expected back sometime today.

Apart from attending Mass and later the courier's meeting, Maureen had the whole day to fill in. She took out a few magazines and found a seat in a shady spot. Her previous experience all those years ago made her aware of the danger of too much sun. She was rubbing on sun tan oil when Caroline O'Hara came over and asked shyly if she might join her. 'Please do. Sit down. You look lovely and cool in that cotton frock.'

'Thank you. I think it's a bit old-fashioned myself but my mother insisted on putting it into my suitcase. It is nice and cool.'

'I think it's very attractive. You'll have all the young men chasing after you,' Maureen laughed. She was thinking of Wayne and Mark. Maureen wondered where those two were this morning. Sleeping off a hangover no doubt. Maureen discreetly brought up the subject of a boyfriend and asked Caroline why hers was not on the holiday with her.

'I'm afraid I don't have a boyfriend,' Caroline confessed.

'Oh, why ever not? You're such an attractive looking young girl.'

'Thanks again. You're very kind. But boyfriends are out for me, I'm afraid.' When she saw Maureen's look of surprise Caroline continued, 'Maybe I'll explain to you sometime.' Maureen was intrigued, but she decided not to pursue the subject.

Caroline picked up a magazine and they both relaxed. Alec Holliday came by but seeing Caroline and Maureen together he just waved and said, 'see you at the courier's meeting later, Maureen,' and passed by. Pity, she would have enjoyed a good talk with him, ask him about his background, find out why he was on holiday on his own. Had he been married? If so, was his wife dead, or were they separated? Maureen could never see herself becoming attached to any man who had left his wife. She often wondered if that was her problem - were her standards too high when it came to living in the present?

Maureen was pleasantly surprised later when, as they were sipping iced drinks and relaxing in the sun, Caroline brought up the subject of Mass. 'Do you know if there is a church nearby?' the younger girl asked.

'I'm delighted you asked,' replied Maureen, 'I was about to go up to my room and get a headscarf. I want to go to 12 o'clock Mass myself.'

'Good, then I'll go with you, if you've no objection...' Caroline said. Maureen was delighted. She looked across the pool to where the three Dublin girls she had noticed at the airport last night, were sprawled on sunbeds. The tall redhead and the good-looking brunette were wearing the skimpiest bikinis she had ever seen. Maureen did not want to be critical, but somehow she doubted if they would be looking for a church to attend Mass!

They found the ancient church in the old part of the town. A few of the older couples who had come over on the flight with them were also at the ceremony. Afterwards they strolled around seeing the sights before choosing an open air restaurant on a height overlooking a section of the beach where they enjoyed a delightful lunch. Despite the age difference, Maureen found Caroline an interesting companion, easy to talk to. But she did notice that while she revealed quite a bit about her background - including her winning £20,000 at Telly Bingo - her young companion skilfully avoided giving too much away about herself.

Was it shyness, Maureen wondered, or was there something in her past that Caroline O'Hara did not want to talk about? Instead they fell to discussing the others in the hotel complex who had flown in with them last night.

'What about that nice Mr Alec Holliday, who is probably waiting to chat you up at the courier's meeting.' Caroline asked grinning. 'If we don't get back to the hotel soon he might think you're ignoring him.' Maureen didn't reply but Caroline noticed she was blushing like a schoolgirl.

The bar was packed when they arrived. She saw Alec Holliday waving her frantically to a seat beside him. He had a drink on the table in front of him and offered to buy herself and Caroline one. Maureen reminded him that she rarely touched alcohol and was surprised when Caroline said she would take a glass of the free Sangria. 'I'd like to taste what it's like, I've heard so much about it,' she laughed.

Maureen was even more surprised when Alec fetched Caroline a glass of Sangria and her young friend finished it off pretty quickly. She's certainly determined to get into the holiday mood! Maureen thought. They listened attentively when Alice the courier mentioned that a special attraction for the more mature holidaymaker would be the Sinatra Nights held three times weekly in another Figueretas hotel. This included dancing to a selection of Sinatra songs.

Doc had always been a Frank Sinatra fan, had a big collection of the singer's long-play records and CDs. Now, while Alice handed out some excursion leaflets, he turned to Maureen, asked her if she liked dancing and would she like to go along to tonight's session in the hotel.

She hesitated for a moment and said, 'I'd love to.'

'Great. We can meet in the lounge after dinner. We'll get a taxi to the hotel. Or maybe we'll walk, see the sights.'

Maureen was about to ask Caroline if she too would like to go to the Sinatra Club tonight but saw that the young man Wayne was chatting her up. Maureen decided not to interfere. Besides, Caroline would probably be seeking something more exciting than the Sinatra Club.

Doc Holliday sat back, a happy man. He was looking forward to the Sinatra Night and the company of Maureen Duff. She seemed a very nice lady, attractive, refined, his type of woman. Maybe he'd have a surprise for his friends in the Ringsend Sports and Social Club when he arrived back in Dublin!

— ☾ —

The courier's meeting was over and Wayne decided to make his move. 'Any of those excursions take your fancy?' he asked Caroline by way of openers.

'Yes, I'd like to go on that coach tour of the island. It sounds interesting.'

'Yeah I was thinking of trying that myself. What about the barbecue on the beach? Barbecues are always good fun, nude swims in the sea and all that - although the food is not always the best.'

'I've never been to a barbecue, I'm not sure I'd enjoy it.' Then her dark eyes flashed mischievously and she added. 'But maybe I'll change my mind and try it.'

'That's the spirit What are you doing tonight? How would you like to come with Mark and myself to a disco?'

Her mother's words about the danger of going out with strange men rang in her ears. Caroline shook her head. 'Not tonight, thanks all the same. Maybe some other time. Now if you'll excuse me I'm going to relax by the pool...' Was she being too cautious, she wondered.

'You got the brush-off there, Wayne. It's my turn to try next.' Mark had arrived just in time to hear Caroline's last remark. It wasn't very often he heard a girl say no to Wayne and he was enjoying it.

Wayne shrugged. 'What the hell, let's go out to the pool and chat up Georgia and the girls. I'll try getting off with that bird some other time. I like the ones who play hard to get.'

Caroline's problem as to how to spend her first night in Figueretas was solved when, strolling around the pool, she came upon one of the Dublin girls sitting alone at a table sipping an iced drink. The girl waved to an empty seat beside her and introduced herself as Bernice.

'Where are your friends?' Caroline asked by way of openers.

'They're over by the poolside bar,' Bernice answered, 'Alison fancies one of the barmen. How about yourself? You seem to be travelling alone, unless you're keeping some handsome hunk locked up in your apartment that you're not telling us about!'

Caroline laughed, 'No, nothing like that, unfortunately! I've no boyfriend with me.' They chatted for a while, Bernice regaling Caroline with some of the antics her two outgoing friends got up to every now and again at some of Dublin's discos at weekends.

She nudged Caroline and they both watched Wayne and Mark making their way towards Georgia and Alison. 'He's like a hound dog in heat,' she observed, referring without a doubt to Wayne. 'He'd do anything to impress a girl!' Just at that moment, Wayne Nolan removed his tee shirt and proceeded to flex his manly muscles and spectacular pecs, to the obvious delight of Georgia and Alison. Georgia appeared very impressed with this virile vision and started to rub Wayne's bulging biceps with the giggling Alison quickly following suit, much to the amusement of the pool-side onlookers.

'Will you look at the carry-on over there,' Bernice said. 'They're throwing themselves at the men already!'

Caroline surprised herself by not being too annoyed. She was enjoying herself. The last time she could remember having such good fun was when she had been sharing the duties in the local youth club with Joe. She wondered what was happening to him. It was months now since they had last seen each other. She might send him a postcard from Figueretas! She might even be daring and write 'wish you were here' on it just for a bit of fun!'

Joe had a knack of being able to make her laugh. She had never dreamed she would find herself sexually attracted to him. He probably didn't want it to happen to them either. That had been the last thing on both their minds. After all, they were both already spoken for, so to speak. Initially, there had been no sexual attraction on Caroline's part. She just remembered thinking about what nice looking eyes he had, and what a lovely smile. As she got to know Joe better, she sensed she had met a warm, kind person in whose company she wanted to be more and more often. As their friendship developed Caroline found herself beginning to wonder what it would be like to be more than just good friends with this fun-loving, young man, even though she knew it could never be. He didn't seem to realise how attractive he was and the effect he was having on her.

The first time he kissed her, it had released an emotion that had been under the surface for some time. They both knew it was wrong but they couldn't help themselves. It was the most tender of kisses, his lips barely brushing hers, but she was left aching for more. It had happened when he was reaching over to let her out of his car after they had locked up the youth club. She had suspected something was about to happen when he had stopped the car some distance from where he usually dropped her off.

'I'm sorry Caroline, I -I shouldn't have done that, taken advantage of you,' he had said, shamefaced.

Caroline couldn't believe it when she heard herself reply quietly, 'Don't blame yourself, I'm glad you did.' What had come over her? She should not be saying things like that.

'Penny for them?' Bernice's voice cut across her thoughts.

'Huh? Oh sorry, I was miles away.'

'I'd guess about a million,' replied Bernice with a curious glance. She looked at Caroline relaxing on the sunbed. What a lovely slim figure she had. I'd die for one like that, Bernice thought to herself. Little wonder that Wayne had made a play for her. Once again Bernice found herself wondering how a girl with a figure like that was on holiday alone.

Caroline got a surprise when Bernice asked her if she would be interested in going to Club Zodiac with herself, Georgia and Alison later. It was apparently quite a famous - or rather infamous - night-club in Ibiza town. 'You should come. It should be good crack.'

'We-e-ll, I'm not sure. I'd like to go but it might be a bit too boisterous for my liking.'

'Boisterous, of course it will be boisterous. What do you think you're going to - a wake? Come on,' urged Bernice. 'It'll be an experience for you. Don't worry, I'll keep an eye on you to make sure you're alright.' What the hell was Caroline about? Was she for real?

'All right then,' Caroline said, excited. 'I'll go!' What on earth was happening to her? Temptation - that was the very thing she had taken time out from her life to avoid. Now here she was all set for a good night out – and looking forward to it into the bargain! 'But don't go running off with some fellow and leave me on my own! I'm not used to the club scene at all really.'

'Me running off with a fella, there's not much hope of that!' Bernice replied disconsolately. Georgia and Alison were always the ones to pick fellows in the clubs. 'I'll go over and let the girls know that you're coming with us.' She headed off to the bar at the opposite end of the pool.

'I'll have to find something suitable to wear for tonight,' Caroline thought to herself. She didn't want to wear anything too conservative, but at the same time, she didn't want to, what was the expression again? - let it all hang out. She snuggled back into her chair, raised her face to the pleasantly warm, late afternoon sun and smiled contentedly. It looked like this soul-searching holiday was going to be a lot more interesting than she had originally intended!

CHAPTER FOUR

Sunday night, their first night on the town, and Georgia, Alison and Bernice were excited. The apartment smelled like a perfume factory as each stood before a mirror and got themselves ready for the action. They each showered, washed their hair, and were now putting the finishing touches to their preparations while they chatted animatedly and flung used tissues into the wastepaper basket – and sometimes onto the floor.

Georgia looked stunning in a pair of silver lame shorts and a black boob tube. Her hair was coiled in a shimmering red mass on top of her head. She zipped up her knee high black suede boots and admired herself in front of the mirror. The reflection showed Alison and Bernice gazing at her.

'Well girls how do I look?' Georgia asked. They turned away without saying anything. 'Club Zodiac, here we come!' Georgia shouted undeterred.

Alison was also dressed in shorts and a skimpy top while Bernice had opted for a flowing white dress slit to halfway up her thigh. They both knew they could never compete with the stunning Georgia. As they were completing their final preparations Bernice announced: ' I forgot to mention that we're meeting Caroline downstairs.'

'Oh, you mean Frigid Brigid,' Alison sneered. 'What on earth did you ask her along for?'

'She's on her own and she seems very nice -' Bernice began to explain.

Georgia made a noise. 'She looks a bit of a downer to me. I only hope she's able to look after herself and doesn't get in our way tonight.' Georgia had seen Wayne chatting Caroline up at the courier's meeting earlier and she was a bit jealous. What on earth had a hunk like Wayne seen in a mousey one like that? Georgia fancied Wayne more than a little. He had told her earlier that himself and Mark would be going to Club Zodiac.

When they arrived down in the foyer they found Caroline sitting alone waiting for them. She was wearing a white blouse with a black skirt just above the knee. Compared to them she was conservatively dressed. But she had a good figure and a very attractive face. She had a cardigan draped over her shoulders.

'Will you get rid of that cardigan, for God's sake,' Alison exploded. 'We're going clubbing – you're like a grannie going to a bingo session!'

Caroline blushed and nipped back up to her room to dump the offending garment. Oh God, she was making a right fool of herself!

They all set out to walk to the Zodiac Club in Ibiza Town. Now that night had fallen the resort had taken on a colourful, somewhat gaudy appearance with couples and groups of young people laughing and parading along the promenade and through the narrow streets. There were some bizarre sights and a wide-eyed Caroline found it difficult at times to separate the males from the females, such was the variety of colourful costumes and outfits on display in the carnival atmosphere. Groups of scantily-clad girls were parading around and seemed all set for a good time.

Caroline felt a bit frightened by it all and it must have shown because Bernice fell into step beside her and said: 'Don't be afraid. People come to Ibiza for a good time. Everyone enjoys themselves here. You just have to let your hair down. Okay. You don't have to become involved if you don't want to.'

Become involved.... Far from reassuring her Bernice's words had added to her fears. What had she meant by becoming involved? Involved in what - and with whom? She looked at her watch. It was approaching midnight. Back home she was usually in bed long before this every night.

Georgia was first through the doors of the Zodiac Club, followed closely by the other girls. The size of the place amazed Caroline. The ground floor had tables and chairs on one level with a sunken dance floor in the middle. Two long bars ran along either side of the club and a balcony which also seemed to be packed with people was on the upper level.

Disco music throbbed and strobe lights flashed in mind-blowing fashion as couples gyrated suggestively on the dance floor. The girls managed to find a deserted table and sat down. A waiter with close-cropped blond hair, dressed in a vest and a very tight pair of jeans, smilingly took their drinks order. Caroline resisted the hard liquor the others asked for a glass of white wine.

'A glass of white wine - are you sure you'll be able for all that?' Alison shrieked to Bernice and Georgia. They all enjoyed a good laugh.

'I wonder will our friends Wayne and Mark be along later,' Caroline asked by way of conversation to hide her embarrassment.

'Who cares,' Georgia shouted above the din. 'Look at all those gorgeous guys eyeing up the talent. Come on girls - let's get up on the dance floor and show them some real action!'

It was the large, glittering revolving orb, suspended from the ceiling and casting a myriad of tiny sparkling lights on the dancers in the Sinatra Club in the Hotel Casablanca,

that did it.......... reminded Alec Holliday of those Sunday
Afternoon dances in the Metropole Ballroom in Dublin.

Ah yes, Dublin in the rare oul' times...... all those girls
he had danced with in the Met in O'Connell Street; girls
he had chatted up, made dates with. The words of the song
ran through his mind........ 'the Pillar and the Met have
gone, and the Royal long since pulled down -'

It was at a Sunday afternoon dance in the Met that he
had caught his first glimpse of Denise. Their eyes had met
and, when a Lady's Choice was called, she had left the
group of girls she was with, crossed the dance floor, and
asked him up. They had hit it off straight away. A date for
later that night was a natural. They had gone to the Gaiety
Theatre, he remembered - the first of their many dates that
had eventually lead to an engagement ring and both of
them making plans to marry.

By then, of course, he had invited her home to
Ringsend to meet the family, his father, mother and his
sister Greta. She was the first girl he had ever brought
home.

What age would he have been then Doc wondered,
gazing up at the sparkling orb as he waited for Maureen
who had gone into the cloakroom to fix her hair... twenty-
five, twenty-six maybe. He was playing soccer for
Shelbourne at the time, training three nights a week,
excited by reports that several big clubs in England were
interested in signing him up...... Alas, it hadn't worked out
with Denise. She had no interest in sport, didn't see why
she had to spend three nights sitting at home while he
trained and then had a few pints with the lads. The
weekends were taken up with him playing matches either
in Dublin or the provinces. And she certainly wasn't
interested in leaving her family and going to live in
England........

'Alec, look - there are some of the people from our
hotel -'. Maureen's voice brought him back to the present.

'Where?' He followed her gaze. Yes, there was the big man Alo Riordan and his wife Mamie. With them at the table were Des Murtagh and his wife Evelyn. The two couples waved a greeting and Doc and Maureen waved back. There was a vacant table not far from them and they went over and sat down.

Earlier in the evening he had joined Maureen for dinner in the Hotel Orlando. Afterwards they had strolled to the Hotel Casablanca, a fifteen minute walk that had given them an opportunity to see some of Figueretas. He found Maureen an easy lady to talk to; she told him how she decided to come on holiday at the last minute after winning £20,000 on RTE's popular Telly Bingo and how later she planned to meet up with her three girlfriends. Maureen had never heard of Ringsend and listened with interest as Doc described his upbringing in Dublin.

'Look at the huge number of people dancing,' Maureen exclaimed, 'I hope they're not all going in for the dance contest we've been told about.'

'Don't worry,' Doc replied, surveying the talent on the dance floor. 'I think we can hold our own with this lot.'

They sat and listened for a while to the trio on stage playing a mixture of quick-steps, foxtrots and slow waltzes, most of them Sinatra favourites. Doc got two drinks from the bar, a 7-Up for Maureen and a pint of lager for himself. When the trio started up another session he asked Maureen up to dance. They were among the first couples on the floor and had some decent space to dance. Within seconds Doc knew that, as a modern ballroom dancer, Maureen Duff was something special. Dancing, he always reckoned, was like football, there were those born with a natural talent, others who just didn't have it. Maureen was a natural.

For her part, she was beginning to enjoy herself. Alec Holliday was an accomplished dancer and very personable.

'Where did you learn to dance?' Doc asked, admiration in his voice. 'You're really good.'

'Thank you. I began dancing when I was a teenager. We went to a dance every week.' He detected a sadness in her voice.

'You said 'we'. You mean someone special?'

'Yes. Very special.'

The dance floor was crowded now and Doc had to concentrate on what he was doing. He wondered who the 'someone special' was that Maureen referred to. He decided not to pursue the matter right now.

They were seated again, enjoying their drinks and chatting, when a roll of the drum signalled the appearance on stage of a dapper man in a dress suit and a small, plump woman attired in a full-length dress that sparkled and glittered. They were Senor Juan Carrasco and his wife Pepita who for some years now had been running the popular weekly dance contest in the Sinatra Club in the hotel. After introducing himself and his wife, Senor Carrasco, in his slightly fractured English, welcomed everyone to the club.

'Tonight we have a big international gathering, dancers from -' he consulted a card - 'the United Kingdom, Germany, Ireland, Sweden, Finland and Iceland. Also even from America. My wife Pepita and I welcome you all. Now I explain the rules. They are simple.....When the band plays, everyone who wishes to take part in the competition comes onto the floor and dances a selection of quick-step, foxtrot, slow and old time waltz, tango and rumba and samba. Everything! This will last approximately twenty minutes and during that time my wife and I will be on the floor eliminating couples by tapping them on the shoulder thus -'

Senor Carrasco demonstrated. 'When you feel that touch you must leave the dance floor - immediatamente!' He emphasised the last word. Paused, then continued: 'Elimination goes on until only three couples are left. Those three couples will be tonight's winners and will each receive a bottle of champagne. On Wednesday night we follow the same procedure; three more couples will be winners and receive champagne. On Saturday night next we have the Grand Finale - My wife will explain.....'

Pepita stepped up to the microphone. 'At eleven p.m. on Saturday night the dance floor will be cleared and the six finalists will dance for twenty minutes. Shortly afterwards my husband and I will announce who is Sinatra Club's champion dancing couple for that week. The prize for the winning couple is a free holiday for a week in the Hotel Casablanca - .' Pepita paused 'On behalf of my husband and myself I wish you good luck!'

There was a burst of applause from the audience. Looking around, Maureen admired the style displayed by many of the women. Some of the dresses were exquisite. They made her own outfit look rather ordinary. She hoped that the quality of the dancing rather than one's mode of dress would be the deciding factor when the winners were announced.

Evelyn Murtagh in particular looked very well, Maureen thought. She was wearing an eye-catching ensemble that exuded good taste, stylish without being showy. If Evelyn's dancing was on par with her dress sense, Maureen reckoned her own chances of winning were disappearing by the minute.

'All set, Maureen?' Doc asked. He sensed that she was nervous.

'I've never danced in a competition before - '

'Don't worry. You'll be fine.' He squeezed her hand and stood up.

The trio had started playing a quickstep. The guitarist was singing, a Sinatra number of course..... 'You Make Me Feel So Young......' It was one of Maureen's favourites. Evelyn Murtagh was already on the floor with her husband. She looked radiant, confident.

Doc coaxed Maureen to her feet. He put his arm around her waist, guided her towards the floor which was now filling up with dancers. They paused at the table where Alo Riordan and Mamie were sitting.

'Not getting up, Alo?' Doc asked.

'No,' the big man answered.

'Why not?'

'He's waiting till they play 'The Walls of Limerick' or the 'Siege of Ennis,' Mamie joked. 'I'm afraid Alo and I are not much good at this modern stuff.'

'Get up and dance anyway,' Doc replied. 'Sure you've nothing to lose. It's only a bit of fun .'

'You're right, Doc. We came here to enjoy ourselves.' He turned to his wife. 'On your feet Mamie girl. We'll show this crowd a step or two that they never saw before!'

On the dance floor Evelyn whispered into Des's ear: 'Be careful, that big fellow Alo and his wife are up dancing. Will you look at him – talk about a bull in a china shop! –'

She had been annoyed earlier in the night when she and Des were sitting at a table and Alo and Mamie had entered and sat down and joined them without as much as asking. Such cheek! Didn't they have any manners down in Co. Clare or wherever it was they came from. Mamie sensed Evelyn's aloofness towards her as the two men chatted but let it pass.

'You'll be up dancing later in the contest, I suppose,' Alo had asked Evelyn. 'I'd say you were a bit of a Ginger Rogers in your day, eh?' He laughed good humouredly.

'I'm afraid Ginger Rogers was before my time.' Evelyn had replied tartly. 'But yes, Des and I will be dancing shortly.' She was glad to see that Alo and Mamie Riordan didn't last long on the dance floor before Senor Carrasco tapped him on the shoulder and gestured towards their table.

For his part Des liked Alo. Chatting at the table the big man had sensed that Des was troubled by something and had invited him to have a discreet chat tomorrow morning over a drink. 'There's no machine that can't be fixed if you study the problem from all angles. That's my motto, Des,' Alo had winked conspiratorially.

Des found himself comparing Alo's open, thoughtful approach to some of his fair-weather friends who, since the word was out that his job was gone, were now becoming increasingly disinterested in his company. This guy is different, very different, Des thought. He's big in stature and in heart. For the first time since he had received the bad news, Des saw a ray of hope.

Wayne Nolan sat impatiently watching Mark Smith finishing his pint.

'Relax. It's early yet, Wayne. We don't want to be first into the disco.' Mark said.

Wayne glanced at his watch. 'It's nearly midnight. I like to get in early to watch the talent arriving. It's difficult to see anything special when the place is crowded.'

Mark was enjoying the music and the craic in Murphy's Irish Bar. The disco was their target tonight, however. He drained his glass. 'Okay, let's go,' he said.

The warm air engulfed them as they walked through Ibiza town to Club Zodiac. The town was throbbing as people looked for the action in the all-night discos at the numerous clubs. When they reached the Zodiac they pushed their way to the bar, ordered drinks, and watched the crowd dancing.

The girls were real beauties. Judging by their outrageous carry-on some of them had already too much to drink. It's amazing the difference a suntan can make, Mark thought. A little sun on the skin and even the plainest girl blossoms and glows. The guys looked good too.

To Wayne, heaven was eyeing-up the scantily-clad Scandinavian babes, strutting their stuff on the dance-floor. He looked forward to the latter part of the disco when he knew he'd see even more of their sexy tanned bodies. Drink usually helped the guys and girls to lose their inhibitions and they would end up on the dance podiums performing all types of exotic dances.

After a few drinks Wayne too, was bumping and grinding to the music. He turned many a head with his good looks and long finely -tuned body. When he returned to his stool Mark nudged him in the ribs to look towards the entrance at the other side of the club where Georgia, Alison, Bernice and Caroline were seated at a table. Both Mark and Wayne were very pleased to see Caroline.

Georgia and Alison made their way onto the dance-floor to bop to the popular Vengaboy's 'We're Going to Ibiza.' Wayne could see that Georgia and her companion were giving them the eye. He and Mark edged their way through the crowd to join them. Bernice and Caroline also joined in. They all gyrated, flirted and laughed as they danced together. Caroline was really enjoying herself. She had just finished her second glass of wine and was beginning to feel very relaxed.

When thirst and exhaustion set-in all returned to the table. Georgia looked searchingly at Wayne and said meaningly. 'My throat feels like sand-paper'.

Wayne took the hint. 'What's everyone drinking?'

Georgia snapped up the cocktail menu and ordered a Pina Colada. 'A large one,' she said, looking wide-eyed and innocent. Alison opted for the same.

'How about you two girls?' Mark asked Bernice and Caroline.

'I'll have the same as Georgia and Alison.' Bernice said.

'What about you, Caroline?' Wayne asked. He wanted to get her a really strong drink, get her tipsy, get her alone somewhere to himself. She wasn't dressed as sexily as the other three but there was something about her he really fancied.

'How about something different for a change?'

'Maybe I'll stick to the white wine,' Caroline was taking no chances.

'You'll get sick drinking all that wine. Leave it to me, I'll get you something exciting!' Wayne assured her. If he played his cards right he was on a winner. Mark could look after himself.

Wayne ordered the drinks and almost fell off the bar-stool when he was presented with the bill. What a steal! - he could have bought a pub in Temple Bar for what he'd paid for that round! This bird Caroline had better come good!

He negotiated his way back to Mark and the girls, placed the well-laden tray on the table. Everyone picked up their drinks except Caroline. Wayne handed her the large, slim glass containing a pinkish liquid with two straws, a tiny parasol and a couple of swizzle sticks.

'Specially for you, Caroline,' he said. 'I think you'll like it.' It had better do the trick, Wayne thought to himself. He had winked at the barman and asked him for something potent. It certainly cost enough!

Caroline smiled a 'thank you' at him, put the multi-coloured straw between her lovely lips and sipped. He could see by her face she quite enjoyed it. She put the second straw into her mouth and syphoned up a large portion of the liquid. That's more like it!, Wayne smiled to himself, watching with interest.

By now the dance floor was very crowded. The podium dancers were in competition with the more brazen punters who took delight in climbing aboard the podiums to strutt their stuff. Georgia and Alison dragged a rather reluctant Wayne up onto the dance floor. Mark decided to go out to the toilet. By now the music was deafening and the strobe lights were working overtime. The Zodiac Club was really jumping!

When Mark returned he noticed an ashen-faced Caroline swaying on her feet, her almost empty glass in front of her and an anxious looking Bernice by her side.

As he approached, Bernice shouted above the din. 'Caroline isn't feeling very well. I think it was that cocktail. She told me she wasn't used to alcohol.'

Mark looked anxiously at Caroline. She looked like she was about to fall down any moment. 'Come on, you need some fresh air. I'll take you back to the apartments. We'll get a taxi.' She didn't offer any resistance as he put his arm around her waist and guided her towards the exit. Mark was glad Wayne was so busy on the dance floor to notice them depart.

By now Wayne had removed his shirt, stripped to the waist, perspiration running off his well muscled body, he jumped onto a podium to join a luscious dark-eyed dancer. They bumped and grinded and did some very sexy movements to the lively Euro beat.

On the floor Georgia was determined to show Wayne that she could also strut her stuff. She too, jumped up onto a podium and slowly and seductively removed her boob-tube to the music, giving it her all. Alcohol had claimed her brain by now and if Ibiza Uncovered camera crew were around she aimed to be the centre of attention.

Georgia finished her routine to cheers as the male podium dancer helped her down onto the floor to rejoin the army of other half-naked male and female bodies. Wayne looked around and wondered where Caroline was. He couldn't see her and reckoned she was in the loo. When he asked and Bernice told him she'd gone home a short while ago with Mark, Wayne nearly flipped. His investment had vanished out of his grasp!

Still the night was young. He looked around..... Georgia was making it with a tall Swede. Wayne allowed himself to be scooped into the midst of a wild group of Scottish girls. He enjoyed their attention, particularly that of a raven-haired beauty called Myra who literally took him to her bosom.

As the first light of dawn appeared they strolled along hand-in-hand into the new day. Outside an all-night bar on the beach Myra asked for a wee night-cap. The wee night-cap lasted three hours and after that Wayne lost track of time!

Ben O'Rourke was determined to make the most of this holiday. After all it was a 25th wedding anniversary trip for himself and Irene. It would help if they had a car. Sitting around a pool all day building up a tan, as they had done today after Irene complained about the unmade bed when they had arrived last night, was not his forte. Besides it made Irene restless, and when Irene got restless.....

It would be nice to visit some of those places off the beaten track, see something interesting for a change. 'We'll hire a car tomorrow, Irene. Get away from the pool and see some of the real Spain. How about it?'

'Good idea, Benjamin. We can tour around, see if we can pick out a nice restaurant where we can have our anniversary dinner next week.'

'What about tonight? How about going to the dance in the Sinatra Club? The courier mentioned a dance contest on there tonight. I was talking to some of the lads - '

Irene turned from the mirror where she was brushing her hair. 'The lads...I suppose you mean Alo Riordan and that Doc what's-his-name. Besides, I don't fancy sitting in a smoky bar on our first night out.' And apart from anything else she never did rate Frank Sinatra as a person because he had been unfaithful to his first wife Nancy.

'We could go just for an hour or so, see the dance competition. We could leave early if you like, get an early start when we hire the car tomorrow morning - '

'Alright Benjamin. We'll go to please you. But be careful not to drink too much.'

The Sinatra Club in the Hotel Casablanca was crowded by the time Irene and Ben arrived. The dance was an ideal weekly promotion guaranteed to attract an international group of dancing enthusiasts. Irene had no intention of entering the dancing competition. It was rather showy and not genteel enough, she felt. As far as she was concerned - dancing was for enjoyment, not for competing for a tawdry prize. She considered herself above all that.

From their vantage point at the edge of the dance floor Irene and Ben watched the dancers twirl by. Doc Holliday and the lady he had become friendly with glided by, as though they were floating on air, both of them obviously enjoying themselves, oblivious to all. Ben wondered what, if anything, was developing between the duo. They made a nice looking couple. A holiday romance between two mature people. The stuff you would read about in one of Irene's women's magazines.....

When the dance competition got under way after about an hour Ben watched Senor Carrasco and his wife eliminate couple after couple until the contest was in its final stages. The excitement among the audience was mounting by the minute. Just six couples left now - and Des and Evelyn Murtagh and Doc and Maureen were among them. Evelyn looked really exquisite and Ben reckoned that she would surely make it to the final.....

Maureen Duff's head was in a whirl. Only six couples left on the dance floor...She had allowed Alec to guide her through the changing rhythms from quick-step to foxtrot, from waltzes to tangoes. Another disappointed couple were making their off the dance floor -

'Keep it going, Maureen my sweet, we're doing great,' Alec whispered in her ear. Senor Carrasco and Pepita had been busy during the past ten minutes or so. At least fifty couples must have felt that dreaded tap on the shoulder; now the dance floor was looking distinctly empty and there was much more space in which to display one's technique. Alec and herself were really flying!

A couple whizzed by, executed some fancy tango steps in a corner of the floor, before disappearing from Maureen's vision.- Evelyn and Des Murtagh! She would recognise that beautiful dress anywhere! They too were still in the running. Maureen was sure they would finish in the top three.

'Two more couples eliminated,' she heard Alec whisper. The rhythm had switched again; now it was a slow waltz. The tension was mounting; only one more couple to be eliminated and the remaining three would go forward to the final on Saturday...Maureen closed her eyes, prayed they would be still dancing at the end.....

Senor Carrasco and his wife were whispering at the side of the dance floor. They nodded their heads in agreement. Every eye in the room was on the short plump figure of Pepita as she advanced into the centre of the dance floor. The quartet of couples swirled around her, the revolving chandelier adding to the atmosphere.

Pepita reached out – and tapped Des Murtagh on the shoulder! There was a gasp from the audience as Des and a very disappointed looking Evelyn left the floor. Maureen almost collapsed with relief as the music stopped and applause burst forth.

Alec and herself had made it to the final! She could hardly believe it – it was nearly as good as winning at Telly Bingo. Alec was smiling at her, guiding her towards the stage where Senor Carrasco waited to make the official announcement. They were joined by an English couple and a duo from Sweden. As their names were announced each couple took a bow and received a bottle of champagne before leaving the stage.

Back at the table all the other couples congratulated them as Doc opened the bottle of champagne with a flourish and poured some into everyone's glass.

'Here's to our champion dancers,' Alo shouted above the din. Glasses were raised and drained. Amid the excitement Maureen saw that Evelyn looked a little disappointed.

'You and your husband came very close,' she said to Evelyn. 'You must try again on Wednesday night.'

'We intend to, don't we Des?' Evelyn replied. Her husband nodded in agreement. Nothing was going right for him these days.

Alec was on his feet. 'I'm going to order two more bottles of champagne,' he said to Maureen. He couldn't spot a waiter so he headed towards the bar.

'Good on you, Doc!', Alo shouted after him.

Doc felt happier than he had been for a long time. He was glad that he had come on holiday alone. Maureen was a nice lady and things were going along smoothly.......

'Hey, amigo,' Doc shouted in his best Spanish to the barman. 'Send two bottles of your best champagne over to that table pronto.'

His words were lost in the hubbub of other thirsty customers shouting orders to the harassed barmen behind the counter. The bottle of champagne that had been presented to himself and Maureen on the stage a few minutes ago had barely survived a round between themselves and the other couples. Doc was on a high; a couple more bottles would see the night off to perfection.

He was endeavouring to attract a barman's attention when he felt a tap on his shoulder. Doc turned. The man in the garish, multi-coloured shirt was grinning beneath his heavy moustache.

'Howya,' there was no mistaking the Dublin accent. 'Alec Holliday, isn't it? Or Doc as we used to call you…'

'That's right.' The newcomer looked vaguely familiar.

'You don't recognise me, do you? I'm not surprised. I've put on a bit of weight since you and I played football together.' He paused. 'Donie Crawford…… we were with Shelbourne, remember?'

'Donie Crawford! Of course!' Now Doc remembered. A face from the past. Donie had certainly put on weight since the last time Doc had seen him. When was that?

Must be nearly thirty years ago now. Donie hadn't lasted long at Shelbourne – not after he had gotten himself involved in a cross-border car scam, been found guilty, and served a year in Mountjoy. He had been kicked out of Shelbourne and had faded from the soccer scene after that. Now he had shown up again - like the proverbial bad penny.

'Put it there -' Donie thrust out his hand. Doc shook it, began searching for an excuse to get away. Donie took a swig from his pint of lager. 'You were from Ringsend, right?'

Doc had caught the barman's eye. He ordered the champagne, pointed out the table. 'It was nice meeting you, Donie,' he lied. 'Pity we can't talk right now. I'm with some friends. Have a nice holiday -'

'Holiday? - I'm not on holiday. I live here.' Donie was swaying slightly. He looked like he'd had one lager too many.

'Really? That must be nice. Retired, I suppose?'

'Retired' Donie let out an expletive. 'You must be joking. I have my own little business -' he winked conspiratorially. 'That's what I want to talk to you about, Doc.'

He had to get away. Maureen would be wondering what was keeping him. 'Sorry, Donie, I can't talk right now. Some other time maybe - Nice meeting you.' He eased his way past his fomer teammate.

'Alright then, some other time. Don't worry, Doc old pal, I'll be in touch - ' Donie called after him.

Phew! - that was a close call. Just his luck to bump into someone like Donie Crawford after all those years. The guy was trouble, always up to something shady. What was he doing in Ibiza? He'd said he had his own business. What was that? Doc wondered. Nothing legitimate, that's for sure!

Doc got back to the table just in time to see Alo Riordan send a champagne cork shooting skywards and hear the screams of delight from the women as the liquid cascaded out into the air. Doc sat down beside Maureen as their glasses were filled.

'Here's to us , Maureen,' he toasted, his eyes straying over to the bar area. Donie Crawford was nowhere to be seen.

'Who was that man you were talking to at the bar?' Maureen asked.

'Oh, nobody important. Just someone I knew years ago' Doc replied easily. He hoped he had seen the last of the man in the multi-coloured shirt. Somehow he doubted it.

CHAPTER FIVE

Doc Holliday jogged his regulation fifteen minutes down the paved promenade, turned, and was now making good progress back towards the Hotel Orlando. The sun was sparkling on the sea and he found the light breeze coming in across the sand very invigorating.

He was about halfway on the return journey along the promenade when he noticed the car pulling into the kerb a short distance in front of him. He didn't give it a second glance. Not until he saw the lissom looking lady with short dark hair and wearing a pair of tinted sun glasses step out onto the pavement and stare in his direction. She was above medium height, wearing the bottom of a track suit and a figure- hugging denim top. She had low heeled leather shoes and there was a smile on her tanned face.

She leaned against the back of one of the many wooden seats that dotted the promenade, watching his approach. Doc was conscious of her studying him but thought nothing of it until he came opposite and she called out:

'Mister Holliday.....' It wasn't an English accent.

He pulled up, surprised. 'Yes?.....'

She had a pleasant smile that showed her small white teeth. 'I am sorry to interrupt your jogging but may I speak with you?'

'Sure.' He hoped she wasn't one of those holiday home time-share freaks!

'You were in the Sinatra Club last night.' It wasn't a question, it was a statement.

'I saw you there. You and the lady.' She smiled again, said admiringly. 'You are a very good dancer, Mister Holliday.'

'Thank you.' Doc took out a handkerchief from the pocket of his shorts, wiped the perspiration from his forehead. It gave him time to think. Who was this woman, and why had she made a point of accosting him on the promenade this morning? 'I'm sure you didn't get up this early just to compliment me on my dancing.......'

She laughed again. 'Of course not -'

'What's the problem then? I did pay for the champagne last night -'

'I'm sorry. I should explain.' The smile had disappeared. She reached into the pocket of her denim top, took out a folded-over identity card, flipped it open.

Doc glanced at it. The word 'Policia' leaped out at him. Underneath the square of cellophane was a snapshot of a slightly younger looking woman than the person standing opposite him. Her name, he noticed, was Yolanda Segguria.

He looked at her with renewed respect. 'So you're a policewoman......?'

She nodded. 'Yes. Ibiza Drug Squad.'

'That's a dangerous game for a young lady like you.'

'I know. But we have a problem with drugs on the island. A big problem. They come in by boat, mainly from north Africa, to the dealers here. That's what I want to discuss with you, Mr. Holliday.'

'Now hold on a minute, lady -' This was getting a bit scary. He'd read about people on holidays being picked up on suspicion of pushing drugs, being thrown into jail, rotting there for months. 'I'm not into drugs. No way. Never touched them. In Ringsend in Dublin where I come from I've seen the terrible tragedies drugs have had on people, on families. You're barking up the wrong tree, lady -'

She was looking at him, puzzled. 'What are you talking about, barking at a tree. What is that?'

He laughed despite himself. 'Sorry, it's an expression we use. It means you're making a mistake. Like I said, I'm not into drugs -'

'Relax, Mr. Holliday. I did not say you were pushing drugs. I just want to talk to you about that man who spoke to you in the Sinatra Club last night. Remember him? His name was Donie Crawford.'

Doc was relieved. 'Is that all? Sure I remember. What do you want to know?' She glanced around. 'I don't like talking in the street. Too many people can see. You probably haven't had breakfast yet. Why don't we go over to that cafe bar across the road. We can have a cappuccino and a roll, talk some more......'

'Be my guest.' He waited for a break in the morning traffic then guided her across the road.

Doc couldn't be sure, but he suspected Yolanda Segguria was studying him intently behind her tinted sunglasses as they waited for the waiter to bring the coffee and rolls. He had also cast his eyes over the woman from the Ibiza Drug Squad and liked what he saw. Late thirties, he reckoned. Obviously kept herself in good shape. Married too, judging by the rings on her fingers.....

'You want to know about Donie Crawford,' he asked. 'We used to play soccer together. Many years ago.....'

'Ah, football,' she cast her eyes skywards. 'My two boys are mad about soccer. They talk about it all the time..... Real Madrid,' she paused, got back to business.

'Your friend - he lives here in Ibiza. He is known to us.'

'Hold on, Donie's not my friend.' Doc corrected her. 'We haven't seen each other for years. To be honest I never did like the guy. Too shifty. I was amazed when he tapped me on the shoulder at the bar the other night.'

'He is a drug pusher. Here. In Ibiza,' she said evenly. 'Heroin mostly.'

'It doesn't surprise me.' Doc replied. 'Thirty years ago he was into smuggling cars. I suppose there's a lot more money to be made in drugs.'

'He has been living here for almost six years. He owns a nice apartment in Ibiza town where he lives with his Spanish girlfriend. We know all about him; our colleagues in Dublin - your Gardai - they gave us his background. He goes to the Sinatra Club a lot, to meet Irish people on holiday. He gets talking to a person, buys them a drink, asks if they would like to make some - how do you say - easy money.'

'Doing what?'

'Smuggling a cellophane packet back to Dublin in a suitcase, past your Customs. Heroin. It is picked up later. He pays 1,000 pounds per trip. Five hundred paid here, the rest when the packet is delivered to his contact in Dublin.' Yolanda Segguria paused, licked some cream from her spoon, her eyes on him. 'Did Donie Crawford ask you to take anything back to Dublin, Mr. Holliday?'

'I never gave him the chance. I brushed him off.'

'Don't worry, he will try again. He operates alone in Ibiza. He is not a big player in the drug business. It is very difficult to catch him in the act..' She paused, said very casually. 'I was hoping you might like to help us.'

'Me? How?'

'You are going to the Sinatra Club again with your lady friend?'

'Yes. Maureen and I plan on going again on Wednesday.' How did she know Maureen wasn't his wife? He liked to think that maybe she had gone to the bother of checking that out.

'Good. I will be there also. Perhaps when Donie Crawford does approach you - and he will, you will play him along, let him think you are interested in bringing a cellophane packet back to Dublin for him.......'

'Why should I do that?' Doc was no fool. He knew that the scumbags who operated in the drug business played rough. Anyone who crossed the drug barons in Dublin was asking for trouble. People who had done so had paid with their lives. He liked to think that he could take care of himself ; still, he had no desire to be found dumped in a canal with a bullet in his head......

'You sure that Donie Crawford operates alone - that he's not connected with a gang?'

'We are certain. He is a small-time player. He has a contact here and two pushers who buy the heroin off him in Dublin. Otherwise he operates on his own. There would of course be some danger...'

Doc considered for a few moments. Helping out meant he would meet Yolanda Segguria again. He would like that. 'What exactly would you want me to do?'

'You arrange for him to hand over the package and the money to you here in Ibiza. We will be waiting. When he does so we pounce, catch him in the act. All the time, of course, you and I will be keeping in touch Mr. Holliday......

'You make that sound like a bonus - you and me keeping in touch....'

He wondered how many times Yolanda Segguria had used that ploy before in the line of duty. 'What does your husband think about you doing this dangerous work, going out to meet with strange men?'

He meant it as a joke but he noticed she wasn't smiling. When she replied he understood why. 'My husband is dead, Mr. Holliday. He also was a policeman; killed three years ago in a car bomb explosion. He was hunting down the drug barons in Ibiza and they did not like it.'

Doc felt like someone who had just been hit by a sledgehammer. He wished that the ground would open up and swallow him. 'I'm sorry. I didn't mean to be insensitive-'

She shrugged. 'It's alright. I am over it now. That's why I do everything in my power to put these criminals into jail. In memory of my late husband and for my two boys....'

He swallowed. 'I'm on your side. I'll do anything you want.' What else could he say after that terrible gaff?

'Thank you, Mr. Holliday. I am very grateful.'

She rose, shook his hand. 'Hasta luego.'

Doc reckoned that probably meant 'see you soon.' 'Yes,' he replied. 'You know where I am - the Hotel Orlando.' He watched her cross the road, get into her car. She waved as she drove off. Doc ordered another cup of coffee from the waiter. He needed time to think.

Paula Sheridan set about her duties in the hotel with less enthusiasm than usual that Monday morning. Thoughts of Ben O'Rourke had filled her mind since yesterday when the name had cropped up. She had checked the hotel register and her worse fears had been confirmed; the O'Rourkes were from Dublin. It must be him....What a despicable trick fate had played.

She had strolled around the vicinity of the poolside yesterday, staying well out of view, surveying the crowds relaxing in the sun. She had been unable to recognise the man who had been her lover, the man who was the father of her daughter Vicki. She would scout around the hotel again today. What if they came upon each other unexpectedly in the hotel and Ben was with his wife. How would she react? What would she do - or say?

Her brief affair with him seemed such a long time ago, but the memory of that unhappy time in her life was still vivid. She was aged twenty at the time and sharing an apartment with her friend Nicola in Malahide, a seaside town with a spread of upper middle-class houses on Dublin's northside. She had decided to invest in her first car and, after perusing the sales columns in the newspapers, had settled for one in O'Rourke's Garage in Glasnevin.

Ben O'Rourke was the perfect salesman: late 30s, debonair, courteous and persuasive. He had come out of his outdoor office to attend to her and Nicola personally. That should have alerted her that he had an eye for the women. While Nicola had stood by amused, Paula and he chatted and bargained - flirted even! Ben O'Rourke had certainly come on to her in a big way - and she had responded. As she and Nicola drove away in her second-hand Toyota Paula had sensed it wasn't the last she would see of him.

'Isn't he just divine,' she had remarked to her friend.

'Who?' Nicola feigned ignorance. She was studying the traffic, playing her own little game.

'Oh, come off it, Nicola. Ben O'Rourke of course!

'Oh, he's a charmer alright. But for heaven's sake Paula, he's much too old for you. Besides he's probably married. I'm sure I saw the mark of a wedding ring on his finger.'

'So what!'

'You were devouring him with your eyes. You're a shameless hussy, Paula Sheridan.'

'Ah go on. You're just jealous. Tell the truth - you fancied him yourself, married or not.' Paula's eyes flashed as she negotiated the coast road. 'I bet you he'll get in touch......'

She was right. She got a telephone call in work two days later. It was Ben O'Rourke , enquiring at first how the car was going - then getting down to the real business of asking her out for a drink after work. Paula was thrilled, but Nicola didn't share her friend's excitement.

'For God's sake Paula, you're asking for trouble. He probably has a wife and a couple of kids. I hope you know what you're getting into.'

Paula was determined to throw caution to the winds. She had never met anyone quite like Ben O'Rourke before. He added up to something more than the morons she met at the discos at the weekends. 'Relax, Nicola, for heaven's sake. Just because I'm going out for a drink with him doesn't mean we're going to move in together.'

She didn't move in with him. But she did the next best thing - over the next month she spent several passionate evenings and the occasional overnight with him in a house in Swords that she later found out was loaned to Ben by a friend of his. Up until then she had only dated inexperienced and immature guys of her own age; with Ben she had her first real sexual experience. Little did she realise then the price she would have to pay for the hours of all-consuming passion that she spent alone with him.

The crisis had begun when Paula had begun to feel unwell and was unable to go to work with Nicola in the Department of Social Welfare offices in Dublin's Store St.

After a week of morning sickness Nicola persuaded her to see a doctor. Paula's worse fears were confirmed with the test. She was pregnant.

Paula was shocked. She knew instinctively she would get no help from Ben. He had never owned up to having a wife but she had suspected all along he was married - even before the night when he was driving her home and she had discovered a Barbie doll at her feet in the car.

'Oh that,' he had laughed it off with the ease of a practised liar, 'that belongs to a young niece of mine. Must give it back to her next time I see her.'

Nicola had done a bit of sleuthing on her own. She had persuaded a male colleague in the Department to drop into O'Rourke's Garage on the pretext of buying a car, getting friendly with one of the salesmen there and making some discreet enquiries about the owner. The salesman confirmed Nicola's worse fears...... his boss was not only married but had two young children. Nicola wondered how she was going to break the terrible news to her friend......

'You said you were going to phone Ben today, tell him all,' Nicola said to Paula when she arrived in from work 'What happened?'

'Nothing. According to his secretary Ben is at the London Motor Show. He won't be back for a few days.' Paula had sighed. 'Funny he never mentioned anything to me about going off to London.....'

Nicola decided that there was no easy way of saying what she had to say. 'Paula, I'm afraid I've got some bad news about Ben. He's married - and he has two children. I'm sorry -'

Paula had stared, devastated. 'Oh God, I was dreading something like this, but I was hoping it wouldn't happen. How could I have been so stupid - '

'The no-good creep! He took advantage of you....'

'What am I going to do, Nicola? He won't leave his wife for me. I know that. I suspected it all along. And my parents.........what am I going to tell them? They'll be devastated when they learn I'm going to have a baby. Everyone at home will be talking. I can't face them...'

Paula had run into the next room and thrown herself on the bed. It was then she had thought of her two friends in Barcelona. They had been to school together at home and were now teaching in a language school in Spain and were always on to her to join them.

Barcelona! .... of course! It would solve all her problems. She would quit work, sell the car - not to O'Rourke's Garage, that's for sure! - telephone her parents and tell them she was fulfilling her long-held dream of working abroad. They would be amazed, of course, try to talk her out of it. But she knew it was the only solution...

Those early years after Vicki was born had been difficult. Her friends in Barcelona had been very helpful when it came to taking care of a young baby. Paula had started off working at night in a bar which left her free to care for Vicki during the day. As Vicki got older and went to kindergarten and later day school, Paula had secured a job as secretary in an American owned shoe company in Barcelona. The shoes were manufactured in Spain and

sold to rich and famous ladies in America and Canada - at
2,000 dollars a pair! Whew!.. what she could have done
with that kind of money! Over the years she had learned
to live with hardship. By now, as far as she was concerned,
Ben O'Rourke was well and truly out of her life. It was a
difficult decision for her to take but she had no regrets. He
had told her lies, cheated her, and for that she could never
find it in her heart to trust him again.

Her friend Nicola had contacted her to tell her that
Ben had been in touch shortly after he had returned from
London. Nicola had fobbed him off by telling him that an
opportunity had arisen for Paula to work abroad and she
had taken it. Ben had been surprised. Where had she
gone?, he had asked. When Nicola had informed him that
Paula was somewhere in Spain she thought she had
detected a sigh of relief coming down the line.

Ben had never got back in touch. As far as he was
concerned his brief affair with Paula had been, in the words
of that famous song, 'just one of those things'. Meanwhile
there would be other attractive - and willing - young ladies
coming in to chat up about doing special deals on cars......

For her part Paula had not tried to get in touch with her
former lover ; as far as she was concerned her young
daughter was better off without that kind of father. Paula
was certainly not going to beg Ben O'Rourke for support.
She had her own life sorted out now; she was in a loving
relationship with Edwin, the German teacher in the
language school at which she and Vicki studied. She knew
she could move in with him any time she fancied, if indeed
she wanted to tie herself to another man.

Of course on occasions down through the years Vicki
had asked questions about her missing father. Like any
child would she wondered how she had no Dad like her
friends. To take her daughter's mind off the subject Paula
had decided on a change of scenery and a change of job so
a few years ago they had moved to Ibiza.

Now, two decades later, Paula's past had caught up with her in the most unlikely fashion. Time for Vicki to meet the father she had never seen. In a rather perverse way Paula was looking forward to meeting Ben again, seeing his reaction when she informed him that he had a daughter. She still had to decide how she would confront her former lover.

What Paula didn't know was that fate would take that decision out of her hands.....

As the early morning rays of the sun shimmered on the surface of the clear blue sea below, Caroline adjusted the artist's pad on her knees and heightened the azure blueness on the paper with her No.3 paintbrush. Down below on the tiny, secluded beach some children played on the sand, their excited cries reaching up to where she was seated on the flat expanse of rock.

She had woken earlier that morning, feeling slightly hung over from the exploits of the night before. She thanked her lucky stars that Mark had come to her rescue and brought her home safely. What on earth had happened to her last night? She should never have taken that exotic cocktail that Wayne had insisted on buying her. It was all his fault. She had told him that she was not accustomed to drinking alcohol, yet he had insisted on buying her a potent cocktail. It must have been very strong for her to lose all sense of control...........

Anxious to get out into the fresh air as soon as possible this morning Caroline had packed her artist's materials and caught a local bus that travelled up the coast from Figueretas. At a suitably isolated spot she had alighted, found a scene that took her fancy overlooking the sea, and sat down on a convenient rock.

She had discovered her love for painting from an early age. She had shone at art at school and even at one stage considered taking it up as a career. She liked the solitude that went with painting. Fate had intervened however, and she had chosen another path. Now she painted merely as a hobby. In the last few hours she had sought to capture on paper the sea, the boats and the pretty sandy cove that lay below her, the shadows cast by the rocky outcrops on the golden sand.

Now it was almost noon, the shadows had shifted and it was time to finish. Besides, it was getting too hot to be sitting out in the full glare of the sun. She moved back into a small area of shade and took out some fruit and a bottle of water to enjoy a snack before heading back to Figueretas.

Caroline accepted that she had very little experience of dancehalls, discos and exotic cocktails. And she had no experience at all of the type of male predator who frequented such establishments. And yet she was not completely innocent. She knew about the dangers of girls accepting drinks from male companions and being taken advantage of. She remembered reading about something called a date rape drug - she could not remember the exact name - that was sometimes slipped into girls' drinks at discos.

Had Wayne tried something like that with her last night? She shuddered at the thought. Her mother was right ; she should not be accepting drinks from comparative strangers. She would have to be more careful in future.

She vaguely remembered Mark's arm around her waist as he helped her out of the Zodiac Club and into a taxi. Wayne of course had been busy dancing at the time and had not even noticed her leaving.

'How are you feeling now, Caroline? Are you alright?' Mark had asked solicitously as they stood on the patio outside her apartment. Every other young male in Ibiza would no doubt have taken advantage of her condition, but she was lucky; Mark had seemed genuinely concerned.

Truth to tell, even though she was feeling light-headed, she had to admit she had enjoyed herself at the disco and now she did not want the night to end. She wanted Mark to put his arms around her again, and hold her close......

Caroline blushed as she thought about it. If her father of her mother knew for one minute how their daughter was behaving!

'I feel a lot better thanks to you,' she had answered Mark. Just as she said that she had swayed slightly. He had reached out and caught her, held her close. Then he kissed her gently on the forehead.

'I think, Caroline, you should go to bed - get a good sleep. You'll feel better tomorrow. Will you be able to manage - '

'Maybe you should come in and put me to bed, tuck me in!' Caroline had surprised herself by saying. Was that teasing tone really her talking? What on earth had come over her? It must be a combination of the glasses of wine and drinking Wayne's lethal cocktail had her acting like this. She had gazed into Mark's eyes, swaying slightly, smiling at him......

'You'd better go in alone. Don't do or say anything you'll be sorry for later.' He waited until she had opened the door to her apartment. Mark knew it was time to leave, otherwise things could get out of hand. He speculated on what Wayne – or practically every red-blooded male in Ibiza! - would have done in similar circumstances.....

'Caroline?'

'Yes Mark?' She had turned her face up to his.

He swallowed. She had beautiful eyes. Didn't she realise how vulnerable she was? 'Er, how would you like to come on a trip with me? Around the island. I'll hire a scooter, we can stay away all day, have some fun......'

She had smiled wanly, hiding her disappointment. 'I'd love to. It sounds exciting.' Not quite as exciting as what she had in mind maybe! But still.....

'Good. I'll see you at the pool tomorrow. We can talk about it then.'

The last thing she had remembered was Mark insisting that she take two Disprin tablets with a glass of water before he said a final goodnight. She had woken up in the early hours lying on her bed - still fully dressed! The Disprins must have worked because she had not suffered a hangover.

As the bus bumped and swayed along the coast road on its way back to Figueretas Caroline thought of what she would say to Wayne Nolan when she saw him again. She would tell him that he was a cheat and a show-off, someone not to be trusted - and he was never to talk to her again.

On the other hand maybe she was being a bit too hard on him. Yes, he was everything she had said he was, but she had to admit he was also very good-looking and exciting to be with, dangerous even.

Ibiza itself was a dangerous place, especially for a lone, inexperienced female like herself. Come to think of it, she was probably the only female on the island who was running away from its hordes of handsome male predators!

Bernice walked down the street. She was scantily clad in shorts and a simple revealing top. The warm air caressed her body. It was early, not yet nine o'clock as she left her companions Alison and Georgia behind in the apartment block, sleeping off the excesses of the night before.

She tilted her face up to the morning sunshine and walked along deep in thought. How quickly the years had gone since she left secondary school. She could hardly believe she would be twenty-four years on her next birthday. She knew there was no great future in the job she was in, she had just drifted into it and remained there. If only she had been as wise when she was eighteen as she was now, but then she thought, better late than never. It had taken all her courage to apply for a place in college this year. No way was she going to sit behind that Spar checkout desk for the rest of her life.

Bernice gave a mental shrug and forced herself back to the present. Maybe she should have called in on Caroline, checked to see how she was after last night. That cocktail of Wayne's had really put her over the top, which was probably what it was meant to do. Luckily Mark had been on the spot. She just hoped that he hadn't taken advantage of Caroline later…

Just then her gaze fell on a row of shops, each one laden with all kinds of souvenirs. Ah! there was her favourite one, the perfume shop, she knew she would return here many times during her stay.

Bernice left the promenade and walked down some steps to the beach. Already people were beginning to claim the umbrellas and sunbeds. She was strolling along lost in thought when suddenly she heard someone calling out. She looked up, saw a young man sitting on a low wall on his own, away from the crowd. He was beckoning frantically to her.

Should she go over to him? Bernice wasn't sure. He looked respectable enough. He was dressed in a pair of shorts and a t-shirt, with dark sandals on his feet. Probably had been drinking into the early hours and had slept out on the beach. And yet, he somehow didn't seem the type. To Bernice his cry for help seemed genuine. And besides, he was rather handsome.

She approached slowly, said 'Hello. Are you alright?'

'No, actually. I- I feel, terrible. Thank you for coming over, answering my SOS. He didn't have an Irish accent, English maybe?

'You look ill, have you been drinking?'

He looked outraged. 'I most certainly have not!'

'You sure?' she studied him carefully.

'Honest. You have my word for it.'

'So.........what's wrong?'

'It's my medication - I forgot to take it this morning before I came out.'

He saw her looking puzzled. 'Look, my name is Brian Casey. I'm from Bristol. I'm over here in Ibiza recovering from a - a very serious operation. I'm under doctor's orders to take my medication regularly , not to miss out. This morning I did and I've paid the price. I must get back to my apartment immediately.' He looked at her pleadingly. 'You do believe me, don't you?'

'Yes, and I'll help you. I'll go up to the promenade and call a taxi - '

'You're so kind. I'm feeling better already.' Bernice was very pleased now that she had answered the handsome stranger's call for help. Not only was he good-looking, he also seemed rather nice.

'Don't move. Wait right there,' she ordered him. She was back in three minutes. 'Come on, I've a taxi waiting. Lean on me......' He put his arm on her shoulder and she put her arm around his waist. She guided him across the sand and up the steps. The taximan gave them a searching look as she helped Brian into the back seat of the vehicle. In Ibiza, he was accustomed to seeing people being poured into his cab.

It was only a short distance to Brian's apartment. As they alighted from the taxi he said he was feeling much better. Bernice insisted on accompanying him to the entrance.

'Would you like me to go up to your apartment with you.?' She hoped she was not being too pushy.

'You're really kind. But I don't think it's necessary, thank you.'

She felt a bit uncomfortable. 'Sorry for thinking you were suffering from too much drink'. She paused. 'My name is Bernice Reynolds, I'm from Dublin and I'm here on holiday with some friends. If I don't to back soon they'll think I'm lost – ' She was joking of course. After last night Georgia and Alison wouldn't surface until the afternoon at least!

Fool, Brian scolded himself as he watched her turn and walk away, why hadn't he asked to see her again? She had been so good to him, so kind to go to so much trouble to get him back to his apartment. Plucking up the courage he shouted after her 'Bernice, could we meet again, where are you staying?'

She turned. 'Orlando Apartments. You'll find me by the pool most mornings. 'Bye and take care!'

Later, when she returned to the apartment, Georgia raised her head from her pillow and asked, 'Where have you been?' Before Bernice could reply Georgia lowered her head and fell fast asleep again. Thus she didn't notice the far-away look in Bernice's eyes as she picked up her swimming togs and headed for the pool. No way would she tell her companions about the handsome guy she had helped on the beach earlier. By now she reckoned Brian had probably forgotten she even existed.

Mark pulled open the curtains letting in the mid-day sunlight. He almost had a seizure when he saw Wayne lying face down on the patio outside. He bent down touching him gently on the side of the neck to check if he was breathing. Wayne swung around suddenly. 'What are you at?' He shouted, still half asleep.

'Wake up, Wayne. How did you end up out here?' There was an unintelligible reply. 'Look at the state of you! You'd have been better wearing that shirt instead of lying on it. The mosquitoes have made a meal of you and your shoulders are beginning to burn.'

Wayne sat up with an effort. 'If I could have gotten in I wouldn't be in this condition,' He rubbed the sleep from his eyes, staggered to his feet. 'Is she gone yet?'

'Who?'

'Don't act the fool.. Caroline of course! You disappeared pretty fast with her from the disco last night.'

'Caroline was never here.'

Wayne stared. 'Are you saying you didn't bring her back here from the disco and then locked me out?'

'I didn't lock you out. I left the key at reception. And as for Caroline, I took her home from the disco in a cab. She wasn't feeling very well thanks to you. I left her back to her apartment.'

'Yeah – and I bet you went in too. Did you have yourself a good time?'

'Wrong again, I never saw the inside of Caroline's apartment. I told you I saw her to her door. Nothing happened between us.'

Wayne looked aghast. 'You mean I slept on the veranda all night for nothing?' he wailed.

'That's right. Look you get some sleep. I'm going down to the beach for a swim. I'll be back in a few hours and we can have those insect bites seen to.'

Wayne flopped onto his bed. He was still annoyed at the way things had turned out last night. An opportunity lost with Caroline, and after he had set her up. He needed some sleep badly.......

When Mark returned to the apartment two hours later- having toured the pool area hoping to see Caroline - the voice of Jose Feliciano belting out 'Guantanamera' assaulted his ears. Wayne was lying in bed playing his ghetto blaster - and letting everyone in the Orlando complex know he had one! As Mark entered the apartment Wayne lowered the music and glowered at him.

'I still can't believe you didn't make it with Caroline last night – after I had set her up for you – '

'You set her up for yourself.'

Wayne was suffering from a hangover and in a bad mood. 'You know Mark, there must be something seriously wrong with you! I wouldn't be surprised if you brought over a teddy bear in your luggage instead of a packet of you-know-what!' Mark didn't reply, just glared. Wayne sat up in bed, scratching at the insect bites on his body. 'When are you seeing her again?'

'Tomorrow, or maybe the day after. I'm hiring a scooter and taking Caroline on a tour of the island.' Mark got a bottle of San Miguel from the fridge, sat down, sipped it casually.

'Hey, back off, mate!' Wayne retorted angrily. 'I fancy Caroline in a big way.'

Mark shrugged. 'I'll put in a good word with her on your behalf.'

Wayne ignored the sarcasm. 'That Caroline, what I wouldn't give to have her to myself for a night. Man, I'd show her some action! There's something about her though, something.....mysterious. No, that's not the word - '

'How about unattainable?' Mark cut in.

Wayne snapped his fingers. 'That's it.......unattainable....out of reach.' He paused, seemed to be speaking to himself. 'Caroline's not unattainable. And I aim to prove it. She's just like every other bird in Ibiza if you get her into the right mood – '

'If I were you,' Mark said calmly, 'I'd forget about Caroline and all those other chicks and concentrate instead on treating those insect bites of yours! They look angry. Let's stroll to the local farmacia and get some ointment, okay?'

'You're better than a mother to me! But you're right, these insect bites are driving me mad.' Wayne jumped out of bed, selected a clean vest, gave Jose Feliciano another loud airing on the ghetto blaster while he went into the bathroom to shave, shower and clean his teeth.

Mark grinned to himself while he waited. Macho Man Wayne was always the one to drink more beer than anyone else, tell more jokes, bed more girls. Only now he was being laid low by a horde of Spanish insects! Serves him right for the shabby trick he had played on Caroline.

Outside Mark and Wayne were strolling through the leafy walk which ran alongside the apartment complex on their way to the farmacia when they heard a male voice calling out- 'Signor! Signor!- uno momento'

They turned around. A stockily built, swarthy young man of about twenty-five was approaching them. 'Pleeze. It is you who play 'Guantanamera' in your apartment so often , yes?' He asked, looking directly at Wayne.

'This is all we need,' thought Mark 'Someone to complain about us.'

'You don't like our music?' Wayne seemed surprised. 'I'm sorry if I was playing it too loud-'

'No, no. You don't understand. We are an Italian family on holiday here. I am Antonio. My brothers Mario and Luigi are hosting a party tonight in our apartment, it is near yours. Pleeze you will both come? We have plenty food and drink- and women! You only bring your cassettes and player.'

Mark looked at Wayne for a reaction. He could see Wayne was interested. 'Did you say you'll have food, drink! - and women?' Wayne asked.

'Si. Very good looking Italian women. You will like them.'

'Good. Then my friend Mark and I will be there!'

'Excellent. I am honoured. Ten o'clock okay?'

'Yes we'll have a few drinks first and we'll bring along some wine.'

'Grazie. Arriverderci.' Antonio disappeared back into the apartment complex.

Wayne still grinning asked Mark. 'Will we honour our new found friend with our presence then?'

'Why not. I love Italian food and we have lots of tapes.'

'Right we'll give them music, Bob Marley, our friend Jose. Even the Dubliners!'

'I wonder would Georgia and the girls be interested in going.' Mark asked 'And how about your Scottish friend Myra?'

'No way are we bringing girls,' Wayne replied sharply. 'Why should we when we can make a play for some of those hot-blooded Italian women!'

After a morning lazing on the beach followed by a leisurely stroll around town, Alo began to wilt in the midday sun. He suggested to Mamie that they should find a restaurant and have a nice lunch in the shade.

During the lunch Alo confided to his wife his concern for Des Murtagh. Even though Des was almost a complete stranger, Mamie knew that Alo would not rest until he got to the root of Des's problem, see if he would be able to help in some way. Mamie had seen her husband do things like that before, usually for people they employed in Alo's farm machinery hire business or in their hardware shop. It was in his nature and in her's too.

'What's Des Murtagh's problem?' Mamie asked.

'I don't know for sure, but whatever it is I can see it in his face. I'm surprised that wife of his hasn't noticed it before now,' Alo replied.

'Evelyn?' Mamie sniffed. 'Sure that lady is so caught up with herself that she's not interested in anything or anyone else around her. When I asked her to come to the boutique with me the other day she made it look like she was doing me a big favour.'

The sun was beginning to sink towards the horizon as Alo and Mamie made their way back to the Hotel. Around the pool people were packing up and heading up to their rooms to shower and get ready to dress for dinner and then enjoy the nightlife in Figueretas or Ibiza. They joined Des and Evelyn whom they spotted relaxing in the lounge.

Leaving the two wives chatting, Alo invited Des for the promised drink in the pool bar. Des seemed more relaxed, now that he did not have to put on a brave face for Evelyn's benefit. He laughed as Alo recounted some of the humorous incidents in his life. He compared Alo's everyday life to his own stressful existence. He had spent years battling his way up the ladder and now he was on the scrap heap.

'So what's this problem that's getting you down Des?' Alo asked when they had two drinks in front of them.

Des was silent, pondering. Maybe it would do him good to talk to someone about what had happened to him, Alo Riordan seemed a decent sort.

'I'll give it to you in a nutshell. A few weeks ago, I was called in and told that my job was gone and I was being made redundant. That also means giving up the company car. I couldn't bring myself to tell Evelyn or the family. I've spent the last of our savings on this holiday. Thankfully, our two children are off our hands now. But for Evelyn and me:...'. Des let his voice trail off in despair. 'So what do you think of that?'

'My God, Des that's tough. I'm sorry for you.' Alo seemed to be at a loss for words. His eyes were fixed on the table. Des was expecting the now all-too -familiar words - 'Well, I have to go now, I have a few things to do' or something of the kind.

But Alo didn't run. Instead, he looked Des straight in the eye. 'I think you and your wife should enjoy this holiday to the full. Don't worry about the future. I have something in mind. Let me think it over for a day or two.' First we'll have a game of golf.'

Des looked surprised. Not a bad idea, he could do with something to take his mind off his problem.

'We'll have a wager on the game.,' Alo went on. 'I'll pay the green fees and the hire of clubs and a buggy. We'll need a buggy in this heat'

Mention of a wager made Des cautious. 'How much will we be betting?' Money was tight. He couldn't afford to wager and maybe lose a big amount.

'Ah, don't worry about it,' Alo waved him aside. 'Something small. We'll work that out later.'

'Are you a good golfer, Alo? Do you play much?' Des had encountered chancers on the golf course before, bandits who upped their handicap when big money or a worthwhile prize was up for grabs.

'I won a local pitch and putt competition a few years ago,' the big man replied proudly, swallowing the last of his pint at a gulp and signalling for two more.

'Pitch and putt?' Des said, relief flowing through him. 'How about the long game? Are you a member of a club?'

'Indeed I'm not! Never had the time. Too busy building up the business. Mamie Riordan would murder me if she thought I was taking a whole day off to play golf!'

Des groaned inwardly, despite the prospect of making some easy money. 'I want to level with you, Alo. I'm a single handicap golfer. In my club, The Grange in Dublin, I play on the Barton Cup team. I'll probably slaughter you.'

'Oh, will you now?' Alo seemed delighted at the prospect 'I want a good handicap then. Give me ten shots.'

'I'll do better than that – I'll give you a shot a hole'

'You're a decent man, Des. But how do you know I'm not conning you – that I'm not another Tiger Woods?'

'You're not a golf bandit, Alo. You're too honest. How on earth did you ever become so successful in business?'

Alo peeled off a 5,000 peseta note from a thick wad, handed it to the waiter as the drinks arrived. He winked at Des. 'Sure Mamie and I don't pay any tax. We have a secret Ansbacher account in the Cayman Islands!' He roared laughing at his own joke.

— ☾ —

Maureen Duff was pleasantly surprised how popular her exploits with Alec Holliday in the Sinatra Club last night had made her. Their achievement in qualifying for the finals of the dance contest next Saturday was evident as soon as she sat down for breakfast. Heads turned at other tables and middle-aged couples nudged each other, staring in her direction. She felt like a minor celebrity. Pity Alec wasn't with her to bask in the glory.

After breakfast, on her way out to the pool area, she was stopped and congratulated on her exquisite display of dancing by an English couple.

'My husband and I will be in the Sinatra Club on Saturday to cheer you on,' the lady said. 'We're members of a dance team ourselves back home and we know good dancing when we see it, don't we, Basil?'

'Yes indeed,' her husband nodded. 'Yourself and your partner are the best we've seen for a long time.'

'Thank you .' Maureen was thrilled.

'If I were a betting man I'd back the two of you to come out on top next Saturday night.'

They said goodbye shortly afterwards and Maureen went into the lounge, found herself a comfortable chair and took out a book. She was surprised that Alec had not yet surfaced this morning. She knew he was an early riser and usually went for a jog along the promenade. Perhaps he had met someone - that man she had seen him speaking to at the bar last night.

By mid-morning Alec had still not appeared. There was no sign of Caroline O'Hara either. Probably sleeping late after a hectic night at a disco with those girls, Maureen supposed. She decided to telephone Joan, Cathleen and Sheila, the three friends from home whom she discovered were staying in the Hotel Nevada. They had informed her at reception that the hotel was at the far end of the beach. She would telephone first and if the trio had recovered from their boat trip of yesterday she would get a taxi over and have lunch with them. Maureen would delight in telling them about Alec - and their exploits at the Casablanca Hotel last night!

Less than an hour later Maureen strolled onto the patio by the pool of the Hotel Nevada where lunch would shortly be served. Her three friends, sitting at a table in the shade sipping long, cool drinks, waved to her. After the initial greetings had been dispensed with and the waiter had brought Maureen an iced drink she looked at the three of them with the makings of a smile on her face and announced:

'Girls -' they always called each other girls although Maureen, at 43, was by far the youngest - 'I have met a man!'.

Had she blurted out that she had just scooped another £20,000 prize on Telly Bingo she would not have created a bigger stir. Her three companions were silent for a few moments then they all began to talk at once.

'That's fast work. You only arrived a few nights ago,' Sheila said, sniffing disdainfully.

'What's he like?.' Cathleen asked eagerly.

'What's his name and where did you meet him?' Joan was equally excited.

Before Maureen could respond Sheila spoke up again. 'I hope he's not after your money!' She wasn't sure if Sheila was joking or if she was serious.

Maureen was delighted with the chaos she had caused. It wasn't often that she got such attention whenever they met. Her three friends were married with grown up families and invariably their get-togethers were taken up with snippets of local gossip lost in long discussions about husbands, how sons and daughters were doing, and - the topic she hated most - whose daughter was having a baby.

Now that she had whetted their appetite for news she decided to make them wait. 'Now girls, steady on, I can only answer one question at a time.' Maureen looked at the three expectant faces in turn, then said slowly. 'His name is Alec Holliday, he comes from a place called Ringsend in Dublin, and he's single. Not even a girlfriend.'

'By the sound of things he has one now!' Cathleen remarked. They all laughed.

Maureen allowed the laugher to die down. 'I didn't say I was his girlfriend. We've only just met.'

'What age is he?' Sheila asked.

'Early fifties.' Maureen answered.

'Thank God!'. Joan said. 'I thought for a minute, Maureen Duff, you might have got yourself a toyboy!' Then she became serious, patted Maureen's hand. 'Only joking, Maureen. We're delighted for you, aren't we, girls?' Cathleen and Sheila both voiced their delight.

'Come on, tell us all. Where did you meet him? How did the two of you get talking?'

The three listened with rapt attention as Maureen recounted how Alec had told her that he had first noticed her at Dublin Airport; how he had taken the first opportunity to help her with her luggage. She told them about the courier's meeting yesterday and how Alec had immediately invited her to the dance at the Sinatra Club.

'Imagine that,' Joan said to the other two. 'She was enjoying herself with a handsome man while we were stranded on a desert island! Some women have all the luck!'

'Apart from him being a very nice man he's also a wonderful dancer.' Maureen said, rubbing it in with a vengeance.

'I take it, my dear, he swept you off your feet in this Sinatra Club.' Sheila said, unable to keep the cutting edge from her voice....

'Too right he did,' riposted Maureen, knowing she was going to trump the lot of them. 'Alec and I qualified for the Grand Final of the Sinatra Club Dance Contest next Saturday night. Pity you girls won't be here to cheer us on.'

There was a stunned silence. Then Joan said, 'Congratulations, Maureen. That's great news.' Maureen knew she really meant it.

'And when are we going to meet your friend Alec?' Sheila asked. There was a slight interruption while the waiter took their order for lunch.

'How about tonight?'. Maureen replied. 'Alec and I will probably have dinner in the hotel. There's an outdoor cabaret by the pool later and dancing. We can have drinks and enjoy the show –'

' – and we might even get to dance with this new man in your life!' Joan laughed.

'Why not.....' Maureen nodded in agreement. She hoped she was doing the right thing in inviting them over to the hotel tonight to meet Alec. After all she had not discussed it with him before she left. For all she knew he might have something else planned. She wondered why he had not appeared at the pool before she left the hotel earlier.

Maureen enjoyed a leisurely lunch with her friends. She had brought her swimming togs with her and before she left they all enjoyed a swim in the hotel pool. She changed back into her ordinary clothes upstairs in their apartment. It was nearly five o'clock in the evening when her taxi arrived back at the Hotel Orlando. As she strolled through the foyer she was relieved to see Alec sitting in one of the plush armchairs chatting to Des and Evelyn Murtagh. They waved a greeting as Alec rose and came over to her.

'Hi. How are you? Had a good day?'

She told him about her visit to her friends in the Hotel Nevada and how she had regaled them with the news of what had happened in the Sinatra Club last night. ' They were amazed – and they're coming over tonight to meet you.'

'Good. I promise to be on my best behaviour.'

'I also promised you would take them all up to dance.'

'Looks like I'm in for a busy night!,' Alec laughed. 'Fancy a drink?'

'No thanks,' Maureen replied. 'I 'm feeling a bit tired. I think I'll go up and have a nap.'

'Sound idea -'

'What did you do today? I didn't see you around before I left?'

She noticed the worried look that replaced the smile on his lips. 'Oh, I - I didn't do much,' Alec replied hesitantly. 'Had some business to attend to this morning.'

As she said goodbye with a 'see you later' Maureen would have given anything to know what exactly that business was. She had an uneasy feeling that Alec was hiding something from her.

— ☽ —

It was near midnight when Mark and Wayne knocked on Antonio's door carrying Wayne's ghetto blaster which he referred to as 'The Ballyfermot Lunch Box,'. They also had a case of cassettes and a couple of bottles of Spanish wine. The other guests were already there, packed tightly into the apartment. Besides Mario and Luigi there were four more of Antonio's brothers. They all looked so alike they could have been cloned. The other guests were made up of wives, girlfriends and friends, little Italy in a Spanish apartment. The men were short and broad and by contrast the women tall and leggy. Mark and Wayne were the only two non-Italians there. Already they were getting some admiring glances from the dark-haired and stunning looking girls.

The aroma of garlic and olive oil filled the air. Mark observed the mouth-watering eats laid out on every available surface. Beer kegs were in operation by the sink unit and bottles of white and red wine stood in clusters between the platters of food.

Wayne and Mark were made very welcome, especially when they set up the music. The girl that caught Wayne's eye was leaning against the wall, just inside the open French window that lead to the balcony. She was young, tall and slender, wearing an aqua-blue silk mini-dress which clung to her body as if crafted especially for it's contours, high at leg, low at her bust. Her smooth tanned skin glowed like freshly polished mahogany. Her rich chestnut brown hair piled high on top of her head held with two aqua-blue butterfly clasps. She had a gold cigarette holder which held a long black cigarette poised seductively between her sensuous red lips.

Mark was quick to follow Wayne's gaze and gasped in admiration. But he knew trouble when he saw it - and the girl was big trouble. He hoped Wayne wouldn't take the bait this time.

A generously proportioned matron whom Antonio introduced as Maria insisted on feeding Mark, intent no doubt on fattening him up, or maybe she had something else in mind! He enjoyed sampling the different dishes, food was one of his greatest joys. He was aware he was the only fair-haired person at the party, and some women, particularly the older woman seemed to find this attractive. Maria was chatting away in broken English and even if the music wasn't quite so loud Mark knew he wouldn't catch a single word that made any sense to him. So he was quite happy to smile and eat.

Wayne was strutting his usual stuff on the margin of the floor cleared for dancing, with one eye still on the smouldering beauty in aqua-blue. She was returning his glances with interest, smiling seductively in his direction. After a short interval Wayne took time out for a cigarette on the balcony, pausing in the doorway briefly and staring back at her before exiting. She followed him out, cigarette at the ready, indicating she needed a light. She did not say a word, simply moved close to him; her eyes looking directly into his. He inhaled her intoxicating perfume and touched her arm as he lit her cigarette, the touch sending electric currents running through his body. The alcohol Wayne had consumed before he had arrived at the party played a big part in lowering his discretion, and he was totally unaware of the dangerous glares of some of the men watching his every move.

Mark had all he could handle with Maria. He hadn't much of an opportunity to keep in touch with the carry-on outside on the balcony, but when he heard several Italian male voices rising in anger he knew there was something wrong – and that Wayne was probably at the centre of it.

Forcibly removing Maria's arms from around his neck he brushed past what appeared to be an angry boyfriend – or maybe the girl's husband! Casually picking up a cassette he moved out onto the balcony. Wayne and the Italian beauty unwrapped themselves from each other and his friend glowered. 'What do you want. Can't you see I'm busy!', he growled at Mark.

'Wayne, you're playing with fire, Mark hissed. 'There's an angry boyfriend inside about to erupt. Let's get out of here while we can still walk - '

'No way! Giulietta and I are just getting to know each other – ' he pulled the girl close to him. 'Aren't we, darling…' She caressed Wayne's cheek, whispered something softly in Italian.

It was that little scenario that lit the fuse. Suddenly, the scowling dark-haired man who had been restrained shouted something and all hell broke loose. Bodies appeared on the balcony and Wayne was dragged back inside. A muscular young man – a friend of the one who had been doing all the shouting - grabbed Wayne in a head-lock, running with him through the crowd intending to rush him through the door of the apartment. Mark grappled with the young man who released his grip on

Wayne. A table was knocked over and plates and bottles flew in every direction.

Male voices were raised in anger, women were screaming and the floor became a sea of broken glass and crockery.

'You're right, Mark, let's get out of here!', Wayne shouted. With that he barged his way out onto the balcony again, climbed over the rail, grabbed a drainpipe and began edging his way down towards ground level. He was the worse for drink now and as the night air hit him his co-ordination wasn't all it should have been. He was making his way down rapidly when suddenly his grip on the drainpipe relaxed and he slid down the remaining few feet, landing awkwardly in a heap on the ground.

Wayne felt himself being grabbed roughly and pulled to his feet. He looked up into the eyes of a stern- faced Spanish policeman.

'Que tal?' the Spanish officer said.

'Wha?' replied Wayne.

'What do you think you are doing?' the policeman asked in English.

'Eh - I was thinking of going to bed.' Wayne thought that was a pretty smart answer considering the condition he was in.

'Si. You are going to bed alright - in my jail!' The policeman clicked his fingers and two younger colleagues materialised from nowhere. They each grabbed Wayne by an arm and frogmarched him around to the front of the Hotel Orlando where the Spanish version of a Garda paddy-wagon was parked. Wayne was bundled inside and over the next fifteen minutes was joined by five scowling Italians as order was restored in the apartment upstairs.

Small groups of residents, returning to the hotel from functions in town, and members of the hotel security staff had gathered and were watching with amusement .

Mark arrived towards the end and also witnessed the action from a safe distance. In the confusion after the melee had broken out he was about to follow Wayne onto the balcony when members of the Gaurdia Civil had come thumping up the stairs and barged into the apartment. Maria had grabbed Mark by the arm and ushered him into a bedroom. She then opened a large wardrobe, pushed Mark inside and squeezed in beside him, closing the door behind them both. Maria had saved him from being arrested and now it was payment time! While the policia restored order outside the two of them wasted no time in getting to know each other better than heretofore!

Later, after the general hubbub had died down outside, Mark had bid an emotional goodbye to Maria, not before she had made him promise to contact her again. Swearing his undying love, he had made his way downstairs just in time to see Wayne and the Italians being driven off.

Mark reckoned Wayne was going to spend an uncomfortable night in jail where he would have more to worry about than his insect bites!

CHAPTER SIX

It was high noon. By the crowded poolside of the Orlando Hotel scores of brown and well oiled bodies were lying about, roasting in the midday sun. The only natives who dared follow the visitors' example of pandering to the burning orb instead of hiding away in the shade were the waiters who were kept busy bringing endless trays of cool drinks to the perspiring masses.

The heart- shaped pool was packed by a mixture of screaming children, anxious parents and serious swimmers in the deep end endeavouring to keep cool and find sufficient space to get some exercise. On dry land people huddled under sun umbrellas to read or enjoy an outdoor siesta.

Apparently oblivious to the bedlam around her a bikini-clad Georgia, under the shade of an umbrella, was busily rubbing in large dollops of Factor 6 to her sensitive skin. No way had she any intention of risking a bad dose of sunburn, or turning herself into a dried-up prune. Judging by the amount of suntan lotion she was lashing on there was little chance of either happening.

Georgia continued rubbing the Factor 6 into her skin, conscious that several pairs of male eyes were watching her. Suddenly she gave a little shriek. 'Oh my God, will you look at that!'

'Look at what?,' groaned Alison, turning her head slowly to follow Georgia's gaze. Alison wasn't feeling too good after all the drink she had consumed last night during a tour of pubs and discos.

'Look at that tall hunk walking over there in the shade of the palm trees.' Georgia replied. Her voice had taken on an awed tone which she used only when she spotted a male who had taken her fancy. 'Isn't he only gorgeous......'

'Not bad at all.' Alison agreed, sitting up and studying the object of Georgia's desire more closely.

'I could go for him in a big way,' Georgia enthused. 'I bet he's great in bed!' When she really fancied someone she wasn't bashful in expressing her feelings.

Bernice opened her eyes. She too followed the gaze of her two friends. Behind the pair of Bono-style wraparound sunglasses which the so-called hunk was wearing she recognised Brian Casey. He had stopped strolling, was surveying the scene and appeared to be looking for somebody.

'Are you girls interested in meeting him?' Bernice asked.

Two heads swivelled in her direction. 'Of course,' Georgia and Alison said in unison.

'Then I'll bring him over and introduce you,' Bernice replied calmly, mischief in her eyes. She rose to her feet and walked towards Brian, leaving the other two gaping after her in amazement.

Brian saw Bernice approaching. 'Hello there, he greeted her.

'Hi' she said. Bernice looked closely at Brian. 'You look much better today, I hope you're doing as the doctor ordered.'

Brian gave a mock bow, 'yes nurse. I'm being very careful. I have to if I want to see more of you. And I do want to see more of you.'

'Come over and meet my friends,' she said, covering her confusion. Bernice was a little flustered. It wasn't often she got off with a handsome hunk.

She brought Brian over to where her friends were. Georgia and Alison devoured him with their eyes as he approached. After the introductions, Georgia patted her sunbed, asked casually: 'Would you like to sit down beside me, Brian, and take off your t-shirt. I'll rub some lotion on your back and then you can rub some on me.'

Much to Georgia's disappointment Brian declined her offer. 'Some other time, perhaps.' He looked at Bernice. 'Would you like to come for a stroll and then go somewhere and have lunch?' he enquired. He extended his hand. Bernice took it and allowed herself to be helped up from her sunbed. She was thrilled.

'See you girls later,' she said gaily to Alison and Georgia. To Brian she said: 'Wait for me in the foyer while I slip into something suitable' She sensed she was leaving two gob-smacked friends in her wake!

An hour later and Georgia was feeling restless. 'Alison, let's go into Ibiza and visit a few of the pubs.' She wanted to meet a few guys , chat them up - have fun!

Right now Alison had her own plans. From the moment she set eyes on Miguel she had planned to get to know him better...... a lot better! Miguel worked behind the bar in the hotel lounge and he was everything Alison wished for in a man. He was handsome, sexy - and he made no secret of the fact that he fancied her..

She would go into town with Georgia – but first she wanted to see Miguel. Every fibre in her body was tingling with anticipation. And to think that he had only started chatting her up at the bar yesterday!

Georgia was annoyed. She was the one who usually made all the running. 'Bernice walks off with Mr. Universe and now you have something going with Miguel.' If she didn't get off her mark soon with someone either Bernice or Alison would claim that bet they had made in the taxi on the way to the airport!

'Have you seen Miguel?', Alison asked. 'Surely you've noticed him. He's a dark version of Leonardo diCaprio,'

Alison knew she was laying it on. 'I really fancy him. I'll be back shortly.'

Miguel was stacking glasses behind the bar when Alison entered. He gave her his most dazzling smile and her heart skipped a beat. His jet black hair was neatly combed and his dark skin was enhanced by the whiteness of his shirt. She sat on a bar stool in her bikini, watched his well manicured hands as he deftly stacked the glasses and wondered what it would be like to be caressed by them.

'So Alison, you remember to come see me.' The way he pronounced her name sent shivers of anticipation through her. If only he knew, she thought, I can't wait to be alone with him again. Last night he had left her back to the apartment, stopping off at a secluded spot under the trees which he had obviously put to good use on other occasions. God, he had been all over her! – like an octopus! It had taken all her willpower to show some restraint and promise him some time soon....She wondered, he stayed in the hotel or did he have his own place in Figueretas. She could hardly wait to find out.

Alison wished she could stay in the lounge looking at him all day but Georgia was waiting so she said 'I have to go into Ibiza with my friend.' He looked so crestfallen that she said immediately 'but I'll be back as soon as I can.'

Instantly the smile returned to his face, 'Then we must meet when I finish work. Will you meet me here at 9 o'clock? I would love to show you my apartment…'

Nine o'clock. It seemed an awful long time away. 'I'll be there,' she promised. Her heart thumping as she left to join the not-too-happy Georgia.

Ben and Irene arrived early to pick up their hired car. It was a lovely day for travelling and it felt good to get behind the wheel of the gleaming Seat. Cars were Ben's abiding passion. He hoped that Irene would enjoy the itinerary he had mapped out for her. Ben was glad they were getting away from the pool area for the day. The screams of the kids were getting to him, although he'd miss the views of the topless babes shamelessly sunning themselves everywhere.

Leaving Figueretas behind, they travelled north. Skirting the town of Ibiza with its crowded streets and teeming bars and restaurants they headed for Santa Eularia. 'This place we are heading for now Irene, is not as well known as Figueretas or Ibiza Town, but it has it's own claim to fame - it is situated on the only river in the Balearics. When you think of all the rivers we have at home we take them for granted.'

Irene was wondering what the restaurants would be like and would they spot a nice one in which to celebrate their 25th wedding anniversary. She hoped Benjamin wouldn't go overboard with his history lessons!.

When they did reach Santa Eularia, they found it a pleasant enough place, with the usual plethora of restaurants and bars vying with each other. They strolled around, admiring the remains of the island's only Roman aqueduct. At a sidewalk restaurant, in very pleasant surroundings, Ben and Irene enjoyed lunch and a leisurely drink before renewing their journey.

Cutting straight across the island and a few kilometres inland Ben and Irene found themselves in an altogether different world. It was hard to believe that the countryside was so unspoiled. The sight of the valley in full bloom, and the spreading fig trees stretching as far as the eye could see, gave the illusion of a multi-coloured carpet.

'Oh Benjamin, we must stop here' exclaimed Irene. They cruised into a lay-by overlooking the picturesque village of San Miquel. 'It's hard to take all this in at a glance. We could spend the rest of the day here, let's enjoy this beautiful place.' Her face was glowing with pleasure.

It was indeed another world. On the dusty roads beyond, the farmers were still using the small horse-drawn carts as transport.

'I read in one of those travel brochures' said Irene, 'that around here we could come across some of the women who still wear the characteristic billowing-skirted costumes. They also have the custom of wearing their hair in a single plait down their backs. They have been doing it for hundreds of years.' As a former school teacher she too was capable of giving a history lesson!

'Wouldn't that couple Alo and Mamie just love this place Irene?' Ben said, taking all in. 'Tell you what, now that we have the car let's surprise them some day during the week and bring them up here. There would be so much to show them.'

Irene was so enthralled by it all that she would have agreed to anything just then. This was so much better than lying on a beach or lazing at the pool. And to cap it all she had found what she had been looking for. In the distance, perched spectacularly on a hill overlooking a marina, was the deluxe Hotel Tropicana.

Irene's eyes lit up. She pointed into the distance. 'That's exactly where I want to celebrate our silver wedding anniversary, Benjamin. Isn't it just beautiful..........'

Ben looked, groaned. A place like that would cost an arm and a leg. Probably two arms and two legs! The lads in the garage would have to service a lot of cars before he would recover from this one!

Aloud Ben said: 'Very nice, Irene. Probably very pricey, though.......'

She wasn't listening. 'I've read about that hotel. It's described in the travel books as a favourite for holidaying sheikhs and honeymoon couples.'

That's alright for cash-rich Arabs, Ben thought. They can afford to write off a couple of oil wells when they stay at a place like the Tropicana. His wife was talking again......

'Drive over and we'll inspect the place. I'll talk to the manager and make the booking. I want to make sure that everything is just perfect for our big night!'

Irene loved dealing with management types. Ben smiled to himself as he drove up the winding road that lead to the entrance of the hotel. This was something with which Irene would regale her friends back home for months. An hour later, after a tour of the hotel, a chat with the duty manager, and a couple of glasses of wine, compliments of the Tropicana, Ben pointed the Seat in the direction of Figueretas.

It was about seven p.m. when he drove into the carpark at the rear of the Hotel Orlando. He had to admit it had been a good day - and one that would cost him when it came to fixing up the bill at the Tropicana. But he mustn't complain; Irene deserved nothing but the best...

The sunbeds were being cleared from the pool area as they strolled across to the hotel entrance. 'I'll get the key and go straight upstairs,' Irene said. 'I think a short lie down is in order. Why don't you treat yourself to a drink, Benjamin. You look like you could do with one.'

Ben accepted his wife's offer gratefully. H could do with a stiff drink. As he headed towards the bar he did not notice the lady standing behind a tree, studying his progress with interest.

After all those years Paula Sheridan knew for certain that she was looking at the father of her beautiful daughter.

— ☯ —

Alison was getting tired traipsing around the narrow winding streets of Ibiza Town with Georgia. It was hot and she just wanted to go into a bar - any bar! - and enjoy a long, cool drink. But Georgia was in one of her perverse moods and insisted on going into practically every shop in the narrow streets of the old town.

Normally Alison would be interested in the shops with their display of colourful goods, but not today. Her mind was on Miguel and those smouldering eyes of his. Last night she had hung on in the bar in the hotel until it had closed – and it had been worth it. She could hardly wait for Nine o'clock! Things were hotting up!

'Let's go in here –' Georgia was already heading towards a not-very- salubrious looking bar with music drifting out from its dark interior. A sign overhead proclaimed it to be 'Jose's Hacienda'. There were tables and chairs with umbrellas outside but they were all empty. Inside a few couples were seated at tables listening to music from a juke- box in the corner. The place had a rather run-down look about it.

Georgia walked up to the bar and ordered two Cokes with ice. The two young men behind the bar nearly tripped each other up vying for the opportunity to serve her. Georgia smiled as she joined Alison at one of the tables. She liked being fussed over.

Alison poured some Coke into her glass, looked around. She was feeling a bit more sociable now. 'You could have picked a livelier place.' she said.

'It is a bit quiet,' Georgia agreed. 'Let's liven things up. Come on, we'll put on some real music–'

They rose and went to the juke-box. The record selection surprised both of them. Alison put in a coin and Georgia pressed a button for the Spice Girls to sing 'Stop'. She turned up the volume, led Alison to the centre of the floor, pushing back a table to make more room. The other couples in the bar began to show an interest.

Out in the centre of the floor Georgia and Alison swayed and sang to the music. Some couples at the tables began singing also....

'You just walk in, I make you smile,
It's cool, but you don't even know me...
Got to slow it down baby, got to have some fun.
Do do do do always be together......'

'Want to see some real dancing?' Georgia asked. Alison recognised that mischievous gleam in her friend's eye. 'Watch me!'

Georgia slipped off her sandals, still swaying provocatively. Every eye in the bar was on her as she stepped up onto a chair, then a table. Her red mane of hair fell across her face as her body swayed to the rhythm of the music. Everyone in the bar began to clap as she gyrated, her long legs and slim body moving in perfect harmony.

Inside in his small office behind the bar Jose, the owner, heard the cheering and clapping. He came out to see what was going on. He stood for a moment his eyes on Georgia, savouring every movement, liking what he saw. It was impossible not to become aroused at the sight of her. Looking at the movements of her long legs and sinuous body a shudder of desire swept through him. The clapping and cheering had brought in other couples and now the bar was doing real business.

Suddenly the record finished. The clapping and whistling got even louder as Georgia, breathless and excited at her success, took a bow still standing on the table.

Jose moved through the crowd towards her and extended his hand. Georgia took it and allowed herself to be helped back onto the floor. The crowd cheered and whistled in appreciation as Jose smilingly kissed the back of her hand.

'Congratulations, senorita, on such a fantastic exhibition of dance,' he said in perfect English.

'Thank you. I'm glad you enjoyed it.'

'You must give us an encore before you leave. Please sit down.' He pulled out chairs for herself and Alison. 'Allow me to introduce myself. I am Jose Simon. I own the bar.......'

Georgia, still slightly breathless, introduced herself and Alison.

'You are Irish?' Jose enquired.

'Yes. How did you know?'

Jose smiled. 'The Irish, they always enjoy themselves in Ibiza! Please come to the bar, I want to get you both a drink. I will create a special cocktail for this special occasion. And you, Georgia, must name it....'

He escorted them both to the bar. Seated on high stools they watched as he mixed the cocktail with dexterity from various bottles, shook it vigorously, then poured it into glasses for Georgia, Alison and himself. With a theatrical gesture he handed a glass to Georgia, then called loudly for silence.

'Please everyone, Senorita Georgia will now name the cocktail I have created specially for her. And after that she will dance for us again.'

Cheers decended into silence as Georgia, smiling and in a clear voice, said clearly, 'I name this cocktail - ' she paused for a moment - 'Ibiza - how are yeh!' There was a burst of applause and when it died down she continued: 'May the mist of love decend on all who drink it!'

The three of them clicked glasses then took a long sip. Georgia noticed that Jose Simon's dark eyes were seeking hers. 'I think your wish is already coming true,' he whispered. 'This name, Ibiza - how are you.' Does it have a special meaning?'

Georgia and Alison both laughed. 'Yes, it's an old Dublin saying. I'll explain it later -'

'And we'll teach you how to say it properly!' Alison promised.

Georgia had become alive. The bar became crowded as people sought to sample the new cocktail. She climbed onto the table top again and did the promised encore. This time the applause was even more prolonged than before. Alison could hardly believe her eyes; less than an hour ago Jose's Hacienda had about as much life as a morgue - now the place was jumping!

When she finished her routine Georgia sat close to Jose and accepted his congratulations. 'You know,' she whispered. 'You could do a lot with this place. It has a good passing trade, great potential - and I'd like to help you.'

Jose's eyes widened. 'That would be excellent, Georgia. I would like that. What would you suggest?'

She was about to put some ideas before him when he held up his hand. 'No please. Wait a minute. I have a better idea. You must have dinner with me tonight. We will discuss it over a bottle of wine.'

Georgia caught her breath. 'Oh Jose. I'd love to.' This was turning into a lucky day after all!

'We shall dine at my favourite La Ventana Restaurant. Afterwards we will come back here. I will make a couple of our special cocktails. And then...' he smiled, 'You can tell me your plans for 'Jose's Hacienda'.

Alison watched entranced as Jose again took Georgia's hand, raised it to his lips, kissed it tenderly. The fellas didn't do that in the discos in Dublin!

Maureen could see that Alec was a ladies' man. He appeared to really enjoy the company of Joan, Cathleen and Sheila. They obviously enjoyed his company too, hanging on to his every word and laughing at all his little jokes. Maureen was aware that none of the three was as good a dancer as herself and she was more than happy to see Alec dance willingly with each of them just as she promised he would.

It was a beautiful night. The tables were set out by the pool so that the guests could admire the lights shimmering underwater as they danced and watched the cabaret acts. There was a scent of pine in the air and the abundance of fairy lights in the trees around the patio lent an an olde-worlde atmosphere to the occasion. Quite a romantic setting. Maureen thought.

'A penny for them' Joan said, as Alec floated by with Cathleen to the tune of an old-time waltz medley.

'Indeed I was just thinking what a magnificent setting for the dancing - a far cry from our young days at home. Will you ever forget the way we used spread the crystals on the floor to make it a bit slippery for the dance?'

'Not to mention the lemonade bar and the raffle for the leg of lamb or the ham before the last dance,' Joan went on wistfully.

Maureen smiled. 'Those were the days. But I love this setting. This whole atmosphere is so romantic. As they say that was then and this is now.'

'Maureen Duff, what's got into you!' Sheila laughed, her eyes twinkling. 'Over the years you had no time for romance, now it's gone to your head!'

Maureen blushed. My God she was talking like a schoolgirl! Better watch it. 'Thanks for the warning, Sheila. I appreciate your concern.'

Sheila glanced to the dance floor where Cathleen was clearly enjoying her old-time waltz with Alec. 'Not to worry, sure any woman would get romantic if she had a man who could dance like that!'

They watched the couples dancing for a few moments then Maureen said: 'Whatever about the romance, perhaps you girls would help me to choose a nice dress for Saturday night.'

'Of course Maureen,' Joan agreed.' You must look your best for the dance final in the Sinatra Club with Alec – '

' - and while you're at it, don't forget a smart pair of shoes and something more appropriate than those pearls you have around your neck!,' Sheila cut in.

When the waltz ended Alec and Cathleen returned to the table. He called for another round of drinks, ordering a pint of Guinness for himself. His fourth so far this night, Maureen noted.. She wished he wouldn't drink so much. Not in front of her friends. She had to admit this was a cause of some concern to her.

Not long afterwards a quick step was called. Alec turned to Maureen. 'I think we should have this one Maureen. It will keep us in shape for Saturday night.' He took her hand and led her out to the dance area. Maureen could feel the three pairs of eyes burning into her back as Alec guided her around to the music. What are they saying about herself and Alec back at the table, she wondered? She was sure her ears were burning!

Back at the table Joan, Cathleen and Sheila were sipping their drinks and trying to keep their eyes from the dance floor.

'Cathleen' said Joan, 'I hope you didn't give Alec too much background on Maureen. You know she's a very private person.'

Cathleen was annoyed. 'What are you hinting I am – the village gossip! 'Why should I tell him all about Maureen. That's none of my business.' She paused, said slyly - 'Alec did seem to want to know everything about her, though.'

'Just look at Maureen' said Sheila with a trace of envy, 'gazing up into his eyes like a love-struck teenager. It's a long time since any of us looked at our husbands like that!.' She sipped her soft drink disconsolately. 'I wish I had ordered a double vodka instead of this rubbish!.'

'My, isn't Alec a lovely dancer,' Joan said sweetly, sighing on purpose. She sometimes enjoyed getting Sheila and Cathleen annoyed. They were envious of Maureen.

'Yes,' replied Cathleen, 'I'd say probably the best dancer Maureen has taken the floor with for a very long time. I do hope she doesn't get too attached to Alec until she finds out more about him. I mean his background and all that.'

Sheila sniffed. 'I wouldn't be surprised if Mr. Alec Holliday has a skeleton or two in the cupboard, or maybe even a lady friend or two back home in Ringsend. I thought he was holding me a little too close when we were dancing.'

'Come off it, Sheila!,' Cathleen laughed. 'That was wishful thinking on your part!'.

Meanwhile, Alec was inviting Maureen to go on a coach tour of the island. 'It would get us away from the pool, all those prying eyes,' he said.

'Yes indeed I'd love that. I also need to buy a suitable dress for Saturday night. The girls have promised to lend moral support and help me choose.'

'The coach tour of the island is tomorrow.' Alec reminded her.

'Oh yes I forgot. Then I'll arrange for us to go shopping another day. I really would love to see the island. I believe there is a great blending of the old and new. Is it true that Ibiza has a fascinating history dating back to 700 BC?'

'I didn't know that.' And he didn't care either. The only thing Alec was interested in about Ibiza was the sun and the quality of the Guinness. 'Let's sit for a while and have a drink. Just the two of us.'

Oh my God, his fifth of the night!, Maureen thought. The girls will think she's taken up with a drunkard!

They choose a nice quiet place near the pool. Maureen who was interested in historic places, returned to the topic. 'We must find out as much as we can about the island. I read somewhere that the rich red soil supports no plant or animal life. Very strange isn't it? Even when I was in East Africa the desert which is normally arid came to life after a good shower of rain, maybe once or twice a year. Lovely little flowers appeared all over the place, creating blankets of colour. The Desert Rose was particularly beautiful. I wonder if it ever rains here at all?'

'So, you were in East Africa?' Now he was showing an interest.

'Yes indeed, many years a go…' She told him about her boyfriend Donal who had qualified as a doctor and had signed up with an aid agency in East Africa for two years. 'I went with him to teach English to a group of pre-nursing students in a Mission Hospital where my Aunt Monica worked. It was a very exciting time for Donal and me. After two years we had planned to come home, get married and settle down….' Maureen paused.

'It didn't work out that way…' Alec took up the story.

'No. Donal died in a plane crash out there and I accompanied his body home.'

'I'm so sorry' he said softly. 'It must be difficult to talk about it, even after all those years,' he said.

'Yes, it is…' Maureen replied. She brightened up. 'Look, here come the girls, I expect they'll be wanting to return to their hotel soon!'

She was right. Alec insisted he would accompany the trio back in a taxi, but Maureen declined and said she would go to bed and get a good night's rest before the tour of the island tomorrow.

Upstairs she strolled out onto the balcony before going to bed. The air was warm and in the distance she could see the headlights of cars snaking their way down a mountain road. Tonight she had spoken of her beloved Donal for the first time in many years. Would Alec Holliday replace him in her life, Maureen wondered, as she listened to the music drifting up from the poolside.

When she did get into bed her mind was in turmoil. She was pleased that she had told Alec about Donal. Alec was of course a good listener and had been very sensitive. She hoped he would understand if she were not too forthcoming in their relationship so far. Better to let things develop slowly between them.

She closed her eyes and tried to sleep. But sleep was slow to come. In a dream she and Donal were together again, he a dedicated young doctor, kind and generous. She still missed him. It had taken her many years to come to terms with the fact that his young life had ended so abruptly in an African desert in the middle of nowhere.

Maureen finally drifted off into a restless sleep.

Evelyn reached for her expensive jar of Lancome face cream. She read the words printed on the frosted glass of the heavy container - 'Fight the ageing process.' Everything was a fight since she turned thirty, she thought. Fighting the flab. Fighting to keep grey hair at bay. Fighting with Des to get him to ask for another pay rise.....

Even on holiday the battle continued. It looked as if she might have to fight the pestering of those two yokels, Alo and Mamie Riordan from taking over their holiday. God Almighty, Des was a push over for those country hicks. You'd think at this stage he would have learned to rub shoulders with a better class of person. Will I always be surrounded by weak men? she thought.

Daddy had been the very same. Mum used die seven deaths if the C.I.E. bus he drove passed her on the street. The neighbours were convinced he was a civil servant. She packed him off to work each morning with his shoes buffed up and his sandwiches in a briefcase having got a solemn promise that he would never appear on the avenue wearing his C.I.E. uniform. If he had been foolish enough to let the neighbours see his cap, it would have been instant divorce. Mum wanted to be an Inspector's wife. And she should have been. But no, Daddy was quite happy to drive his bus back to the garage in the evening and spend his leisure time playing darts with a bunch of no hopers. Is it my fate,

Evelyn thought, to spend my days in the company of people with no ambition?

Even if we had qualified for the final of that dance competition in the Sinatra Club it wouldn't have been too bad, but to have been beaten by a pair of hicks, like that country one with the pearls and that flash Harry from Ringsend. What an indignity, Evelyn thought, as she smoothed the anti-ageing cream over her neck and throat. Now she and Des will have to try again tomorrow night. And silly Des had been talked into playing golf that morning.....

Her mind went back to Barry Moran, her first boyfriend. He now owned a chain of electrical shops and was rolling in money. They had met in the Crystal Ballroom in Dublin when she was sixteen. He swept her on to the floor and off her feet. Even at that age Barry had the look of a young man going places. He was eighteen then with jet-black hair and hazel eyes that never left her face as they whirled around the dance floor. He worked for his father and drove a rusty blue van.

His father ran an equipment hire shop in town supplying everything from a ladder to a cement mixer. Barry used grin and say, 'Watch me Evelyn, in ten years time I'll have a string of shops and a pad in Castlenock,' even though when they went for pertol in the scruffy blue van he only ever had enough money to bring the needle on the gauge barely past the E.

Evelyn saw a feature about him a year or so ago in Business and Finance Magazine. She remembered staring intently at the photograph at the top of the page. Apart from a bit of grey on the temples, he looked the same old Barry. He was now married to someone called Serena and had one son named Edward. According to the magazine they lived in a Georgian mansion in Castlenock. 'My own fault' thought Evelyn 'for not hanging in there.'

But she was an innocent eighteen years of age when Des came along. Des was very handsome in those days.

He wore smart suits and drove a Ford Cortina. It was a company car but that didn't matter. Her Mum had welcomed him in with open arms.

'Don't waste your time with Barry Moran,' she would say, 'Des Murtagh is going places.' How wrong she was.

And then there was that spectacular disastrous night. In the back of a Cortina, for heaven's sake! The shock, the shame and the look of betrayal in her mother's eyes, and then the hurried preparations for the wedding. They were married five months when Samantha was born but Mum never got over it. When I remember, Evelyn thought, of having to phone before we visited, so she could have the garage doors open for us so we could drive straight in. The neighbours never saw Samantha or her carrycot. Later on they must have wondered where the toddler came from.

Des watched from the bed as Evelyn applied her make-up. She certainly looked after her appearance, he thought. She was a stunner twenty odd years ago, with her long slim legs and beautiful wide eyes. He read somewhere that the eyes were the mirror of the soul - but what did they mirror in Evelyn now? Evelyn was never satisfied, the house was too small, the neighbours were too common, there was never enough money.

The children were a disappointment to her Des knew, even though she never voiced it. Graduations of the offspring of family or friends were guaranteed to produce a bout of sulking and bad temper. Samantha and Gary had never given her one of those big days out and she resented this.

All this would pale into insignificance when he unburdened himself of his loss-of-job secret. He felt his throat going dry at the thought of telling her the bad news. Evelyn would take his news as yet another humiliation. He knew he shouldn't feel like this but he was suddenly overwhelmed by an enormous sense of shame.

At least I'll get a few hours peace on the golf course with Alo Riordan, he thought. He was quite looking forward to the game. He was glad that he had brought the white tailored Bermuda shorts. The latter would never get an outing at the Grange! Alo seemed a very decent type, it was refreshing in the sales management game to talk to anyone who actually listened.

— ☯ —

'How do I look girls?' Georgia asked, with the confidence of someone who already knew what the answer would be.

'Stunning,' replied Alison. Then she added, a touch of envy in her voice, 'although you can forget dancing on the table top for Jose in that outfit!'

'You look terrific, Georgia.' Bernice agreed. 'You must really fancy this fella Jose in a big way.'

'You'd have fallen for him too if you'd been with us earlier today.' Georgia replied, still studying herself in the mirror. She was dressed in a black mini dress held up with slim straps. The scooped neckline showed an amount of cleavage that would probably have got her arrested for indecent exposure had she been anywhere else but Ibiza. She would have to be careful walking anywhere in her three inch black stiletto heel shoes which showed off her long, shapely legs to perfection. Her red hair was tied behind with a green band. Georgia was a vision to behold - and she knew it.

The telephone in their apartment shrilled. 'That's probably the taxi!,' Georgia exclaimed. She watched Bernice pick up the telephone. 'Thank you, she'll be down in a moment.' Bernice confirmed.

'Well, girls, wish me luck -' Georgia picked up her tiny shoulder bag and headed for the door. They both watched her teetering on her high heels across the apartment.

'Bye. I don't suppose we'll be seeing you again until tomorrow morning'. Bernice said, winking at Alison.

'The cheek of you!' Georgia feigned shock. 'You know I'm not that type of girl. The is strictly business. Jose wants me to give him some advise about how to improve business at his bar. Isn't that right, Alison?'

'That's part of the plan alright,' Alison replied drily. 'Although I wouldn't be surprised if he has something else on the menu!'

Georgia shrieked laughing. 'Good bye girls. Don't wait up for me. I'll tell you all about it tomorrow morning!' With that she slammed the door and was gone.

Bernice rose from the couch from where, in between looking at Georgia getting ready, she had been passing the time glancing at a Spanish version of 'Fair City' on television. 'I'm having a shower. Georgia's not the only one who has been invited out to dinner. - Brian and I are going out on the town. How about yourself, Alison? Not sitting in I hope?'

'No way!,' Alison was riled at the indignity of the question. 'I'm seeing Miguel later, after he has finished in the bar. He's promised to show me his apartment.....'

For Georgia, the candlelit dinner with Jose in La Ventana Restaurant in Por d'es Torrent on the west coast of the island was terribly romantic. She had never experienced anything like it before in her life. It was certainly a long way from Finglas!

Jose was the perfect dinner date, charming, attentive to her every wish, knowledgeable about the food they were eating and the wines they were drinking. He possessed an old-world charm, and when he looked at her with those soft brown eyes and covered her hand with his as they sipped the wine and watched the moon in the sky through the giant window which gave the restaurant it's name, Georgia reckoned that this was about as good as it gets. Well, almost!

'Tell me about yourself, Georgia. Who are you? What do you do for a living in Dublin? Was it fate that sent you to this island so that we would meet? How come of all the bars in Ibiza today you walk into Jose's Hacienda.?....'

Oh God, Georgia thought, how can I tell him about the area of Finglas where I live? All the houses, the kids playing football on the streets, riding horses on the greens, making fires outdoors and sitting around them at night? He would never understand.

'Forget about me, Jose,' Georgia replied evasively. 'Let's talk about you instead. You and your bar. You want to hear what I think you should do to make it popular.....'

For a time it didn't look like Georgia's ruse would work. Jose seemed just as reluctant to talk about himself as she did about her own background. But eventually her girlish pleading paid off.

Jose told her that he was an only son. Georgia groaned inwardly at that bit of information. Just her luck, she thought. Surely not a Mammy's boy like a lot of Irishmen! His father had died when Jose was young and the family had an estate in the country about thirty kilometres from Ibiza where his elderly mother lived with an unmarried sister. He kept referring to his mother as 'the Condesa' and when Georgia asked was that his nickname for her he had laughed but had not bothered to explain.

Jose had explained that, some years ago, he had tired of life on the farm and, wanting to be part of the tourism boom that had hit Ibiza, he had moved into the town and bought the bar hoping to make his fortune. So far without much success.

'That is until you came into my life today, Georgia. Now I feel my luck has changed. You are my destiny. Tell me what you have planned for my bar...' His brown eyes gazed into hers, melting her soul.

Georgia came back down to earth. 'You could get the place painted for a start.' she replied bluntly. 'Brighten it up from the outside. Let me pick some colourful tablecloths. And get some real action going at night like what Alison and I had going this afternoon. And another thing - introduce a Happy Hour from 5pm to 7pm, two drinks for the price of one. They really go for that in Dublin!'

Georgia was really worked up now. 'Alison and our other friend Bernice will be over tomorrow and we'll introduce everybody to your new cocktail 'Ibiza how are yeh'. We'll have a gala re-opening of Jose's Hacienda maybe some night next week and I'll even devise a special dance for the occasion. We'll put posters around the town advertising the event and the girls and I will get a crowd from our hotel to come along.' Georgia paused, slightly out of breath. 'How's that for starters?'

Jose was ecstatic. 'Georgia, querida mia, this is amazing. You are a genius - a beautiful genius!' He leaned across the table and kissed her. It was meant to be a congratulatory gesture, but somehow it developed into a passionate embrace that was prevented from continuing to its natural conclusion by the table in between.

Georgia could feel her senses swirling. She broke away reluctantly, breathless. Jose was looking at her with those liquid brown eyes. He really was gorgeous. The girls weren't expecting her back until tomorrow morning. What the hell...She wasn't going to disappoint them!

'We must leave now. You will come back to my place....' Jose stood up, signalled for the bill, extended his hand and helped Georgia to her feet. He made it sound so natural, like it was all planned so long ago. She was feeling light-headed and wondered if it was the wine. In the taxi going back to Ibiza she closed her eyes, leaned her head on his shoulder.....

The bar was doing reasonable business when they arrived. Jose lead the way through the back entrance and into to his office in which he sometimes stayed overnight. He closed the door behind them and they stood in semi-darkness. Jose advanced on her and when he took her in his arms she made no protest. Winding her arms around his neck she clung to him. He pressed her body to his, kissed her, a long passionate kiss that aroused them both.........

They broke apart eventually, staring silently at each other. Georgia reached up, slid the straps of her dress from her shoulders. It slid to the floor at her feet. She stepped out of her shoes, undid the clasp and let her hair fall loose. She watched as Jose began to undress in front of her.

He lifted her in his arms, Georgia laughed, let her head fall back as he carried her to the large bed in the corner and laid her on it. He continued to kiss her as his hands moved down below and deftly removed her underwear. Georgia was so consumed with passion that she tore what remained of his clothes from his body. He was a demanding lover and she was his match.

For the next few hours they continued to pleasure each other, sipping occasionally from glasses of wine, before once more allowing their bodies to merge into one. Dawn was breaking when, finally exhausted, they slept.

CHAPTER SEVEN

Wayne lay awake in bed watching the hands of his travel alarm clock move slowly towards 9am. He intended to rise and go jogging before the sun got any hotter. That episode at the Italian party the other night after which he had been carted off to spend a night in jail had been a shock to his system. Despite his wild ways he had never before landed in jail. It had not been a good experience and he would have to be careful in future.

Apart from everything the news of his punch-up with the Italians and his landing in jail had filtered around the Orlando complex and had not done his reputation any good. After Mark had shown up early yesterday morning at the jail and pleaded for him to be released the two of them had kept a low profile during the rest of the day. Last night they had gone into Ibiza, visited a few pubs and had kept out of trouble. He wondered just how long he could keep on the straight and narrow.

Wayne rose, donned a vest, shorts, thick white socks and his well-worn Nike joggers. Mark was snoring away and he was careful not to waken him. He went out onto the balcony and did a dozen warm-up press-ups. Then he made his way out of the apartment, closing the door on his still sleeping friend.

He had to admit that the huge amount of alcohol he'd consumed over the past few nights was finally catching up with him. Maybe he should slow things down lest he'd spoil the rest of his holiday.

As he jogged along steadily towards Ibiza his thoughts turned to his mother, Kate. He hadn't phoned her since he had arrived in Ibiza a week ago. He wondered what she'd say if she heard he spent a night in a police cell, for being drunk and disorderly! No way would he tell her, the shock might kill her. And if the newspapers back home got hold of the story he'd surely be front page news. Since his dad died four years ago he'd seen just how vulnerable she, a strong Dublin woman, had become.

The very thought of that overnight stay in the Spanish jail brought eerie sensations down his spine. Although he often tried to act macho when the occasion called for it, he was really quite tame. He now had some guilty feelings about the events which led up to his Italian neighbours being provoked by his actions and causing a major disturbance. It was a volatile situation to end up in a prison cell with five of the Italian party, plus a couple local men crammed into that tiny space.

The first few hours were terrifying; in his drunken state he remembered thinking he wouldn't get out alive. But the Italians were all noise and really were not as violent as they sounded. When they had been thrown into the cell the Italian whose girlfriend had started all the trouble had been very aggressive and tried to start a fight, but fortunately he had been restrained by his friends. After that they had all shook hands and everyone cooled down.

Being locked up did have it's funny moments. One of the local Spaniards had kept attempting to sing what sounded like a rebel Spanish song, only to be sat on each attempt by two of the Italian brothers who took exception to the noise the local was creating.

As he jogged along Wayne recalled how he had dozed on and off sitting on the filthy jail floor, squashed in between an Italian and a Spaniard. The stench of sweat, urine and stale beer hung sickeningly in the air. The heat was the hardest to bear, with only one tiny barred window for ventilation. He was a very happy man when he heard Mark's voice early the following morning and had been released. Before leaving he had apologised to the Italians for the trouble he had caused and they had shook hands and ended up kissing him!

As he jogged along the promenade in the early morning sunshine, Wayne enjoyed the sun and the fresh air. The sea looked like a John Hinde picture postcard. The air was filled with the scent of lavender, which somehow stirred up thoughts of Caroline. He would love to get her alone sometime, try to get beneath her icy exterior........There he was again lusting after a female. So much for his vow to turn over a new leaf!

Wayne reached the end of the promenade. It was an area where a lot of pleasure boats selling trips around the island tied up. He quit jogging, strolled along studying the various sale points for the various sea tours. He was struggling to unscrew the cap on his now tepid bottle of water when a garish poster caught his attention.

—— CRADLE CRUISE ——

✦

— For under 25's only—

✦

Join Captain Bonaparte
and his Pirate Crew

✦

For a full day cruise around this here island!

✦

Lots of wine, music, guys and gals, and fun below deck!

✦

Also includes beach party, swimming, dancing.

✦

Price — 4,500 pts.

He could almost picture the scene... wet, wild and wicked, the girls in skimpy costumes, the guys chasing them all over the boat. Just what he was looking for!

To hell with his turning over a new leaf. A plan was forming in his mind on how he could entice the unsuspecting ice maiden Caroline along as his co-pirate!

— ☺ —

Bernice sat on the balcony of her apartment, putting the finishing touches to painting her last toe-nail. She stretched out her legs and flexed her toes admiring the pale pink varnish that glistened in the morning sunshine.

She had spent last night in the apartment alone. Neither Alison nor Georgia had returned to sleep there. Surprise! Surprise! This was nothing unusual for the duo especially on holidays. Bernice was accustomed to Georgia and Alison scoring with fellas. Between them they had more one night-stands than Duffy's Circus! Bernice was confident they would turn up sometime during the morning.

She was not, however, confident that Brian Casey would turn up for their arranged meeting at the pool at 11am. She had had a lovely time with Brian last night. After they had met they had set out for a long romantic walk along the beach in their bare feet, weaving in and out of the sea as the fancy took them. It was a time to get to know each other, to learn about each other's background. A time to be alone among the screaming masses, an opportunity even to flirt a little.

As they walked hand-in-hand Brian told her that he was 27, the eldest of two children. He had a sister three years his junior. His parents were originally from Co. Meath, they had met and married in Bristol, some thirty years previously.

Brian told her that he was a chartered accountant. It was during his final exams, late last year, that he neglected a bad cold, it subsequently turned to pleurisy and left a shadow on his left lung. The doctor assured Brian that he would make a full recovery and advised him to take a month or two in the Spanish sunshine.

They had left the beach and entered Ibiza's famous old walled town, known as D'alt Vila. This area was a warren of narrow streets lined with small shops, chic restaurants and bars.

'Let's go to Alfredo's for lunch, it is located on the Vara del Rey, serves typical local cuisine, I just know you'll enjoy it, Bernice.' Brian sounded very knowledgeable.

They had a leisurely meal, and went to the beach later for a swim. By the time Brian walked Bernice back to her apartment , late in the evening, it seemed as if they had known each other all their lives. Outside the apartment Brian had leaned forward and kissed her. A tender kiss that exploded into something more for both of them. Bernice was astounded at the intensity of her feelings, it took all her willpower to push him away.

'What is it? Have I done something wrong?' Brian had asked, concern in his voice.

Bernice was in a state of confusion. She really liked him, fancied him in a big way, even though they had known each other only a few days. Was he, too, like the modern man that expected sex on a first date? How would he react when she told him she was an old fashioned girl with old fashioned ideals? There was nothing for it only to tell him how she felt.

'Brian,' she said. 'I don't agree with promiscuous holiday romances. You know what I mean, the type where a fellow chats up a girl and expects her to jump into bed with him.' Bernice held her breath, she had been dropped so many times before for making this same declaration, standing by her principles.

Brian threw back his head and laughed. I've blown it, again, Bernice thought to herself. She blushed. She had made a fool of herself. That's why he was laughing at her.

A good-looking guy like Brian would probably expect a girl to fall for his charms in a big way. She was nothing if not a realist; she knew Georgia and Alison were glamour girls and sexy into the bargain. Fellows went for them automatically instead of her. That's why she had been reluctant to take part in the 'who'll score first' bet on the way to the airport in the taxi.

'So that's what you're worried about? You think I only want sex from you.- ' He laughed again. 'I thought I smelled of B.O. or something awful like that with the way you pushed me away.' He looked at her earnestly. 'To be honest I quite agree with you.' He saw Bernice's look of surprise. 'How about I see you to-morrow at the pool. OK with you?'

Bernice was relieved. He was so matter of fact about it. 'Of course, Brian,' After a goodbye kiss she said 'Be careful on the way back, I don't want anything to happen to you. See you to-morrow.'

Now, glancing at her watch she realised that she would know shortly whether he would keep their appointment by the pool. Meanwhile she had better tidy the apartment. Alison and Georgia were so untidy, the place was littered with their clothes and bits and pieces. Bernice picked up everything and placed it on the girls' beds.

She was just finished when the door of the apartment opened to reveal a very tired looking Alison. She didn't look like she had too much sleep! 'Hi Alison, how are you?' What a silly question, Bernice thought.

'I'm fine.' Alison's eyes were dreamy. 'Tired but very happy.' She began to slip out of her clothes. 'What an animal that Miguel is!' She yawned. 'I'll tell you all about it when I've had a sleep. By the way, I see Brian down by the pool, are you expecting him?' Alison was too tired to notice the relief on Bernice's face.

'Yes, we arranged to meet at 11am. Why don't you join us down there for lunch about 2pm? Georgia too, if she's back, by then.'

Alison giggled. 'Georgia is probably still between satin sheets right now. Her new boyfriend, Jose, is really something. Very sophisticated - and sexy. We had a great time in his bar and he really fancied Georgia. To be honest it wouldn't surprise me if we don't see much of her for the rest of the holiday! Anyway I'm off to bed now. See you later.'

Bernice checked her appearance in the mirror. She was wearing a black bikini top and white shorts. She favoured the shorts, although they didn't make her look any slimmer. She picked up her towel and bag and made her way to the pool area.

She found Brian lying by the side of the pool on a sunbed, well shaded with an umbrella. He jumped up as soon as he saw her approach.

'I've got two beds, side by side and two umbrellas. I hope that's o.k.'

'It's fine, Brian. Thank you. How are you to-day? You look better each time I see you.'

'I feel fine, Bernice. I'm looking forward to us spending the day together. If you can put up with me.' During a companionable silence Brian reached over and placed her hand in his own. Bernice felt that this was his way of assuring her that he wanted to be with her, and her alone.

Fiona and Gerry meandered hand-in-hand around the outdoor market in Punta Arabi, her mind rambling back over the past couple of days. She and Gerry were having such a lovely time touring the island by hired car. Mind you, she could have done without enduring a few of the more boring tourist attractions along the way, such as those silly old caves at Port de Sant Miquel. She had broken the heel of one of her favourite Gucci shoes there. Not to mention having to visit those numerous, pokey, old museums. Even the smallest village seemed to have one. Boring!

They had also however, been to some great spots like Portinax, Fiona had been thrilled to find out that it had been the setting for some of the scenes from the film 'South Pacific.' On today's tour Fiona and Gerry had decided to make Punta Arabi their final stop before returning to Figueretas. The district was well known for its weekly hippie market and fleets of coaches and specially chartered boats from Ibiza and San Antoni were laid on every Wednesday to ferry the peseta laden tourists to it.

When they had reached the market Gerry had suggested that they split up for a while, as he wanted to buy presents for Sandra and the kids and he knew it would only bore Fiona. She seemed happy enough to comply and Gerry was relieved. He felt he needed a bit of time and peace to himself, even if only for half an hour or so.

He wandered around browsing, going from stall to stall, on the look out for suitable presents. He had never seen such a large, colourful marketplace. Sandra would have loved it, he thought guiltily. She would have been in her element buying presents for Jake and Rosie and knick-knacks for the house.

He wondered how she and the children were getting on. He had promised to ring her at some stage today at her mother's house, she often went to stay with her when he was away at some conference or other. That was where she believed him to be now in fact; a series of conferences in London. He had purposefully left his mobile at home so she couldn't contact him. He decided he would ring her when he got back to the hotel later on.

When Gerry had finished buying his presents, he still had a few minutes to spare. Feeling rather hungry, he moved to one of the food stalls to grab a bite to eat whilst waiting for Fiona.

Fiona meanwhile, wasn't having much luck in finding presents for her friends. All the merchandise was much too cheap and tacky to even consider purchasing. She would have to head into Ibiza town where there were supposedly a handful of little designer boutiques which would do nicely; in Fiona's circle, you were a nobody unless you were dressed from head to toe in designer wear.

Fiona quite enjoyed the status attached to being involved with the 'Ladies who Lunch circle' back in Dublin, even if it meant having to do some work now and then. The feeling that many of the well-heeled ladies did the charity work out of boredom didn't bother her. She knew her close friends on the committee were aware that she was having an affair, but it didn't worry her. Several of her colleagues were in the same position as herself. And although over a glass of wine the women could be bitchy and reveal certain things within the group, they all knew it would go no further than themselves.

However, there was one thing Fiona never discussed and which she dreaded the others finding out about. Her past! All of the women she worked with on the committee were extremely high profile and as far as she was aware had come from wealthy backgrounds – mainly from snaring a rich husband and of having rich and influential in-laws. They had wallowed in wealth all their lives and had experienced nothing of the poverty and shame she had suffered while growing up in the northside Dublin suburb of Ballymun.

God, how she had loathed living there! Existing in one of those awful, ugly, towering, blocks of concrete that the Corporation had built to house the countless families in the 70's. Fiona had hated the lifts that were forever broken and out of order, the graffiti-covered walls, and the filthy stairways that perpetually smelled of urine. There were even a couple of families who were known to keep their horses in their sitting rooms!

She could have cried with joy the day she escaped the place forever. It was he only positive memory of Ballymun that she took away with her.

Her family still lived there, including her mother Joan, and her older brother and sister, Paul and Tracy. But she had abandoned them years ago and was never in touch.

Fiona's father had left her mother and cleared off years ago. She didn't know whether she hated him for it, or admired him for having the guts to get out while he could. During her formative years her mother might as well not have been present for all the help she was to the family. She had spent most of her nights down at the local pub aptly named The Towers. Often as not Joan would run short of funds to feed her habit, and as a result, it was not unknown for a series of men to arrive and skulk through the sitting room where the children were watching telly, and enter their mother's bedroom for twenty minutes or so. Fiona would frequently have to turn the volume up on the television to drown out the moaning and groaning which emanated through the paper thin walls. After the last man had left, purse topped up once more, Joan would head downtown into Dublin and its more salubrious establishments. It was not unknown for her to bring back a man along with a takeaway!

Fiona had little time for her older brother or sister either. Paul had been very wild and undisciplined as a child. He was ever ready with his fists and was frequently in trouble with the neighbourhood kids. As he got older the Gardai took an interest in him and had warned him to change his ways or else he would land up in Mountjoy. Fiona was praying that wouldn't happen and spoil everything for her.

She reckoned that Tracy was heading the same way as her brother. She was aware that Tracy had started drinking at a young age, and if the graffiti that covered the walls of Ballymun was anything to go by, she was granting favours of a particular nature to her male contemporaries.

As for herself, with her good looks and attractive figure, Fiona had realised at an early age that she could attract men. She figured that her body would be her tool for getting out of Ballymun and away from her embarrassment of a family.

Attractive and ambitious, Fiona reckoned that in order to attract independent, financially stable young guys who could buy her the luxuries she desired she would have to patronise the more upmarket pubs and hotel bars. In fact it was in the 'Dubliner's Bar' in Jury's Hotel after a rugby match at Lansdowne Road that she had allowed herself be chatted up by a handsome, young accountant named Shane. A week later she had moved into Shane's city centre apartment. She was eighteen years old and one step up the ladder to the riches she had dreamt of.

Fiona stayed with Shane for the better part of a year. He was devastated when she left him for another older- and -richer man. Fiona had drained as much as possible from the relationship with Shane, so it was time to move on and give him his cards as far as she was concerned. By this time, she had completed a commercial course after leaving school and was now working as a junior clerk in an insurance office.

Over the next few years she had liaisons with a succession of wealthy men, each better off than the one before, and finally at the age of 24, she had started work for Sean as his personal assistant. This had come about thanks to David, her boyfriend at the time knowing someone in the personnel department; not realising of course that she planned to ditch him as soon as he had got her the position.

Once Fiona had one foot in the door she set about carrying out her well laid plans with the utmost care. No longer would it be good enough for her to show some leg and smile seductively at Sean like she had with her previous partners. Sean was already married – as many of her conquests before had been – and it would have been easy to end up as his mistress. But Fiona had aimed her sights much higher; she had had enough of staring at ceilings in order to get what she wanted. This time she would aim for the top and become the new Mrs. Sean Davenport.

Sean Davenport saw Fiona initially as a very hardworking, efficient assistant. She was more than willing to stay behind after work with him and do some overtime in order to help him out through their busiest periods. It was at such periods of stress that he found it becoming more and more difficult to concentrate on his work instead of glancing at Fiona and being unable to take his eyes off her young, slim body, invariably encased in a tailor made outfit that showed off her assets to perfection.

Fiona sometimes left the top button of the silk blouse which lay beneath her suit undone. She sensed he appreciated it and that it drove him mad with desire; it hinted at what lay beyond, and he could sample the goods if ever he wanted.

Sean had her checked out and knew that she had a boyfriend, indeed several. It proved that she was available although it drove him crazy to think that other men were availing of the pleasures which he was denying himself. And all the time he was admiring her shapely young body....

Poor vulnerable Sean – he was such an easy conquest. Soon he was seeking some very lame excuses to keep her late at the office. Finally Sean could hold his desire back no longer. She knew she had him when he asked her out for a late night drink one night.....Not unnaturally they landed up in her bed, with Sean driven mad with desire and wanting to demonstrate just how crazy he was about her.

Fiona was triumphant. All her months of hard work had paid off. Sean got a shock the next night when Fiona informed him that she had high standards and no way did she plan on becoming a mere mistress. Sean got the message, and most importantly his wife got it also – along with a quickie divorce and a sizeable chunk of his fortune to allow her to enjoy life to the full.

'Fiona! Fiona! Over here.' She looked around. Gerry was waving to her. 'Did you find any presents for your friends, darling?' he called out.

'No, a lot of the things here are very tacky. I'll check out the shops in Ibiza another day. I'll be sure to find something there. How about yourself? Did you get everything you needed?'

'Just about. Listen, I don't know about you, but I think I've seen all I want to see. Besides the heat is killing. Shall we start heading back to Figueretas? I've a couple of phone calls to make. Then we'll have a rest before head to the Hotel Casablanca for dinner.'

'Fabulous! That suits me,' replied Fiona as they walked hand in hand back to the car. She liked the idea of yet another romantic interlude with Gerry. What niggled her was him wanting to make phone calls home. Did that mean he was thinking of Sandra? If so, she knew one sure way of taking his mind off his wife.....

As Gerry placed his purchases in the boot of the small car, Fiona made her way into the passenger seat and turned on the radio. This had to be the hottest day of the holiday so far, surely, she thought. Much too hot to be wearing her tee shirt which had become damp and sticky after walking around the marketplace for the last hour!

Slowly, she pulled off her tee shirt, lowered her seat back and fanned herself seductively with the little paper fan Gerry had sweetly made for her earlier on. She waited for him to get into the car.

When Gerry eased his way into the driving seat a few moments later, his eyes fell on her slim, nubile bronzed body, stretched out seductively. Fiona was smiling her eyes on him, watching his reaction. She certainly knew how to turn a man on!

Fiona read the desire in his eyes. They were a mirror of her own. Gerry ran his hand through his hair and looked about himself furtively. They were in a fairly deserted corner of the dusty, rubble-strewn square that served as a car park where there were hardly any people around. Gerry watched transfixed, as Fiona teasingly reached up and opened her bikini top which fastened to the front. Her bikini top slid open, revealing her beautiful rounded breasts......

Gerry could contain himself no longer and gave way graciously to Fiona's obvious charms. Figueretas and that phone call to Sandra would just have to wait. He had more pressing matters to attend to right now.

— ☻ —

Mamie had asked Evelyn if she would go with her to a local market in Cula Llonga, about five miles from Figueretas. A local bus would take them there. Evelyn had reluctantly agreed to go, it sounded like a good opportunity to pick up some inexpensive presents.

She found Mamie hard going as they travelled on the local bus to the market. The heat of the packed bus and the overpowering smell of Mamie's perfume were just too much. 'Is that Chanel you're wearing?', Evelyn enquired, knowing full well it wasn't.

'Arra no,' Mamie had to shout to make herself heard, 'sure it's only lavender water, I believe it's good for keeping the midges away.'

'It would keep more than midges away,' Evelyn sniffed as she looked out the window at the dry shrubbery and the parched Spanish earth.

The market was crowded with tourists and locals alike when they got there. Luckily the rows of stalls kept out the sun but it was still hot and sticky. Evelyn hated bargaining, she felt it was degrading. Mamie, on the other hand, was in her element as she dragged Evelyn from stall to stall. Evelyn winced as she heard Mamie's strident voice calling her from across the way. 'Over here Evvie, I've found just the thing.'

She watched as Mamie haggled with a dark-skinned Romany type who was in charge of the stall. Mamie was holding up the ugliest bag Evelyn had ever seen. It was real leather and quite expensive, but it was a sickly khaki colour. What on earth could she possibly wear with that? Evelyn thought to herself. Does this woman know what co-ordination means! She looked at the outfit Mamie was wearing. Obviously not!

'It's good quality alright, but has it got a designer label?,' enquired Evelyn. She could see that Mamie didn't share her interest in labels and watched as her companion handed the fellow a wad of peseta notes to pay for the hideous bag. Money didn't seem to be any problem with Mamie Riordan, Evelyn thought as she looked on enviously.

'That's enough haggling for now Evelyn, let's go for a coffee and a cool drink' Mamie said. They found a cafe bar and sat down in the shade. Evelyn watched as Mamie threw two lumps of sugar into a cup of black coffee no bigger than an eggcup. She herself had a cappuccino without sugar.

Mamie stole a look at Evelyn who was studying herself in a hand mirror. 'That woman has so many hang-ups' she thought, 'she is looking so hard at finding fault with the world that she has forgotten how to enjoy herself.' She looked at Evelyn's face, a pretty face, but not a happy one, a face filled with apprehension and suspicion.

'What else did you buy' enquired Evelyn as she eyed the assortment of carrier bags on the chair beside Mamie.

'Ah, only a few bits and pieces for the girls,' replied Mamie. 'I must say the jewellery is gorgeous - what do you think of these?' She fished a wad of tissue paper out of one of the bags and opened it carefully on the table. It contained three gold link bracelets. Evelyn whipped off her sunglasses and lifted one for inspection. Yes - these were the real thing, 18 ct. gold was printed on the tiny labels attached to the bracelets.

'They're for the young ones' said Mamie, 'I got something special for the others.' She opened a flashy black bag with gold writing on it and took out two little velvet-covered boxes. Inside were the most beautiful earrings Evelyn had ever seen outside of Weirs of Grafton St. They consisted of a cluster of little diamonds, at least six to each earring, which sparkled even in the shade.

'Now I have to admit these were quite expensive,' Mamie confided. 'We'd need a calculator to convert the price of these into punts!' She gave a roar of laughter, snapping shut the lids of the boxes and replacing them in the bag.

Evelyn felt her throat tighten as she forced a smile. 'Very nice' she said, hoping Mamie wouldn't know what she was feeling. She wouldn't be buying the likes of those for Samantha now or ever. She glanced at the straw handbag on the chair beside her. It contained a few trinkets she had bought for the family - a key ring with Figueretas written on it for Gary, a lipstick case for Samantha, and a fridge magnet for her sister Imelda. Des had warned that money was tight. She had been at him to use his banker's card but he had refused point blank. What on earth was wrong with the man?

'Well for her,' thought Evelyn as she looked across the table at Mamie - 'ugly as sin but she still managed to get a man with money.' Life just wasn't fair.

They noticed the people hurrying out of the cafe and making for the far side of the square. The dusty blue and white bus was already there and filling up with happy shoppers laden down with bags.

'Alo won't be sorry he missed this' said Mamie. 'He is a devil to bring shopping. I usually take one day every fortnight to go shopping in Dublin. Alo loves that day because he can golf, have a drink and not be expected home at a set time.' Evelyn noticed that her voice softened when she spoke of Alo, obviously she loved him very much. Evelyn felt the familiar surge of envy. 'This woman has everything' she thought.

On the coach back to Figueretas, Mamie recalled the Enid Blyton books she used read to the girls when they were small. The characters in the stories always went home 'tired but happy' when their adventures were over. This was exactly how she felt. She rested her head against the warm leather of the seat and glanced sideways at Evelyn who had closed her eyes and was dozing. Even in repose Evelyn didn't look happy.

To Bernice's surprise, Alison and Georgia joined herself and Brian at the pool side cafe for lunch.

'You look tired, Georgia. What have you been up to' asked Brian.

Before Georgia could reply Alison cut in. 'She was making sure she was winning a little bet from Bernice and me. Am I right Georgia, dear?'

Georgia lowered her lashes and smiled at Brian and began to tell him about Jose. 'Oh! I met this terrific guy. He owns a bar in the old part of Ibiza Town. Alison and I were there yesterday. The place was a bit dead until we walked in. We soon livened things up. Jose and I became very friendly and he invited me out to dinner last night. We promised to go back today and liven things up a bit. You and Bernice should come along too. You're sure to enjoy yourself.'

'Let's get a taxi later then' suggested Bernice. 'I'd love to see this latest hunk of yours.' They all agreed that a taxi was a good idea and they settled down to enjoy a light lunch.

As they entered Jose's Hacienda, Georgia was quick to notice that some of her ideas had already been implemented. The tables were covered with red and white squared cloths and in the centre of each was a candle encased in a red glass bowl. Scattered around the walls were several posters imploring the clientele to 'Enjoy Jose's new cocktail - Ibiza How Are Yeh! It's something special!' Already several customers were trying out the new cocktail. Georgia was pleased. Jose had been waiting for her and he walked over and hugged her warmly and kissed her passionately.

'Querida - Mia, you are so welcome, also your friends.' He shook hands with Bernice and Brian and invited them to have one of the special cocktails. Then Jose called for silence and announced to the clientele; 'Ladies and Gentleman, I want to introduce you to this lovely lady, her name is Georgia and she is from Dublin, Ireland. I named our new cocktail in her honour because she was the inspiration. I think I am falling in love with her.' With that Jose grabbed Georgia again and kissed her passionately as everyone in the bar cheered loudly.

Georgia walked over to the juke box, choose a few of her favourite tunes and turned up the sound. Jose joined her, pulled her into an alcove and again put his arms around her, pulled her to him and gave her a long passionate kiss.

'Jose,' declared Georgia, breathlessly when he at last released her 'how can I concentrate on improving this place if you distract my attention.' She pulled his face down to hers and whispered in his ear. 'There will be plenty of time for that to-night. First we must look after business, get a bit of life into this place.'

The throbbing beat of the music began to attract attention from outside and a steady flow of young people came in and began to sit down at the tables. 'Now is the time to serve some half-price cocktails.' Georgia said turning to Jose. 'Announce that for the next hour we will serve two for the price of one. That way everyone will buy and get to know about them.' Jose looked surprised.

He was not used to being ordered about. But he did what Georgia commanded.

Georgia became very much the hostess, finding seats for everyone, chatting them up and asking them what their favourite tune was. Suddenly the bar became alive, Jose and his two barmen were mixing and serving Ibiza, How Are Yeh! as fast as they could make the cocktails. Couples were up dancing and gyrating on the floor.

Brian sat on a high stool and was amazed at the way the place had come to life. Georgia walked over and took his hand. 'Come along Brian,' she said softly 'I want you to dance with me.'

Bernice felt the alarm bells ringing. What was Georgia at, was she trying to make Jose jealous?

'Oh no Georgia, not me, I have two left feet,' Brian pleaded.

'See that you don't trip yourself up then' Georgia pulled him to the centre of the floor. Brian did his best to move to the music like the other couples but compared to Georgia he was like a dromedary.

Shouting over the loud music, Brian complimented Georgia on her dancing and asked 'Where did you learn to dance? I think I could do with a few lessons.'

'I've been dancing since I was five years old, Georgia declared. 'It's easy, just keep to the beat of the music. I think I was born dancing. I went to the famous Billy Barry Dance School in Dublin for 14 years and I loved every minute of it.'

'You're sensational Georgia. Really hot stuff.' Brian said. The crowd in the bar were really enjoying the show she was putting on.

'Perhaps I was a dancer in a previous life. Know what - I'd love to do Salome's Dance of the Seven Veils!' Georgia looked as if she was about to perform the sexy dance there and then. She had gone to see the play at the Gate Theatre in Dublin and had been knocked out by Salome's sexy dance scene.

'Why don't you suggest to Jose that you do it as a special act in his club.?' Brian said. 'You'd be sensational.

'Hey, that's a great idea' Georgia replied. 'I could buy some see-through material around town and really liven this place up.' The more Georgia thought about it the more she liked the idea.

'This is a bit strenuous for me, mind if I sit down for a while?' Brian asked.

Georgia thought he was looking a little green around the gills. 'Sit down and I'll get you a cool drink,' she said. He might be a big handsome guy, Georgia thought, but he'd never survive a night in some of the discos in Dublin!

There was great applause as they left the floor. Jose came out from behind the bar and put his arm around Georgia. His intention was obvious, he wanted to make it clear to Brian and all present that Georgia was spoken for. Georgia told him she fancied performing the Dance of the Seven Veils in his bar and Jose agreed it was a great idea.

Jose looked into Georgia's eyes. 'Come into my office and we'll discuss it further,' he said. Georgia was only too willing to oblige. No sooner was the door closed than the two of them fell into each other's arms.

'I thought we were going to discuss my dance,' she said, holding Jose off momentarily.

'Later,' he whispered. She could feel herself weakening as they kissed. For Jose, it was a long time since any girl made such an impact on him. In his heart, he knew, he had already fallen in love with her. 'You will dine with me again to-night, will you not, querida mia,?' he said, when they at last broke apart. 'Then we will spend the whole night together and you will make me as happy as you did last night.'

Georgia could feel her heart pounding. She too wished to relive last night. She smiled her consent and he held her close for a moment.

'I will not be in the bar tomorrow,' he said. 'I have to go to the country and visit La Condesa, my mother. I wish to tell her all about you, Georgia.'

'She's not a real Contessa, is she?' Georgia asked.

'Oh yes, of course. You may find her a bit old fashioned, but do not worry.'

Oh! God, thought Georgia. What am I letting myself in for? Yes she fancied Jose in a big way. But his mother - she was probably a real Spanish dragon, one that thought no girl was good enough for her son. And she was a real Contessa. Jose had admitted that she was old fashioned... that probably meant she was very strict.

Georgia managed a smile, 'I'd love to meet your mother sometime, Jose darling' she lied.

'Good. I will tell her what you have done here, how you have made me very happy.'

'Better not go into too much detail about our goings - on' Georgia laughed.

'My mother, she is very, very wise. I do not have to tell her all. She will guess. You will come to visit her - for dinner - on Sunday. Okay?'

Oh God! Georgia thought, She didn't fancy meeting his mother so soon. She'll probably think I am trying to steal her only son. Jose had told her last night when they were together that his father was dead and that he was the only one in the family. No doubt Jose's mother would like to see him marrying someone - a nice Spanish senorita, who would give him plenty of children - not a redheaded Irish girl who planned to do The Dance of the Seven Veils on a table top in her son's bar!

Georgia was already making plans to find a boutique where she could buy some diaphanous material for her upcoming performance. If only she didn't have to meet Jose's mother. That was one trip into the country on Sunday she wasn't looking forward to.........

CHAPTER EIGHT

Paula Sheridan busied herself during the morning tidying the apartment.

Wednesday was a day she could take some hours off and when she had finished her domestic chores she planned on making a trip to the bank. Later she would return to the apartment, make herself a cup of coffee and study her German language textbook for at least an hour before lunch.

Vicki was at college and would not be home until late afternoon. Vicki also did part-time work as a waitress in the Sinatra Club, where she earned some useful pocket money. Paula had heard that an Irish couple from the Hotel Orlando had already qualified for the final. Maybe she would drop in there tonight ....

Paula grabbed her handbag and set out to walk along the promenade towards the bank. She ignored the noisy crowds on the beach and turned her gaze instead to the masses of colourful flowers and shrubs that abounded on the other side of the road. It was a beautiful day. It was also going to be an eventful one.....

She cut up a narrow street into the busy centre of Figueretas and crossed the road towards the Banco Hispano. As she pushed at the swing doors a man was exiting from the other side, Paula's heart missed a beat. She recognised him immediately.

'Ben! Ben O'Rourke!' She blurted out the name before she could stop herself. He paused, peered at her. Suddenly recognition dawned. 'Paula! Paula Sheridan!

'Oh my God! I don't believe it. How are you for heaven's sake?'

'I'm fine. And you?.....' He had gained some weight, lost a lot of hair. And now he wore glasses. They gave him a distinguished look, but he wasn't the Ben O'Rourke she remembered.

'I'm fine too.' His eyes travelled unashamedly over her body in admiration. 'You're looking well, Paula. What are you doing here?' He grinned, 'Holidays, I suppose.'

'No,' Paula replied. 'Actually I work here in Figueretas.'

'Oh........That's interesting. Where?'

Didn't he realise how smug he sounded? Paula knew she was going to enjoy the next couple of minutes. 'The Hotel Orlando.' She smiled when she said it, savouring the effect she knew it would have on him.

Ben looked like she had slapped him across the face, an action that had indeed occurred to Paula to perform. 'You're joking? -'

'I'm not.'

He tried a smile, but it was a weak effort. 'Would you believe it I'm staying there too.'

'Yes. I know. With your wife.' She smiled again. 'Irene isn't it?'

He was getting really worried now. And it showed. 'Er, yes, that's right. Irene.....' He was about to ask her how she knew his wife's name when she said: 'I saw it on my register at the hotel when she complained about the beds.'

'Oh yes. So she did. That's Irene....A stickler, complains about a lot of things......'

'I'd love to meet her sometime,' Paula said sweetly. 'I mean any woman that inspires such loyalty in a man must be someone special. Don't you think so?'

Ben knew Paula was getting at him, twisting the knife. He could see disaster ahead. He looked around as though afraid his wife was right behind him. 'Look Paula, we can't talk here. How about a drink? Just for old times sake? To be honest I could do with a stiff one myself -'

Why not, Paula reasoned. She was really enjoying herself. She was in control, held all the aces. Ben was scared, confused, disorientated, didn't know what was going to happen next. He looked like he had aged a few years in the last couple of minutes. Paula reckoned he was about to age some more in the next few minutes. She allowed him to guide her towards a nearby bar where they sat outside in the shade.

'What'll you have, Paula?'

'Same as I used to in the old days - a Campari and soda please. With ice.'

'I'll need something stronger than that!' He gestured to a waiter, ordered Paula's drink and a double Hennessy brandy and a mixer for himself. She sat back relaxed waited for him to say something.

Ben could not believe this was happening. He and his wife had come to Ibiza to celebrate a very special occasion - their silver wedding. Twenty-five years of married bliss, if one was to judge by all the outside appearances. A closer look at his and Irene's marriage might prove otherwise. And now to make things worse, his past was catching up with him. If Irene got a whiff of what had happened between him and Paula all those years ago there would be hell to pay. He must prevent that at all costs.

'You must think I'm a right no-good. I mean not getting in touch with you after your friend - what's this her name was, Nicola? - had told me you had gone abroad......'

The waiter came with the drinks. Ben was glad for the respite. Why was Paula smiling at him with that half smile on her face? Why doesn't she say something! 'I'm afraid my friend Nicola didn't tell you everything, Ben darling.....'

Ben darling! Oh-oh! Alarm bells were definitely ringing now. There was something more. 'I left Ireland because I was expecting a baby. Your daughter. Her name is Victoria....'

Ben nearly fell of his chair Holy God, he thought. I stroll out on a beautiful morning to change some travellers' cheques and the whole world is collapsing around me! What next?

'A daughter. Mine... Are you sure Paula....?'

A silence. She glared at him. 'I rather suspected you'd say something like that, Ben. But then you know what they say.... once a no-good always a no-good....'

He had the good grace to look embarrassed, but recovered himself quickly, 'I'm sorry, Paula. I didn't mean it that way. But you do understand, this is a terrible shock.'

Despite herself she laughed. Loudly this time. 'Vicki is your daughter, Ben. I was never more sure of anything in all my life.'

Ben finished half his brandy at a gulp. 'A daughter..... I can't believe it. What is she like? I'd love to meet her sometime.'

'Don't worry you will.'

'When?'

'Tonight maybe.'

Once again Ben looked shocked. 'Tonight! You mean to say she's here - in Figueretas?'

'Of course. Where did you think she was? Needless to say she's been asking about you a lot over the years.......'

'Why didn't you write, Paula, telephone me. I'd have helped. You know I would -' Her icy glare stopped him in mid-sentence.

A crowd of young people, Vicki's age mostly, passed up from the beach, giggling and joking with each other, oblivious to the drama being played out under their noses.

Ben stared at the rest of the liquid in his glass, swilled it around. When he spoke again it was like he was talking to himself....'Who would believe it......Of all the crummy hotels in the crummy towns on the crummiest island in the world - I had to pick the Hotel Orlando for a holiday!'. He had always liked that line Humphrey Bogart line from his favourite film 'Casablanca'. He never thought he would be using it!

Bogart and Bergman had rekindled their relationship in Rick's Bar in Morocco. Maybe he and Paula could do the same here in Ibiza.......

He reached across the table, covered her hand with his. 'You've grown into a beautiful, mature woman, Paula. I'm so happy we've met after all these years. Are you married –' he paused – 'in a relationship perhaps....'

Paula carefully removed her hand from under his. 'Don't you want to hear about Victoria, your lovely daughter?' she asked levelly.

'Of course. I was about to ask. What age is she now -'

'She's eighteen. She attends college here.'

'Eighteen – and at college...Excellent.' He looked pleased. 'I suppose she looks a bit like her dad,' he said, and for a moment he was the confident car salesman again.

Paula paused. She would have to tell Ben the truth. 'Yes, Vicki does resemble you a little. But I would like to think she has my character. She cares about people - and she's also very trustworthy.'

Ben knew what Paula was hinting at. But he decided to ignore the barb.

'Victoria......What a beautiful name. I have to see her, Paula. I must see her before we leave Ibiza.?'

'I don't know that you deserve to meet Vicki, Ben. I'm not sure I want you to - '

'Please, Paula......' He was really pleading. She took a sip of her drink before replying .

'Alright, Ben, you can meet Vicki - ' Relief flooded his face. 'On one condition......'

'What's that?'

'That when I tell you where Victoria will be tonight you'll bring Irene along. I'd like to meet her - ' She saw the surprise or maybe it was fear, in his eyes. 'Don't worry, Ben, I won't tell Irene who Victoria is, or about our affair for that matter. What you want to tell your wife is entirely up to you. I won't even, let Victoria know that she will be meeting her father. I'll tell her myself tomorrow, when we're alone. Then we will all meet the next day in my apartment.'

She could see that Ben was both puzzled and afraid. Bringing Paula and Irene together, introducing them to each other, was fraught with danger. He knew that. But he so wanted to see his new daughter......

'Okay. So are we meeting someplace tonight?'

'Yes. The Sinatra Club in the Hotel Casablanca. Vicki works there a few nights a week for pocket money. There's a dance competition on there tonight. Some of your friends from the Hotel Orlando are going. Bring Irene along.'

Ben groaned. 'Irene won't fancy going. She's a bit of a snob, hates crowded bars and pubs, that sort of thing.' Paula thought it rather ungallant for him to speak about his wife like that. That was Ben's problem, however.

'Too bad, Ben. Pity, it may be the only chance you'll get to see your daughter.' Paula finished off her drink stood up. 'Now I must go. It was interesting meeting you again.'

Ben was taken by surprise. 'Hey Paula, please wait a minute -' But she had already turned on her heel and was walking smartly back towards the Banco Hispano. Ben O'Rourke sat staring after her. Only one word could describe how he felt - Gobsmacked!

Doc Holliday spotted Yolanda Segguria as he approached the cafe/bar. She was seated in the shade outside the entrance, at the same table they had occupied earlier in the week. When she saw him she smiled a greeting.

'Sorry I'm late,' he apologised as he sat down beside her. Yolanda had telephoned him at the hotel late last night, asking him to meet her. She was anxious to hear what happened now that Donie Crawford had made contact again.

'I'm glad you could come. I saw our friend speaking to you last night....'

'Yes. We had a very interesting chat,' Doc replied. 'You were right, he asked me how I'd like to make a thousand pounds - five hundred in pesetas now and five Irish when I deliver the goods to a man in the car park at Dublin Airport.'

'Heroin?' she asked.

Doc nodded. 'Wrapped in cellophane. Donie assures me it will be easy to hide in my luggage.'

He ordered coffee and rolls for them both, sat back and relaxed in the cool, mid-morning sunshine. Yolanda Segguria was looking very pretty this morning, Doc thought. She had cast aside the track suit bottoms and denim top of their first meeting for a crisp white blouse tucked into a loose patterned skirt. Her dark hair was held back from her face with a short red headscarf. She had removed her tinted sunglasses and he admired her soft brown eyes.

'You pretended to Donie that you were interested? What happened?'

'I always do what pretty women tell me,' he smiled. 'I followed your instructions to the letter.'

'Good. And thank you for the compliment. Now, I must know when and where he is passing the heroin and the money over to you. Then we can make an arrest -'

She paused while the waiter brought the coffee and rolls. When he had departed Doc said: 'Donie won't hand it over until sometime next week, near the end of the holiday. He's very cautious. Probably afraid I'll try to sell it here, make some easy money -'

'Don't even think about it, Mr. Holliday. These men are ruthless. Believe me I know what I am talking about. I told you how they killed my husband. It was probably the one time he got careless and didn't check underneath his car…

A silence fell between them. Yolanda Segguria looked across the road, out towards the blue sea where small boats were sailing in the distance. She seemed lost in thought. Doc stirred his coffee and said: 'One thing I'd like you to do for me…'

She turned her gaze to him. 'What is that, Mr. Holliday?'

'Stop calling me Mr. Holliday. It's so formal. I mean if we're going to work together we should be on more friendly terms, more relaxed. Don't you think so - '

She laughed, her teeth showing white against her tanned skin. 'Of course. You are correct. From now you call me Yolanda -'

'And you call me Alec - or Doc if you prefer. Doc's a nickname.'

She puckered up her nose in disgust. 'I prefer Alec. It's nice, suits you better.'

He smiled. ' Whatever you wish….' Just like Maureen, he thought. Funny the way only men seemed to like nicknames, while women tended to ignore them.

'I appreciate the risk you are taking to help us fight the drug trade here in Ibiza,' Yolanda remarked. 'It is muy peligroso - very dangerous, and for you there is no reward.….'

Doc shrugged. 'Think nothing of it. It brought us together, that's reward enough for me.' He paused, said 'I'm going to enjoy working with you, Yolanda.' Doc knew he was taking a chance; she could feel threatened, think he was pushing things between them, tell him to back off and mind his own business. Instead she looked pleased.

'Thank you. I think I will enjoy working with you also. But then I suppose you pay compliments to all your lady friends - Maureen included.'

'Maureen and I only met on the plane coming over. We like each other but.......' he paused. 'At the moment we are a dance partnership in the Sinatra Club, that's as far as we've got.'

'I see. Now I understand.'

He was enjoying this second meeting with Yolanda Segguria. He found her attractive and interesting. Despite the tragedy she had endured she seemed determined not to let the death of her husband at the hands of the island's drug dealers ruin her life. He found her easy to talk to and he liked the way she laughed easily. It was as though they had known each other for a long time instead of having met just a few days ago.

And what about Maureen? Would that relationship ever pass the dancing stage? They had planned a half-day trip this afternoon around the island and he was looking forward to it. But, what would happen when the holiday was over for them both? Would they see each other again when they returned home? Funny the way he had met two women, both of whom had endured tragedy in their lives. Maureen had a different personality to Yolanda. Of course that would have to do with their different backgrounds. Maureen was more reserved, not quite as upfront or as outgoing as Yolanda Segguria. Maybe he would introduce the women to each other, see how they would get on together......

'Like all detectives I like to ask questions,' Yolanda's voice cut across his reverie.

' What about - our friend Donie Crawford?'

'No Alec, I wish to know more about you. What line of business are you in? What do you work at in Dublin?'

She was interested when he informed her that he had worked in the famous Guinness brewery all his life.

She listened attentively as he recounted how his father and grandfather had also worked there. 'When new technology was brought in I got a good offer and decided to take early retirement - '

'Why did you not come to Spain to live? A lot of Irish people have bought homes on the Costa del Sol.'

'And we could have got to know each other a lot sooner, eh?' He shrugged. 'I have a nice house in an area called Ringsend in Dublin, and I have a lot of good friends there -'

'And lady friends too, no doubt. A wife perhaps?'

'Lady friends yes. A wife - no.'

'Why not? You are a handsome man. And you keep yourself fit. You run, you swim -' She was smiling across the table at him. 'Many ladies would find you attractive!' He wasn't sure whether she was teasing him or being serious. He decided to play her at her own game.

'Does that include you Yolanda?'

She was amused. 'Alec, I ask questions strictly in the line of duty. I like to know everything about the person I am working with.' She paused. 'Do you believe me?'

'Frankly, no!'

She laughed, but didn't say he was wrong. 'Now we must get back to business. I have to be going soon. I have work to do....' She paused, said: 'About Donie Crawford, you must let me know as soon as he contacts you again.'

'I will. But how about us meeting before that? I'd like to.......' It was three years since her husband had been killed. He wondered if she was involved with someone else. He would soon find out.

'I'll be at the Sinatra Club again on Saturday night for the dance final. You and your friend Maureen will be there, of course -'

'Yes, so will a lot of our friends from the hotel. We won't have much of an opportunity to continue this little chat.'

Yolanda studied him for a short while, as though deciding something in her mind. Finally she said. 'I wish to repay you for helping us to trap a drug pusher.......How about you coming to dinner tomorrow night, in my apartment in the town.? -'

The invite took Doc by surprise. Things were happening much faster than he had anticipated. A romantic meal alone with Yolanda. And in her place too. Surely an offer he couldn't refuse! 'Thanks, Yolanda, that's very nice of you. I'd love to - '

As though reading his thoughts she said. 'My two boys will also be there. I would like you to meet them. You may not be so enthusiastic when you taste my cooking!'

They both laughed. ' Here is my address.' She handed him a card. 'It is near the cathedral. The boys and I eat late, around nine o'clock.'

'Nine o'clock will be fine.'

Yolanda and Doc had been so engrossed in conversation that neither of them noticed the three ladies who had paused on the pavement opposite as they were passing the bar.

'Girls, look over there. I do believe that's Maureen's friend Alec chatting to a woman outside that bar.' Cathleen observed.

Joan and Sheila followed their friend's gaze. 'You're right. Cathleen,' Sheila said triumphantly. 'That's our friend Alec. And doesn't he look like he's enjoying himself!'

'For heaven's sake what of it. What's wrong with a man having an innocent chat with a lady over a couple of coffees.' Joan countered.

'Innocent my foot.' Sheila observed slyly. 'Look at the way they're gazing into each other's eyes! There's something going on over there between those two, mark my words.'

Joan had to admit that Alec Holliday did seem to be enjoying his chat with the lady. He was so caught up being in her company that it was doubtful if he was conscious of whoever else was passing by. She was a little perturbed to see Maureen's friend talking to another woman but, she was not going to let Sheila and Cathleen see that she was worried.

They had kept walking and were now past the bar. 'Well now girls,' Sheila said, smirking. 'Won't we have something very interesting to tell Maureen tomorrow when we meet?'

As soon as Irene had opened her eyes that morning she knew she was in trouble. The sun was streaming through a chink in the bedroom curtains, and even that shaft of sunlight made her close her eyes more tightly. Her migraine headache had struck again.

This was her recurring nightmare. She lifted her head off the pillow but the demonic dance in her temples forced her to lie back in abject misery. Could she not even get two weeks free of this torment! She looked at Benjamin, bustling around the apartment - for this once why couldn't it be him!

Irene dozed fitfully. She knew Benjamin was going to make himself scarce, as he usually did when these 'aberrations' as he called them occurred. He hated the dark room.

'I'll go into town for the morning, Irene. I've to visit the bank. Maybe you'll feel better when I get back. I'll phone the Hotel Tropicana and confirm the booking for our anniversary dinner - that is if you've really decided that it's the best place. What do you think?'

'Oh, just go and do what you have to do, Benjamin.' She was beyond caring what he did.

Irene didn't answer the cleaning staff when they knocked twice during the morning. They went away again and she slept. But now a persistent loud banging roused her. She looked at the clock. It was early afternoon.

'Come in,' she called out.

Paula Sheridan swiped her entry card, braced her shoulders and entered Irene O'Rourke's bedroom. When she had returned to the hotel from town and her meeting with Ben she had been told that the lady in Room 405 was ill. It was her responsibility to investigate.

She knew this was Ben and Irene's apartment. She would be meeting Irene sooner than she expected. What if Ben arrived back and found the two of them chatting in the apartment! Not so long ago she had left Ben in a rather flustered state. Now she was coming face to face with his wife.

'Good afternoon, Mrs O'Rourke. Irene, isn't it? I'm Paula Sheridan, Staff Supervisor. It was reported to me that you may be unwell. I came to check, see if there is anything you require.'

'That's very good of you...' Irene struggled to sit up. Paula felt sympathy for her. Right now Ben's wife wasn't looking her best. 'My husband went into town this morning. He said he would be back in an hour or two. I can't believe he's not back yet.'

'Can I get you something to eat or drink?' Paula asked. 'I can contact the kitchen and one of the staff will bring you up a light snack.'

Irene was hardly listening to what Paula was saying. Where was Benjamin? He should be back by now. He certainly wasn't showing much sympathy. 'Thanks, that's very good of you. My husband Benjamin went off to finalise arrangements for our silver wedding celebrations next week -'

Paula felt a pang of envy 'That's very nice.' she heard herself say. 'Congratulations.'

'We're having dinner at the Hotel Tropicana. Do you know it?'

'Oh yes. It's an excellent hotel. You'll have a lovely dinner there.'

'That husband of mine- he must have stopped off for a drink....' Irene lay back on her pillow.

What would you say if I told you that your darling husband and I had an affair - and that he's the father of my daughter? Paula mused. That would give you more than a migraine headache to worry about!

'Do I look dreadful?' Irene asked.

Paula blushed. She must have been staring. 'You just relax. I'll go down and see what's on offer in the kitchen.'

'You're very kind.'

Paula opened the door. 'It's nice to have met you, Mrs. O'Rourke. Oh, by the way If you've recovered you and your husband should go along to the Sinatra Club tonight to see the dance contest. I'll be there with my teenage daughter Vicki. I think you'll enjoy yourself. Goodbye.' With that Paula Sheridan exited.

Irene got up and managed to get into her silk dressing-gown. She splashed some 4711 on her aching forehead. Like myself, that's gone out of fashion too, she thought. Where is Benjamin? What excuse is he going to come up with this time, Irene fumed.

Paula Sheridan was as good as her word - a nicely displayed tray with appetising tit-bits and a carafe of iced orange arrived. Irene had almost finished eating when Ben burst into the apartment. He looked flustered and strangely out of breath.

'Steady on there, don't take the door off the hinges. Where have you been all morning?'

'Irene, I'm sorry to be so late. There was a big queue in the bank and afterwards I went for a stroll.' He paused for breath. 'I did telephone the Hotel Tropicana. Everything has been taken care of. No need to worry. You'll enjoy our special night. How are you? You look a bit brighter.'

'No thanks to you!' Irene snapped. 'If Paula Sheridan hadn't come to check on me I'd still be in bed.'

'Paula Sheridan!' Ben gasped. ' I thought it was her day off. She was here, talking to you?'

Irene's eyes narrowed. 'How did you know it was her day off?'

Ben swallowed, looked guilty. Holy God he'd have to be careful or he would give everything away. 'Oh, I met Doc Holliday in town. He - he had been told to report a missing watch to the Staff Supervisor which of course is Paula Sheridan. He told me she went off duty. It was a false alarm in the end - Doc found his watch under the bed.' Ben laughed shakily.

'Paula was worried about my being ill. She wanted to know what caused the upset.'

'It was only a migraine, wasn't it? You didn't have to go into any details about yourself or me, did you?'

'Why should we be discussing you, for heaven's sake? I was the one with the headache.' Irene snapped.

'Of course. Did she say she would be back again?'

'Benjamin, were you and that fellow Doc Holliday off drinking? You're all on edge. Calm down and relax. What were you really doing all day? I have a feeling you're not telling me everything. Lucky you didn't come in with a bunch of flowers behind your back - that would really have made me suspicious! I must have a word with your man Doc to see what exactly the pair of you were up to!'

Ben sat down. His knees felt weak and he was breaking out in a cold sweat. All these questions... Irene was suspicious and he was having to invent lie after lie. And if she checked with Doc.... Ben planned on having a word with him first!

Since he had met Paula Sheridan this morning his whole world had come crashing down. And to think he had come away on this holiday to relax! The shock news that she had had a daughter - his daughter - had left him reeling. Her name was Victoria, she was beautiful, eighteen - and he was going to meet her tonight at the Sinatra Club - and Irene would be there!

Paula had asked him if he was going to tell Irene about Vicki. No way! That would mean having to tell of their affair. Of course he couldn't ruin Irene's holiday - and their wedding anniversary. And of course his marriage. But what about Paula? How would she react over the rest of the holiday?'. She was in the driving seat!

He was thankful when Irene went in to have a shower. Later she emerged from the bathroom, put on a fresh pink linen frock and white sandals. Colour was gradually returning to her cheeks. She agreed when Ben suggested they should go down to the pool side and get some fresh air.

She wasn't too agreeable when, sipping iced drinks in the shade and relaxing in the cool breeze, Ben said they should go to the Sinata Club tonight to see the second final of the dance contest. Des and Evelyn would be trying to make it to the final on Saturday night and quite a few people from the hotel were going to cheer them on. They should lend their support, Ben said.

Irene grimaced. But Benjamin was looking after her so well right now that she decided to accommodate him. 'The noise of the band and all that talk - I hope it doesn't bring on another migraine. If it does I'll blame you, Benjamin O'Rourke!' Irene said. Ben sighed. Irene's migrane was the least of his worries!

— ☯ —

'Ah, so you are both going golfing this morning?' The receptionist remarked to Des as he and Alo ordered a taxi. 'The golf course at Roca Llisa is not too far from Figueretas. Fifteen minutes drive into the mountains. It has beautiful views but - ' he shrugged apologetically....

'But what?' asked Des. He didn't like the sound of this.

'I am afraid it is not what one would call a first class golf course. Not like some of the excellent ones you have in Ireland.'

Des and Alo looked at each other. 'I've played golf in Spain a few times,' Des confided to Alo. 'Right enough while the well known courses here are top class, some of the others are below par. Hacked out of the side of mountains, that sort of thing...'

'Shure it won't make a blind bit of difference to me,' Alo replied philosophically. 'Not the way I play golf! Anyway we're only going for a bit of fun.'

'Is Roca Llisa the best course there is in Ibiza?' he asked the receptionist.

'It is the best because it is the only one!' the receptionist grinned. Des groaned. As a single handicap golfer he was accustomed to playing on good golf courses. Still, he should have no problem beating Alo and earning a few pesetas.

Evelyn was standing in the background listening. She wasn't too keen on Des going golfing this morning with herself having to spend the day with Mamie; she would have preferred to spend the day relaxing by the pool. Although by accompanying Des to the golf course she'd make sure he didn't have too much to drink. She wanted him in good fettle for the Sinatra Club tonight.

Mamie Riordan had insisted on going with Evelyn 'to keep you company,' as she put it. 'We'll have a nice lunch in the clubhouse while the men play golf. And a bottle of wine, of course. And don't worry, Evelyn dear, this is my treat. I'll pick up the bill.' The cheek of her, Evelyn thought. She must think Des and I are paupers!

As like yesterday when they had gone to the market, Mamie kept up a continuous line of patter as the taxi left the streets of Figueretas behind, wound its way into the countryside and up into the mountains.

'Do you know what I'm going to tell you, Alo Riordan,' Mamie tapped her husband, who was seated beside the driver, on the shoulder. She had been looking out of the window at men in straw hats and sweat-soaked t-shirts toiling behind oxen turning the hay in the sun-baked fields. 'You'd make a fortune if you opened up a branch of Riordan's Farm Machinery for Hire out here in Ibiza!'

'Will you have a bit of sense, woman!' Alo shouted back above the noise of the taxi engine. 'Look at those poor men - shure they haven't two pesetas to rub together! Where do you think they'd get the finance to hire out expensive machinery. I'll make more in a week when I open our new branch in Naas than I'd make out here in a year. Amn't I right , Des?'

Evelyn sighed. She was squeezed in the back seat between Mamie and Des. With her girth Mamie needed about half the seat to herself. Didn't the woman ever hear of Weightwatchers! She seemed to be expanding by the minute. Evelyn's arms were pinioned by her side and the only part of her body she could move with any degree of comfort was her head. What a way to prepare for her big night in the Sinatra Club!

'Desmond!,' Evelyn turned her head, hissed at her husband.

'Yes dear? What is it? - don't ask me to move up on this seat. I'm crushed to death as it is!'

'About your Bermuda shorts.......'

'What about my Bermuda shorts?'

'You're not wearing them today traipsing around that golf course!'

What on earth was wrong with Evelyn? Was the sun finally getting to her. 'Why not? Alo is wearing his.'

'Alo is not dancing in the Sinatra Club tonight. I'm afraid you'll get sunburn on the backs of your legs and you won't be able to dance properly.'

Des groaned. No sense in arguing with Evelyn when she was in this mood. 'As you wish, dear,' he acquiesced.

'And another thing.....'

'What's it this time?' He was beginning to sound like Hyacinth's husband in the tv series Keeping Up Appearances!

'Wear a proper hat and not one of those skimpy sun visors. If your bald patch gets sunburned you know what happens - you get a terrible headache!'

Evelyn was relieved when five minutes later the taxi drove into the Roca Liisa golf complex. When they alighted she had to rub both her arms to get the blood circulating. She made a mental note never to share the back seat of a taxi with Mamie Riordan again!

While the ladies scouted around, Alo and Des headed for the professional's shop. Inside Alo negotiated the hire of two sets of golf clubs, an electric buggy and half a dozen golf balls each. He brushed aside Des's offer to pay half of the cost.

While Alo went into the locker room to change, Des heard his name been called. He looked up and saw Evelyn and Mamie sitting at a table on the clubhouse balcony. 'We've discovered a beautiful outdoor swimming pool.' Mamie shouted down. 'After Evelyn and I have had lunch we're going to have a swim and a laze in the sun. Enjoy your golf!' Des sighed with relief. Thank God! That took care of Evelyn for the afternoon!

He drove over to the first tee in the buggy and waited for Alo. When the big man appeared a few minutes later Des tried not to laugh outright. Alo was wearing the most lurid, multi- coloured pair of Bermuda shorts he had ever seen. Des reckoned he'd take a photograph later to show his friends in the golf club when he got home.....

Des was still smiling as he placed a ball on the tee, swung his driver, and smashed a drive over 200 yards down the first fairway.

'Be the hokey your man Tiger Woods would be pleased with that one!' Alo bellowed, much to the amusement of another group waiting to tee off.

Then it was his turn. Alo looked ungainly and had a golf swing more suited to a hurley player. Des winced, but the centre of Alo's driver made perfect contact with the ball and sent it straight down the fairway like a rocket, landing twenty yards ahead of Des's drive. Alo beamed with delight. It was the best shot Alo was to hit all day.

While Des hit the green with his second shot setting up a comfortable par, Alo pulled an 8-iron badly to the right, fluffed a chip, managed to get his next onto the green but then three putted for a seven. Des breathed a sigh of relief!

Worse was to follow for Alo. On the second hole Des again hit the fairway off his drive. He winced as his opponent again swung at his ball like he was wielding a hurley. This time the golf club didn't contact the ball spot-on. The ball took off like a boomerang, cleared a belt of trees on the right of the fairway and was never seen again.

Shame-faced, Alo placed another ball on the tee. 'This time hit an iron for safety and don't try hit the ball out of sight,' Des advised. The big man followed the advice and that ball survived for another three holes before Alo fell back into his old habit and it too disappeared down a ravine. Des commiserated with him and passed on as much advice as he dared without embarrassing Alo.

By the time they walked off the 18th green almost three hours later Alo had not only run out of golf balls, he had also lost three belonging to Des. 'Ah well,' he laughed as they were in the shower later, 'I bet Tiger Woods would be a wash-out selling farm machinery!'

Des roared laughing. He liked Alo Riordan. The big man might never make a golfer, but unlike a lot of others he enjoyed himself on the golf course and could laugh at his misfortunes. And at least when the holiday had ended Alo had a thriving business to go back to, as well as his beloved Mamie. Des reckoned Alo deserved everything that had come his way.

He admired Alo a lot more when they were dressed and he found a large wad of pesetas being thrust into his hand. Des looked at the amount and was amazed. 'Hey, wait a minute, Alo' he exclaimed. 'What's this?'

'That's out bet. You won.'

'Don't be ridiculous.' He did a quick count. 'There's at least two hundred pounds in pesetas here. I didn't win all that.'

'Two hundred and fifty pounds to be exact,' Alo replied calmly. He held up his hand when he saw Des about to reply. 'Listen Des, you're going through a tough time right now, losing the job and all that. Mamie and I are the opposite – things couldn't be better. Business is booming and we're having our first holiday in years - and enjoying ourselves thanks to you and your good wife. Mamie is really enjoying Evelyn's company, and I'm enjoying yours. We want to give you both something back in return....'

Des was choked. He felt guilty, hearing Alo's words of praise for Evelyn, knowing how she looked down on Mamie, criticising inconsequential things about Alo's wife. The two of them were the salt of the earth, an expression his mother used to describe good people. Social climbing would be anathema to them.

'I can't take this money, Alo. I don't know what to say.'

'Don't say anything, Des. Just take it. Now let's go upstairs and collect the two ladies. Evelyn will be anxious to get back and get glammed up for your big night...'

You're so right, Des thought grimly. He wasn't exactly looking forward to the Sinatra Club tonight. If he and Evelyn didn't qualify for the final on Saturday no doubt he'd feel the cutting edge of her tongue.

On the other hand if they did qualify she would be on a high. With the few glasses of champagne inside her it might present a good opportunity to break the news that he had no job to go to when they returned to Dublin after the holiday...

— ☯ —

Caroline leaned forward excitedly, arms wrapped around Mark's stalwart middle, her young, supple body pressed firmly against his. She had never been on a motorcycle or a scooter before, and was half afraid she would fall off if she didn't hold onto Mark tightly enough. Mark meanwhile, was thoroughly enjoying himself experiencing the closeness of Caroline's body pressed to his. He was disappointed when, after a while, she became more confident and relaxed her grip on him slightly.

It was midday and the two of them had just set off on their pre-arranged scooter tour of the island. It looked set to be another gloriously sunny day and Caroline was in an elated mood as they sped through the open countryside, winding their way occasionally through tiny inland villages that basked in the sun, surrounded by acres of almond and olive groves. They had spent a very enjoyable morning driving around, stopping off at some of the recommended out-of-the-way tourist spots recommended by Alice the courier, including the spectacular drive from Sant Miquel to Sant Antonio. They had great fun travelling the little roads, hardly better than dirt tracks, off the main highway and Caroline in particular was fascinated by Cabo Norro, a cave with walls covered in what were ostensibly paintings from the Bronze Age.

She had also been fascinated by one sleepy little town named Santa Gertrudis de Fruitera which to her delight contained no less than four art galleries. Caroline had enjoyed walking around each painting or object d'art pointing out the different compositions, tonal and shading features to an attentive Mark. Although much of her discourse had gone over his head, he feigned interest for her sake.

For his part, he preferred to study Caroline more than the paintings. He reckoned she looked very desirable and sexy, her eyes bright and her face aglow as she talked about her favourite subject with enthusiasm and passion.

Later they went into Can Costa, the village bar which was a popular hangout for the arty set. Ensconced in a corner, they studied the clientele, some of whom were very weirdly dressed indeed and looked like they could do with a bath! Caroline was unsure what to drink and left the choice to Mark. He recommended 'herbes', a native Ibizan drink popular in the area. It consisted of a tasty aromatic concoction of herbs that had been stewed in alcohol and tasted very nice.

They chatted about what they had seen so far on the island tour and how they would spend the rest of the day. Then the conversation turned around to Wayne and to the other holidaymakers who had travelled to Ibiza with them.

'How did you meet Wayne?', Caroline enquired. 'You seem a most unlikely pair, if you don't mind my saying so.'

'I've known him for years. We go back a long way. We were in school together from a young age.'

'You mean you've put up with his carry-on all those years?', she exclaimed. 'You must have the patience of a saint.'

'He could do with a saint looking after him,' Mark agreed, laughing. 'Seriously though, he's really a nice guy once you get to know him. He just puts on that macho image to hide his insecurities.'

She smiled fondly at him, touched his hand on the table. 'You're a nice guy yourself, Mark. I've no doubt you got Wayne out of some scrapes in his time....'

'You bet your life, Caroline!' He recounted the uproarious goings-on at the Italian party the other night and how he had had to make a visit to the local policia station the following morning to bail his friend out of jail.

'Poor Wayne.' Mark wasn't worried about Wayne. He was very aware of Caroline's hand on his. He longed to hold her to him, kiss her passionately, see if she would return his passion. She was holding back, he sensed that. He also sensed that she was unsure of her own feelings towards him. He did not want to make any move that might frighten her off – but he was finding it increasingly more difficult to keep his hands off her!

'I think it's about time we made a move. There are a few more places we have to see. And we might even squeeze in a swim somewhere...' Caroline stood up, stretched. Mark admired her shapely body. A swim!....Caroline – hopefully – in a skimpy bikini! The thought galvanised him into action!

Back astride the scooter, enjoying the sensation of her arms tightly around his middle again, he reckoned that Wayne would give anything to be in his position right now. He headed for Es Cavallet, a well-known nudist beach situated beyond an ancient water tower. The journey was relatively short and when they got to the beach they were amazed to see naked male and female bodies lying in the sun, or sitting at beach cafes enjoying a drink. Mark was enjoying the view but he could see that Caroline was embarrassed and so they did not stay long. Maybe he'd return another day with Wayne – they would have some fun in a place like this!

Towards the end of their excursion and as they neared Figueretas, Caroline suggested that they make a final stop at the tiny beach where she had spent the morning painting a few days previously. They would catch the last rays of the sun....Mark needed no persuading. A short while later they were relaxing on a blanket which Caroline spread out on the golden sand of the almost deserted little cove.

'This is the life!,' Mark exclaimed as he closed his eyes and lay back with hands behind his head. He had flung off his shorts and tee shirt and was wearing the swimming togs he'd had on underneath. Caroline had thrown caution to the winds and wore a bikini underneath the shorts and top which she had now discarded. She couldn't help but notice his lean, tanned body, his wide shoulders and well-proportioned torso tapering down to a trim waist. She blushed when he suddenly opened his eyes and saw her looking at him so intently. To her inordinate relief, however, he pretended not to have noticed and challenged her to a race into the sea.

'You're on!,' Caroline replied, rising to the challenge.

She jumped up. 'Hey, come back here!', Mark yelled as she took off at speed. He took off in pursuit and Caroline squealed in mock terror.

Mark was quite happy enjoying the view of Caroline running across the sand and did not make contact with her until they were both in the water. She had had second thoughts about cavorting solely in a bikini and indeed had worn white tee-shirt to feel more secure. Thankfully the tee-shirt didn't hide her long, tapering legs which, like the rest of her body, were now turning to a golden tan under the Ibizan sun.

As they playfully ducked each other under the crashing waves, Mark was relieved that they were waist deep in the sea; he had become deeply aroused by the sight of Caroline as she cavorted innocently, her tee-shirt now soaking wet and clinging to her feminine curves in a way that left little to the imagination!

She seemed oblivious to the effect she was having on him. At one stage one huge wave knocked her off balance and she had to cling to Mark for security. He held her close; she was screaming and holding him tightly, her arms around his neck. When she opened her eyes they stood staring at each other for what seemed an eternity. He bent to kiss her but she pushed him away, laughing again, and the moment was lost.

All too soon she had enough of the sea – or else she reckoned that danger lurked there in the shape of Mark. She decided to call it a day and headed back to the beach to dry off. He followed her and tried not to look as she removed her sodden tee-shirt, wrapping herself in her towel and scrubbing herself dry. He would have given anything to be asked to do that task for her...

'Sorry, Mark, I seem to be having a bit of trouble with the knot of this bikini. Could you untie it for me?'

He could hardly believe his luck! 'Sure Caroline, no problem.' He fumbled with the string at the back of her neck, his hands brushing against her soft skin. He eyes dwelt on the graceful curve of her neck beneath the wet strands of her dark hair. He could resist temptation no longer! He leaned forward, placed his hands gently on her shoulder, and tenderly kissed her tanned skin.

He felt Caroline shiver at his touch. When she turned to face him neither of them spoke. There was no need, her eyes said it all. Mark placed a hand under Caroline's chin and gently tilted her face up to his. He bent down and placed a warm, tender kiss upon her full, inviting lips. She tasted diving, a touch of saltiness lingering from the sea.

For several delicious moments they stayed kneeling on the sand, kissing and enjoying their romantic interlude. Passion and fervour however, soon took possession of them both. Almost without noticing it, they found themselves stretched out on the blanket, Mark, slowly beginning to tug at the towel which Caroline had draped around her. Alas, the movement brought Caroline back to her senses, alerting her that danger lurked....

She moved sideways, sat up. 'I'm sorry, Mark. We have to stop right now. I can't go through with it!' She was agitated.

'What's wrong, Caroline? he asked. It surely can't be something I've done. Did I push you too far?' He studied her face, concern in his eyes.

'It's nothing to do with you, Mark. It's me. I'm the one with the problem!' She pulled her shorts on over her bikini bottoms.

'What do you mean? What problem? Why don't you tell me what it is. I'll understand...

'I can't say any more Mark. Not right now. Please don't ask me to explain. Just take me back to the apartments – '

Mark was disappointed. She was obviously unwilling to elaborate on the cause of her distress, but he didn't want to push it too hard. It was still early days and there would be other opportunities. They left the cove, got back on the scooter and headed back towards Figueretas. Caroline clung tightly to him but didn't say anything. When they reached the complex she looked a bit crestfallen.

'I'm sorry. I hope I didn't spoil your day – '

'Of course you didn't. He raised his hand to brush aside a non-conforming wisp of still damp hair from her forehead. But she pulled back quickly when his hand touched her. There was an awkward pause.

'How about dinner tonight, Caroline?' Mark asked. Ibiza was packed with stunning girls practically all of them willing to fall into bed with someone like himself and yet here he was begging to see Caroline tonight.

She hesitated, looked for a moment like she was going to accept, then said: 'Thanks for the offer, but it's been a long day and I think I'll have an early night tonight. Hope you don't mind.'

Of course he was disappointed. But he didn't want to let her see that he was. 'Of course, I understand.' He was turning away when he paused. 'Remember Caroline, if you ever want to tell me about whatever it is that's worrying you…'

'I know. And thanks for today. I really did have a lovely time.' To his surprise she stepped close, kissed him quickly, then vanished behind her apartment door.

Inside, Caroline threw her hold-all on the floor, leaned back against the closed door and glanced heavenwards. 'Please give me the strength to tell him sometime,' she said aloud. Why was she allowing this to happen to her again, she wondered? She had come to Ibiza to sort herself out and all she had succeeded in doing was adding to her problem. She made a decision – when the first opportunity arose she would tell Mark the truth about herself. If he was like the average young man, out for only one thing, that would be sure to frighten him off!

Or would it? Maybe he wasn't like the others -. Then a thought struck her. Oh God, what if he was falling in love with her? Caroline lay down on the bed, stared at the ceiling. And what if she found herself falling in love with him…….

— ☾ —

Mamie and Alo Riordan hailed Irene and Ben as they entered the Sinatra Club. Although they had arrived relatively early many of the tables were already occupied. The three-piece outfit on stage were playing nice dreamy music and several couples were on the dance floor.

'Sit over here,' Mamie called out. 'Des and Evelyn haven't arrived yet. We were with them earlier on the golf course. We'll have a grand view of the dancing from here.'

'I'm not sure I should be here tonight,' Irene said as she sat down.

'She's had a migrane most of the day,' Ben said as he held the chair for his wife.

'Oh, you poor thing,' Mamie looked at Irene solicitiously. 'If I'd known, Irene, I'd have called to your room to see if you needed anything.'

'Thank you, but Paula Sheridan, the supervisor lady dropped in to check on me. She's Irish, you know. Lucky I had someone to help because Benjamin was in town most of the morning. I still don't know what kept you so long.'

'I, er, bumped into Doc Holliday and we had a chat – '

'He's here somewhere with Maureen,' Alo remarked. 'I was talking to him a few minutes. I thought he said they both spent the morning walking on the beach…'

Ben pretended not to hear. 'Everyone alright for drinks?', he asked, hoping to divert the conversation. 'I'm going to the bar to order…' He'd better get to Doc and arrange an alibi.

Just then Des and Evelyn Murtagh entered. Evelyn looked stunning in a dress slit to mid-thigh that succeeded in turning several male heads, while Des sported a pale blue jacket and matching bow tie that showed off his tan, acquired during his round of golf with Alo earlier. 'Am I glad to sit down,' he whispered to Alo. 'All that walking on the golf course didn't do my feet much good. I soaked them in the bath all afternoon.'

Ben came back from the bar with the drinks for himself and Irene. She noted he been talking to Doc Holliday. Now he was glancing around as though looking for someone.

They were all laughing and joking and sipping drinks when Irene said suddenly, 'Oh look, there's Paula Sheridan – and she seems to be on her own. Benjamin, stand up and catch her attention.'

Ben got such a shock that he almost spilled his drink. 'Maybe she's meeting someone,' he said.

'Go over and find out. Ask her to join us if she's on her own.'

Ben stood up and made his way towards Paula. Irene saw them converse briefly before making their way back to the table.

'Get another chair from somewhere Benjamin – Paula can have yours.' Irene began introducing Paula to everyone at the table. 'You know my husband Benjamin of course – '

'Oh yes,' Paula smiled at Ben. 'Nice to meet you – again.'. The last word hung in the air. 'You don't seem to remember me, do you Ben?'

A silence fell. Everyone at the table was listening. 'Oh, have you and Benjamin met before?', Irene asked. Paula hadn't mentioned that when they were talking this morning.

'Yes indeed. Your husband and I are old friends. We did a little bit of business some years ago. Don't you remember, Ben?'

'We did?' Ben's throat had gone suddenly dry. 'I - I'm afraid I don't remember. He hardly recognised his own voice. What was Paula going to say next!

'You sold me a car once. At your garage…'

'I did?' He managed a laugh. 'Fancy that – but then I've sold a lot of cars in my time – '

'Ah yes, but this was something special as I remember – ' Paula was enjoying herself, teasing him.

'I hope you got a bargain off my husband, Paula…' Irene laughed.

'As a matter of fact I did. As I recall there was an extra bonus attached to the sale. I just couldn't resist the deal Ben came up with at the time!'

'I'm certainly glad to hear that,' Irene replied. 'Benjamin, order a drink for Paula. And get another round while you're at it.'

Ben was glad of the opportunity to escape. But before he could get away Paula cut in. 'I'll get my daughter Vicki to take the order,' she said. 'She works part-time here and she's on duty tonight…' Paula looked around, waved. 'There she is. She's coming across to you, Ben…'

Ben couldn't believe this was happening. His daughter, whose existence he had learned about only this morning, was coming over to take a drinks order from him – with Irene sitting there smiling. If she only knew!

Suddenly Victoria was at the table. She was really pretty, tall and slim like her mother, her auburn hair falling about her shoulders. She looked at Ben, smiling. 'You wish to order some drinks?'

'Er, yes.' He ordered the round in a daze. Victoria jotted them down on a pad, very efficient and pleasant. Did she know who he was?, he wondered.

'That's a very pretty daughter you have,' Irene commented to Paula when Victoria departed.

'Thank you, Irene,' Paula replied.

'She reminds me of someone – ' She broke off. 'Of course – our own daughter. Don't you think so, Benjamin?'

Ben was feeling weak from the tension. He was sorry he had ever set foot inside the Sinatra Club tonight. And to think he had brought Irene along! He was grateful when Senor Carrasco came on stage a short while later and announced that the second elimination stage of the dance competition was about to commence. The band struck up a slow waltz and Des and Evelyn rose and made their way towards the dance floor. Ben breathed a sigh of relief.

As Des guided Evelyn around he prayed he would not receive that dreaded tap on the shoulder from either Senor Carrasco or his wife. There seemed to be an awful lot of couples competing tonight. He could do with a bit of good fortune for a change. If they won this heat of the competition it could be the start of happier times.

Senor Carrasco and his wife were busy darting in and out through the dancers, eliminating couples at a rapid pace. Now it was time for the Latin American numbers. Evelyn loved to tango – and tonight she felt she was dancing on air. Okay, so Desmond was no Fred Astaire, but tonight she was certainly as good as Ginger Rogers and no doubt she would inspire him...

Only six couples left! Oh God, Evelyn thought, if they were eliminated now she would die of embarrassment. No way would she and Des go back to the table if that happened – they'd get a taxi straight back to the hotel! But they weren't going to be eliminated – she just knew they were going to do the business tonight!

Des whirled her around, and Evelyn did a spectacular sidestep that showed her leg off to perfection through the slit in her dress. She had to admit he really was in top form tonight. Then suddenly there was a burst of applause. Evelyn glanced around; another couple had been eliminated and now there were only three couples left on the dance floor.

'Evelyn, we've done it! We're through to the final!' The music had stopped and Des was hugging and kissing her. Evelyn responded. She felt elated, like she had just won the Lotto! Maureen Duff and Doc Holliday rushed onto the dance floor to congratulate them.

'Both of you were superb,' Maureen said. 'Alec and I will face very stiff competition from you both on Saturday night.'

Senor Carrasco brought the three winning couples onto the stage and his wife presented each of the ladies with a bouquet while the men received a bottle of champagne. Evelyn positively glowed as herself and Des made their way back to the table. Alo and Mamie had already bought a couple of bottles of champagne in preparation for the celebration.

Evelyn was on such a high that she hardly noticed Victoria, Paula's daughter filling the glasses with bubbly, neither did she see how intently Ben O'Rourke followed the young girl's every movement. Indeed Evelyn was on an even greater high when, after a celebratory night-cap in the Orlando Hotel bar, herself and Des finally closed their apartment door behind them.

'Desmond darling,' she said as she slipped out of her dress. 'May I say you were only magnificent tonight.'

'Thank you, pet,' he replied. 'But then you were only magnificent yourself. Ginger Rogers eat your heart out!'

He went into the bathroom. This was an ideal time to come clean about losing the job. Evelyn is flying after all that champagne. There would never be a better opportunity…

'Evelyn darling,' he called out. 'There's something I want to tell you.'

'Really?' He recognised that tone. Slow, slightly giggly. He hadn't heard her like that for a long time. 'Good news, I hope?'

'Not exactly – '

'Never mind. Whatever it is let it wait until you're in bed –' Another giggle.

'Alright, dear – '

'I think I know what it is…' Des froze, looked at himself in the mirror.

'You've damaged the company car, haven't you? – that's why we couldn't take it to the airport…'

He exited from the bathroom. Evelyn was sitting up in bed, her hair mussed and falling over one eye. Her nightie had slipped loose from one shoulder and she was smiling, a sexy, seductive smile.

He couldn't remember the last time he had seen her in this mood. What a night this promised to be – and if he told her the truth about being made redundant it would spoil it all. Maybe tomorrow…

'Come here to me, Desmond darling…' Evelyn patted the bed beside her. 'You look like you need a something special. Who cares about the damn company car!'

CHAPTER NINE

On Thursday morning Paula decided to have a talk with Vicki. It was time to tell her daughter about her father. Paula would have preferred to wait for another year or so until Vicki had finished school and then tell her who her father was. But the incredible coincidence of Ben O'Rourke and his wife showing up at the Hotel Orlando for a holiday meant a change of plan.

Several times over the past few days Vicki had noticed her mother looking at her, as though she had something important to say to her. Then the moment would pass. She wondered what was bothering her mother.

'When you come home from school today, Vicki, I want to have a chat before you go to tennis,' Paula had told her daughter before she left that morning.

'What is it Mama?,' Vicki had looked worried. 'Have I done something wrong?'

'No darling. It's nothing like that. Now go to school and don't worry. It's just something important that involves us both. See you later....'

Vicki liked school and was especially keen on music and art. Sometimes she would persuade her mother to bring her out into the countryside where she would paint landscapes. All during her childhood the only cloud on her horizon was the absence of her father. Her best friend, Miranda, didn't have a father either. He had died at an early age leaving a wife and three children. But at least

Miranda, who was ten years old then, could talk about him and describe how he had made their lives so happy.

'If only I knew who my father was, I too could talk about him,' Vicki often thought to herself when Miranda mentioned her dad.

As she had grown older Vicki assumed that she had been born out of wedlock. When she brought up the subject of her father, her mother had promised to tell her, but so far she had not done so.

Last night while working in the Sinatra Club Vicki had experienced a most peculiar feeling. Usually her mother didn't get involved socially with tourists staying in the hotel, but last night was an exception. Vicki had watched her mother talking with two men at the bar. She had noticed them glancing in her direction every now and then.

'Vicki,' her mother had called out. When she joined them her mother had introduced her to the men, neither of whom she had met before. She had gestured to the tall one first.

'I'd like you to meet Mr. Alec Holliday,' Paula had said. The man had smiled and said how pleased he was to meet such a beautiful young lady – a compliment which made Vicki blush. After a slight pause her mother continued, '- and this gentleman is Mr. Ben O'Rourke…'

It was then that Vicki had experienced that rather peculiar feeling. Was it the manner in which her mother had introduced the second man, or was it the way he was staring at her, as though he was seeing a ghost?

'Pleased to meet you, Mr. O'Rourke,' she had said brightly.

'Victoria…'He pronounced her full name, then stopped, staring. Why had he not called her by the shortened version like everyone else? She felt a little uncomfortable as he continued to stare. He was holding her hand as if he didn't ever want to let it go.

'Mr. O'Rourke and I are old friends,' she heard her mother say, 'We met in Dublin many years ago. I bought my first car from him back then.'

Mr. O'Rourke looked at Paula. Then he turned to Vicki, smiled and said, 'My friend Doc Holliday is right. You are a beautiful young lady...'

'Thank you, thank you both. I'm sorry but I must go now. We're very busy tonight. Perhaps I'll see you both later – '

Vicki smiled at her mother. For some reason she felt uneasy, confused. She had not spoken to the charming Mr. O'Rourke again that night, but several times as she was rushing around serving drinks she had glanced over to the table where he was seated with her mother and the other Irish couples – and always his eyes were on her.

Now, on her way to college, Vicki had pondered over what her mother had said, about wanting to discuss something very important with her. She was certain it had to do with events that had happened in the recent past. Perhaps her mother was planning one of her infrequent visits back to Ireland, wanting to visit her own parents who were now getting on in years. Vicki was forever hearing from her mother of the aunts, uncles and cousins she had in Ireland. She looked forward to meeting them some day.

Paula made sure she kept busy during the day. Work was her therapy for survival whenever something was troubling her. This was the day she had been dreading since Vicki was old enough to ask questions about her father.

It was 5pm when Paula finished work in the hotel, locked up her office and left. She had prepared lasagne and a fresh salad before leaving for work. Vicki had arrived home before her and had already set the table. 'We'll eat first and then have our talk,' her mother decided.

Vicki's stomach was churning as they both tucked into the lasagne, which Paula washed down with a glass of red wine. Finally the meal was finished and they brought their coffees out onto the balcony.

Paula braced herself and started right at the beginning. She told Vicki that after she finished school she had come to Dublin to work in the civil service. She had met Nicola and the other girls and they had shared a flat. Paula recounted how after a year in Dublin she had decided to buy a car and how they had visited a garage in Glasnevin.

'The garage was owned by Ben O'Rourke, whom you met in the Sinatra Club last night. He was much older than me but I found him very attractive, very mature. He was much more charming than any other boyfriend I had had up to then and – ' Vicki saw her mother smile shyly – 'being not much older than you I fell head over heels in love with him, even though I suspected he was a married man.'

Paula broke off, took her daughter's hand in hers, said, 'I was young, immature I suppose. Like I said I fell in love and I became pregnant…' She broke off. 'At that time in Ireland a young girl expecting a baby out of wedlock brought terrible shame on her family, especially if they lived in a rural area like mine did. I didn't want to do that to my parents – '

'What about Ben O'Rourke?,' Vicki cut in. 'Didn't he help?'

'When I tried to get in touch I was told he was away in London on business. He never did get in touch and I was too proud to go crawling after him. Instead I told my parents I was going abroad to meet up with some of my former school friends and find work….I never regretted having you, Vicki. It's the best thing that ever happened to me…'

'Oh Mama!' Vicki rose, threw her arms around her mother, kissed her. Both of them were in tears. 'I'm so lucky to be your daughter. You have been so brave and have given me such a happy childhood.'

Paula smiled through her tears. 'I'm so sorry you haven't had a father like your friends when you were growing up,' she said. She told Vicki how she had bumped into Ben O'Rourke yesterday morning in Ibiza, arranged for him to be in the Sinatra Club last night.

'The man who is your father is here with his wife to celebrate their silver wedding anniversary,' Paula explained. 'We must not spoil their big occasion. Irene does not know what happened between her husband and myself all those years ago and she must not hear it from us, Vicki. I want you to be nice to your father when he comes here tomorrow.'

'My father is coming to visit us?' Vicki was surprised and elated at the same time.

'Yes, I invited him. I want you both to meet and talk to each other. You must remember he is in a very difficult situation. He is married with a grown up family and will find himself face to face with a daughter he says he didn't know he had. And of course there is his wife to consider also....'

Paula squeezed her daughter's hand, comforting her, and continued. 'Fate has dealt us these unexpected cards and we must play them with care. Promise me, Vicki, that you help your father and me in this difficult situation?'

'Oh I will, Mama, I will!' Vicki had tears in her eyes also. Mother and daughter fell into each other's arms, sobbing.

— ☽ —

Whenever they went on a sun holiday, Des and Evelyn liked to get away as often as possible from the crowd. Hiring a car was the simplest method of escape.

Promptly at 9am a bright young man met them in the hotel lobby and gave them a set of keys for a Fiat seiscento. Having wished them safe motoring in fractured English he left. Half an hour later they took off northwards in search of a not-too-crowded beach. It was in a small cove called Los Arboles, a beach appropriately approached through an avenue of trees, that they met a German couple Karl and Maria.

That was after Des had heaved the picnic basket out of the car boot and placed it on the sand beside the rug they has spread on the sand. Evelyn had discovered a little tapas bar in Figueretas and had charmed the patron into packing the picnic basket with delicacies, plus a bottle of wine and two glasses, for their little adventure.

'Isn't this just beautiful?', Evelyn exclaimed, surveying the expanse of blue sea shimmering in the distance. She had on a wide-brimmed straw hat and was in her favourite polka-dot bikini. She had ordered Des to buy a parasol which he was now struggling to spear into the sand. When he had finally succeeded he lay down on the rug and decided to have a nap.

It was some time after he had drifted off that he became aware of Evelyn's voice. She wasn't talking to him; he knew that because she was using what was known in family circles as 'mother's upmarket voice,' reserved solely for strangers.

'Yes indeed, Ibiza is quite stunning,' Evelyn's voice drifted into his consciousness. 'My husband and I are staying in a hotel down the coast...'

He opened one eye to see whom she was addressing. A couple were perched on a nearby rock. They were about their own age and both were very blond and tanned. The woman wore a well-filled black bikini and the man looked like he would not be out of place on a film set. His swimming togs were the briefest Des had ever seen. Evelyn was sitting bolt upright facing the couple, smiling and being her charming self.

Des closed his eye, pretended to be asleep. In the name of all that's holy she's at it again! He decided not to get involved. He listened, however, as the couple introduced themselves as Karl and Maria. They were Germans and they owned a summer villa in Es Cana, just several kilometres away.

Evelyn let out a screech of excitement at this latest bit of information. 'A villa. I'd love one of those, in fact we're thinking of buying one,' she said airily. Des nearly choked when he heard this.

'Karl is sales director of one of the biggest drug companies in Germany,' he heard Maria say.

'Isn't that amazing,' Evelyn gushed, 'my husband is the senior sales representative for the biggest drug company in Ireland.' Always one better, Des thought. He felt a jab in the ribs. 'Des, Des, wake up. We have visitors I'd like you to meet…'

Des groaned inwardly, sat up and apologised for having been asleep. He shook hands with the couple. Maria was fair haired and attractive looking, with a good figure. Karl reminded Des of a film star whose name escaped him at the moment.

'Darling, Karl and Maria own a villa nearby. He's a senior salesman in a drug firm like yourself , so you both should have a lot to talk about.' This was Evelyn's shorthand for 'be on your best behaviour, Des, or you'll answer to me later!'

'Pull over that rock and join us,' Des joked. Karl and Maria had brought lunch with them, including a bottle of white wine. They settled themselves down and the four of them spent the afternoon together. Evelyn was in her element and herself and Karl seemed to hit it off immediately. Des got the impression that Maria was accustomed to seeing her husband being charming to other women and he found it hard going trying to keep her in conversation.

Des waited patiently for Evelyn to finally regale the German couple with the story of how herself and Des had danced their way to success in the Sinatra Club last night.

'You and Karl must come and cheer us on in the final on Saturday night,' she said to Maria. Karl's wife wasn't exactly over the moon with the invitation, but Karl said they would be there. The Spanish sun grew warmer and Karl suggested they go to their villa and relax in the shade and perhaps cool off in the pool. Evelyn jumped at the suggestion; it was as though all her birthdays had come together.

Des had to admit that he really enjoyed the afternoon. The Germans had a beautiful villa and took pleasure in showing it off. They had a swim in the pool – Karl was not only an excellent swimmer but showed off his diving skills as well – and then they sat around sipping wine. It was into the evening when Des and Evelyn rose from the cool of the cream coloured couch in their new friends' spacious lounge.

'You must come to visit us at our hotel, be our guests,' Evelyn said expansively as they left. 'Why not come for dinner tomorrow night? We'd love to have you both, wouldn't we, Desmond?' You mean you'd love to have Karl for company again, Des thought to himself as he nodded his approval.

'Maria and I will be there,' Karl said. Evelyn was thrilled. She adored the way Karl looked at her. He had very sexy eyes, and since they had met they were invariably locked into hers. She wondered if he fancied her.

'Such wonderful people,' Evelyn remarked later, her voice returning to normal as they drove along the highway that would bring them back to Figueretas. 'There's plenty of money there – did you notice the paintings. If they have that kind of style in their holiday villa what must their home in Bavaria be like!'

Des didn't reply. In his mind's eye he kept seeing Karl in his skimpy swimming togs, slicing through the water or doing a somersault into the pool. And Evelyn – she had hung on to his every word!

'You know, Des, I think we should seriously think about investing in an apartment in Spain.'

'What!' Des almost drove into the ditch in shock.

'Why not? Everybody's doing it nowadays. We'll miss the boat if we don't do it now. We'll start making enquiries tomorrow.'

Des was about to tell her what she could do with her villa in Spain but thought better of it. 'Evelyn, don't get carried away,' he cautioned. 'Those two, Karl and Maria, are loaded. We're not. We can't afford a place in Spain. We couldn't afford to buy a dog kennel here this minute!' God if she only knew the real picture!

'Oh, you're too tight – too conservative. I should have married someone like Karl. He's obviously not afraid to spend his money.'

He has it to spend, Des thought as they entered the outskirts of Figueretas. Evelyn was speaking again, 'I'm going to keep an eye out for a place advertising villas for sale here in Ibiza. Some properties are going for a song.'

A song…Des began to hum the melody of 'There could be trouble ahead…'

— ☽ —

Maureen met the girls for lunch in their hotel. She was looking forward to having a leisurely meal and telling them about the marvellous coach tour of the island herself and Alec had enjoyed yesterday afternoon. Later they planned to stroll into Ibiza Town where her friends would help Maureen choose a new dress for the dance final in the Sinatra Club on Saturday night.

She had never been in a boutique before. What would she be doing in a place like that at her age? Down home she would be the talk of the town if she were seen coming out of such an establishment.

They were hardly seated at their favourite table by the poolside, sipping drinks, when Sheila spoke up. 'Well Maureen, will we be welcoming your friend Alec to

Tipperary after the holiday?' She smiled as she asked the question.

Maureen noticed Joan and Cathleen exchange furtive glances. Trust Sheila to bring up the subject! Maureen sensed this wasn't part of the light-hearted banter that they usually engaged in when they met; there was a serious intent behind the question.

'Alec and I haven't really reached that stage yet,' Maureen replied cooly. 'I did joke him about the family who used to come down to Tipperary from Dublin years ago. The children used to tell us they were down to get some fresh air. So the locals called them 'the fresh airs.' Maureen laughed at the recollection while her three companions smiled.

'Ah come on now Maureen,' Sheila said. 'I'm sure you and Alec discussed more than fresh air when you were away together all day yesterday. Does he ever mention any other girlfriends?'

'Sheila!', Joan hissed. 'Will you stop this minute! That's entirely Maureen's business. She must think we're a trio of busybodies. We shouldn't be embarrassing Maureen by asking her about Alec.'

'I agree.' Cathleen spoke up. 'Let's enjoy our lunch.'

The waiter arriving to take their order gave Maureen some breathing space. She was glad for Joan's intervention. What on earth was going on? Something to do with herself and Alec obviously – and it wasn't just old fashioned curiosity.

She had enjoyed yesterday's tour with Alec. The half-day tour had circled the complete island, cutting inland away from the popular coastal resorts to allow the coach passengers to catch occasional glances of the real Ibiza. When they did skirt the coast the sea sparkled as if someone had sprinkled glitter on it.

Maureen enjoyed the inland scenes of men and women haymaking, dressed in their colourful clothes. She turned to Alec on one occasion and remarked: 'the hay will dry very quickly in that lovely sunshine.'

'I suppose that's what's called haymaking,' he said. 'Looks like hard work to me.'

'Country people like working in the fields. Have you no country cousins in your family, Alec?'

'Nary a one. I'm a Dub through and through.'

'You must sample country air sometime. The quality at the foot of Sliabh na mBan in my area is very invigorating.'

He had glanced at her sideways. 'Is that an invitation, Maureen?'

'Yes,' she replied. 'If you care to take it up.'

Alec had laughed. 'Careful, when we get home I might just do that!'

Later, at a wine-tasting in a bodega in the mountains, Maureen had another insight into Alec Holliday's Dublin psyche. As Maureen sipped a glass of sparkling white wine Alec looked at the slim glass and said: 'I'd rather have a good pint of Guinness in The Oarsman's than all the wine here.'

Maureen pretended to be shocked. 'Alec, you're a member of the European Union. You'll have to adapt, try new things. I've noticed you're very fond of your pint of Guinness. How many can you take in a night?'

'Oh, it varies.'

'Would you say what you drank the night I had the girls over in the hotel was your limit?' Maureen persisted.

'No way! I can handle twice as much as that and still be sober. You see Maureen, I started young.'

Maureen didn't like men who drank too much. And she was unsure of how she felt about Alec Holliday. He was kind and thoughtful and had a good sense of humour, but she sensed that she wasn't the first woman he had chatted up in his time. Was he a ladies' man, she wondered? Was that what the girls were trying to warn her about earlier?

What if Alec wanted their relationship to continue when the holiday ended? Would she want that? She was in her mid-40s now, and had not been in a relationship since she and Donal had been together. Most of her family were married and had moved from the farm. Soon she would be the only one left. Now another man had entered her life and shortly she would have to decide whether she wanted their friendship to develop further.

'I hope Maureen, we find the type of dress you're looking for in a boutique – ' Sheila's voice brought Maureen back to the present. 'I mean boutiques are very trendy - '

'Then maybe it's about time I got a bit trendy too!', Maureen riposted. 'I'm going to try a boutique anyway.'

After they had finished lunch, when Maureen suggested that they stroll along the busy promenade with its bars and restaurants, Joan, Sheila and Cathleen seemed a little reluctant to go along with the idea. 'Why don't we get a taxi there and back. It's difficult walking in this heat.' Joan said. When the other two lent their support Maureen reluctantly agreed. What on earth had gotten into them today?, she wondered. They all seemed ill-at-ease.

Fortune smiled on them in the very first boutique they entered. Strolling around the shop, Maureen's eye fell on a lovely lavender creation.

'Look girls,' she took the dress off the rack. 'Isn't this just beautiful?'

As usual Sheila was the first to respond. 'Personally I think it's a bit young looking for you, Maureen. And will you look at the sweetheart neckline. Surely at your age that's going a bit far!'

Why does Sheila take the good out of everything, Maureen wondered. What pleasure does it give her downgrading people? Fortunately Joan sprung to the attack. 'For goodness sake, Sheila, will you ever give over. 'Come on, Maureen, into the fitting room and try it on.'

Maureen loved the dress. In the old days the material was called plain and simple voile. Nowadays it was labelled something more sophisticated. It was the shade she liked, lilac or lavender suited her colouring. She liked the style also, it was simply styled with a full flowing skirt, figure-hugging at the waist and the sweetheart neckline that had irked Sheila. For that reason alone Maureen suspected she would buy it!

When she tried it on it fitted to perfection. Lucky for her she had kept her trim figure with all the walking and swimming over the years. She felt very confident when she emerged from the fitting room. She pirouetted while Joan and Cathleen 'oohed' and 'aahed' in appreciation. Sheile reluctantly admitted that the dress was 'nice'.

A pair of stylish dancing shoes was next on Maureen's list. She had never favoured much jewellery, but fortunately on yesterday's tour, during a stop at a town perched on a hillside boasting local artistic work, Alec had insisted on buying her a beautiful multi-coloured traditional necklace with matching ear-rings.

'That's to bring both of us luck in the dance final on Saturday,' Alec had said. 'You'll be the belle of the ball, Maureen.'

She laughingly recounted this to her three friends when, laden down with purchases, they were enjoying coffee and cakes at an outdoor café in Ibiza before taking a taxi back to Figueretas. Once again at the mention of Alec Holliday's name she detected a sense of unease.

'Is there something worrying you three, something I should know, something to do with Alec, perhaps?' Maureen looked at them each in turn.

Nobody spoke up. Finally Cathleen said, 'Joan, I think you should be the one to tell her.'

'Tell me what?'

Another silence, shorter this time. Then Joan said in a low voice, 'Maureen dear, the three of us were strolling back to the hotel yesterday around lunchtime when, across the road, we saw Alec sitting in a bar talking to a rather attractive Spanish looking-lady. I have to say they both seemed to be enjoying each other's company…'

'We thought you should know,' Sheila added.

The three of them were looking at Maureen. She was silent, but they could see she was trying not to look too concerned. The news had come as a shock to her, no doubt about that. Maybe they should not have mentioned it after all, Joan thought.

'He didn't say anything to you about her when you were on the tour yesterday, did he?' Cathleen asked.

'No, he didn't. And I'm not going to ask him either,' Maureen replied. It was none of her business really. Neither had he said anything to her about that sleazy looking character she had seen him talking to in the Sinatra Club on both nights they were there. Suddenly the excitement of her shopping spree was evaporating. And as for the necklace and ear-rings Alec had bought her on the tour yesterday….

'We didn't really want to tell you, Maureen, but we decided it might be better – for your sake,' Joan said.

'Yes, of course. Thank you for your kind thoughts – ' Maureen put down her cream cake. Even that had lost its attraction.

'For all we know Alec may be planning on telling you about the lady himself,' Cathleen volunteered. 'He may have a simple explanation.'

'I'd like to hear what Mr. Alec Holliday has to say for himself,' Sheila sniffed. 'Men – women shouldn't trust them!'

— ☽ —

Night had fallen and the quaint Spanish restaurant with the candle-lit tables was pleasantly full. It had a charming ambiance, with cosy tables for twosomes situated discreetly in alcoves. The tabletop candles seemed to beckon customers in with their little flickering fingers of flame.

'What a lovely romantic spot you've chosen, Gerry,' Fiona complimented him as she study the menu. Judging by the prices there would be no riff-raff patronising this restaurant, she surmised.

They ordered and while awaiting the food they held hands across the table, gazing adoringly into each other's eyes and sipped wine. For Gerry it was a frieze-frame from the recent past – a reminder of the first time he had laid eyes on Fiona...

He and Sandra had been invited to dine with Sean, Fiona's husband and his boss, at their ultra-modern five-bedroomed house on the Meath-Dublin border. It was a magnificent home which Sean lost no time in telling them that it had cost one and a half million pounds to build. 'I reckon it's worth nearly double that now, thanks to the Celtic Tiger,' he had informed them. He had made his fortune by being one of the first in Ireland to invest in the computer software business from which he had successfully diversified.

Occasionally he liked to invite his top employees to dinner with their wives or partners. It was a sign one was upwardly mobile in the company and Gerry was particularly excited that he and Sandra had received the special accolade. He had been with the firm a relatively short time and already it looked like fate was smiling on him. He remembered being annoyed with Sandra that night; he didn't particularly like her dress and she didn't appear to realise how important the dinner date was for them both.

He had been told by his male colleagues at work that Sean's wife Fiona was a beauty, but nothing could have prepared for the gorgeous creature who smiled at him and shook his hand when they were introduced.

As their two eyes met he had been struck by the hidden force that drew him to her. He sensed that Fiona was experiencing the same sensation. She was really stunning, with her long, silky black hair, her almond shaped eyes of purest emerald and her long, slender figure. Gerry found her both exotic and erotic with a feline sensuality. Beside her, Sandra had looked very ordinary indeed.

'Remember that first time we met at the dinner party...'

'How can I forget – '

Fiona's green eyes smouldered in the candlelight. 'I wanted you there and then. It was all I could do not to kiss you in front of Sean and that wife of yours...'

She remembered how Sean had been going on about this go-ahead young whiz kid who had recently joined the company's ranks. She had endured a succession of dinner dates with Sean's executives, but this time was different. There was never any doubt in her mind from the first time she had locked eyes with Gerry that they would end up having an affair. It was the first time she had ever tried it on with one of the company employees.

The fact that both of them were already married wasn't a barrier; as far as Fiona was concerned it added to the excitement. How an attractive guy like Gerry had ended up with the rather ordinary looking Sandra she would never know. All Sandra had talked about that night were her children, bringing up vile subjects like how Rosie had kept them awake the previous night with diarrhoea and how she prayed that little Jake wouldn't come down with the same thing. What a subject to bring up at a dinner table!

Fiona knew she would never have to worry about Sean straying. He was mad about her, lavished gifts on her, gave her whatever she wanted. She was not too unhappy that his business interests took up a lot of his time, there were always attractive men like Gerry around on the social scene on whom she could weave her magic spell...

'I was just thinking...' Gerry's voice cut across her thoughts. 'Now that we have a car how about us visiting that famous hotel your friend Charmaine recommended to you?'

'Good idea, darling. It's called Pike's Hotel and it's in a place called Sa Vorera. Grace Jones and George Michael are said to be regular visitors. Charmaine said some of the rock stars often hold outrageously wild parties there.'

'Hhmm, sounds interesting,' Gerry retorted, although personally he was getting fed up hearing what Fiona's fancy friends thought. He wished she wasn't so influenced by the opinions and goings-on of that so called Ladies who Lunch bunch. All that crowd were interested in was getting their names attached to charities and seeing their photographs in the newspapers.

Instinctively he leaned across the table and kissed Fiona. 'My goodness, what did I do to deserve that,' she asked, secretly pleased.

'You've introduced me to real sex,' Gerry replied. They kissed again, oblivious to the stares from other diners. They were interrupted by the discreet 'ahem' of the waiter as he arrived with their starters.

'When we go back to the apartment we'll have a special dessert to finish off the night,' Fiona promised.

CHAPTER TEN

The well- groomed young woman looked up from her desk in the spacious reception area as she heard the elevator come to a stop on the sixth floor of one of Dublin's centre city's office blocks. She viewed the approach of the man as he made his way towards her, the rain glistening on his coat.

'Good morning, sir. May I help you?'

He returned the greeting with a smile, his eyes taking in the trim figure and nicely coiffured shoulder length hair. 'Mr. Davenport is expecting me. I have an appointment for eleven o'clock.'

'I see. And your name is…?'

'Taylor. Michael Taylor. Mr. Davenport will know why I'm here.'

The receptionist scanned her appointments book. 'Ah yes, that's fine, Mr. Taylor. Friday eleven a.m. Please take a seat. Perhaps you'd like to hang up your coat while I check if Mr. Davenport is ready to see you….' As he sat down she smiled, said pleasantly, 'Isn't the weather dreadful for this time of year? We're having our usual Irish summer.' He watched her trim figure disappear down the corridor.

As he relaxed in the tastefully furnished waiting area Michael Taylor speculated on why his services were required by someone like Sean Davenport. Industrial espionage maybe, or perhaps someone in the organisation was helping themselves to more than their fair share of the profits? He would find out soon enough.

'Mr. Davenport will see you now, Mr. Taylor.' The girl's voice cut across his thoughts. He rose, followed her down the carpeted corridor past several offices with names on doors. Halfway down she knocked discreetly on the beechwood door, different from the others, and opened it. She gestured the newcomer inside.

Sean Davenport came forward from behind a large desk, unsmiling, shook Michael Taylor's hand, and gestured to a chair.

'Thank you, Carol.' he said to his receptionist. 'Please see that I'm not disturbed for the next half-hour.' The girl nodded and exited.

Michael Taylor followed his usual procedure and studied his client as he saw down. Early fifties, he reckoned, compactly built, distinguished looking with his steely grey hair brushed back from a broad face. Sean Davenport looked exactly what he was, a no-nonsense millionaire businessman capable of making tough decisions. Right now though , he seemed a trifle ill at ease.

Taylor recognised the signs. He reckoned his client's problem was personal rather than a financial one. He decided not to waste any time. 'What can I do for you, Mr. Davenport?'

The man now seated behind the desk also came directly to the point. 'I want you to find my wife.' The voice was crisp, devoid of emotion.

'I see. Gone missing has she?'

'No. She has gone on holiday. To Ibiza with, I suspect, a man. I suspect she is having an affair. I want you to find her, photograph them together, bring me back the evidence.'

'Of course' Taylor paused. 'Should be no problem., Mr. Davenport. ' He coughed discreetly. 'What makes you so sure that your wife is having an affair?'

Davenport didn't answer immediately. Instead he rose from his chair, turned his back on his visitor and stared out of the window. 'I'm not a stupid man, Mr. Taylor. All the signs are there. Fiona putting the telephone down when I walk into a room; telling me she has been staying with friends overnight when I know in fact she has not. And now this bogus holiday – '

'Bogus? What makes you think it's bogus?'

Davenport turned back from the window. 'My wife informed me about a month ago that she had been invited to spend two weeks at a villa in Ibiza with some friends of hers – a couple with whom she is involved on one of her many charity committees. Before she left I made it my business to meet the lady's husband at a function, asked him where he and his wife were going on holiday.' A pause. 'He told me that he and his wife were planning a cruise this summer....'

Davenport paused, smiled thinly. 'I managed to get a look at Fiona's air ticket. It was a flight to Ibiza sure enough. She is staying at the Hotel Orlando in Figueretas.'

'I see. Mind my asking how you found that out, Mr. Davenport?'

'If you must know I have good friends in many areas of business – including the travel trade, Mr. Taylor.'

'You seem to have all the details you require about your wife already. Why do you need me?'

'Because, Mr. Taylor, if I wish to divorce my wife – and that is a distinct possibility – I will need evidence of her consorting with another – her lover. You know that, no doubt you've done this sort of thing before. I need a video, photographs of them together – ' Davenport broke off. 'What chance is there of bugging their apartment?'

'You mean their bedroom?'

'Of course.'

This guy obviously meant business, Taylor thought to himself. Aloud he said, 'That I'm sure would be very difficult. I'll try, suss out the opportunities – ' He paused, chose his next words carefully. 'Do you have any idea with whom your wife is having this affair?'

Davenport didn't reply immediately. He thought for a moment in silence. 'I have my suspicions. I want you to find out for sure.'

'Leave it to me.'

'I presume these sordid affairs follow a pattern. Am I right?'

Taylor hesitated before replying, decided to be forthright with this client. 'As often as not, Mr. Davenport, the lover is someone that the husband knows and indeed knows quite well. It is not always a total stranger involved. Might be a friend, possibly a work colleague...' He watched Davenport's face closely to see what effect his words would have.

As though sensing this Davenport turned towards the window again. 'Hmmmm...' He stared out, lost in thought. Finally he turned and said. 'Do you need anything else, Mr. Taylor?' The tone was brusque, business-like, impatient.

Michael Taylor smiled. 'A photograph of your wife would be useful,' he said drily.

'Of course. Stupid of me.' Davenport reached into a drawer of his desk, took out a photograph. He looked at it for a moment, his face expressionless, then passed it across to the man sitting opposite.

Taylor looked at the picture of the smiling dark-haired young woman, photographed from the waist up, posing in a rather revealing low-cut top on what looked like a yacht – probably her husband's.

Mama mia!, he thought to himself, this one is a stunner! He was now looking forward to this assignment with a lot more interest! Several days in the sun, photographing one of the most beautiful young women he had seen in a long time. He had expected a wife closer in age to his client. But in this business you knew never to take anything for granted. 'Expect the unexpected', that was his motto.

Michael Taylor put the photograph into his briefcase. 'When do you wish me to leave?', he asked.

'Tomorrow.' It was an order that brooked no argument. Taylor watched as Davenport reached into the drawer again and took out an A4 brown envelope.

Taylor didn't like being ordered around so casually. Davenport might be a big business wheeler-dealer, used to getting his own way, ordering people around, but there were limits. If he treated everyone like this – his wife included – it was no wonder she was off enjoying herself with someone else! Taylor decided to be a little awkward.

'Getting a ticket for a popular place like Ibiza this weekend might present a big problem – '

Davenport waved him to silence. 'I'm afraid you underestimate me, Mr. Taylor,' the voice had a triumphal ring. 'I took the liberty of booking a flight for you as soon as I found out where my wife was staying.' He held up the envelope. 'This contains your plane ticket and expenses. I think you'll find the latter more than adequate. All you have to do when you arrive is find somewhere to stay. I have booked an early return flight for you on Thursday next. You will report to me here when you leave the airport. My wife is not due back until a week from tomorrow.' Davenport paused briefly. 'Any questions?'

'No. I think we've covered everything.' There were several further questions that Michael Taylor would have liked to ask, but for good client relations decided against. For instance did Sean Davenport still love his wife? Why had the relationship broken down? Did he really want his wife back or was he doing this for revenge? What the hell, Taylor reckoned, it was none of his business. Get to Ibiza, get the job done, return with the evidence and get paid – move on to the next job.

The interview was at an end. He stood up, said goodbye, shook hands with Sean Davenport and exited. The nice-looking receptionist gave him a nod and a smile as he passed by.

Inside his office Sean Davenport returned to his large, comfortable leather chair, swivelled around to face the wall - to - wall window and gazed unseeing at the corporate skyline that lay before him. Why? And for what reason? He had rescued her from her humble beginnings, gave everything she wanted. And the question he didn't really want to answer – with whom? Yes, with whom? What if she was with the person he suspected? That would add insult to injury. It would be so embarrassing, so humiliating. He could never forgive Fiona, however much he wanted her.

He could see them now, his wife and her lover, touching each other on a beach, whispering intimacies to each other by the pool, making love at night in their room and laughing at him all the while.

Sean Davenport gripped the armrests of the leather chair until the white of his knuckles showed. He was angry, humiliated. Nobody was going to make a fool of him and get away with it.

It was as they strolled leisurely back from the beach, in the heat of the midday sun, that the young girl on a moped stopped beside Des and Evelyn Murtagh and engaged them in conversation.

After a preliminary cheery 'hello' the young girl asked 'Are you both on honeymoon? How about buying a timeshare or maybe an apartment here in lovely Ibiza?'

What a clever opener, Des thought cynically. They had been warned about this type of scam already by their courier. Before he could tell the girl that no way were they interested in buying an apartment on the island – or anywhere else for that matter! – to his horror he heard Evelyn say, 'The very thing. Only yesterday I raised the question of buying a property here with my husband. Didn't I dear?'

'You did, and I told you in no uncertain terms – '

But Evelyn wasn't listening. Instead she was talking to the girl again. 'Where are these apartments you're talking about?'

'At Es Cana,' the girl replied. Already she was off her moped and producing brochures from a briefcase. 'Es Cana is a small town set in a beautiful bay on the north east of the island, only twenty minutes drive from here. It has a lovely little harbour and an exquisite sandy beach. It's so beautiful…' The adjectives were just tripping off the young girl's tongue.

'Do you hear that, Des!', Evelyn screeched. 'Es Cana – that's where our friends Karl and Maria have their holiday home! Remember they did tell us that it had a lovely little harbour and an exquisite sandy beach - '

'Evelyn will you stop! You're sounding off worst than she is!' He turned to the girl. 'Tell me,' he asked, his voice heavy with sarcasm, 'What other kind of beach would you expect to have in a place like this – marble maybe!'

The girl, who had introduced herself as Tracey and who spoke with a pronounced English accent, smiled through her teeth. She ignored Des, handed Evelyn a coloured brochure. 'Here, see for yourself. Perhaps you both would like to sit down at that table. We can discuss it over a coffee.'

'Oh, just think about it, Des,' Evelyn gushed, her eyes dancing with excitement after they had all sat down. She was scanning the brochure while the waiter brought the coffees. 'Our own apartment in Ibiza, near our friends Karl and Maria. We could visit each other every week, have intimate parties, go dancing together…'

'Could we now? Karl and Maria aren't friends of ours – we barely know them – '

Evelyn was barely listening. She was tingling all over as she saw herself lounging by the apartment pool in a bikini, Karl nearby, dancing attendance on her, refilling her glass with sparkling white wine, bending over her so close she could get a whiff of the perfumed oil on his lean, bronzed body....

'Evelyn, I don't remember you answering the final question on Who Wants To Be A Millionaire? Before we came away.'

'Don't be sarcastic, Desmond dear!'

'Are you out of your mind or what, woman! Do you know how much an apartment here would cost? I'll tell you – the best part of a hundred grand. Probably more!'

'Not really,' Tracey smiled sweetly, 'We have some on offer at half that price. Sterling of course.'

'Now Des – did you hear that...Only fifty thousand. We could surely afford one. Maybe even something more luxurious like Karl and Maria - '

'I'm telling you we can't!,' Des shouted. Fifty thousand grand – and him after being made redundant just before they came away. Why hadn't he told Evelyn before that he had no job to go back to. Maybe he should tell her the bad news now before it was too late -

Tracey sipped her coffee hiding her amusement. As an apartment/timeshare rep she had witnessed this scenario many times before. Wives tended to be swept away by the prospect of a villa in the sun; husbands on the other hand generally threw cold water on the idea, just as this agitated one was doing now.

'Don't be a spoilsport, darling. You know we can afford it. Everyone at home is buying villas in the sun nowadays - '

Des fought to control his mounting anger. 'Your friend Karl has a big job. He's rolling in money – a near millionaire, according to himself. Me – I'm – I'm – ' He almost got the word 'redundant' out but it just wouldn't come. Instead he said. 'How on earth can we afford an apartment, Evelyn? Go on, answer me that.'

'Simple, darling – ' He wished she would stop calling him darling. Evelyn was putting on her posh accent, acting like that woman Hyacinth Bucket on television. But this was for real – and it wasn't funny!

Evelyn was speaking to him again. 'You're due for promotion soon, aren't you?' She flashed a smile at Tracey. 'He hates me talking about his profession.'

Promotion! Holy God – he didn't even have a job!

' – that means a raise in salary, ' Evelyn went on. 'We're very comfortable, our house is paid for, no mortgage, and at today's prices it must be worth at least a quarter of a million pounds. The children are working, we have no bills, no overheads – and the banks are shovelling money at people at present' – She broke off, smiled at Tracey. 'You've heard about the Celtic Tiger, my dear. Haven't you?'

'Oh yes,' Tracey smiled back. 'Who hasn't heard of the Celtic Tiger…' What on earth is this woman on about? Celtic Tiger – does that mean she can pay cash up front?

Des nearly swooned. He just couldn't believe what he was hearing. Please God, give me the willpower to tell my wife the truth so that she will come back down to earth, he prayed. Alas God didn't respond and Des kept silent. He sensed he was fighting a losing battle.

He would wait until after the dance contest final in the Sinatra Club tomorrow night to tell Evelyn everything. No sense in upsetting her before then. If they won the dance contest she would be in a good mood, especially with a few glasses of celebratory champagne inside her. Yes, better leave it until then.

'How do we get to Es Cana to see the villas?', Des heard his wife ask. Now she was describing them as villas! Not for Evelyn a humble timeshare. Nothing but the best and to hell with the expense.

'No problem. We collect you by taxi from your hotel and bring you back later,' Tracey replied brightly. 'There will be other couples selecting properties, of course. We serve champagne as you stroll about. The atmosphere is very relaxed and everyone enjoys themselves. And remember there is no pressure on either yourself or your husband to sign anything unless you really want to...'

'You hear that, Desmond? No pressure. Isn't that nice?'

Bullshit!, thought Des. 'Marvellous,' he heard Evelyn say. 'When may we go to see these beautiful properties?'

'Would Sunday afternoon suit?', Tracey asked.

'Sunday would be just fine,' Evelyn responded. 'My husband and I are looking forward to visiting Es Cana, aren't we, Desmond darling?'

He could only nod. Had his wife addressed him as 'Richard' as Hyacinth Bucket did with hers he would not have been surprised. 'If you say so, my dear,' Des replied. He cringed inwardly – he was even beginning to answer like Richard!

A delighted Tracey jotted down their names and their hotel on a small pad, gave them her business card, leaped astride her moped, waved and was soon swallowed up in the passing traffic..

What a fruitful day it had been thus far, Evelyn thought to herself as she and Des strolled along the promenade back towards the Hotel Orlando. Dinner with their friends Karl and Maria tonight in the hotel, the dance final in the Sinatra Cluc tomorrow night – she planned to ask Karl and Maria to come along – plus a trip to Es Cana on Sunday to view a holiday villa which hopefully would soon be theirs.

Life, Evelyn reckoned, could not be better. Des on the other hand reckoned he could do with a stiff drink!

Doc Holliday paid the driver and alighted from the taxi. He paused on the pavement, looked around. Yolanda Segguria's apartment was in the centre of Ibiza Town, practically in the shadow of the cathedral. He glanced at his watch, reckoned he had a few minutes to spare. Yolanda had said she and the boys didn't usually eat until nine o'clock; back home in Ringsend he'd be getting ready to go out for a drink to The Oarsman's or the social club at this time.

Across the road he spotted a florist shop, its entrance almost covered in a myriad of coloured blooms. Just what he was looking for! He crossed over, selected a large bouquet of roses and had them wrapped by one of the young lady assistants. Outside the sun had disappeared behind the roofs of the houses and the streets were crowded with tourists and local families out for a stroll in the cool evening air.

Doc found the apartmeht block easily enough, ran his finger down the list of tenants and pressed the appropriate bell. Yolanda's voice answered almost immediately over the inter-com.

'Yes?' Her voice was barely above a whisper.

'Hello. Alec here.'

'Good. You are on time.' There was a warm tone to her voice. 'Push the front door open and cross the courtyard to the elevator opposite. We're on the fourth floor. I'll be waiting.'

The stone-flagged courtyard was an oasis of cool. There were a couple of small trees and fronds of greenery hung everywhere. The elevator whisked Doc to the fourth floor.

Yolanda was waiting outside the door of the apartment. She looked very different out of her police uniform and for a moment he didn't recognise her. She looked exquisite. She was wearing a silk sheath dress to her ankles, her dark hair coiffed and shining, framing her face. She smiled a welcome as he walked towards her.

'Yolanda, you look smashing.' He was not one for showering women with compliments, but she really did look beautiful.

He saw her looking puzzled. 'Smashing? What is that?'

'It means you look beautiful.' Doc kicked himself mentally. He would have to be careful with these Dublin expressions.

She laughed. 'Thank you. You are looking very handsome yourself. Muy macho'.

'For you…' He held out the flowers. 'Beautiful roses for a beautiful lady.' If his mates in Ringsend could only hear him now. Cary Grant eat your heart out!

'Gracias.' She took the flowers in one hand, put the other on his shoulder, stood on tiptoe and kissed him lightly on both cheeks. Doc got the faint whiff of her perfume. In the muted lighting they stared into each other's eyes for what seemed to him an eternity. Finally Yolanda said, 'Come in. Meet my boys.'

He followed her inside the apartment. The first thing he noticed when he entered the spacious sitting-room was the shrine. It was set in the wall, the framed photo of the square-jawed, handsome man in police uniform as the centre piece. In front was a small electric altar lamp that glowed red. He could make out the wording on top of the framed photograph. It read: Juan Segguria 1954 – 1998. There was some smaller Spanish script underneath.

He crossed the room. 'Your husband?'

'Si. That is Juan.'

Doc was silent. He didn't quite know what to say. 'He was very handsome.' He knew it sounded trite but it was the best he could do given the circumstances.

'Yes.' She smiled. 'He liked me to tell him that.'

'The lettering underneath….what does it say?'

'It reads 'Remembered always by your loving wife Yolanda and our two sons Carlos and Jose Maria. We pray for you every day.' Her voice was barely audible and Doc was afraid she was going to cry. If she did should he put his arm around her, comfort her. He was glad he had brought along one of his new handkerchiefs!

He need not have worried. The moment passed when Yolanda called out: 'Carlos, Jose Maria, come and meet our guest.'

The two boys emerged from the room where Doc guessed they had been waiting to be summoned. Carlos was the eldest, in his early teens, Doc guessed, while his brother looked about three years younger. They were both dark-haired and had inherited their father's strong features. Doc could see them breaking a few female hearts in the not too distant future.

The two youngsters shook Doc's hand politely, surprising him by saying 'Hello, how are you?' in English.

'They are learning the language in school,' Yolanda explained, adding laughingly, 'but I think they pick up more from watching English soccer on television!'

'So you are both interested in football,' Doc said. 'I suppose Manchester United is your favourite team?'

'Si. Real Madrid and Manchester United,' Carlos piped up.

'Good. I have a surprise for you both.' Doc handed each of them one of the paper-wrapped parcels he had brought with him. He and Yolanda watched as the boys broke the cellophane seals, removed the paper wrapper and held up the famous red shirt with a name emblazoned in white across the back.

'Look Momma. I got Giggs!', Jose Maria exclaimed excitedly.

'And I got Roy Keane!,' Carlos shouted, brandishing his jersey.

Doc smiled to himself. He had bought the two outfits in the Manchester United shop at Dublin Airport before flying out. They had been purchased with his two nephews in mind; Doc reckoned they were even more appreciated by Yolanda's two boys.

Carlos and Jose Maria both thanked him, then said something in Spanish to their mother before disappearing into the bedroom.

'They asked my permission to wear them at dinner,' Yolanda explained. 'And talking about dinner....' Her eyes sparkled. 'I have prepared a typical Spanish dish in your honour.'

'That's nice. What is it?' He hoped it wasn't anything too exotic. Good, plain food was his dish.

'Paella! You've heard of paella, Alec? Come and see....'

Yes, he had heard of paella. Had never tasted it, though. He knew it contained things like fried rice, lots of fish, squid, mussels and prawns mostly. Coming from Ringsend as he did Alec reckoned he would be able to handle that.

He followed Yolanda into the kitchen. On the cooker was a giant black frying pan, the biggest he had ever seen, its flat surface sizzling with the mass of ingredients that made up paella. As he watched Yolanda poured on some olive oil, followed by a dollop of wine from one of the several bottles within arm's reach. A great billow of steam rose towards the ceiling. The extractor and the cool air fans were working at full blast.

Yolanda had donned an apron and now she handed Doc a bottle of wine. 'Now senor, out of my kitchen,' she ordered, picking up a large wooden spoon and stirring the paella. 'Pour yourself a glass of wine and sit out on the balcony where it is cool. Dinner will be ready in five minutes...'

The meal was superb. Doc couldn't claim to be an expert on paella, but it tasted delicious although at times he had no idea what exactly he was eating. Yolanda was pleased no end when he requested a second helping from the huge pan. He even condescended to wash the food down with several glasses of strong red wine.

When he had finished he said, 'That was excellent, Yolanda. One of the best meals I have ever had..

She beamed with delight. 'Bueno. I am pleased. I wanted you to taste a typical Spanish dish.'

'When you come to Dublin I will make you a typical Irish dish – a Dublin coddle. I'm an expert. Would you like that?'

'Of course. But first I must be invited to Dublin…'

'Yolanda, as from now you and the boys have an open invite from me any time you want to accept. You'll be my guest, stay at my home.'

'Thank you, Alec. That is kind of you. We shall see.'

Later, while the boys cleared the dishes away to the kitchen, Doc and Yolanda sat out on the balcony. Yolanda made a pot of coffee and she also bought out two brandies in well cut goblets on the tray.

She handed a brandy to Doc, raised hers. 'Thanks to you, Alec, this is a very special night for me. It is the first occasion since my husband died that I have invited anyone to dinner in my apartment, other than some of my girlfriends.' As they drank he noticed that her eyes were meeting his over the rim of her brandy glass.

The balcony overlooked the crowded street and they were able to see the groups of people below as they passed to and fro. Most of them were young, dressed for a night out, chatting and laughing among themselves. Away to the right the shadow of the cathedral towered into the night sky. To Doc, it seemed the balcony had become their own private world.

'Juan and I would often come out here at night when the boys were asleep,' Yolanda said, as though talking to herself. 'Sometimes in the summer we would sit out here all night, watch the sun rise in the early morning. It was very romantic.'

Doc remained silent, unwilling to break the spell. Finally he said, 'You still miss him a lot, don't you, Yolanda?'

'Yes, very much,' she said softly. She rose from her chair, looked over the balcony, pointed. 'You see down there, that black patch across the road outside the newspaper shop.....?' He looked to where she was still gazing, to where a black patch covered part of the pavement and roadway. 'That is where it happened...'

'You mean....' Doc's voice trailed off.

'Juan had his car parked there. It was eight o'clock in the morning. I was still in bed and the boys were asleep. As soon as I heard the explosion I knew it was him. When I looked down I knew he was dead. No one could have survived that terrible blast. I screamed....'

'Outside your own doorway. It must have been terrible for you and the boys – '

'It was. Thank God Juan died instantly, that he did not experience much pain.' She paused. Her face, half hidden in shadow, was sad, beautiful. Doc was reminded of a painting of the Madonna in St. Patrick's in Ringsend. 'But I know I must not go on mourning my husband forever. He would not have wanted that because it is not good for me. He made me promise that if anything happened to him and if I met someone else....

She turned, looked at him with moist eyes. 'I have vowed to continue his work, to put as many drug pushers as possible behind bars so that they do not ruin young lives. I am very happy that you are helping us, Alec.'

He shrugged. 'It's nothing – '

'You don't understand, Alec. These people are ruthless, and that includes your friend Donie Crawford. You must be careful in the Sinatra Club tomorrow night. I do not want anything to happen to you.'

'You're really concerned for me, Yolanda, aren't you?'

'Yes.'

'Is that a Spanish police officer talking. Or do you have other reasons...'

She didn't reply immediately. Instead she went to the balcony and looked down at the street below to the black patch on the pavement. 'Tonight, for the first time since my husband died, I wanted to be alone with a man. I wanted to experience that feeling again, and I have. Do you know what I am trying to say, Alec?'

He moved to her side, covered her hand with his. 'Of course, Yolanda. I'm very pleased I came...'

He wanted to kiss her then, but reckoned she might think he was taking advantage of the situation. He was glad when Yolanda changed the direction of their conversation. 'Did you tell your friend Maureen that you were going out to dinner tonight – with a mysterious lady?'

'You warned me not to tell anyone about our relationship, remember?'

She laughed. 'Of course. Alec, I am – how you say? – teasing you about your other woman...'

'Don't worry, I'm used to people joking me about women. Back home I get it all the time.'

They stayed talking on the balcony until the bells of the cathedral rang out a single chime into the night. Doc checked his watch. 'I'd better be getting back, Yolanda. I don't want to keep you up too late...' He rose from the chair. 'Thanks for everything.'

'De nada,' she replied. 'I also enjoyed it very much.' She had risen to her feet and they found themselves standing very close together. A breeze stirred and again Doc got the delicious whiff of her perfume. He leaned forward and kissed Yolanda very tenderly on the lips. She responded momentarily, then the moment passed and she stepped back. They stared at each other. They both sensed there would share many such occasions in the future.

'Will you have dinner with me again sometime?', Doc whispered.

'Of course. In Dublin – in your house. I will make you your favourite paella!'

They tiptoed across the darkened apartment. The boys' bedroom door was slightly open but no light showed. Outside in the hallway Doc paused. 'Don't bother coming down. I will find my own way out.'

'Buenos noches, Alec.'

'Buenos noches, Yolanda.'

Down in the elevator, across the moonlit courtyard. He opened the main door and stepped into the street. There were still groups of people sitting at tables outside a bar. Doc crossed the road and on impulse looked back towards the apartment.

Yolanda was on the balcony, watching for him. As he looked up he saw her wave, then she stopped and her hand flew to her mouth in a gesture of shock. Puzzled, Doc looked down – and understood why. He was standing in the blackened area where Juan Segguria's car had been when it was blown to smithereens three years ago. Scolding himself for being such a clumsy idiot, he turned and hurried off down the street.

Despite the lateness of the hour Doc decided to walk the two miles back to Figueretas. He needed some fresh air – and some time to think.

CHAPTER ELEVEN

Maureen Duff arranged to hitch a lift to the airport in the coach with her three friends. Joan, Sheila and Cathleen were flying back to Dublin this morning and she knew she would miss their support at the Sinatra Club tonight. Pity though, that they had spotted Alec with a lady, no doubt it was a big topic of conversation between them.

'Maureen, come and sit beside me.' Sheila called out.

Oh Lord, Maureen thought as she reluctantly took the seat beside Sheila; another lecture in behavioural science, she supposed, the dangers of a lonely middle-aged woman falling for a ladies' man. She wished she had been seated with either Joan or Cathleen. Sheila would surely bring up the subject of Alec.

'Oh well, we had a lovely holiday, ' Sheila began as the coach pulled away from their hotel. 'I hope, Maureen, you'll be able to say the same when you arrive home next week, ' she added slyly.

'And why shouldn't I?' , Maureen replied levelly. She would not let Sheila annoy her.

'A lot can happen in a week, mark my words, ' Sheila went on. 'They say a week is a long time in politics -as far as I can see a day is a long time in Figueretas! I mean who would have thought that you would have picked up such a handsome dancing partner like Alec the first day you arrived here.'

'Would you say it was my personality, Sheila, or was it providential or what?' Maureen asked sweetly.

'You must be joking Maureen. How could it be providential? Chance maybe, but not providential.'

'You know, Sheila, I have often heard it said that nothing happens by chance. There is a reason for everything. The man above has it all planned out.

Sheila looked at her in amazement. 'Ah, come off it. ...reasons for everything and raisins in a cake. For goodness sake what's got into you and at such an early hour in the morning. You are not thinking straight. Did you sleep well last night?'

'Of course I did' Maureen said irritably. ' Anyway what has sleep got to do with it.'

Sheila gave her a searching look. 'You know Maureen, I'm really worried, leaving you here all alone for a whole week. ,

'What are you worried about? That I'll get desperate and pick up with somebody else and let Alec see I am not depending on him? You know very well I'm not that type. I'll be careful.'

'I'm suspicious of Alec, Maureen, and I'm usually right. True enough, he can be a charming dancing partner, but for goodness sake leave it at that. Don't do anything foolish my dear. You are at a very vulnerable age. Last chance to get a man and all that '

Maureen fought hard to keep her temper under control. 'Sheila, would you ever forget about my age. I'm not ancient you know. I do enjoy a bit of fun, but don't worry I am not desperate to grab any man that comes along.'

'Well Maureen, there's fun and fun! Just don't do anything foolish.'

Sheila was like a dog with a bone. She just wouldn't let go. After a short pause she started up again. ' I do wish you and Alec all the best in the competition tonight, and in the future of course -providing you two have a future. ,

'Thank you Sheila. I'll phone Joan later tonight to let you and Cathleen know how Alec and I get on in the

Sinatra Club.' Maureen breathed a sigh of relief as the coach drew up at the Airport.

Joan checked in first and left her friends to come back and talk to Maureen. 'I hope Sheila didn't annoy you too much. She insisted I sit with Cathleen."

'No not really. We had quite a philosophical conversation about chance versus providence. She is very worried about my wellbeing. Would you ever calm her down on the way home.'

'And when you get home Joan, for God's sake tone down any yarns she may be telling about me. I'm worried that she will make me out to be man mad, picking up men in every bar in Figueretas!'

Joan laughed. 'We all know what Sheila is like, don't we? She has a kind heart even if she lets her tongue wag too often. And don't worry, Maureen, I'm sure there will be a simple explanation about Alec and that lady we saw talking to him the other day.'

'I'm not worried. Alec is perfectly entitled to talk to any lady he wants. Right now we are really dancing partners.' Maureen was mortified. She didn't want her friends to see her as a lovesick teenager or a desperate spinster, anxious to grab the first man who came along.

'My main concern, Joan, is that there won't be any tension between Alec and myself tonight. It is important to be relaxed on the dance floor.'

'Of course. I have a gut feeling that everything will turn out fine between you and Alec' Joan reassured her.

'I hope so. But please don't be worrying about me.'

Just then Sheila and Cathleen rejoined them. Maureen said she would have to go as she was getting a lift back in the coach. She wished them a safe journey home and complimented them on how well they were looking after their two week holiday in the sun. Frankly she was glad her friends were returning home. She would have a week all to herself.

When Maureen arrived back to the hotel she saw Alec in the foyer. She had not seen him around the hotel last night. She wondered where he had been. ...

'Hello Alec. I'm just back from seeing my friends off' she greeted him.

'We'll miss them cheering for us tonight. How are you feeling Maureen? 'Not too nervous I hope.'

'On the contrary I'm looking forward to the dance competition, I think we have a pretty good chance.

'We must have a chat about tonight over coffee or maybe a drink by the pool' Alec said. ' I believe there are quite a few from the hotel going along to the Sinatra Club tonight for the show. We'll sit in the shade and not take any chances of getting sunburned!'

'I'm afraid I won't have much time to chat, Alec, I have an important engagement in town in about an hour.'

'Oh' He looked surprised, and for a moment appeared as if he was going to ask who she was going into Ibiza to see, but he thought better of it. Maureen was pleased. She didn't tell him that it was only an appointment to have her hair styled.

Let Alec think he had a rival - that she was meeting someone, a dashing Spanish senor perhaps! Her friend Sheila had said a lot could happen in a week, and there was still a week of her holiday left!

It was mid-morning on Saturday when Georgia arrived back at the girls' apartment. Alison and Bernice were not long out of bed and had just finished breakfast after a late night out on the town.

There was no need for them to ask Georgia where she had spent the night. Both Alison and Bernice had long conceded that Georgia had won the bet they had made on the ways to Dublin Airport in the taxi!

At one time during the night the four of them, Alison and Miguel and Bernice and Brian, had met up in Jose's Hacienda where Georgia had spent the night behind the bar with Jose surveying the scene and sampling the atmosphere. Georgia's cocktail Ibiza-How Are Yeh! was now a firm favourite with the clientele and several times during the evening Jose had announced over the microphone that a highlight of the gala night next Wednesday would be Georgia from Dublin performing her sensational Dance of the Seven Veils .This was greeted with loud cheers from the audience.

'I thought you were going to give us a sample of what we can expect on Wednesday', Bernice said as Georgia tucked into a breakfast of coffee and fresh bread rolls available at the supermercado in the apartments. 'Everyone last night was looking forward to you doing a bit of a striptease.'

'Salome's dance is not a striptease. I'll have you know it's looked upon as art, not pornography,' Georgia replied haughtily.

Bernice and Alison exchanged glances. 'The posters being put up around Ibiza advertising the show look more sexy than arty to me' Alison remarked.

'I'm not worried how they look as long as they attract an audience for Jose' Georgia sipped her coffee, looked thoughtful. 'Anyway, I have more than Salome's dance to worry bout right now'.

They both looked at her, waited for her to continue. It must be serious; Georgia wasn't the worrying kind. She was looking serious. 'Jose is bringing me out to his house in the country tomorrow to meet his mother and I've nothing proper to wear.'

'Georgia, you must be joking', Bernice laughed. 'Your wardrobe is bulging with clothes.'

'I know' Georgia answered. 'All skimpy, sexy things.' She sighed. 'You two don't understand. According to Jose his mother is an old fashioned lady, very strict, after years of the old Spain under your man Franco. She dresses in black from head to toe every day. Everything I have is geared to show off my legs and my boobs. I can't go to meet Jose's mother looking like that. She'll expect me to show up dressed like a nun!

Bernice snapped her fingers. 'I have it - why don't you borrow something from Caroline? She's not exactly a top of the range dresser. More like a nun if you ask me!' They all laughed, even Georgia.

'She has a black skirt that would be perfect for you, Georgia- ' Bernice went on. 'I saw her wearing it the other day. It looked like she was going to a funeral! ,

' - and she has some blouses that button up to her chin!', Alison cut in. 'Why don't I go down to her apartment and see if she's in, ask her to let you borrow some of her stuff?' With that Alison exited.

A few minutes later she burst back into their apartment with some clothes folded over her arm. 'Here you are, Georgia. No doubt your future mammy-in-law will approve of these. Take your pick.' She dumped them on the bed. 'Caroline was thrilled when I told her that you wanted to see some of her gear. She took it as a compliment. I didn't tell her the real reason!'

Georgia slipped off her top and shorts and stepped into the black skirt. It fitted her perfectly.

Alison and Bernice were doubled up on the bed laughing. Bernice picked up a sleeveless blouse and passed it to Georgia. 'Here, try this for size.'

Georgia did so. She looked in the mirror, grimaced. 'Oh my God. I look awful! I can imagine what Jose will think, but it will have to do. All I need now is a pair of black sandals. None of us have any.'

'I'll try Caroline again. She's sure to have a pair.'

'And while you're at bring the rest of her clothes back,' Georgia commanded. 'Tell her thanks very much.'

Alison looked at Bernice. 'She must fancy Jose in a big way to be doing all this for him. She can see herself in a few years time, ordering the servants around like she had them at home in Finglas!' Alison curtsied in front of Georgia. 'Anything else you wish for, madam?'

By the time Alison returned with the required pair of black sandals Georgia was once again in her brief top and shorts. She folded Caroline's clothes and put them into a beach bag.

'Thanks a lot for the help, girls. Wish me luck tomorrow. And say a prayer that Jose's mother likes me. ' Georgia paused. 'Will any of you be over to the Hacienda tonight?'

'I won't,' Bernice said. 'I promised Caroline that myself and Brian would go to the finals of the dancing competition in the Sinatra Club with her. I probably won't see you tomorrow, Georgia. But I hope everything goes well with you and Jose's mammy.'

'And watch that she doesn't catch you sneaking into his bedroom!' Alison laughed.

'What about you Alison, will I be seeing you tonight?'

'I doubt it, Georgia. Miguel has asked me out tonight. I think he has something really exciting planned for me!'

'Hmm, that sounds interesting. I expect you'll be gone for a few days!', Georgia exclaimed. They all burst into gales of laughter.

The Sinatra Club in the Hotel Casablanca was filling up rapidly when Maureen Duff and Alec Holliday entered around 8 p.m. Obviously word that the Grand Final of the modem dance competition was taking place had got around, and a lot of people wanted to be there for the big occasion.

Doc and Maureen looked over the sea of tables, most of them already occupied. 'There's our crowd over there'

Alec exclaimed, pointing to the far side of the ballroom. 'At least we will have some support tonight, Maureen. Look, Alo is waving us over.

Maureen had been looking forward to this night all week. Now the big occasion was getting to her and she felt slightly nervous. The thought of being one of six couples dancing for a fifteen minute session in the final under a spotlight was daunting. But then Alec was a very good dancer; he would look after her.

She wasn't the only woman Alec was looking after, if what Joan and her other friends had told her was true. So what if he liked chatting up other women, Maureen had consoled herself. Lots of men do. Why should she be feeling jealous? There was nothing serious between them - there was no reason to believe that their relationship would progress further than the dance floor.

Alec and Maureen were wending their way through the tables when they heard their names being called. Evelyn Murtagh was waving to them. She was seated at a table with Des and a handsome looking man and his blonde wife.

'Good evening to you both' Evelyn said expansively. 'Maureen and Alec, I'd like you to meet our friends, Karl and Maria. They're German and they have a villa here. They have graciously come along tonight to cheer Des and myself on in the final,' Turning to her German friends Evelyn went on, 'This is the other Irish couple I told you about who are also in the final.'

Maureen and Alec shook hands with Maria and Karl. 'Good luck. I wish you both well', Karl said.

'Karl, darling, you are such a diplomat', Evelyn shrilled. 'You'd like everyone to win!'. Des looked a little embarrassed while Karl's wife just looked bored.

Maureen thought that Evelyn looked marvellous. She was wearing the most stunning looking off the shoulder full-length creation that Maureen had ever seen. It showed off Evelyn's tanned shoulders and cleavage to perfection and it was dotted with sequins that sparkled in the semi darkness. Maureen felt her own new dress very ordinary in the circumstances.

'Your dress is lovely, Evelyn,' Maureen complimented her.

'Thank you Maureen. Yours is lovely too' Evelyn replied, without conviction. 'We'd love to ask you and Alec to sit with us but as you can see this table only accommodates four. Besides, you're probably joining your other friends?'

It was brush-off time, no doubt about that. Alec and Maureen said goodbye, made their way through the tables and joined Alo and Mamie and Ben and Irene, also the lady supervisor from the hotel, Paula Sheridan, whose young daughter Vicki was on duty as a waitress.

'Ye'll have your work cut out winning the dance final tonight', Alo remarked when they were seated. 'Our friend Evelyn is dressed to kill. She looks as though she means business! ,

'Will you be quiet Alo Riordan', Mamie cut in. 'Sure what would you know about women's fashions. It's the dancing that counts, not how you're dressed. Aren't I right Alec?'

Doc thought back to last night to the dinner with Yolanda Segguria in her apartment. She would also be somewhere in the Sinatra Club tonight, observing all, keeping an eye on both himself and Donie. He would make contact with Donie later. ..

Doc lost no time in asking Maureen up to dance. 'We'd better get in some practice before the final starts,' he said. 'How are you feeling Maureen?'

'A little nervous, Alec, to be honest.'

'Good. That means you are alert, ready to perform. When I played football I always liked to feel nervous before a big game. It's a good sign. You know, Maureen, I have a feeling we are going to win tonight!'

The two of them spent a good part of the next two hours on the dance floor, under the large revolving orb, trying several new routines and getting accustomed to each other's dance movements. The sessions of quicksteps, waltzes and tangos helped to ease Maureen's nervousness and she began to relax and enjoy herself.

She wasn't the only finalist to shine on the dance floor. Evelyn was first out to dance at every opportunity , sharing her favours not only with her husband, but also with the dashing Karl. The German was a really fine dancer and brought the best out in Evelyn. They were the centre of attraction whenever they got up to dance together, causing Doc to remark to Maureen.

'I'm glad Evelyn is partnering Des in the final and not Karl. She seems to take on a new life when she dances with that German guy.'

Excitement in the Sinatra Club reached fever pitch when the rotund figure of Senor Carrasco, accompanied by his wife Pepita, appeared on stage to request the floor to be cleared preparatory to the dance final taking place.

'Would the six couples please come forward and take their places, so that we can commence.' He announced. As they lined up Senor Carrasco explained. 'There is one change for the final. No couple will be eliminated during the dancing. Instead, there will be fifteen minutes of continuous dancing, and at the end my wife Pepita and I will decide which is the winning couple. I will announce the winners from the stage immediately the dancing is finished. Thank you. Now let us begin!'.

The six dance partnerships were introduced individually before the contest commenced, a spotlight picking them out as each couple was named., Maureen noted that in addition to themselves and Evelyn and Des, couples from England, Sweden, Germany and Scotland had also made the final.

As the lights dimmed in the Sinatra Club and the three-piece struck up a quickstep, Maureen offered up a silent prayer to Saint Jude that herself and Alec would win. Then she remembered Saint Jude was the saint of lost causes!

Whether it was prayer or sheer excitement, Maureen never knew, but suddenly her nervousness disappeared and before she realised it, she and Alec were out on the dance floor, twirling and gliding around as though they had been dancing together for years. It was all so easy, so exhilarating. She felt like she was floating on air!

'Hey, steady on!' Maureen heard Alec whisper as they changed tempo for a waltz. His arm tightened slightly around her waist. 'Keep it nice and simple. Let's not get too fancy. You 're doing fine, Maureen.' His words of encouragement steadied her and she relaxed even more. Maureen really enjoyed the waltz and hoped the band might play another before the contest was over. The crowd applauded as the tempo switched once again and the rhythm changed to a tango. She closed her eyes, deciding not to concentrate on anything but the music.

Suddenly Maureen heard a huge gasp from the audience. 'Oh my God!', she heard Alec's shocked whisper. For a split second he lost his concentration and faltered, but he quickly regained the tempo and continued.

Maureen opened her eyes, looked over Alec's shoulder as he twirled her around. She couldn't believe her eyes at what she saw. Evelyn and Des had fallen right in the middle of the dance floor! Every person in the audience was looking on in horror. Des was helping his wife up, whispering to her, while the remaining five couples danced on.

'What happened?' Maureen asked.

'They were tangoing right in front of Karl and Maria. I think Evelyn wanted to show off, trying something elaborate for their guests. It didn't work, suddenly they were both on the floor'. Doc broke off, 'Keep dancing', he said. 'We're doing fine!'

The audience saw Evelyn say something to her husband, then storm off the floor. Des followed her, looking crestfallen. At their table Evelyn was being comforted by Karl and Maria.

Meanwhile the drama was continuing on the dance floor with the contest about to come to an end. Already the tragedy of one of the Irish couples crashing ignominiously out of the final was pushed into the back of the audience's minds as the band finished with a rousing South American set, the dancers completed one last twirl, stopped, and waited breathlessly for the winners to be announced.

'Poor Evelyn and Des. What a terrible thing to happen. They must be very disappointed', Maureen whispered to Alec as Senor Carrasco made his way onto the stage.

'They won't be half as disappointed as me if we don't win here tonight', Alec whispered back, wiping perspiration from his brow with a handkerchief.

Senor Carrasco held his hand up for silence, then in a solemn voice announced, 'Ladies and gentlemen, we have seen some exquisite modem dancing here tonight, and on your behalf I would like to congratulate the six couples who reached the final. I would also like to commiserate with the couple who suffered that unfortunate accident'. He paused for the round of sympathetic applause. Des and Evelyn were not in the Sinatra Club to hear it. They had already departed with their German friends.

'And now, to the winners of the contest I present this magnificent prize.' Senor Carrasco paused. 'A week's holiday for two here in the beautiful Casablanca Hotel in Ibiza next April.' Another pause. ' And the winners are…from Ireland - Maureen Duff and Alec Holliday!'

A huge burst of cheering and applause greeted the announcement. 'We've done it!' Alec hugged Maureen, gave her a congratulatory kiss. Maureen was so breathless she could hardly speak. Alo Riordan was standing up and cheering loudly.

Doc led Maureen up on stage and they received their prize from a beaming Senor Carrasco and his wife. Flashbulbs popped as people took photographs as souvenirs. Maureen was thrilled, she felt like a film star! As the cheering and applause continued Doc turned to her and handed her the envelope containing the prize.

'You hold onto that Maureen. Come next April if you want to avail of the free holiday in Ibiza, I'll be only too happy to oblige. On the other hand, if you wish to bring one of your lady friends, that's fine by me.'

Maureen took the envelope. She wondered what was in Alec' s mind. She suspected that he did not want to put any pressure on her~ or on their relationship such as it was.

'Thank you, Alec' she said. 'That's a very nice gesture.'

Back at the table there was pandemonium. Alo had ordered several bottles of champagne and everyone had a glass in their hand. Maureen and Doc were overwhelmed with congratulations from those at the table and from total strangers.

Nobody was anxious to mention the catastrophe that had befallen Des and Evelyn Murtagh; it was too embarrassing to discuss.

In the midst of the celebrations Maureen whispered to Alec that she wanted to telephone Joan back home as she had promised and tell her the good news. Doc gave her his mobile phone, showed her how to use it, and suggested she go out into the foyer of the hotel where there was less noise. As soon as Maureen had disappeared from view Doc excused himself. Time to talk to Donie Crawford.

Doc found him in his usual place at the bar. 'Well, well, well, if it isn't Fred Astaire himself', Donie greeted him. ' Congratulations me oul' pal.'

Doc let the gibe pass. Donie as usual looked the worse for drink. 'I'm here to talk business, Donie. That deal you were hinting at the other night...'

Donie seemed to sober up quickly. 'You interested?' he asked, voice lowered, eyes darting around to make sure they were not being overheard.

'Yes, I could do with a few extra pesetas to see me through this holiday'.

'Good. Now listen carefully....' Donie leaned so close that Doc could smell the beer off his breath. 'There's a little park with a children's playground in it at the far end of the harbour. It's very popular, lots of parents bring their kids there every evening – '

'I know it. I jog by it every morning.'

'Good. Meet me there next Thursday, 8 p.m. Got that?"

Doc nodded. 'What about payment?'

'I'll give you five hundred pounds sterling, in pesetas with the heroin on Thursday. You get the remainder of the money when you hand over the stuff to a man after you've passed through Dublin Airport.'

'Where do I meet this character?'

Donie took a gulp of his drink. 'The carpark pay machines opposite the arrivals exit. Wait at the right hand machine. I'll describe you to my contact. O.K. ?'

'O.K.' Doc was anxious to get away. 'See you Thursday evening – '

'What's the rush. Let me buy you a drink.'

Doc shook his head. 'Some other time, Donie. I've got to go back to my friends'. Doc turned away. Donie called after him. 'You know something, Doc. You're a better dancer than you ever were a footballer!'

Doc didn't reply. He wondered if Yolanda Segguria had witnessed the scene.

Meanwhile, in the relative quiet of the hotel foyer, Maureen was dialling Joan's number. Her friend must have been waiting right beside the phone. It was answered immediately and Maureen had barely time to say 'hello' when Joan blurted out:

'I knew it would be you Maureen. What's the news? I have Sheila and Cathleen right here beside me. We lit a candle for Alec and yourself today. Oh we are so excited. Couldn't think of anything else all day. Tell us all!'

'Now Joan, if you will only give me a chance to talk I'll tell you.'

Sheila butted in, 'Hello Maureen, we're dying to know how it all went. How did Evelyn and Des do? Did she look gorgeous? We have so many questions to ask you. Maureen, you have us on tenterhooks here. Here's Joan again.'

'Maureen', Joan sounded exasperated, 'before I am interrupted again, tell me how did you and Alec do in the dance competition?'

'We won!' Maureen shouted into the mobile phone. She then heard Joan scream and shout to the others 'Maureen and Alec won. I knew they would. Isn't it great!'

'Joan, for goodness sake will you calm down and let me get on with it. Yes Alec and I won first prize, champagne on the house and a week for two in the Hotel Casablanca next April. Are you jealous?' She said, laughing.

'No indeed I'm delighted for you Maureen. Congratulations, you deserve it. Wait till I tell Sheila and Cathleen about your prize!'

'Don't be long.' Maureen wanted to get back to the celebrations in the ballroom.

In no time at all Sheila was back on the phone. 'Delighted to hear the good news Maureen. How are things between Alec and yourself. Are you heeding my warning? What's going to happen about the holiday? Do be careful Maureen. Don't make a fool of yourself. Remember we all love you.'

'I know that Sheila, thanks a lot. I promise to be very careful. Now, will you put Joan back on.'

'In a minute. Tell me how did Des and the beautiful Evelyn do? She must have looked stunning. And how did your dress look? Did you get your hair done nicely? Be sure and have lots of photos when you come home.'

'Sheila, I can only answer one question at a time. Yes, Evelyn did look beautiful but would you believe, she slipped on the dance floor and poor Des fell on top of her!'

'What, Evelyn fell? Sheila screamed. 'Wait till I tell Joan and Cathleen.' Maureen heard her shout out the news 'Girls Evelyn and Des fell!'

Maureen shouted out, 'Sheila, please pass the phone to Joan. When Joan came back on Maureen said, 'Joan I'm going to hang up if you don't hold fast to that phone.'

'Please try to understand Maureen, we're all so delighted for you. We want you to know everything. Are you feeling alright? You're not tipsy are you? Have you had too much champagne?'

'I never felt better Joan. And what if I do have several glasses of champagne too many so what. It's an evening for celebrating you know.' Maureen tried to end the conversation but before she could bring it to a close, Sheila took over the phone again.

'Maureen, I was just thinking, what are you going to do about the week for two that you and Alec won?"

'I'm going to avail of it of course.'

'With Alec?'

'Perhaps, who knows.'

'What do you mean 'who knows'. Would you ever talk plain English and cut the riddles.'

'I think the riddles make it more exciting, don't you? Alec gave me the voucher to do it as I wish.'

'And what are you going to do?' Sheila was persistent.

'That's a bit difficult to answer right now. Maybe when the time comes I'll have a lucky dip between the three of you. Now, if you'll excuse me I just have to return to the celebrations or they'll think I'm lost.'

Reluctantly Sheila handed the phone back to Joan. 'Good nights' were exchanged all round and the trio promised that they would be at Dublin Airport to meet Maureen the following Saturday night.

Maureen knew in her heart that it wasn't only herself her girlfriends were anxious to meet when she arrived home. They would be more than anxious to see if she had Alec Holliday on her arm!

CHAPTER TWELVE

Sunday morning dawned very hot in Figueretas, the sun shining from a blue sky without a trace of cloud. Georgia and Jose had just finished breakfast on the veranda of his apartment and were relaxing and enjoying the view. Georgia was feeling rather apprehensive about the upcoming visit to Jose's family home to meet his mother.

They had spent a very romantic night together and had already showered and dressed. Jose was about to collect his car from the underground carpark. 'Will you be ready in five minutes, querida?' he asked.

Georgia nodded. 'Yes, Jose darling. I just have to comb my hair and touch up my make-up. I'll meet you outside the front entrance.'

He came over, kissed her gently on the temple. 'I am so proud of you, Georgia. I am sure the Contessa will be too. You are so beautiful and talented.'

Beautiful and talented. ...No one had ever said that to her before. She adored the way Jose paid her compliments. He seemed to get great pleasure out of saying nice things about her. She wondered if all the Continental men were like that. She had never heard her Da say things like that to her Ma.

When he was gone Georgia studied herself in the mirror. My God didn't she look hideous in Caroline's black skirt and white blouse. If only she could wear some of her own sexy outfits. She stepped out of the black sandals, slipped on a pair of fashionable high-heel shoes. She glanced again at herself in the mirror, opened another button at the top of the blouse. Surely Jose's mother couldn't be too old fashioned if she was living in a place like Ibiza!

Yes, that was a little better. At least she didn't feel like a nun. She put on her sunglasses and picked up her hat and bag, glanced again at her reflection in the mirror. Behave yourself today Georgia, for Jose's sake', she cautioned herself aloud.

Jose drove up at speed to where Georgia was waiting. She was impressed with his car, a red sports convertible, sleek and shiny. It was almost worth the trauma of having to meet mother, to go for a spin in such a car. Jose complimented her on outfit, kissed her hand and told her how lovely she looked. It was obvious he wanted Georgia to make a good impression on his mother; he was his own man, but it would be so much easier if he had his mother's blessing when he chooses a bride.

It was just past ten a.m. when Jose settled Georgia into his car. The rooftop was back and he made sure that she had her wide brimmed hat on to save her from the sun. He placed a cool box in the boot of the car containing soft drinks, bottled wine and some fruit. As Jose steered the car though the streets of Figueretas he explained to Georgia: 'We will be cutting straight across the island towards the north coast. We will travel six kilometers past Ibiza Town and then branch off to the right heading towards Partinax.

Georgia relaxed and took in every detail of the countryside. The burnt red fields looked so different to the green fields of Ireland, but then how could olive trees and trees like the ones she was looking at now, grow in the Irish climate. They passed a plantation of melons. Georgia asked Jose what his mother grew the farm.

'When we get there I will take you for a walk and show you everything" he said. 'I forgot to tell you to bring some walking shoes, but never mind, we'll borrow some.'

They sped along, passing small houses tucked away in the fields, each one brightly painted and surrounded by flowers of all colours. Georgia was enjoying the trip, at least she was seeing some of the real Spain. On her holidays to the sun she usually saw only the interiors of bars, shops and discos.

'We will stop for a little while and have a cold drink, Georgia, and then it will take another 35 minutes. I am really taking you on a scenic tour of the island. Are you feeling alright? You are not nervous are you?'

'Of course not Jose.' Georgia hoped she sounded convincing. 'A cold drink would be lovely.'

When they continued on their journey Georgia was wondering what sort of house Jose's mother lived in. They must be near it now, she thought. Suddenly Jose drove in through a pair of very impressive looking gates and up a short, steep drive. On a large plateau was a beautiful white hacienda. It was so large that Georgia throught it was a hotel.

'Why are we are we stopping here Jose' she asked.

'This is my home, Georgia. Come, meet everyone.'

Georgia gazed wide-eyed at the beautiful big dwelling. In her mind's eye she had a vision of her family's Corporation house in Finglas. What on earth was she getting herself into, she wondered?

Jose took Georgia's hand and escorted her in through the main door. Her high heels clicked on the tiles in the large cool entrance hall; it was almost too much for to take in. Jose propelled her towards a door, he opened it and they stepped into a large sitting room. Two elderly ladies were seated on a cushioned settee. Both were dressed in black, their white hair piled high on their heads, held in place with identical Spanish combs.

Jose placed his arm around Georgia and introduced her to the smaller of the ladies. 'Georgia, may I present my mother, The Contessa Madelina Elena Simon.' Then to his mother he said. 'This is Georgia, I told you about her on my last visit.'

The Contessa held out a delicate hand to Georgia. 'I am happy to meet you.' The tone was cool, not very welcoming. 'Let me present my sister-in-law Senorita Pilar Simon,'

Pilar took Georgia's hand. 'Welcome, sit down please, it is so hot today...'

Georgia was glad to sit down. Her legs felt weak. She was in a state of shock. Jose's mother was a Contessa! She wasn't exactly sure what a Contessa was but she knew it was a sort of title. Georgia was bewildered. What did that leave Jose? He must be a Count, having inherited the title from his late father. Georgia could hardly believe this was happening to her.

The Contessa remained silent, deep in thought. The girl seemed out of her depth, but it was obvious even at this early stage that Jose was in love with her. Why couldn't he have fallen for a Spanish girl?. If Jose married this Irish girl, what would her grandchildren look like with that red hair!.

The Contessa stood up. 'Perhaps you would like to freshen up before lunch,' she said to Georgia.

'Yes please' , Georgia replied gratefully. Truth to tell she needed to be alone for a few minutes to gather her thoughts. As she stood up she said. 'Your home is very beautiful, Contessa.' It was a trite remark but at least it was something.

'Thank you. I have always thought so.' the Contessa replied,. 'I came here as a young wife 50 years ago and I have loved it since.' She paused, and when she spoke again she looked directly at Georgia as though to make sure her message was understood. 'When Jose takes a bride I hope she will live here with me. It would not be suitable for her to live in Figueretas. But then he will give up his interests in Figueretas and live here and look after his plantations. Jose is fortunate to have a dependable foreman here.' The Contessa paused again. 'But we can talk over lunch. Pilar will take you to the guest room to freshen up.'

Pilar stood up. She was tall and slim and her face was still beautiful. What a pity Georgia thought, that Jose's aunt was dressed in black. It made her look older than she was. Georgia could see that there was a great resemblance between Jose and his mother. The elegant good looks were still very much apparent, even though she was dressed in a rather dowdy manner.

Pilar stretched out a hand to Georgia. 'Come my dear, I will show you where to go.'

Once out of the room Pilar relaxed. She was delighted to get Georgia alone. She loved the company of young people and she also wanted to get to know Georgia. They walked down the long corridor, each side of which was adorned with pictures and relics of the past. Pilar stopped and opened a door on her right. She ushered Georgia into the room. It was a very big bedroom decorated in peach and cream. The dark wooden floor was scattered with rugs that were soft and luxurious under foot. Pilar crossed the room and opened another door to reveal a marble bathroom with shower. It was as big as her mother's front room back home in Finglas!

'When you are ready, come out to me through the French windows on the right. Take your time, there is no hurry'.

Pilar went out and sat down. In the distance she could hear Georgia singing softly. She seemed a happy enough young lady. Pilar wanted to be sure that Georgia would make Jose happy. She remembered the day Jose was born. His mother, Madelina had long since given up hope of having a child and after eighteen years of marriage, Jose arrived. What a day that had been. The nine long anxious months behind them, and a perfect baby boy to love and cherish. Madelina had taken a long time to recover from the birth. Pilar had watched over him as if he were her own. There was a special bond between herself and Jose, and all that she wanted was for him to be happy.

Georgia exited through the french windows. Pilar patted the seat beside her and invited Georgia to sit down. 'We can talk for a few minutes before we join the others.'

Georgia turned to Pilar and asked, 'Have you always lived here? It is so beautiful.'

'Yes' replied Pilar. 'Just once in my lifetime I nearly left here for a man, but it was not to be. You see, Georgia, in those days marriages were arranged between families. There was a marriage arranged for me with a man I did not love. He was wealthy had vast estates, but I did not love and I would not marry him.'

Pilar paused for a moment, a look of sadness on her face. 'Perhaps I should have tried, but you see I already loved someone else. This other man was not rich and so my parents would not let us marry. I did consider going away with him but that would been a disgrace to both our families, and we could not do it.' She paused, 'Things are very different now, Georgia, but I still believe that a marriage without love will never last.'

Georgia remained silent. Pilar wondered if perhaps she had being too inquisitive. 'Forgive me, my dear, I do not wish to pry into your personal life, but please do not hurt Jose. I want him to know the beauty of true love. I don't ever want him to have regrets like I have myself.'

Georgia touched Pilar's hand. ' I understand, and I promise whatever I do I'll be honest and not hurt Jose.' She looked at her watch and said to Pilar, 'Perhaps we should join the others for lunch.'

'Yes, let's go and find them. We are having lunch in the open today. You will meet some of the plantation workers. We will have some music and dancing. Come let us go and enjoy the festivities.' Pilar placed her arm through Georgia's and in doing so Georgia felt that Jose's aunt was offering her friendship. Two women, so different in appearance, age and outlook, stepped out into the sunshine.

Georgia was surprised to see so many people gathered. Jose introduced her to lots of people and to her surprise she found she was enjoying herself. The long tables were covered with white linen cloths and decked with bowls of food, bottles of wine, baskets of crisp rolls and fruit. Over to the side there was a barbecue with steaks, sausages and burgers being prepared. It was self service and for once Georgia forgot about her figure and tried a selection of food, regardless of the fat content.

Afterwards the music and dancing started. Two guitarists played Spanish music and couples got up to dance. Georgia was fascinated. She found herself swept up by the atmosphere. Urged on by Jose, she jumped into the circle of dancers, and to applause from the locals, joined in a Flamenco. When she finished Jose was escorting her back to her seat, Pilar rose to her feet and hugged her with delight. Even Jose's mother had lost her stern look and was smiling.

As the evening wore on Jose and Georgia slipped away and walked through fruit groves. They held hands like lovers normally do, they kissed and were happy to be together. After a while Georgia stopped and looked at Jose, 'I have so enjoyed today', she said. 'Your home is beautiful, very peaceful. How can you bear to be away from it and go to live in a place like Ibiza?'

Jose looked out to the distant hills, fading now in the dusk. He was not smiling and in fact looked rather sad. 'I have never found anyone to share all this with; not until now, that is.' He stopped and looked into Georgia's eyes, blurted out, 'Marry me Georgia, be my wife as well as my lover.'

Georgia was stunned. This was so totally unexpected.

'Jose, you just can't ask someone to marry you when you have known them less than a week' Georgia replied. Did Jose know what he was doing? She thought her own humble background. Oh God, this was getting out of hand.

'One week, one month, one year, what does it matter when you have found the you want, the person you want to be with for the rest of one's life. And you are that one for me.' Jose moved closer to her. 'Do not worry, Georgia, you do not need to give me an answer tonight. I did not intend to ask you to marry me so soon, I wanted you to get to know me first, but time is not on my side. All too soon you will be back with your family and I will miss you so much.'

Back at the house the Contessa was waiting for them. Once again she was looking rather stern, her chiselled features unsmiling.

'Jose, Georgia, we were getting worried about you. Where have you been?'

'We were strolling among the olive trees and discussing our future together, ' Jose answered.

If her son's answer disturbed his mother she did not show it. 'Sit here, Georgia, and have some coffee before you retire. You also, Jose.'

They did as they were told. Georgia felt like a schoolgirl who had been found out late with a boy, facing the headmistress the following morning. The Contessa was looking at her, still unsmiling. 'Now, querida,' she said, 'I wish for you to tell me something about yourself and your family.'

On Sunday morning Maureen and Caroline went to Mass together in Ibiza. Afterwards they had a light lunch in one of the pretty restaurants on the promenade. Maureen was basking in the heady afterglow of the previous night in the Sinatra Club and the success of herself and Alec in the dance competition.

Caroline was rather quite throughout lunch. Maureen observed her during the meal and sensed that her young companion's mind was elsewhere. 'You don't seem yourself today, Caroline,' Maureen said. 'Is there something bothering you?'

'Since you ask, yes there is,' Caroline said. 'I'm a bit uptight and very confused over something. I keep asking myself the question 'what is life really about?'

'And have you found the answer?'

'No. I'm not in a receptive mood. I feel that I'm not being true to myself.' Caroline paused, said reflectively, 'I suppose you could say I'm a sham.'

Maureen was shocked to hear such a lovely young girl voicing such thoughts. Especially so in Ibiza, the island of youth. What was disturbing Caroline? she wondered.

'Really Caroline,' Maureen's tone was comforting, 'You're being very hard on yourself. Lots of girls would give anything to have your looks – not to mention the fact that you have two young fellows like Mark and Wayne chasing you all over the island!'

The jocose remark failed to lift Caroline. 'That's part of the problem,' she said wistfully, 'I don't want young men chasing after me. It's only making things worse. That's not what I came to Ibiza for.'

'What did you come for then?'. Maureen asked. 'It wasn't for a holiday, was it?'

Caroline didn't answer. Instead she said, 'How about us going to the beach this afternoon for a swim, Maureen? I'll tell you all about it there.'

'Good. I'd like that.'

They had almost finished their coffee. 'I'm lucky to have someone like you to listen to my problems. Someone who listens and tries to understand…'

Maureen brushed the compliment aside. 'Let's go back to the hotel and pick up our togs and our towels,' she said. 'I'm just dying for a dip in the sea.'

On their way they noted the large number of Spanish family groups who had come into Ibiza from the countryside to enjoy a Sunday at the beach. After their swim in the sea Maureen and Caroline stretched out on their towels and relaxed beneath a cloudless blue sky. They chatted for a while and as it was lovely and warm, and despite the chatter of the children nearby, Maureen eventually found herself dozing off. She was about to fall asleep when she heard Caroline say, 'Maureen, there's something I just have to tell you…'

Maureen had her eyes closed. 'What is it, Caroline?' she asked dreamily.

'I'm a nun.'

At first Maureen thought she was dreaming'. She opened her eyes, saw the serious look on Caroline's face. 'What did you say?' she asked.

'I said I'm nun.' Caroline's voice was a mere whisper. 'I've been meaning to tell you for the last few days…'

Maureen sat up. 'Really.' She wasn't sure what to say next. Her young friend a nun…things were beginning to full into place.

'I'm what you might call a mixed-up nun, but I'm a nun nevertheless.'

Maureen stared at Caroline. 'If you are what you are, what on earth are you doing here – in Ibiza of all places!'

Caroline gazed out to sea before replying. 'What I'm going to tell you, Maureen, is strictly between the two of us. Nobody at the hotel must know. Not yet, anyway.'

'You can trust me, Caroline.' This holiday is turning up some very interesting people!, Maureen thought to herself.

'I've been given leave from my Superior for a few months to sort myself out, reflect on my vocation,' Caroline explained. 'Back home myself and a young curate called Father Joe, whom I helped to run a local youth club, were becoming very close – ' She paused. 'I suppose you could say we were becoming very fond of each other –'

'I see,' Maureen said quietly.

'I actually teach in a primary school where Fr. Joe and I met initially. We were becoming such good friends that

Reverend Mother suggested that I take time out and to reflect on what exactly I wanted to do with my life – '

'I doubt if Reverend Mother had a break in Ibiza in mind,' Maureen opined drily.

Caroline laughed despite herself. 'No doubt you're right. You see I'm an only child, adopted by a wonderful married couple. They don't know about Fr. Joe and myself – I told them I was allowed home for a break before taking my final vows. They thought I looked a bit stressed and I convinced them that a holiday in the sun would do me good. I came to Ibiza not knowing what it was really like.'

'If you ask me you've jumped out of the frying pan into the fire! Why on earth did you pick a wild place like Ibiza'

'I didn't exactly pick it. Everywhere was booked up and this was the only holiday that was available. I assumed Ibiza was just an ordinary holiday resort like everywhere else. I didn't know it would be so, so wild – ' Caroline broke off. 'I realise now, Maureen, that I've missed out a lot on life. You see I went from boarding school straight into the convent. Nowadays it's recommended that young girls do some training before entering. Had I done that I'd have been more mature – not that I've regretted entering the convent – expecially now that I see some of the carry-on outside!'

'So where do you go from here, Caroline?'

'I'm not sure. Tomorrow I'm supposed to be going on a cruise around the island with Wayne and Mark – '

'No, no,' Maureen sighed. 'What I mean is - have you decided on your future? And are you going to tell Wayne and Mark that you're a nun? Mark seems very keen on you.'

Caroline pondered a moment. 'The answer to both questions is that I don't know yet what I'm going to do. I haven't made up my mind. I came on this holiday to think some things out and have a bit of harmless fun – '

'Harmless fun – in Ibiza! I don't want to sound like your Reverend Mother, but I hope that God will direct you, Caroline, see that you don't do anything that you'll regret later.'

'Will you say a prayer for me, Maureen?'

'Of course. I hope you're praying also. Apart from going to Mass on Sunday I hope you're saying some prayers every day for guidance.'

Caroline looked a bit guilty. 'I'm afraid I've been taking a few short cuts,' she said sheepishly.

'At least you're honest. Maybe we should attend Mass together a few days this coming week. I hope you don't think I'm interfering, but I'd like to discuss your situation further. Would you like that?'

'I would. And thanks, Maureen. You're very kind. I've been a bit lonely this past week. You were lucky, you met Alec, who seems very nice – ' She broke off. 'Incidentally, what about yourself and Alec? I think he's interested in you – '

'Alec is my dancing partner and a charming one at that, but nothing else,' Maureen replied, rather primly, Caroline thought. 'Who knows, we may meet sometime when we return home for a chat.'

'Is that all? Now you don't seem very definite about what you want to do in the future.'

Maureen paused before saying, 'To be honest, Caroline, I too am at a crossroads in my life'....She played with the sand at her feet. 'When you come to a place like Ibiza and see what goes on you realise that a lot of people are leading empty lives.'

'Do you have any idea what it is you want to do with your life?', Caroline asked.

'Yes,' the older woman replied. 'When I was about your age I worked in a hospital in Africa, teaching English to young girls anxious to pursue a nursing career. I had no formal training as a teacher but I found I had a talent for the job and that it was very fulfilling...'

'I hope I can work abroad like that sometime.' Caroline cut in.

'Unfortunately something happened that changed the whole course of my life,' Maureen continued. She told

Caroline about her late fiancé, Donal, with whom she had gone to Africa and how their plans to marry had been cut short by his untimely death in a aeroplane crash there. Caroline listened attentively.

'Donal's death must have been a terrible shock to you, Maureen. And here I am boring you with my troubles.. '

'You're not boring me, I was always a good listener. But yes, it took me a long time to get over Donal's death. I never met anyone else that could take his place in my life.'

'Were you angry with God for having taken him away so suddenly, that you didn't enjoy a full life together?'

Maureen smiled wistfully. 'No, I don't blame God for what happened. I feel that crosses like that are sent to us in life to test us, see how strong we are. If you survive them then you are a better person. It happened to me, Caroline, and I believe you also will come out of your little crisis a better person.'

Caroline wasn't so sure, but she felt a weight had been lifted off her shoulders now that she had unburdened herself to Maureen. It was like she had had a heart-to-heart talk with her Reverend Mother! She told Maureen and they both had a good laugh.

Then Maureen became serious again. 'I genuinely want to do something really worthwhile with the rest of my life. My father died a few years ago and the younger brothers and sisters I looked after are all independent now. Some are married with families and businesses of their own and have left the farm. I don't want to remain on the farm for the rest of my life. I feel I'm ready to move on, change direction so to speak.'

'Good for you, Maureen. We both have important decisions to make about what to do in the future. Who knows, maybe we can work on something together' – Caroline jumped to her feet. She felt there had been enough soul-searching for one day. 'Come on, ' she urged, 'let's have another swim!'

They enjoyed themselves among the waves for a second time. Later, back in the hotel foyer, they bumped into Alec who invited both of them to the Sinatra Club for the dance that evening.

Caroline declined the offer. She promised herself an early night in expectation of what she reckoned would be an all-action day tomorrow on the cruise around the island with Mark and Wayne. First she would take a stroll alone later, reflect on her talk with Maureen. Regarding that cruise with the lads...she wondered what on earth she had let herself in for!

Evelyn pretended to be asleep. The bedroom was shaded from the mid-morning sun and she was conscious of Des moving quietly around the room.

Memories of last night came flooding back. What a disaster! She buried her face in the pillow. Imagine falling down in front of everyone -and particularly with Karl present! The memory of it was so painful Evelyn wanted to scream out in anguish. What must she have looked like, sprawled on the floor minus one of her patent leather slingbacks? Karl had gallantly retrieved it while Des was helping her to her feet. God- the shame of it all! It had all been Des's fault, of course. When it came to dancing he wasn't in her class. He should stick to his stupid golf!

She opened her eyes, saw he had put his head around the door. 'Hello, love. How are you feeling?'

Evelyn nearly exploded. 'How do you think I'm feeling - bloody awful!'

'Sorry about last night. Try not to think about it. I know it was awful for you – '

'How can I not think about it. I'm the laughing stock of Ibiza! How am I ever going to show my face around the pool again?'

'Karl was on the telephone while you were asleep, asking about you' Des said. He knew that would cheer her up. 'I told him you were disappointed about last night. He said you were not to let it worry you and that he's looking forward to seeing you this afternoon when we're viewing the apartments....'

The fact that Karl had been on asking about her almost made last night's disaster worthwhile. When Des left she consoled herself, remembering the feel of Karl's arm around her waist as he helped her back to the table. He had offered his handkerchief when the tears flowed. Maria had offered some consoling words too, but Evelyn suspected she was highly amused by it all.

Evelyn brightened up. She pushed the bedclothes aside and swung her feet onto the floor. I'll survive, she thought to herself. Herself and Des would have a snack and travel to Es Cana by taxi. The least he could do would be to agree to buying her a luxury apartment - maybe even a villa!

The taxi arrived promptly at three o'clock. Evelyn and Des were waiting outside on the hotel steps. Evelyn had insisted on that. 'We don't want the driver shouting our names all over the lobby. The less people like Mamie and Alo Riordan know about our comings and goings the better.'

A middle-aged- couple were already ensconced on the back seat of the large taxi. Des and Evelyn sat on the seat opposite. The couple introduced themselves as Doris and Jim. In the half-hour that it took to get to Es Cana they learned that Doris and Jim were from Sheffield and had two daughters and three grandchildren. Jim had taken early retirement from his job in the steel industry and now spent most of his time in their nice council house looking after Monty, his whippet.

Evelyn shivered; how any wife would allow her husband to have a whippet as a pet was beyond her. We'll shake these two off as soon as we arrive at the apartments,

Evelyn thought to herself as Doris continued to natter on about their boring life in Sheffield.

'This is the sixth trip to view apartments we've had since we arrived last week, .Doris gloated. 'We enjoy the taxi trips and the free champagne, don't we, luv?' she said as her husband nodded agreement.

The luxury home development, situated on a hill overlooking the bay, was very impressive. The apartments were painted a bright yellow and had white wooden shutters, with newly planted bougainvillaes trailing down the gable walls. They were greeted at the main apartment by a handsome, thirtyish man in a beige linen suit and white open necked shirt who spoke excellent English.

Des felt vaguely uncomfortable at the ease with which Evelyn joined with other couples in asking questions of the handsome man. Couples were invited to cross the spacious room to a desk where an older man with greying hair had a site plan spread before him. Clusters of little red and blue coloured pins dotted the drawing.

An attractive young girl was in a corner of the room pouring champagne into tall glasses. Des helped himself to a glass and looked around for Evelyn. She had a half-empty drink in her hand as she chatted to a well-dressed couple over by the open fireplace. As he approached she drained her glass, helped herself to his.

'Go get two more from that girl,' Evelyn said.

'For God's sake go easy on that stuff,' Des hissed. 'It may not be vintage but it has a kick in it.'

'Good. It will help me to forget last night,' Evelyn smiled, glancing around to see if Karl and Maria had arrived yet.

A short while later Des and Evelyn and as many as could fit into the bathroom with the smooth-talking Spaniard were admiring the white marble floor with the star-shaped green design when they heard a familiar female voice.

'Wouldn't that be a great yoke for soaking your feet in after a hard day's work, Alo.' They looked behind them. Sure enough there was Mamie Riordan gazing into the bidet, grinning at the same time. There was no escape; the bathroom was too crowded.

Just then Mamie straightened up, turned, and spotted Evelyn and Des. 'Well fancy meeting you two here. Would you like to own one of these apartments?, ' she asked Evelyn.

'They are rather small. We're actually thinking about a villa, aren't we, Desmond?'

Des managed a weak smile. He was beginning to wish they hadn't come to Es Cana. Before he could reply he heard Mamie say, 'By the way Evelyn, your two friends have just arrived. We saw them outside, didn't we, Alo?'

Evelyn's eyes lit up with excitement. 'We'd better go out and say hello to Karl and Maria, Desmond darling,' she said. It was a good excuse to get away from Alo and Mamie. Outside the bathroom she said, 'Get me another glass of champagne while I look for them.'

By the time he got two glasses of champagne Karl was already talking to Evelyn and they were strolling outside into the sunshine. Des spotted Maria coming downstairs into the room and gave her the glass of champagne instead.

Evelyn was hanging onto Karl's every word. 'I know the people who developed this property, ' he said. 'It is an excellent investment. I'd advise you and Des to buy.'

She looked up into his eyes. He was very handsome, Evelyn thought. Worldly, that was the word she was seeking, a man who was never out of his depth, was exciting to talk to. Buy a villa in Es Cana where Karl would be a near-neighbour….she could hardly wait to put pen to paper!

A line of lemon trees took them out of view of the other couples. Karl moved close to her, said, 'It would be good if you convinced Des to buy. You and I could see more of each other....' He touched her arm...

Oh my God, he's flirting with me, Evelyn thought! What will I do? Could he hear her heart pounding? This sort of thing happened only in those women's magazines she bought at home – English ones mainly. They all followed the same line, bored wife with boring husband on holiday meets handsome stranger. There is an immediate chemistry between them. She's tempted, should she have an affair? A once-off fling, something she will treasure for the rest of her life. Would she dare?

Evelyn got the whiff of Karl's after-shave. Des never used after-shave, he said it gave him pimples. If she turned to face him she was sure he would kiss her - !

'I – I think we should rejoin the others,' Evelyn said without looking at him. Her throat felt dry. She could do with another glass of champagne!

'If you wish...' He took her arm, guided her through the lemon trees back to the villa. Looking out from an upstairs window, Mamie Riordan followed Karl and Evelyn's progress with amusement. She had not heard the conversation between Evelyn and her handsome escort, but their body language said it all. Some women have all the luck, Mamie thought!

While Karl rejoined Des and Maria, Evelyn approached the desk and listened as the man with the plans discussed finance with a client who spoke with a strong London accent. 'Yes Senor,' the salesman was saying, 'ten thousand pounds will be quite adequate as a down payment on one of our villas...'

Evelyn could hardly believe her ears. The man began nonchalantly signing a cheque for the amount. Holy God! – if that docker could lash out that kind of money on a Spanish property surely her Des could certainly afford one! The Londoner wore a vest revealing tattoos on both arms. Evelyn shuddered. The tattoos indicated that 'Mavis' and

'Mother' were the two women in this man's life. The woman beside him – whom Evelyn assumed was Mavis – had blonde highlights in her hair and tight white trousers that clung to her ample posterior. Judging by the large wheels suspended from her earlobes she was trying to bring back the hoola-hoop era!

Where do these people get the money to buy Spanish properties, Evelyn asked herself? Not by honest means, that's for sure. Common as muck! She would make sure the London couple didn't end up as their neighbours. She watched as the tattooed man and the salesman shook hands while Mavis, with a satisfied smile, accepted another glass of champagne.

Evelyn looked across the room. 'Desmond!', she called out. Her husband looked over. 'Come across here, darling,' she commanded. That Des, he had no spirit of adventure. All these lovely villas being snapped up and he had still to make a move. She glanced across gardens to where swimming pools glistened in the early evening sun. She pictured herself pouring a gin and tonic and plucking a lemon from one's own tree, while Karl watched her every move. Sheer bliss!

'Yes?' Des was beside her, an anxious look on his face.

Evelyn was brusque. 'I've seen enough. Time we got down to business.' The man with the site plans overheard, smiled at them.

'If you are interested we have one property left facing south-east. Two bedrooms, with balcony, its own private swimming-pool and superbly fitted kitchen and bathroom.' He pointed to one of the coloured pins on the site plan. 'It could be yours, Senora, when it is completed next April –'

Evelyn almost swooned with excitement. She turned to Des. 'See, we have lots of time. It won't be ready until April next. We can save extra and your bonus will be through by then. Oh Des, we must have it!'

In her excitement she failed to notice the shocked look on her husband's face. It was the mention of the bonus that pushed Des over the edge.

'Damn it woman, you're talking rubbish!,' Des shouted. A hush decended on the room and heads turned. 'Don't you understand – there is no bloody bonus! There will be no villa in Spain because I have no bloody job! I was made redundant the week before we came away on holiday!'

In the deathly silence that followed Des's outburst people turned away, embarrassed. The man behind the desk stopped smiling and shuffled his papers nervously.

'Des, Des,' Evelyn said in a strained voice. 'What are you saying?' Shock was etched across her face. She put her half finished glass of champagne down on the desk. What a weekend this was turning out to be; last night the disaster at the Sinatra Club in front of all their friends, now this humiliation. 'Don't you realise, even yobbos with tattoos can afford to buy a villa!'

'I don't care about them. All I know is that we can't and that's that!' Des shouted. Now that he had broken the bad news he realised he had to go all the way.

Evelyn was conscious that everyone in the room was listening to the drama. She caught sight of Alo and Mamie, saw them turning away in embarrassment. Thank God she couldn't see Karl and Maria. Maybe they had left before Des's outburst. She saw Mavis the brassy blonde and her husband grinning.

Evelyn fled across the room and out through the front door, her eyes full of tears and her cheeks burning. As she ran down the pathway a car reversed out, drove past her. As it did so Evelyn caught a glimpse of the occupants; Maria was driving and Karl was sitting in the seat beside her, staring ahead. Neither of them waved goodbye or even glanced her way.

— ☾ —

Caroline was strolling down towards the pool area when she first noticed the man with the camcorder. He had it pointed directly towards the pool area and he was so engrossed in what he was filming that he didn't notice her approaching.

Of course it was not unusual to see someone with a camera filming at the poolside. People did it all the time, shooting off rolls of film of friends or family lazing he sunshine or of the children playing in the pool, a memento of the holiday which they would enjoy viewing back home during the winter months.

Still, there was something about the young man with the camera that made Caroline stare as she passed by. He had positioned himself behind a tree, out of sight of the people at the pool area. Perhaps he wanted to catch his subject off guard, Caroline thought. She had a sneaking suspicion, however, that he was not filming for fun.

As she came level with the man he lowered the camera and saw her staring. He looked a bit guilty, then smiled. He was thirtyish, athletic looking, wearing a nice line in designer shorts and top.

'Hello,' he said pleasantly.

'Good evening,' Caroline replied politely. 'Doing a spot of filming? That's an expensive looking camera you have there – ' It wasn't exactly sparkling conversation but it was the best she could muster under the circumstances.

'Er – yes,' he said hesitantly. 'Professionals like myself always use top equipment.'

Caroline looked towards the area of the pool where he had had his camera focused. 'Are you interested in that couple, Gerry and Fiona? They came out on the flight with us. Do you know them?'

'Know them….?' He hesitated. 'Er, yes. Matter of fact I do. Sort of.'

He didn't seem very sure. 'We suspect they're on honeymoon,' Caroline said, 'although they haven't said as much.' In the distance she could see Fiona rubbing sun tan oil onto Gerry's back. 'I suppose you're shooting a film of them as a memento. A surprise. Am I right?'

'Good guess. It'll be a surprise wedding present for them – from a friend - when they return to Dublin.' He smiled. 'You won't tell them, will you? I mean it would spoil everything.' The ability to think on one's feet was a vital element of his profession. 'By the way, I didn't catch your name?'

'It's Caroline. I didn't catch yours…'

He hesitated again. 'Just call me Michael. Are you staying here, in the hotel?'

'Yes. The apartments.'

'You see a lot of Fiona and her – her new husband then?'

'Not really. They keep very much to themselves. They've hired a car and go touring almost every day. I've only spoken to them once since I arrived…' She saw he was putting his camcorder back into a leather bag. 'Have you finished filming for the day?'

'Yes. I reckon I've got all I want for the moment. I'm going to enjoy a nice cool drink. Care to join me, Caroline?'

She shook her head. 'Thanks for the offer. But I'd rather just stroll around if you don't mind. Maybe another time if you're still around.' As she smiled and waved him goodbye, Caroline wondered what her mother would think if she knew her daughter was being offered drink by strange men. She could feel his eyes following her as she continued her walk.

Michael Taylor watched Caroline until she was out of sight around the trees. He scolded himself for being so careless. Private investigators were not supposed to be caught red handed filming their quarry. He shrugged. The film he had of Sean Davenport's beautiful young wife laughing and whispering seductively as she rubbed sun tan oil onto her companion's back spoke louder than words. It was exactly the type of evidence he was being paid to produce.

He looked over and saw Fiona and her boyfriend rise from their sunbeds, both of them slipping into sandals and tops. Michael Taylor watched as they headed towards the poolside bar, saw them select a table shaded by trees and give the waiter an order. So they were going to have a cool drink. His eyes switched to the empty table beside them. If he was lucky he might just be able to record their conversation. It was worth a try….

Neither Fiona nor Gerry gave a second glance to the lone man in the shades who took a seat at the table just a short distance from them. In fact he was not in their eyeline. Michael Taylor selected the chair directly behind Fiona's boyfriend that had him hidden from their view. It allowed him dangle his pin-headed, super-sensitive recording device over he side of his table nearest the couple. He was so close that he could even hear snatches of their conversation.

Their good humour had evaporated and now they seemed to be having a bit of a spat.

'Oh, for heaven's sake Gerry darling,' he heard Davenport's erring wife say, 'will you stop worrying about your kids. You're spoiling the last few days of our holiday!'

'Sorry Fiona. I just can't help it. I suppose it's all the kids playing around that reminds me…'

'Get them out of your mind,' Fiona snapped. 'It's becoming a bit boring. Besides – ' she smiled, 'you had other things on your mind last night, as I recall…'

'We both had too much to drink,' Gerry muttered. 'I had anyway.'

'Nonsense darling. You were superb. Ten out of ten.'

'That all? I thought I might have done a bit better than that!'

'Actually you did. Make that eleven.' They both laughed, waited until the waiter had served their drinks and departed.

'Of course I expect an encore tonight, my pet,' Fiona looked at him over the rim of her glass.

'My God, Fiona, you're insatiable!'

'And you're divine, Gerry darling.' More laughter. Gerry seemed to have suddenly forgotten about his kids.

After a while he said, 'What about Sean?'

'What about him?'

'Supposing he finds out about us?'

'Will you stop worrying! He won't find out about us.'

'What makes you so sure, Fiona?'

'Because my dear devoted husband is so busy making money he doesn't have time for anything else. To Sean making money is better than sex!'

'He's no fool. He must suspect something.'

'So what if he does?', Fiona replied irritably. 'You leave my husband to me. I know how to handle him.'

'You do love him, I suppose?'

Fiona didn't answer. Instead she began to sing the Tina Turner number…'What's love got to do, got to do, got to do with it – ' She broke off, laughed. 'Of course I love my husband. Not sexually, though – ' A giggle this time. 'I have you for that, Gerry darling…'

Gerry toyed with his bottle of Bud, sighed. 'You know, I still can't believe I've got myself involved with the boss's wife.'

'Well you have, and in case you have forgotten you didn't need much coaxing. Now stop worrying and let's enjoy the rest of the holiday.' Fiona paused, then went on. 'Remember you're not the only husband who's straying. I know several of my married girlfriends who have enjoyed the odd fling. It's a nice change from our work for charity, gives us something to giggle about!'

'These friends of yours – the so-called Ladies Who Lunch – don't they obey any rules?'

'Of course they do, silly – when it suits them!' A sigh. 'The trouble with you, Gerry, is that you have a guilty conscience. Now finish up your drink, I want you back at the pool to rub some Factor Five on my shoulders. Oh, and Gerry darling, do try to look like you're enjoying being with me!'

Michael Taylor watched them as they retracted their steps back towards the pool. His work for the day wasn't finished just yet. His eyes were glued on the departing Fiona and her sway of her shapely posterior under the sarong she had tied at her waist. He had to admit that she was some beauty. He would get some pleasure from filming her lying down topless on her sunbed, having her shoulders rubbed by Gerry. The evidence would be for Sean Davenport's eyes only.

CHAPTER THIRTEEN

Jose had intended to return with Georgia to Figueretas on Sunday evening, but it was so pleasant relaxing in the large room with his mother and aunt, and with Georgia by his side, that he was perfectly happy.

When he announced that they would stay in the villa overnight Georgia thought the Contessa looked a little alarmed. Despite the fleeting look his mother said, 'Jose, this is your home and you don't have to ask permission to stay. I will ask Maria to check that the guest room is ready and that your young lady has everything she needs.' Georgia noted that the Contessa did not call her by her first name.

Pilar stood up. 'I will tell Maria to check the room. Whenever you wish, Madelina, you can retire to bed and I will look after Georgia.'

The Contessa was pleased. If her sister-in-law said she would look after Jose's girl she would do just that, even if she had to sit up all night. Madelina and her sister-in-law got on well together; she was always there when needed and ever ready to help. Herself and Pilar were about the same age but Pilar was by far more forward-looking than the Contessa.

About an hour later the ladies decided to retire for the night. Jose kissed them both goodnight, said he would retire also. He knew his aunt too well for him to try to slip into Georgia's room during the night. Pilar fussed over Georgia, making sure that she was comfortable in the rather old-style bedroom with its large bed and timbered ceiling. When the older woman left the room it was well past midnight.

Before leaving, Pilar told Georgia some stories of Jose's childhood and the joy he had brought into her own life. Now that Jose had grown into manhood his mother was anxious he should marry so that in time his children could inherit the estate. But it wasn't always easy; Jose had had many girlfriends and had brought several prospective wives home to meet his mother. Always the Contessa had voiced disapproval of her son's choice.

Before she departed Pilar turned and said rather wistfully, 'Remember Georgia, love is the only thing worth fighting for in this life. When you find it grasp it with both hands and never let go. When I was your age I unfortunately did not take that advice.' With that she closed the door softly behind her and was gone.

The words ran through Georgia's mind time and time again as she got undressed. She put on the full-length nightie that Maria the maid had laid out for her. Despite her best efforts she could not fall asleep, her mind was so active with the day's events. As she listened to the stillness the only sound was the chimes each quarter-hour of the big clock in the entrance hall. She thought of her own small bedroom back in Finglas; it would be no hardship to get accustomed to these surroundings, she thought! Wealth and good taste exuded from every room in the Contessa's house. Nothing was too loud or too vulgar.

Surely everyone was asleep by now. Georgia listened, slipped out of bed and put on the wrap that had been placed at the end of the bed. If she was careful and tip-toed down to Jose's room perhaps no one would hear her. She would love to slip in beside him, feel his body close to hers. He was probably waiting for her... Moonlight was streaming in through the window as, with the skill of a burglar, she gently opened her bedroom door. She was halfway down the oak walled corridor when she trod on a loose board. It squeeked and she froze. To her horror a door opened.

'Georgia dear' Pilar whispered, 'do you wish for something?'

Georgia had to think quickly. 'I -I'm going to the kitchen. I need a drink of water – '

Pilar frowned. 'I instructed Maria to leave you a cool drink beside your bed? Come, let us check...'

Caught! Pilar lead the way into the room, switched on the light, pointed. 'There. Maria is so thorough. Let me pour you a drink and then you must go to sleep. You have an early start in the morning.'

Georgia accepted the drink, sipped it. 'Thank you, Pilar. I hope I did not waken you.'

Pilar smiled, gathered her dressing-gown around her slim figure. 'I was not asleep. I was listening for Jose. He has a nasty habit of walking in his sleep when he brings girlfriends home!' She laughed. 'Do not worry, Georgia, the Contessa will not be told.'

Seconds later Georgia was back in bed, feeling frustrated, staring at the ceiling in the moonlight. So much for a nocturnal visit to Jose. She would do what she did at home when she could not sleep - count sheep!

It came as something of a relief several hours later when Maria entered the bedroom to tell Georgia that breakfast would be served for herself and Jose in about 15 minutes. It didn't take Georgia very long to have a shower and slip into the blouse and skirt she had worn the previous day. In the kitchen Jose was already seated and tucking into his breakfast. Georgia accepted a cup of strong coffee but refused to have anything to eat. She did not tell Jose about her nocturnal encounter with Pilar during the night. She prayed that Pilar would keep her word and not say anything about it also. Even though the Contessa wasn't present she could feel the influence of Jose's mother.

On the drive back to Figueretas in the open-top car Georgia closed her eyes and let the breeze fan her face. Jose glanced sideways at her. 'What are you thinking of querida?' he asked.

Georgia kept her eyes closed. 'The Number 34 bus from Finglas!' she laughed. It wasn't the truth. She had actually been thinking of what would have happened had Pilar not intervened in the process of sneaking into Jose's room during the night. But she wasn't going to tell Jose that. When he looked puzzled she went on, 'I have to queue every morning for the No.34 bus to get to work, she explained.'

Jose took one of his hands off the steering wheel and squeezed hers. 'When we are married and you come to live here you will drive your own car. Then there will be room for one more person on that bus,' he vowed.

Back in Figueretas, outside the Hotel Orlando, Georgia refused his offer for lunch but promised to call into his bar later. He kissed her tenderly and whispered 'Not too much1ater, please. I wish to be with you every moment of the day.'

She entered the apartment quietly, tip-toeing past the bedroom where Bernice and Alison were still asleep and out onto the balcony. She wondered if Alison had had a date last night with Miguel and if so and why she was back in her own bed.

Out on the balcony she relaxed and let the early morning sun warm her face. She was about to doze off when Alison appeared. She looked like she had been crying.

'Alison, what's wrong?' Georgia asked, concerned.

'It's Miguel. He's been cheating on me. I was coming back into our apartment to get ready for our date last night when I saw him with a tall blonde under the trees. They were kissing passionately!'

'What did you do?'

'Nothing. It was so embarrassing. Miguel looked up and saw me. They went inside into her apartment, Alison let out a wail. 'He's a rat. I hate him!'

'Of course you do. But you're old enough to know that the Miguel's of this world are like the bumble bee, they fly from flower to flower – '

'Is that so?' Alison wasn't impressed with Georgia's slice of philosophy. She had expected more sympathy from her friend. 'What about your Jose?', she snapped. 'How d'you know he's not a bumble bee too?

Georgina realised Alison must really fancy Miguel. This was a serious romance – at least on her side but obviously not on Miguel's. 'Sit there, Alison,' she said. 'Dry your tears and I'll make some coffee. We'll have a chat. There's something I have to tell you and Bernice.'

Bernice joined them on the balcony when Georgia brought out the coffee. 'What are you two doing today?, ' she asked.

'Brian has to go to the hospital for a blood test. He told me it would take most of the day so Alison and I booked on a cruise around the island. It should be fun, there's music and partying on board – '

'I don't feel like going now. ' Alison said. 'Not after seeing what Miguel was up to with that blonde - '

'Forget about Miguel. Let him see you're not depending on him,' Georgia advised. 'That cruise sounds fun. There'll be a lot of male talent there.' Alison didn't look too impressed.

'Anyway, never mind about us, Georgia. Tell us how you got on in the country with Jose's mother.' Bernice nudged Alison. 'Was she nice?'

This was Georgia's big moment and she made the most of it. Her Da always said that truth was stranger than fiction. Not that he was into reading books; studying the racing pages of the newspapers was more in his line. But still, for once she had to agree with him.

'Girls, ' she said. 'What would you say if I told you that you are now looking at the future Contessa Georgia Simon?' She put on what she presumed to be a regal air.

Alison and Bernice stared at her. She could see she had their undivided attention. 'We're looking at what?' Bernice asked.

'A Contessa, ' Georgia replied

Alison had suddenly forgotten about Miguel. 'You – a Contessa?. Isn't that someone with a title?' She gave a sneering laugh. 'Come off it, Georgia – I know the sort of title they'd give you in Finglas!'

'What's a Contessa?' Bernice asked again quickly. Anxious to avoid a slanging match between her two friends.

Georgia gave Bernice a withering look. 'A Contessa is the wife of a Count' , she answered.

'A Count! -You mean as in Count Dracula? ' Bernice looked puzzled.

'Georgia, you have as much chance of becoming a Contessa as I have of becoming one of the Spice Girls?' , Alison snorted. She was taking her break-up with Miguel very badly.

'If I agree to marry Jose that's what I'll become in time' Georgia replied calmly. 'His mother is very rich. You should see their hacienda – when I saw it first I thought it was a hotel!'

Alison and Bernice both stared again. 'You mean Jose asked you to marry him?' , Bernice's eyes were wide with amazement.

'Yes, when we were walking under the lemon trees. It was very romantic.'

'Oh Georgia, we're delighted for you. Aren't we, Alison?' When there was no response Bernice went on. 'When is the wedding?'

'I don't know. I haven't accepted Jose's proposal yet. A girl has to keep a man waiting. If it happens I'll want both of you as my bridesmaids.'

Alison sniffed. 'Thanks very much, but I'm not holding my breath!' Trust Georgia to fall on her feet. It was always the same. Georgia ends up with a title while I couldn't even hang on to a barman! 'What will your Ma say when you tell her you're going to marry a Count?'

'My Ma - I mean my mother - will probably be delighted. Who else in Finglas has married into high society?'

'The nearest would be Miranda O'Brien who lives four doors from you', Bernice answered. 'She's an air hostess with Ryanair! She walks around with her nose in the air. My father says she's permanently on the look-out for aeroplanes!' They all laughed.

Alison and Bernice were anxious to hear more about Jose and his mother the Contessa, but Georgia said she was exhausted. She decided to go to bed for a few hours to get some sleep. She had a lot to think about and wanted to be alone.

'Come on, Alison, we'd better be getting ready for this cruise,' Bernice said. She would have much preferred to spend the day with Brian - they were getting on so well together it was almost too good to be true - but Alison needed cheering up. They spent the next hour getting ready while Georgia retired to the bedroom.

Later. when they alighted from the taxi and were climbing aboard the sailing ship with its skull-and-crossbones flag and the handsome male crew members dressed as pirates, Bernice began to think that maybe they were in for a good time after all.

Wayne was chuffed at his own genius in getting Caroline to accompany him on the pirate cruise around the island. It hadn't been easy, but so far so good. On the pier waiting to board Wayne looked around the other eager faces about to spend the day afloat. There was some great female talent on show. He could hardly wait for the action to start!

Caroline found it difficult to trust Wayne, especially after his behaviour at the disco a week ago when he had tried to get her drunk. This cruise was by way of an apology for his actions, he had told her contritely. Caroline would never have taken up his offer only he'd sworn Mark was to accompany them. But where was Mark? So far there was no sign of him.

She turned her thoughts to the pirate ship they were to spend the day cruising on. It certainly stood out among the other craft at the pier. Flashily painted, the masthead had a carved top half of a voluptuous woman winking broadly. A Jolly Roger flag on the mast fluttered in the breeze. The 'Pretty Molly' looked like something straight out of a cartoon. Caroline gazed in awe at the queue of young people waiting to board for the pirate cruise. Some of the skimpy outfits the girls were wearing left a lot to be desired!

'Well Caroline, what do you think?', Wayne asked.

'Sorry, what did you say. I was miles away – '

'The ship, doesn't it look great?' Wayne asked, lowering his Raybans for the first time that morning. 'I bet we're in for a good time.'

'It's certainly looks different from any ship I've seen,' Caroline said. She was beginning to have misgivings about having agreed to this island cruise.

She had her swimsuit on under a white blouse and black walking shorts. This crowd were well out of her league. The fellow in front of her had earrings in each ear! She began to panic at the thought of spending a day with this already rowdy bunch. What if Mark didn't turn up? Oh God, she felt weak at the knees.

'Caroline! Caroline! Up here.' Someone was calling out to her. She looked up. On deck at the bow of the ship, Bernice and Alison were frantically waving down at her.

'Hello Bernice! Hello Alison!' Caroline waved, delirious with relief at seeing someone she knew. 'Look Wayne who's aboard,' she said.

That's ruined it, Wayne thought to himself, scowling behind his dark glasses. Just his luck! He tried not to let Caroline notice his reaction. Alison and Bernice were spoilsports, turning up where they weren't wanted. His plan to have Caroline to himself for the whole day was in tatters. Stupid cows!

A tall, tanned young man - Captain Boney according to the gold lettering on his sailor's cap – stood at the gangplank welcoming everyone on board. He promised everyone a fun-filled day aboard his ship, pleased to see that the mixture of males to females was just about right.

Up on deck bodies were sprawled on sunbeds catching the sun's rays. Caroline insisted on keeping a spare sunbed for Mark although she suspected he wasn't on board. She cleverly placed the sunbed between herself and Wayne. She had intended joining Bernice and Alison after boarding but there was no room to stretch out where they were.

A short while after they set sail crew members weaved in and out of the sunbathers serving long, cool glasses of Sangria from the ship's bar. The sun was now high in the sky and bottles of sun tan lotion began to make their appearance.

Caroline was relaxing on her stomach with her eyes closed when she felt cold drops of lotion falling on her bare back. Opening her eyes she saw that Wayne had moved across and was preparing to rub the sun tan oil into her skin.

'What do you think you're doing?' she asked coldly.

'Sorry Caroline, I don't want you burning up. You need some protection on your back and legs – '

'It seems the only thing I need protection from is you Wayne,' she answered indignantly. 'I'm capable of rubbing my own sun tan oil on myself!'

'Hey handsome, you can oil me up anytime you like. That's an offer. What do you say?' A female voice cut in. Caroline swung right around swiftly. She came face to face with a stunning looking girl, lying unashamedly topless on the sunbed next to her. Caroline tried to avert her eyes. She knew she was blushing from head to toe with embarrassment. The girl was smiling invitingly across at Wayne.

Caroline wished she was somewhere else, anywhere! She glanced at Wayne. He was smirking, his eyes well hidden behind those darn sunglasses, enjoying the acres of flesh Miss Universe was putting on display.

How did I ever allow myself be talked into this dreadful cruise Caroline scolded herself as she picked up her beach bag and towel and went off in search of Bernice, her head throbbing to the beat of the loud music blaring out as the Pretty Molly nosed it's way out of the harbour and into the open sea.

Wayne was close on her heels but at that moment she could not have cared less if he jumped overboard, she felt bitterly angry with him for having asked her to go on this terrible cruise with him.

What have I done now? Wayne was thinking. Caroline sure is hard to fathom. I've never met such a complicated female before in my life. What am I doing wrong? I only wanted her to break free of that antiquated swimsuit she clings to!

They were about an hour sailing when Captain Boney announced it was time for games. The first game, 'an ice breaker' he called it. An ice breaker? Caroline thought this was funny considering the heat. And when it started she found herself laughing out loud at the antics of some of the competitors. An orange was passed from one person to another without using hands, just the chin. It engaged the players in some very funny entanglements, especially when the orange rolled into the most unlikely hollows and crevices of the various bodies, large and small. Caroline doubled up with laughter, although she was mortified also, at the antics of the various couples. Herself, Alison and Bernice refrained from having a go themselves, but Wayne the eternal ego-tripper had a hilarious innings with his partner in the game, a lissom Swedish blonde whose actions gave the game a whole new meaning,

'Look at what you're missing, Caroline, that could have been you out there wrapped around Wayne,' Bernice said jokingly. Seeing what Wayne and the Swedish girl were getting up to made Caroline shudder. She couldn't believe young people could behave in this manner. Didn't they have morals anymore?

There was ample time for swimming when the 'Pretty Molly' anchored. Wayne enjoyed showing off his diving skills to several female admirers. A pirate plank was the diving board, although some adventurous swimmers dived off the ship. By now all of the female swimmers were topless and those who didn't go in for a swim found themselves other games to engage in aboard ship.

The sea was breathtakingly beautiful. Caroline was very happy to sit on board and look out at the swirling waves and changing blues and abundant colourful marine life it had to offer, her artist's eye taking in everything to adorn a future canvas.

She couldn't help thinking about Mark and why he didn't shown up. She came to the conclusion he didn't know anything about the cruise. Wayne had obviously pulled a trick on both of them. Caroline couldn't see Mark throwing her at Wayne's mercy for an hour never mind a whole day!

She was right; Mark had spent the morning in a bank in Ibiza Town, endeavouring to retrieve his laundered money. He had sat patiently awaiting the manager's verdict on the fragments of over fifteen 5,000 peseta notes, about 400 Irish punts, he had taken in, wrapped in tinfoil. The money had mysteriously ended up in the apartment washing machine with his shorts and T-shirts, washed and tattered almost beyond recognition. He knew he had not left the last of his cash - which he'd changed from travellers' cheques the day before - in the pocket of his shorts. He remembered vividly putting the notes into the apartment safe, which he shared with Wayne.

Wayne obviously had something to do with his money ending up in the wash. Just another one of his crazy pranks. Where had Wayne disappeared to anyway? Mark had not seen him all morning. Caroline was nowhere to be seen either. He had searched the hotel and around the pool without success.

Mark's long wait in the bank ended when a cashier beckoned him enter the manager's office. Good news! Three-quarters of his bank-notes were salvaged! Mark reckoned he was lucky to come out so well, he could have been left penniless for the rest of his holiday. He had a few questions to ask Wayne when he saw him next.

Back on the Pretty Molly the afternoon barbecue and disco was taking place on a beach as part of the cruise. All the passengers and crew invaded the unspoiled white sands where food and drinks were liberally dispensed. The disco dancing became wilder and wilder as the wine and exotic cocktails began to take effect.

'Hey, this is even better than 'Ibiza Uncovered' on Sky One!' Bernice remarked to Alison and Caroline.

An intoxicated Wayne became a real pain, lusting after Caroline, asking her to go topless like most of the other girls. It was a slightly tipsy Alison who obliged instead, flinging off her top and dancing wildly with Wayne while Bernice and Caroline looked on amazed. Bernice explained to Caroline that Alison had been two-timed by Miguel, offering this as an excuse for her friend's behaviour. After an hour of cavorting in the sun it was time to get back on board to sail to the home port.

Back on dry land once more, Caroline, Bernice and a still tipsy Alison walked from the pier arm in arm. Wayne stumbled off happily with a group of Swedish guys and girls, asking Alison to join him. But Bernice persuaded her friend to come back with them to the hotel. Caroline was relieved when she got back to her apartment. She had had her eyes opened to the behaviour of today's young people. Was she a prude to think that morals had declined? Maybe so, but no way would she ever behave in the way she had seen some girls do on the cruise. She certainly had some interesting things to discuss with her friend Maureen Duff next time they met.

Georgia woke up, changed into some fresh clothes, and decided to find a telephone kiosk from which to telephone home. Time to break the news about Jose and herself to her Ma and Da. They were in for a bit of a culture shock!

When she found an empty kiosk she carefully stacked up a supply of coins and dialled the number in Finglas. When she got through heard her mother's voice. 'Hello?'. 'Hello Ma. It's me, Georgia.'

'Georgia! How are you, pet?' She could hear a man's voice in the background. 'Wait till I tell your Da - ' She heard her mother calling him. 'Hello Ma,' Georgia began again. 'What's Da doing at home this time of day? Why isn't he at work?' Her father worked in the Waterworks Department of Dublin Corporation.

'He'd had a bit of an accident - ' 'Oh my God!' Georgia's heart missed a beat. 'An accident! What happened? Is he badly injured?' 'No. Not really, ' her Ma answered casually. 'They were lifting a manhole cover and it fell on his foot. He's not hurt - lucky he had his reinforced boots on, the ones with the steel toecap. His big toe is a bit bruised, that's all.'

'Why isn't he in work then?'

'I'll give you one guess – he's looking for compensation. There's no flies on your Da. He's putting in a claim. Says he's crippled with pain. But it hasn't stopped him wearing a path down to the bookies and the pub. Anyway, how's the holiday going pet?'

'Great Ma. The weather's lovely and we're having a fabulous time.' Georgia hesitated. 'I've something to tell you, Ma, something very important.'

'Important! Oh God! – Georgia! I hope you're not – '
'No Ma, it's nothing like that!'.

'Oh Thank God! Parents can't be sure of anything with the carry-on of you young people nowadays. What is it then if you're not pregnant?' Georgia could hear her mother calling out. 'Paddy, she's something important to tell us – '

'I've met a fella over here, Ma – '

'Is that all!?' Her mother was disappointed. Georgia was always meeting fellas. She could hear the news been being shouted out with relief. 'Your Da wants to know if the fella's from Finglas?,' her mother asked.

'No. He's not from Finglas. His name is Jose.'

'Jose? That's not Irish.'

'Of course it's not. Jose's Spanish. He's mad about me and he's asked me to marry him. He's a Count – '

She could hear her Ma's intake of breath. 'Georgia Fitzgerald, you watch your language now, Miss! You didn't hear that kind of talk in this house!'

Georgia sighed. 'I said he's a Count. Ma. Not the other thing!' She was getting exasperated. ' Tell Da. He'll know what a Count is - ' a short, muffled conversation between in the background, then her Ma came back on the line.

'Your Da wants to know is your boyfriend a count, like that fellow in the film The Count of Monte Cristo?'

Georgia groaned. 'Yes. Tell him yes. Like I said he's gorgeous.'

'Georgia, are you sure this fella is not just fooling you?'

'No Ma. He's genuine. I've met his mother and I've been in his house. It's huge. A hacienda. And guess what - he also owns a bar!'

'A bar! Georgia, that's fantastic! Wait till I tell your Da!' Her mother was shouting out the news. When she came on again she asked: 'Your Da wants to know is your boyfriend's bar as big as The Cappagh House?'

'No Ma, it's not as big as that – '

'Does it sell Guinness? Your Da wants to know does it sell Guinness?'

'Yes Ma, it sell's Guinness. Bottles, and pints on draught-'

'Lovely! Paddy'll be delighted!' Georgia could hear her Da shouting again. 'He says he can't wait to meet Jose. He wants to know how much is the pint in your boyfriend's place? Is it cheaper than The Cappagh House?'

Georgia was beginning to regret telephoning home. 'I don't know, Ma. And I don't care either –' She paused. 'Ma, one more thing before I go – '

'What's that, Georgia?'

'Do you mind if from now I stop calling you both Ma and Da and say Mother and Father instead. I think it sounds nicer.'

'Of course not, Georgia pet. It does sound more respectable. And I mean if you're going to marry a Count...'

'Thanks Ma – I mean Mother!'

The conversation was suddenly interrupted by a scream from her Mother. 'Sorry Georgia, I have to go now.' It sounded like an emergency.

'What's wrong? What happened?'

'It's that stray dog your father brought home from the pub last night. It's barking at the postman. The poor man has dropped all his letters and he's now outside the gate! He'll sue us. 'Bye, pet. Ring again before you come home!'

The line went dead. Georgia sighed, looked at her watch. She would have lunch with Jose, discuss the plans for the gala opening on Wednesday night featuring her Dance of the Seven Veils. Jose was having posters put up in Figueretas and Ibiza and a big crowd was expected. Herself and the girls would organise a group from the Orlando.

Unfortunately the Contessa was coming also. Georgia wasn't looking forward to that.

CHAPTER FOURTEEN

Caroline could barely wait to tell Maureen Duff about her adventures on yesterday's cruise around the island. The carry-on aboard Cap'n Bonaparte's Pretty Molly with its splendid masts and olde-worlde creaking timbers had certainly opened her eyes. In her innocence Caroline had expected a leisurely sail around Ibiza's rugged coast, enjoying the sunshine and the scenery. Nobody had prepared her for the antics of Cap'n Bonaparte's lusty crew and the sex-mad young crowd of revellers – both male and female - who had climbed aboard at Figueretas.

'But wasn't Mark with you? Didn't he look after you?' Maureen asked.

'Mark never showed up,' Caroline explained. 'Wayne invited me along and I assumed that Mark would be there also. Thank God Bernice and Alison came; I don't know what I'd have done without them.'

'You should find out what happened to Mark, ' Maureen said. 'I'm sure there's a reason why he didn't go along.'

'I have a feeling that Wayne had a hand in it, Maureen.'

'How so?'

'Wayne thinks he's real macho but he's really very childish. He likes to be the centre of attention and he expects every girl to fall victim to his charms. I still haven't forgiven him for giving me that very strong drink that first night when I went with the girls to the disco.'

'I rather liked him when I first talked to him and Mark on the way out here', Maureen replied. 'He was very nice to me, he helped me with my luggage, that sort of thing. I accept that his behaviour does turn some people off but I think there's another side to him.'

'He soon lost interest in me when he saw what was available on board the ship. You should have seen his carry-on with some of those girls. I couldn't believe my eyes! ' Caroline paused. 'I have to say he wasn't the only one to - what's the expression? - let it all hang out!'

'No doubt he got lots of encouragement from the others on board,' Maureen replied. She was glad the Reverend Superior wasn't around to hear her young novice nun using the 'let it all hang out' expression. Caroline would have to watch her language when she went back to the convent!

'You wouldn't believe the way some of those girls behaved, ' Caroline said. 'Don't girls have any respect for themselves anymore? I know that sounds prudish, but there are limits.'

Maureen laughed. 'Your forgetting you're in Ibiza, Caroline. Many of those young people who went on that cruise yesterday obviously threw their morals overboard.'

'They certainly did! Bernice and Alison went below decks to see what was going on but I hadn't got the nerve! When they told me what they saw I was glad I didn't go.'

'Did you enjoy anything at all about the trip?' Maureen asked.

'We did stop in a lovely little bay at one stage and almost everyone including Bernice, Alison and myself, had a swim over the side. That was fun.' Caroline paused, laughed despite herself. 'I think we were the only ones wearing swimsuit tops!

'So how do you feel about things now?,' Maureen asked. 'Are you sorry you came to Ibiza?'

'Not at all. I'm seeing a whole new world I never thought existed. Not my kind of world. mind you. But interesting nevertheless.' Caroline paused. 'Maybe seeing how the other half lives is the best thing that could have happened to me. Amazing the way God works. isn't it, Maureen?'

'Sounds like you're getting yourself sorted out. I presume you're get a chance to tell Wayne and the girls about your being a nun and the convent and all that?'

'You must be joking! Had I mentioned I was a nun on that trip I'd have been thrown overboard!'

They were relaxing in a small park overlooking the beach. The profusion of colour from the flowers and shrubs was eye-catching and Caroline knew she would be returning with her pad and paints before the holiday was over. 'What have been the highlights of your holiday so far, Caroline?'

'The beautiful countryside has been ideal for someone like myself who likes sketching. I've been fortunate to get some scenes down on paper. And of course I also enjoyed the trip around the island with Mark.'

'Have you thought about the discussion we had on Sunday?'

'Yes. Talking over my problems with you, Maureen, and going on that cruise yesterday, has really helped me see my situation more clearly. I'm looking forward to getting back and moving on with my life.'

'I take it then you've made up your mind about where you're going, what you want to do?'

Caroline nodded. 'There's an old Chinese proverb which says 'God writes straight with crooked lines' .I understand what that means now.'

'Good. Now, to other things. Are you going to the gala night in Jose's Hacienda tomorrow?'

'Yes. I suppose as a nun I shouldn't say this, but I'm looking forward to seeing Georgia doing Salome's Dance of the Seven Veils. The posters are very daring. I expect the place will be packed - mainly with men! 'Caroline laughed. 'That's when I seem to get into trouble!'

'Don't worry Caroline dear, I'll be there to keep an eye on you.'

Despite her experience on the cruise yesterday Caroline wondered if she really wanted her friend Maureen as a minder tomorrow night. After all this could well be her last opportunity to enjoy herself, let her hair down. First thing she would have to do when she went home would be to go to Confession!

Later that afternoon. Caroline was strolling among a vast number of bodies sunning themselves at the poolside seeking an empty sunbed when she spotted Fiona and Gerry. It brought to mind the photographer she had come across videoing them from the trees a couple of days ago. She had not seen the young man since. Maybe he had completed his video on the honeymooning couple and gone home.

In her innocence Caroline had always assumed that both Fiona and Gerry were on their honeymoon. As far as she was concerned the fact that they kept so much to themselves and rarely mixed with other couples gave the game away.

She was surprised when Fiona looked up from the book the was reading and smiled a greeting. 'Hi.' Fiona said. 'Going to have a swim?'

'I will shortly,' Caroline replied. 'I want to get some sun first -if I can get an empty sunbed. They all seem occupied. I've never seen so many people lying out in the sun. ...'

'Here. take mine. ' Gerry offered. He stood up 'I want to have a plunge. Unlike Fiona I can't take too much sun.' He rose, went to the edge of the pool, dived in.

They watched him do a powerful crawl stroke towards the far end.

'Enjoying the holiday?'. Fiona asked.

'Oh yes. but aren't the days flying in. It's hard to believe we're nearly halfway into our second week already.'

'Meet any fellas?' Fiona smiled. 'Those two handsome hunks that came over on our flight seemed to fancy you no end. Have you been out with either of them?'

'Er, yes. I went on a cruise around the island with Wayne yesterday.' Caroline paused.

'Well go on, what happened? Did you have a good time?'

'Not really. The carry-on on board was embarrassing. A lot of people had too much to drink. Wayne included. It wasn't very nice.'

'What did you expect?' Fiona laughed. 'This is Ibiza, the island where anything goes. That's why Gerry and I hired a car for the fortnight. We avoid the riff-raff. We've had an absolutely fabulous time so far.' She paused. 'What about Wayne's buddy? He looks nice.'

'Mark is very nice, ' Caroline agree. 'but I didn't come to Ibiza to meet a fella. Quite the opposite in fact.'

'Really?' She saw Fiona studying her. 'You must be the only girl on this island who isn't interested in men! What did you come here for if not to have fun?'

'I came to relax, enjoy the sun, do some sketching, sort myself out.' She wished she hadn't said that last bit. It sounded like she was a nut case with big problems. Maybe she was!

'Look. take my advice. Caroline. enjoy yourself while the going is good. You're an attractive girl with a good figure. You could have a really good time with the blokes. So what's your problem?'

Caroline shrugged. 'I'd rather not talk about it if you don't mind,' she said. She decided she had better change the subject. She didn't want Fiona delving into her past. 'You've got a lovely tan, ' she said.

'Thank You.' Fiona got the message. A broken romance, she supposed, a marriage break-up, or a question of sexuality. Whatever it was Caroline obviously didn't want to delve into it. Oh well, time was too short to worry about other people's problems. 'Gerry makes sure I have lots of cream on so that I don't peel.' Fiona smiled, her small, perfect white teeth showing up in her tanned face.

'He's very attentive, your husband,' Caroline said. She had opened her bottle of sun tan lotion and was covering her legs and shoulders. 'You're both on honeymoon, aren't you?'

This time Fiona laughed outright. 'However did you guess? Oh, I suppose it shows – '

'The man with the camera said so.'

She saw Fiona's smile freeze, then fade. 'Man? What man?'

'Oh, I wasn't supposed to tell you. A man with an expensive camera -a camcorder, I think they call them. I noticed him on Sunday when I was walking down towards the pool. He was filming yourself and Gerry –'

'Really?' Fiona put down her book.

'He was behind one of those trees over there.' Caroline pointed. 'I think he was a bit annoyed that I spotted him. We got chatting and I asked him what he was doing.'

'Good for you, Caroline. What did he say?'

'He said he was filming yourself and Gerry on your honeymoon. I know I probably shouldn't be telling you this, Fiona, it was supposed to be a surprise for you -,

'A surprise? It certainly is that,' Fiona muttered, as if talking to herself. 'But then again....' She paused, brightened up, smiled. 'Of course, I know what it's all about-' Caroline waited for her to continue. 'I suspect Gerry is behind it. He's planning this film of our honeymoon as a surprise for me. ' She laughed. He's such a darling –'

'Oh, and I've gone and spoiled it for you, Fiona. I'm sorry, I shouldn't have told you. -' Caroline was mortified.

'Not at all, Caroline. I'm glad you did. Don't worry. I won't say anything to Gerry. I'll let him surprise me when we get home. Be a dear and don't mention anything to anyone about this, will you?'

'If you wish.' Caroline thought it odd that Fiona looked so worried. She decided to change the subject yet again. 'Are you and Gerry going to Jose's Hacienda tomorrow

night? There's a big group going from our hotel to see
Georgia performing there.'

Fiona's thoughts were still on the mysterious
cameraman. 'What is Jose's Hacienda and who is Georgia?'
she asked absent-mindedly. When Caroline explained
about the gala night and Georgia performing her Dance of
the Seven Veils, Fiona shook her head disdainfully.

'Sorry. I'm afraid that's not our scene,' she said. 'Besides,
Gerry and I have planned a romantic evening in the
Sacapella Restaurant in San Antonio tomorrow night.
They say they serve the best seafood on the island there.'

They chatted for a few more minutes until Gerry
returned dripping from the pool. Caroline rose from the
sunbed and decided to find one for herself. She had the
distinct impression that Fiona wanted to be alone with
Gerry. She said goodbye and moved off.

They both watched Caroline make her way to a vacant
sunbed over the other side of the pool. 'Not a bad looker'.
Gerry remarked.

Fiona turned to him. 'Darling, I think we're in trouble.'

'Trouble?' He stopped drying his hair with the towel.
He could see by Fiona's expression this was serious. 'What
do you mean?'

She filled him in on what Caroline had told her about
the man in the trees with the camcorder. He looked
concerned. He collapsed rather than sat down on his
sunbed'. staring at her. 'You think Sean is behind this?' he
asked.

'Who else?'

Gerry's tan had turned rather pasty. 'But you've phoned
him a couple of times since we arrived here, pretended you
were in he south of France with your friends. You told me
that Sean didn't suspect a thing. So how come – '

'How the hell do I know,' Fiona cut in sharply.

'You must have got careless, Fiona, told one of your
friends about us.'

'That's right! Go on, blame me! How do I know you didn't say something stupid to that wife of yours before we came away!' They were at each other's throats now, on a guiltrip, not caring what they said.

Gerry looked strained. 'Oh God. What if Sandra finds out? She'll leave me, take the kids – '

'What about me!' Fiona hissed 'Sean will kick me out. I'll be left with nothing!'

The two of them were silent, lost in their own thoughts, oblivious to the shouts and screams coming from the crowded pool.

'What are we going to do, Fiona?' Gerry asked after a while. 'I think we should catch the next plane home, face the music, try to sort things out – '

Gerry was panicking, Fiona could sense it. As soon as things go wrong he wants back with his dowdy wife and the kids. Well, she wasn't prepared to wave the white flag just yet. 'We'll find out first if Sean really knows what's going on between us. When we know for sure we'll make up our minds on what to do.'

Gerry looked at her aghast. 'You're not going to telephone him are you?'

'Don't be silly, Gerry. I'm not that stupid,' she hissed. My God he really was cracking up.

'How will you find out then?' he asked.

He saw Fiona smile. 'I'll do what I would do if I was on Who Wants To Be A Millionaire –

'What's that, for God's sake?'

Fiona rose before replying. 'I'm going to phone a friend!'

Gerry watched her bikinied figure weave in and out of the sunbeds. He saw several male heads turn and study Fiona's progress with interest. He was beginning to wish he had never set foot in Ibiza.

— ☽ —

Irene applied the cream to her white shoes and left them in the sun to dry. She felt lazy today and decided to crash out on the lounger on the balcony until Benjamin came back from his swim.

She lay down and let her mind wander. Hard to believe that they were coming towards the last days of the holiday. It seemed like only yesterday that they had flown out from Dublin Airport. The group of people they had come to the Hotel Orlando with had bonded well. All except that couple Gerry and Fiona, they rarely mixed and when they did appear at the poolside they spent more time rubbing sun cream on each other. Irene wondered if they were married a all. Honeymooners? – she had her suspicions!

As for Des and Evelyn Murtagh, they reminded her of Benjamin and herself – everything alright on the surface, but underneath things not going well. But then a lot of couples were like that. It had taken this holiday to show up the rut herself and Benjamin had sunk into.

Of course Ben always did have an eye for a pretty woman. Why then had she been surprised when Paula Sheridan had let it slip that she had known Benjamin in Dublin when she was a young civil servant? Was it jealousy on her part? Paula was a lovely lady - and when they had met Benjamin would have been old enough to be her father! Funny the way he was always on edge when Paula was near. ...

Irene genuinely liked Paula and her lovely daughter Vicki, who was not unlike their own daughter Deirdre and was almost the same age. She wondered what Benjamin would say to her idea of inviting Vicki to come to Dublin and visit them sometime.

She heard Benjamin let himself into the apartment. He came out onto the balcony. 'You look nice and relaxed,' he said, giving her a peck on the cheek. 'Pity you didn't come for a swim in the sea. The water was lovely.'

'Lucky for you I didn't', Irene said, without opening her eyes.

'What do you mean?'

'I went for a bit of a stroll myself, met Paula Sheridan and Vicki in the foyer when I came back. They had been to the beach also. Vicki left and Paula and I had a bit of a chat –'Irene opened her eyes, shaded them from the sun when she looked at him.

'And?'

'She enquired about you. Asked where you were'

Ben didn't say anything. He was wary of discussing anything about Paula with Irene. He leaned on the balcony and stared down to the pool area below. It was crowded with sun worshippers as usual.

Irene was speaking again. 'Paula said the manager at the Hotel Tropicana where we're having our anniversary dinner is a personal friend of hers. She has offered to contact him to ask the head chef to prepare a special meal for us on Thursday night – '

'Has she now? How very kind of her.'

'You don't sound very pleased with her offer, Benjamin.'

'I'm not. It's our anniversary, Irene. Couldn't we arrange one night out on our own without all this fuss.' Ben was uneasy. He got even more so when Irene spoke again.

'Paula says she has arranged a surprise for us on the night –'

'A surprise?' Ben turned from studying the pool area, looked at Irene. He didn't like the sound of this. 'What sort of surprise?'

'She wouldn't tell me –except to say I was to make sure you took me up to dance.'

What did that mean? Why did Paula want him up dancing? She was up to something, Ben was convinced of that. He didn't want a surprise on his anniversary, he'd had enough surprises already on this holiday! Aloud he said, 'Paula has done enough for us already. I wish she would leave it be and let us enjoy ourselves.'

'Don't be so ungracious, Benjamin,' Irene said sharply. 'She's only trying to help. I like Paula Sheridan. I find her very nice, interesting to talk to. Not like some of them on this holiday whom we won't mention. When I had that migraine last week Paula was very sympathetic, looked after me.'

Ben was getting nervous, exasperated. 'I thought, Irene, we came to Ibiza for a nice relaxing holiday and to celebrate our wedding anniversary. I wish you'd let us get on with doing just that!' Irene was taken aback. Benjamin had never spoken to her like that before!

With that Ben turned on his heel and exited. He went downstairs and out into the sunshine. He needed a drink. If only he had someone to confide in, someone he could unburden himself to. He began to walk.

Not far from the hotel was the Gardenia Bar. Ben decided it was just the place he was looking for. Inside it was cool, quiet and at that time of day almost empty. Ben sat at a table in the corner, ordered a beer. He was lost in thought when he heard a voice.

'Ben, my oul' mate. On your own are you. Mind if I join you'?

He looked up. It was Doc Holliday, looking resplendent in a canary yellow T-shirt and white slacks. 'Hello Doc, how are things? Get yourself a drink and sit down.'

When Doc had done just that he said breezily, 'Well Ben, I suppose you and Irene are going to the gala night in Jose's Hacienda tomorrow night? Maureen and I are going, and so are a lot of people from the hotel. Georgia's boyfriend is organising a special table for all of us. I must say I'm looking forward to seeing that Georgia one doing the Dance of the Seven Veils. It promises to be some night!'

Ben hadn't a clue what Doc was talking about. But when his companion explained what the gala night was about he was interested. Irene might turn up her nose, but like Doc, he wasn't going to miss the chance of seeing that young redhead with the fine figure dancing about in see-through veils. No way!

'Irene and I will be there. It's just the tonic I need right now,' Ben said.

Doc studied him closely. 'Something wrong?' he asked. 'You look a bit down in the dumps. What's the problem, Ben? Want to talk about it? ,

Ben was silent, thinking. It would be good to talk to someone. He had been bottling this whole thing up inside for days. 'I'm going to tell you something, Doc,' he said sombrely, 'and I want you to give me your word that it'll remain a secret between you and me.'

The smile disappeared from Doc's face. He reckoned it must be something serious for Ben O'Rourke to talk like that. 'You have my word, Ben. What's bothering you?'

Ben toyed with his drink. 'You're a betting man Doc. What odds would you give on me bringing my wife on holiday to Ibiza, and for me to bump into an old flame with whom I had a brief fling in Dublin many moons ago, and her with a beautiful teenage daughter that I never knew I had?'

It took Doc several seconds to take it all in. Slowly he absorbed what Ben had recounted. Doc had had his own adventures thus far on this holiday, but what had happened to Ben O'Rourke was something else. A former girlfriend with a teenage daughter suddenly appearing from nowhere…

'What about Irene. Does she suspect anything?'

'That's the worst part. Sometimes I feel she does. Irene knows that the lady and I met years ago in Dublin. The two of them have met here in Ibiza and really get on very well together. The lady is even helping to set up a special twenty-fifth anniversary dinner for Irene and myself!' Ben paused, took a swig of his drink. 'The tension is getting to me, Doc. I feel like I'm cracking up.'

'I'm not surprised Ben. It's a tough one to deal with.' Poor Ben - he was living on a knife edge. 'Mind my asking who this lady is? You don't have to tell me if you don't want to, Ben.'

Ben swallowed another mouthful of brandy and ginger. 'You won't believe this, Doc. It's Paula Sheridan!'

Doc couldn't hide his surprise. 'You mean our Paula - the Irish lady who works in the hotel?' When Ben nodded Doc stared in disbelief.

'I still can't believe something like this is happening to me. It was all so long ago. What am I going to do. Doc?'

Doc considered for a moment. 'What's Paula doing or saying in all of this?'

'I feel she's secretly enjoying seeing me squirm. I have to admit I didn't go out of my way to find out what happened to her after we split up and she had the baby.' Ben sighed. 'Now it looks like it's payback time for Paula.'

'Do you think she'll tell Irene about your affair?' Doc asked.

'She has promised not to.' Ben replied. 'I couldn't cope if the story came out now after all those years. It would ruin our marriage. And just imagine the whispers among the neighbours and the crowd in our local pub. I can't figure out if Paula is playing a game. getting all friendly with Irene. She told me she won't hurt Irene but I'm afraid something will slip out. What will I do then?'

Doc sat back in his chair, pondered a moment. 'I appreciate you telling me all this. Ben. Want to know what I would do? I'd make sure Irene enjoys the rest of the holiday - especially your anniversary dinner. Pull out all the stops, buy her a special piece of jewellery for the occasion, a bunch of flowers - the lot. Reverse the downward spiral and get the old romance back on track!'

For the first time that day Ben felt relieved. 'Thanks, Doc. That's not a bad bit of advice. I feel happier now that I've talked to you.'

Doc smiled. 'Think nothing of it. Now maybe you can give me a bit of advice. You know that Maureen Duff and I have hit it off together - and I don't mean only on the dance floor!

'Yes, and a very nice lady too. Has a touch of class about her. You wouldn't be doing too badly if you threw your cap in there, Doc – if you wanted to, that is.'

'That's part of the problem, Ben, do I want to - and does Maureen want to? The other part of the problem is I've met this Spanish lady. Very attractive, a widow with two teenage sons -' Doc paused. 'I can't go into too many details about her, anyway get two more drinks and I'll fill you in a bit more..'

Alo looked up from his Agatha Christie novel as Mamie approached. His wife had been for a swim in the pool and she obviously had neglected to wear a bathing hat. Her hair was standing up like forks of lightning and the stripey beach towel which she had used to dry it was slung loosely around her shoulders. Her flip-flops did just that as she hurried towards him.

'You know, Alo, I haven't seen or heard sight or sound of our friend Evelyn these past few days. That dreadful episode that happened when we were viewing those new apartments last Sunday must have really shook her, poor thing.'

Alo put his whodunnit down on the table top. He was thankful to be sitting in the shade of the umbrella. The sun was really hot. Mamie flopped down in the chair beside him.

'Now that you mention it, Mamie, I haven't seen Evelyn lately either', he answered. 'I've caught a glance of Des a few times. He seems to be keeping his distance from everyone.'

'Thank God we didn't tell anyone what happened at those holiday bungaloes in Es Cana on Sunday, It must have been an awful shock him losing his job and Evelyn finding out like that. The Celtic tiger didn't do much for poor Des'. Mamie paused, the sun had almost dried her off completely. 'I take it then, Alo, that you haven't talked to Des yet about that other thing?'

'How could I when he's been missing these last few days. He doesn't even come into the bar – '

'Maybe you should go up and knock on their apartment door?'

'I wouldn't like doing that. Evelyn is probably hiding indoors, in the horrors. I'd rather get Des on his own, spring it as a surprise on him.'

'I hope they're going along to that gala night we're all invited to tomorrow in Jose's Hacienda. Surely they won't miss that.'

Alo shook his head. 'I doubt that they'll go. Not after what happened on Sunday. I'm sure it's ruined their holiday.' He sighed. 'The problem is time is running out. I'll have to talk to Des soon. I'll take a stroll around, see if I can spot him.'

'And I'll go up to our room and lash lots of conditioner on this hair of mine,' Mamie said, rising. 'I'll see you later, Alo.' He smiled and watched his wife flip-flop her way towards the lift.

Up in her apartment, Evelyn Murtagh lay in the darkened room with her face turned towards the wall. Her eyes and throat ached from the continuous sobbing of the past two days. She eased herfelf out of the bed and went to the bathroom. The bright light made her eyes feel even worse. Evelyn rooted in her make-up bag until she found the tablets. Filling a glass of water she swallowed two. She gagged when her now empty stomach protested.

She could barely remember when she had last had something to eat. It must have been on Sunday before they set out for that fateful journey to view the villas. She cringed at the memory; falling to the dance floor in the Sinatra Club had been a disaster, but the humiliation she had suffered on Sunday, in front of Karl and his wife...Damn those apartments, she thought, tears filling her eyes and spilling uncontrollably down her cheeks.

She got back into bed, closed her eyes, prayed for sleep. Maybe over the years she had unconsciously been putting pressure on Des over the house, his job, seeking a better standard of living. She had hoped that what he said about being made redundant wasn't true, that he was only saying it to stop her signing on for one of those apartments.

But it was true. Des had lost his job. He was fifty-five now and his prospects of getting something substantial on the jobs front, anything at all in fact, - were slim. She would have to accept that. Evelyn dreaded the thought of going home to Templeogue when the holiday was over. Facing the neighbours, watching Des leaving every week to sign on the dole.

For all she knew maybe there was more horror to come; bills to be paid, a second mortgage having to be taken out on the house to stave off debts. Why had Des not been able to tell her before they came away that he had lost his job and that they really could not afford the holiday? Was it her fault? Had she put so much pressure on him that communication between them had broken down? Oh God, if only they had another chance she would see things differently.

A few days ago the world had been a lovely place. Now everything had changed. How could Des have shouted at her like that in front of Karl and the others? She could still see Karl driving by, too embarrassed to look at her, with that jealous bitch of a wife of his at the wheel, a smug smile on her face.

There had been a spark of romance between herself and Karl. Nothing serious, of course - she would never have allowed it to develop any further than friendship. Or would she, Evelyn wondered? She would never know. How was she going to get out of bed and face the world -not to mention Mamie Riordan and the other wives down at the pool.

And Des – he was probably in some taverna or other drowning his sorrows. He would be back soon trying to cheer her up, telling her that he still loved her, that they still had each other and that they would see out this crisis together. Wasn't that what marriage was all about?, he would say. Evelyn turned her face to the wall.

Down at the beach, Des Murtagh sat on a towel spread on the sand and watched the waves endlessly rolling onto the shore. The sun was setting and spaces were beginning to open up around him as people packed up and headed back to the hotels and apartments to get ready for dinner.

Des looked enviously at some of the couples remaining, lying side by side, talking and laughing. A wave of sadness engulfed him. Apart from strangers in the hotel restaurant, he had not spoken to a soul since Sunday. Nor did he want to. He wished it was Saturday so that he would be getting out of Ibiza. Of course then he would have to face the music back home..

He felt guilty now the way he had shouted at Evelyn in those apartments last Sunday, but he had been driven to it. No way could he have allowed her to sign that form and put themselves into debt. In the taxi back to Figueretas Evelyn had not spoken a word, but when they had arrived back in their apartment the shock had worn off and she had exploded.

She had told him he was a failure; her mother and father had known it, her in-laws knew it – even the dogs in the street knew it! Through it all Des had remained silent, he couldn't give her an argument on that score. He had winced when she had hurled at him that she would never have married him only he had made her pregnant.

Even during their worse rows, and there had been many over the years, she had never thrown that up at him.

A shadow fell across him. Des looked up and saw Alo looking down at him. 'Des old son. I've been looking for you these past couple of days. Where in the name of God did you get yourself to?'

'Oh, here and there'. Des replied off-handedly. He hoped Alo wouldn't ask after Evelyn.

'Come over here to that beachside cafe and we'll have a drink. There's something I want to put to you –'

'I'm not really in the mood for talking, Alo. I have to get back to the apartment. Evelyn hasn't been too well.'

'This will only take a few minutes. Come on, it could solve all your problems - Evelyn's too.'

Des got to his feet reluctantly. The sand was still warm as they made their way across the beach. They sat at a table outside the cafe and Alo ordered two bottles of San Miguel. Des waited for him to begin.

'Look, you can tell me to mind my own business if you wish, but ever since you told me about losing your job myself and Mamie have been worrying about yourself and Evelyn. Now I've been thinking. My farm machinery business is expanding rapidly and as soon as I return from this holiday I'll be opening a new plant hire in Naas –'

Alo paused and Des was wondering where all this was leading. 'I've made a few phone calls home during the last few days, Des -one of them to a friend of mine in the Irish Management Institute - and I'm told you're a pretty good salesman – one of the best in the business was how this fellow described you.' Alo looked him straight in the eye. 'How would you like to run the Naas plant for me? I'll match whatever salary you had with Digitor and in addition you'll be on commission. The job also includes a company car – '

Des was stunned by the offer. He wasn't quite sure what to say. Was Alo Riordan doing this merely out of sympathy or was Alo sure he could do the job? Alo's next words answered that question.

'It's a great opportunity but I warn you Des, I'm not in the business of doing favours for anyone. I'll expect good results and you'll work under your own initiative. I'm not one for interfering if a man is doing a good job – '

'But Alo, I know nothing about farm machinery –'

'You won't have to know everything. Not at first anyway. To start up I'll give you a man who will fill you in on that end of the business. Don't worry, you'll learn in good time. Well, are you interested, Des?'

Des knew he was being thrown a lifeline.' Of course. And thanks a million, Alo! But I'll have to discuss it with Evelyn first ‑ With the M50 motorway on his doorstep he'd be in Naas in half-an-hour from Templeogue. Evelyn would love big money coming in again. She loved style. And maybe they could still buy that villa in Spain!

'Will we have two more San Miguels?' Des asked his benefactor.

'Better not,' Alo replied. 'I think you have urgent business back at your apartment.'

Fifteen minutes later Des quietly opened the bedroom door. He opened the shutters, letting in the weak rays of the setting sun. Evelyn stirred in the bed.

'Evelyn, wake up. I've something important to tell you–'

She opened her eyes. 'Oh Des, I had a funny dream. I dreamt we had no money and you kept wanting to buy champagne all the time –'

'Voila!' Des produced the bottle of champagne from behind his back. 'Darling, your dream has come true – '

Evelyn sat up in the bed, looked on in horror. 'Des Murtagh, have you gone mad! Drinking champagne is not going to solve our problems!'

Des brushed her protests aside. 'Listen to me, woman. Our problems are solved! Your nightmare days have ended.

We've got something to celebrate. Get out two glasses quickly.'

As he loosened the cork in the bottle Des began to sing.

'Happy days are here again. ...' Suddenly the cork shot out of the bottle and Evelyn screamed as she was enveloped in a spray of champagne.

Mark Smith sat on the apartment veranda, sipping a black coffee and watching the poolside, hoping that Caroline might turn up to have a swim. It was nearly noon and he wasn't long out of bed. He hadn't seen Wayne for over twenty-four hours, he hadn't a clue where his friend might be. There was no need to worry; like the proverbial bad penny Wayne was bound to turn up.

He could have phoned Wayne on his mobile to check that he was okay, but of course Wayne's phone had become a write-off on the second night of their holiday when he dropped it down the toilet where it had been found by Mark next morning.

It was another glorious day. As the sun beamed down Mark watched the golden bodies soaking up the sun and splashing about in the azure heart-shaped pool. He was anxious to see Caroline; last night had been just magic!

Earlier in the evening he had had a phone call from his brother Ray in Dublin, informing him some of Ray's musical friends were in Ibiza on holiday. He gave Mark the name of their hotel and said he should get in touch with them and enjoy a session.

A session was just what Mark needed. Ray's friends were excellent part-time musicians and the craic was mighty wherever they performed. He had telephoned their hotel yesterday but they were out. No problem - he would have no bother coming across them later in one of the Irish pubs.

So it was in The Ould Triangle at the far end of the beach last night that Mark had ended up with Kev, Fez, Hammer and Collie and their wives and girlfriends. The pub's resident trio had no objections to the lads joining them for a session and a good night was had by all. Mark's older brother Ray had not come to Ibiza as his wife Aoife was expecting their first baby back in Dublin. It was after four a.m. when Mark eventually returned to the empty apartment to fall asleep immediately.

Looking at the poolside Mark saw it had become very crowded. He decided to stroll down to the beach for a swim. He had not strolled very far when he spotted Bernice returning with groceries from the local supermarket. He crossed over to her side of the road.

'Hi Bernice. Have you seen Caroline lately?'

'No. Alison and I were with her yesterday on the cruise around the island. She was with Wayne.' Bernice paused. 'What happened to you Mark? You never showed up. Caroline was disappointed.'

'A cruise? What cruise?, I had no idea -' She could see by his expression that he had known nothing about a boat trip. His friend Wayne had obviously kept it a secret from him. 'What was it? Did Caroline enjoy it?' he asked.

'The answer to your first question is that the cruise was wild! Really wild! Even Alison and I were amazed – and as you know we like a good time. Caroline wasn't too impressed with the carry-on, and especially with Wayne who really enjoyed himself with the girls. Alison and I looked after Caroline and yeah, we had a bit of a laugh.'

Mark could picture the scene only too well. Typical Wayne jumping in head first without considering anyone else's feelings. 'Thanks, Bernice, for filling me in. You're a pal.'

Bernice turned, called after him. 'Are you inviting Caroline along to Jose's Hacienda tomorrow night to see Georgia do her stuff -'

'Of course. Wouldn't miss that for all the beer in Ibiza.' Great - another opportunity to be with Caroline.

Later in the day he came across Caroline relaxing on a sunbed by the pool, having just enjoyed a swim. Mark stopped for a chat and took the opportunity to invite her out to dinner later. 'I came across a lovely little Italian restaurant earlier today that I thought we might try.'

'Hhmmm, sounds interesting,' Caroline said. It would be a good lead-up to her having a real heart-to-heart talk with Mark.

'And do you like ballads?' he asked. When she said she did Mark told her about Ray's friends. 'They're playing in a hotel in the town tonight. We can go along there after we've had dinner. How about that?'

'Fine,' she smiled. She would try at some stage to go on a long walk with Mark, have a serious talk with him. Caroline sensed that he was falling in love with her. She would have to be honest and tell him about her background before time ran out. Tonight would be a good opportunity.

'I'm going to relax here in the sun for a few hours. You're welcome to join me, Mark, if you can find a sunbed.'

Mark managed to find an empty sunbed which he moved closer to Caroline's. He then fetched two long cool drinks from the poolside bar. Not too far away he saw Gerry and Fiona, both of whom were looking rather serious and who seemed to be having an earnest discussion. They were such a handsome looking couple; he hoped nothing was happening to spoil their holiday.

He explained to Caroline why he had not gone along on the cruise yesterday – 'Wayne obviously wanted you all go himself' – and he pretended to be horrified when Caroline described some of the antics of the crowd. In reality Mark had been on several such cruises over the years and knew the score. Never in his wildest dreams would he have invited Caroline along on such an escapade.

Later that evening Mark was about to leave the apartment for his dinner date with Caroline when a bleary-eyed Wayne arrived back. He looked like someone who had been mugged. It took all Mark's willpower to be civil to him. 'Where on earth have you been?' he asked.

Wayne rubbed a stubbly chin. 'That's a good question,' he replied. 'Let's just say with a girl - or two or three!'

'You look dreadful.'

'I'm not surprised. I feel dreadful. I need a good sleep. I'll grab a few hours before heading out tonight -' Wayne paused before entering the bedroom. 'You've got yourself all shined up. Where are you off to?'

'I've a date with Caroline, ' Mark replied. An idea was forming in his head.

'Where are you taking her?'

'I'm thinking of taking her to that big party on over in San Antonio, 'Mark lied. 'A foam party, you know the scene..Lots of girls, drink, sloshing around in foam in wet t-shirts and tops, the lot. I saw a poster about it in town today. The party's being held in a nightclub at the far end of the beach in San Antonio –'

Wayne's eyes lit up. 'Hey, I'm all for that. A few hours sleep and I'll be ready to go. See you over in San Antonio later. Thanks for telling me about the party!'

'Bye' Mark smiled to himself as he left. He owed Wayne that one!

The dinner in the Italian restaurant later that evening was intimate and romantic. Mark thought Caroline looked really beautiful as she sat across the candlelit table. Amazing how desirable she could look in a slinky cerise coloured dress, her dark hair framing her oval face, accentuating her high cheekbones. When he complimented her on the dress she told him she had bought it specially for tonight. He took that as a good omen. He enjoyed watching her eat, felt easy and relaxed. Is this what love feels like?, he thought to himself. He saw Caroline blush and knew his staring had embarrassed her.

'More wine?' he asked. He wondered if Wayne was enjoying the foam party.

'Yes, please.' She watched him pour. 'The dinner was perfect, Mark, Thank you for a lovely evening,'

'The night isn't over yet, ' he said, covering her hand with his.

She looked at him across the table. Her eyes seemed to burn into his very soul. 'Mark, there's something I want to tell you. Something very important. It concerns both of us–'

Mark's heart pounded. 'Yes? What is it, Caroline?'

Caroline hesitated. He had fallen seriously in love with her, she sensed that instinctively. Even a nun like her could tell that! She had let it happen again, first Father Joe, now Mark. Oh God, give her strength, the willpower to do the right thing.

God mustn't have been listening just at that moment. Caroline wavered; if she told Mark now it would spoil a lovely evening. Perhaps she would leave it until later. Yes, she would tell him later on the way home. Definitely, she had made up her mind.

'It's something to do with yourself, isn't it, Caroline?', Mark said. He could guess what it was. She already had a boyfriend, a lover -maybe even a husband! Perhaps she had separated from him - so many relationships were breaking up nowadays.

'Don't ask me just now, please. I'll tell you about it later, I promise.' She scolded herself for backing off.

When they had finished dinner they made their way to the Ambassador Hotel, a short distance from the restaurant. As they entered the foyer they heard the nostalgic sound of The Marino Waltz wafting out. They entered the packed function room to see Pez, Kev,

Hammer and Collie of the Dubs Angels doing their stuff on stage. Mark and Caroline found a table, relaxed and enjoyed the ballads and the craic.

At one stage Caroline asked where Wayne was tonight. 'At this moment I'd say he is up to his ears in foam in San Antonio,' Mark laughed. When she looked puzzled he explained how he had gotten rid of his pal for a the night. 'Let's not worry about Wayne, he can look after himself.'

It was as they were strolling hand-in-hand along the promenade on their way back to the hotel that Caroline stopped. 'Mark, that something I wanted to tell you about earlier - ' she began. 'Let's sit on this seat.'

They sat side by side, facing the sea, he still holding her hand, the sound of the waves breaking on the sand in the distance. He turned, looked at her. 'There's someone else, isn't there?' he said. He had been foolish to think that someone as lovely as Caroline, and as genuinely nice, would not have someone else seeking her affections.

'Yes. There is someone else, but not what you are thinking.' She paused, seeking the right words. 'Mark, I came away on this holiday to do some thinking, sort myself out – ', Another pause. 'You see, I've been in a convent now for a few years. In fact I'm only months away from my final vows...' She looked away, out towards the sea, saw the moonlight glistening on the water.

'You mean -' Mark too was fighting to find the right words - 'You're telling me, Caroline, that you're a nun!'.

She took a deep breath. 'Yes. Almost.'

'Holy God! ' He sat transfixed, as if posing for a still-life portrait. The silence was unbearable.

'Mark, for God's sake say something. I've tried several times to tell you because I knew you were – I knew we both liked each other a lot. I know I really liked you -.' Caroline broke off. 'Oh, I'm so confused at the moment!'

'A nun!' Mark repeated, almost to himself. She heard him laugh. 'Believe it or not, Caroline, in a way this is a relief. When you told me before that you had a problem I thought....1 thought lots of things. Oh, never mind what I thought! ' He paused. 'If you're planning on becoming a nun, Caroline, what the hell – sorry! - what on earth are you doing herein a place like Ibiza?'

'Let me try to explain. You're right, there was someone else involved. It was my fault. I was ruining his life too. I realise now I was being selfish, thinking only of myself.' Caroline paused. 'I know I'm not making much sense, Mark, and I'd prefer not to go into too much detail if you don't mind – '

He realised it was painful for her to talk about it. 'You don't have to explain it all if you don't feel like it, Caroline.'

'Thank you for understanding, Mark. All I know is that I desperately needed to get away to sort myself out.'

'And you have sorted yourself out - '

'Yes.' She paused, looked at him. 'I'm returning to the convent, Mark. I hope you understand.'

He squeezed her hand. 'Of course.' He was devastated but he hoped it didn't show. 'Remember if ever you change your mind...'

'I value your friendship, Mark, and if circumstances were different I'd want you as more than a friend. But I'm sure you'll find someone else, and she'll be a very lucky person, believe me.'

They got up from the seat and began walking again. In no time it seemed, they were back at the Hotel Orlando. Mark had hoped he would have ended up kissing her tenderly, both of them enjoying a passionate goodnight, but he reckoned that was out of the question now. Or was it? What if he tried....

Putting temptation her way, that would be unfair. Instead he held her close. brushed his lips lightly on the forehead. Mark was mildly surprised when she did not try to break away.

'You had better go to bed immediately and get some sleep, Caroline.' he whispered softly. 'It'll be a late night at Jose's place tomorrow night.' When he released her and walked away he looked back and saw that she was still gazing after him.

When it came to getting a good night's sleep Mark couldn't take his own advice. Thankfully Wayne hadn't yet returned from San Antonio so he didn't have to answer any questions. He tossed and turned in his bed, unable to get Caroline out of his mind. He had gone out on the date earlier so much in love and now his world had come crashing down around his ears. Mark got out of bed, donned a sweater, shorts and a pair of sneakers and decided to go on a long walk on the beach.

CHAPTER FIFTEEN

Doc Holliday was really enjoying the gala night in Jose's Hacienda. Earlier in the day he had asked Maureen Duff if she would like to to accompany him for the evening and she had readily agreed. There had been a lot of talk during the past few days among the Irish contingent in the hotel about Georgia and the dance she would perform in the club bar owned by her Spanish boyfriend. It was adding a bit of spice to the holiday!

The posters advertising the event dotted around Figueretas showed Georgia in a very seductive dance pose, covered in see-through material that left little to the imagination. It certainly looked like those who could get into Jose's bar on the night were in for a good night's entertainment!

Doc and Maureen had shared a taxi to the show with Caroline and Mark. Doc had seen the young couple together quite a bit and wondered if they would be an item when the holiday ended and they were back in Dublin. He had asked Maureen what she thought about the relationship and she had inferred that if Mark was serious about Caroline then he was in for something of a surprise!

When Des Murtagh and Evelyn arrived into Jose's bar there had been an awkward silence at the table, but Alo had jumped to his feet and waved them over and the moment had passed. Everyone was on their best behaviour and greeted Des and Evelyn as though nothing embarrassing had happened. Somehow during the past few days the word had got out at poolside about the shouting match that had ensued on Sunday afternoon last when the Murtaghs had gone out inspecting holiday homes with their German friends. Evelyn had been in hiding ever since, poor dear.

Now here she was entering on the arm of her husband, smiling and looking radiant as usual. What had happened to bring about the change, those in the know at the table wondered? The mystery was solved when, after Des had knocked back a couple of drinks, he got to his feet, called for silence, and on behalf of Evelyn and himself thanked Alo and Mamie Riordan for coming up with a job offer that Des said he was only too happy to accept. Alo looked suitably bashful and tried to brush his good deed aside, but Des ordered a couple of bottles of champagne and insisted on everyone raising a glass and drinking a toast to their benefactors from Co. Clare.

'To Ibiza, the island where dreams come true and everyone has a good time,' Des began his speech. 'I came here a very distressed person. I don't mind telling you I had been let go from my job just days before Evelyn and I set off for this holiday. It was a terrible shock and I took the decision not to tell my wife the bad news for fear it would spoil our holiday – '

Des paused. 'Well, you all know now that things went somewhat pear shaped and unfortunately Evelyn learned the bad news the hard way. But I'm glad to say that while Ireland may not be the Island of Saints and Scholars that we learned about in school, we still have some very fine people there – and we are privileged to have two of them with us tonight. So my friends – ' Des raised his glass – 'rise and let us drink a toast to Alo and Mamie Riordan!'

Couples at the other tables looked on and some joined in the applause as everyone at the big table jumped to their feet and toasted the blushing couple. Des too got a big round of applause as he sat down.

Evelyn joined in, then took a drink of champagne. The bubbles stung her nose and she felt like sneezing. She had found Des's speech a bit embarrassing. She didn't want to be an object of pity, still she had better have the good grace to be pleasant. She leaned over and clinked her glass with Mamie and Alo. A couple like that were, as her mother might say, 'the salt of the earth…'

'Isn't it marvellous that we've all got on so well together on this holiday and that we're having such a good time,' Doc said expansively.

'Speak for yourself, Doc!', Wayne shouted up. 'I've already spent a night in jail and most of the other nights I can't remember where I was!' Everyone laughed.

'And what about that honeymoon couple that came over with us,' Alo said to nobody in particular. 'They were a peculiar pair, never mixed with anybody and never passed myself or Mamie the time of day. Why aren't they with us tonight? Did anyone think of inviting them? Maybe they think we're ignoring them - ' Alo always believed in giving people the benefit of the doubt.

'They knew about the gala night alright,' Caroline spoke up. 'I told them about it yesterday when I chatted to them at the pool.'

'I think I know why they're not here…' All eyes at the table turned towards Irene O'Rourke, Ben's wife. She and Ben were sitting beside Paula Sheridan whom they had invited for the evening. 'The honeymoon couple, as we called Gerry and Fiona, are no longer in the hotel. Isn't that right, Paula?'

Now the attention was on Paula, who nodded. 'That's quite correct. That couple checked out this morning. I had their apartment cleaned out today.'

'I saw them leaving early this morning – with their luggage,' Irene spoke up again, delighted to be the centre of attention. 'I was sitting in the foyer at the time, minding my own business, when they came down with their suitcases.' She paused. 'They didn't look too happy, and they certainly didn't look like honeymooners – if indeed they were on honeymoon. They seemed to be arguing with each other as they got into the taxi.'

Mamie Riordan sniffed. 'I don't think that couple were married at all. Too luvey-duvey for my liking. We never went on like that when we went on our honeymoon, did we, Alo?' Her husband remained silent; no way could he answer that question and come out winning!

Listening to the conversation, Doc remembered the whisperings of Gerry and Fiona in the seat beside him on the flight out before he had dropped off to sleep. If it was true they weren't married imagine what was facing them when they landed back in Dublin.

'Ah well, they aren't the first couple to slip away for a passionate two weeks together. Am I right there, Ben?'

Ben O'Rourke nearly choked on his drink. What the hell was Doc at – and Irene sitting there listening! And him after confiding his affair with Paula to Doc only yesterday. He wished Doc would be more careful with his throwaway remarks. 'I suppose you're right there,' Ben replied, hoping that his wife would let things rest. No such luck; Irene had climbed aboard her moral high horse and was on the warpath.

'Benjamin O'Rourke,' Irene barked, glaring at her husband, 'does that mean you approve of what that couple were up to?'

Ben coughed, tried to give himself time to think. Out of the corner of his eye he thought he saw Paula smiling. 'Of course not, love,' he replied quickly. 'I– I didn't mean it that way.' Before Irene could come back at him again he asked: 'Does anyone have any idea why Gerry and Fiona had to leave the hotel so quickly?'

To Ben's relief the young girl Caroline spoke up. 'It might have had something to do with that photographer I told them about.'

'Photographer?' What photographer?', someone asked.

Now it was Caroline's turn to become the centre of attention. Everyone at the table listened attentively as she recounted her conversation with the mysterious photographer she saw the other day filming Fiona and Gerry together by the pool, and how he had told her that he was shooting a surprise film of them on their honeymoon.

'And don't tell me you believed him,' Wayne shouted up from the end of the long table. He seemed to be drinking too much as usual.

'Of course. Why not?'

'Well Holy God – aren't you the little innocent!' Wayne responded sarcastically. Everyone laughed and Caroline was glad that in the semi-darkness of Jose's Hacienda nobody saw her blushing.

She was not the only member of the group to get a surprise before Georgia did her dancing act. Doc Holliday was enjoying the conversation and the light-hearted banter at the table when he happened to glance idly around the room. To his surprise he saw Yolanda Segguria beckoning him discreetly from the far end of the bar.

Had she not warned him that they must not be seen talking together for fear of jeopardising her undercover work? – yet here she was in a crowded bar trying to catch his attention. Doc reckoned that something serious must have happened to make her break that rule.

He rose from the table, excused himself to Maureen, and slipped away. He made his way by a circuitous route to where Yolanda was standing.

'Yolanda! What are you doing here?'

'I had to see you Alec, it is urgent.'

'Why didn't you telephone me at the hotel?'

'I am also on duty here tonight. Our fight against drugs takes us to places like this where there will be a big crowd of young people. But I wanted to talk to you anyway. About tomorrow night – '

'What about tomorrow night? It's still on, isn't it? I show up at the kids' playground and collect the drugs and the money from Donie Crawford, then your men jump in and arrest him – '

'Something has happened.' He saw the worried look on Yolanda's face. 'There is danger.'

'What do you mean?'

'Your friend Donie … He does not trust you. He suspects you are, how you say, setting him up.'

Doc stared at her. He didn't like the sound of this. 'How do you know that, Yolanda?'

'We have inside information – from our contacts close to the drug scene. If our information is true, Alec, and we think it is, you could be in danger. These people make big money from drugs and they are ruthless.'

Who are you telling!, Doc thought to himself. He knew that from the scene in Dublin. He was no coward but he still didn't fancy ending up in a canal with a bullet in his head. And yet he wanted to help Yolanda – and also to have something exciting to tell his buddies back in Ringsend. No, he couldn't pull out now…

'You'll have a lot of your men in that playground tomorrow night when I meet up with Donie, won't, you?'

'Yes. We will take no chances.'

Doc shrugged. 'Well then….I'm game.' He hoped he sounded more confident than he felt.

Yolanda wasn't sure what that expression meant, so she asked: 'You still want to do this for me?' When he nodded she looked into his eyes. She would have liked to kiss him lightly on the cheek but it was too risky, there were too many people around. Already she had taken a big chance by speaking to him in a crowded bar.

'You are a brave man, Alec. Thank you very much. But you must be careful. I do not want anything to happen to you…' The way she looked at him made his heart miss a beat. 'Now I must go. Until tomorrow night. Adios.'

Doc watched her disappear into the crowd. When he glanced over to the table he saw Maureen Duff staring at him through a haze of cigarette smoke. If she asked any awkward questions he knew he would have to fend them off.

What on earth had he let himself in for tomorrow night? Despite her concern, for all he knew Yolanda Segguria could be using him, putting his life in danger to further her own career. Was he being blinded by what had happened between them on the balcony of Yolanda's apartment after dinner the other night, the soft look in her eyes, the whiff of her perfume, the closeness of her body…?

He had come to Ibiza for a fun holiday and here he was putting himself in danger for a woman he hardly knew. His pals in The Oarsman's pub in Ringsend would probably say he was crazy! Doc made his way back to the table. He hated to admit it, but he was a worried man, scared about tomorrow night. As he waited for Georgia to appear and do her dance he was glad that Maureen Duff didn't ply him with any questions…

Meanwhile, outside in the street, Jose Simon was pleased to see the groups of people entering his show bar. People were arriving by taxi and on foot to see the exotic Dance of the Seven Veils being performed by the red-headed Irish girl called Georgia. Inside the tables were filling so rapidly that Jose knew that shortly he would have to turn people away. That had never happened before!

He looked with pride at the miniature rows of bunting fluttering in the breeze and the fresh coat of paint which had transformed Jose's Hacienda overnight. Also the full-sized poster of Georgia placed in a prominent position on the pavement, showing off her stunning figure and her long shapely legs to perfection. Jose hoped the Contessa would be pleased when she saw it.

Just then he turned and saw the family Mercedes limousine nose its way through the traffic towards the entrance with Pedro, the farm overseer who acted as chauffeur to his mother, at the wheel. He could see the figures of the Contessa and his Aunt Pilar seated in the back.

Jose waited until Pedro opened the car doors and helped the two women onto the pavement. In contrast to the extravagantly dressed couples milling about his mother was dressed as usual in severe black. Aunt Pilar in contrast looked a picture in a midnight blue full-length dress. His mother expertly swished open her fan and cooled herself in the evening heat, pausing only when Jose greeted them both with a kiss on the cheek.

'Welcome to Jose's Hacienda,' he said, guiding them towards the entrance. 'This is a long overdue visit. Thus far the Contessa had not deigned to visit his humble establishment. Now his mother stood on the pavement and took all in with her usual cold gaze.

'Please come in and meet my guests. Georgia has invited a group of her Irish friends from the hotel to her performance. She will be going on stage as soon as you both are seated…'

Jose broke off, looked over his shoulder. His mother had stopped in front of Georgia's full-length poster. From the manner in which she was gazing at it it was obvious that she did not approve. She said something in a low tone to Pilar then followed Jose inside.

As he lead them both to their specially reserved table in front of the stage he admired how beautiful his Aunt Pilar looked. 'You are looking very elegant tonight,' he whispered in her ear as he settled her into her seat. Pilar blushed and gave him a warm smile. Jose poured each a glass of Tia Maria – his mother's favourite drink – from the bottle then said: 'I will join both of you ladies later. Right now I have something to do. Please excuse me…'

By now the show bar was packed to capacity and the security man on the door was not allowing anyone else in.

Every candlelit table was occupied and even the bar area was packed. Jose had never experienced anything like it before – his Georgia was a star before her show even opened!

He glanced over to the table where Georgia's Irish friends were gathered. He recognised Bernice and her new boyfriend, also Alison, sitting between two young men and another dark-haired girl, and several middle-aged couples. Everyone seemed to be having a good time. There was an air of expectancy as everyone awaited Georgia's entrance.

Jose went backstage to his office which Georgia was using as a dressing-room. He kissed her and wished her good luck.

'Jose, I'm very nervous,' Georgia confessed, 'and I'm even more nervous with your mother sitting out front!' She had peeped out at the audience and had seen the Contessa, unsmiling, sipping her wine, waiting for the show to begin.

Jose looked at Georgia. The diaphanous veils barely covered her figure and he was glad she was wearing a pair of flesh-coloured briefs underneath. The males in the audience were in for an eyeful! He wasn't too sure what his mother would think!

'Georgia, my darling, do not worry about the Contessa. Or anybody else. You will be a sensation, I promise you.' He kissed her again. 'Now I must go out front and introduce you…'

When Jose stepped onstage a spotlight picked him up and the crowd fell silent. He had prepared a short, introductory speech which he delivered first in English, then Spanish and finally in German. The audience applauded and he exited.

The spotlight was extinguished and the show bar was lit by candles only. Exotic Spanish music started up, the beat slow and sensuous. The spotlight burst forth again and focused on the side of the stage. The faint tingle of bells was heard, then a long, bare leg appeared, a string of small bells around the shapely ankle…

As the music increased in tempo the lovely Georgia appeared in all her glory, her mane of red hair contrasting with her slim, white body. There was a collective intake of breath from the audience and someone at the Irish table let out a long, plaintive wolf whistle. Alison kicked an already boozy Wayne in the shins and gave him a blistering look.

Georgia began her dance on the small stage and after a short while discarded one of her diaphanous veils, to much applause from the audience. Then there was another gasp from the audience as, in one fluid movement and keeping in tempo with the music, she stepped down from the stage and was among the tables, dancing sensuously between them. At appropriate intervals she discarded a veil during a performance that was at once captivating, in good taste, and thoroughly entertaining.

She earned the loudest burst of applause when, gyrating past the Irish table, she deftly discarded a veil which floated down through the air and landed on Wayne Hanlon's face as he was openly admiring her close-up body.

Minutes later Georgia was back on stage, dancing erotically. The music reached a crescendo as the final piece of chiffon was discarded a split second before the spotlight was switched off. There was silence for a moment, then the audience burst into spontaneous applause.

As the lights in the club bar came on again Pilar looked at her sister-in-law. 'Well Madeleina, did you enjoy the performance? Wasn't Georgia's dancing exquisite?'

The Contessa didn't reply immediately. Instead she looked over to where Pedro was at the bar. She beckoned him over with an impatient gesture. As he made his way through the tables she turned to Pilar and said:

'I am glad you enjoyed the performance. I did not. I thought it was cheap, disgusting.' To Pedro she snapped:

'Bring the car around to the front at once. And if you see that son of mine tell him we're leaving – immediately!'

'Si, Senora.'

Jose caught up with his mother and Pilar as they made their way towards the exit. 'Mother, you are leaving so soon? Georgia is changing, she will be joining us shortly –'

Madeleine gave her son a frosty look. 'From what I have seen that girl has very little to change! Inform her I did not like her performance. I will not discuss the matter here. Now please escort me to my car.'

Outside Pedro was already holding the car door open for them. Jose gave his mother and aunt a goodnight kiss and wished them a safe journey home. He watched with a heavy heart as the big Mercedes eased its way out into the traffic.

After a while Pilar stole a sideways glance at Madeleina. She knew by the set of her sister-in-law's jaw and the thin line that was her lips that she was seething with fury. Pilar endeavoured to make a diplomatic comment about the evening.

'I watched Jose during the performance. Like the members of the audience he seemed to be enjoying it – '

'Then I was the only person in that place who did not enjoy it. My God, the prospect of my son marrying that girl fills me with horror. She is no better than a – what are they called – a stripper. In my time she would not have been allowed to give such a performance.'

'Madeleina, you must understand that this is the new century. Time has moved on and we must learn to move with the times. Tonight Georgia gave her interpretation of the Dance of the Seven Veils. The audience enjoyed it – and for what it is worth so did I!'

Madeleina took out a white lace trimmed handkerchief and wiped a tear from her eye. 'Why cannot Jose marry Inez Montoya. She is a local girl, she comes from an aristocratic family and she has breeding – '

'She is also as ugly as sin and you know it! That is why Inez Montoya is still seeking a husband – and will be doing so until it is too late. She also has a vicious temper like all the Montoyas. Thank God Jose had the good sense to see that he would never find happiness with her!'

There was silence between them for a while. Pilar again broke it and said, 'Madeleina, you must accept that your time – our time – is past. We cannot turn back the clock. Ibiza has changed for the worst but it is our home. Georgia is a girl of today and your son loves her. She may not be of aristocratic stock as you would wish, but I have a feeling in my heart that she will be good for Jose.'

There were tears now also in Pilar's eyes. As she was speaking she was recalling a time long ago when she too had loved someone in similar circumstances. Then, she had not followed her heart and had paid the price. It was something she had deeply regretted ever since.

As the Mercedes sped through the countryside into the night Pilar felt it incumbent to make one more observation. 'If you are wise, Madeleina, you will stay out of Jose's life, allow him to marry whom he wishes. He is a man now, let him make up his own mind. That way you will not lose him and he will be happy.'

The older woman did not reply. She stared straight ahead, lost in her own thoughts. Her only comment as the car sped through the night was: 'Pedro, there is a chill in the air. Please switch on the heating.'

Back in Jose's Hacienda, however, the temperature was reaching boiling point - especially so for Ben O'Rourke. Seated at the table between his wife Irene and Paula Sheridan, they had, like the others, enjoyed Georgia's sensuous performance and now the drink was flowing freely. A floor space had been cleared and some couples were already up dancing.

'Come on old girl, let's get up and trip the light fantastic,' Ben said to Irene. Sitting so close to Paula all night had brought back memories he knew he could never re-live.

'Less of the old girl bit if you don't mind,' Irene responded. She turned to Paula. 'Men can be so insensitive sometimes.'

'Oh, I'm sure Ben meant it in the nicest possible way,' Paula smiled. 'I do agree that paying compliments to ladies is not the Irishman's strongest point. Give me the romantic Continentals any time.'

Thanks a bunch, Ben thought. These two were getting very palsy-walsy. He didn't know whether to be pleased with the situation or not. 'Oh, sorry if I offended, dear. I'll try again.' He bowed before Irene, 'Madame, will you do me the honour of dancing with me – ' Ben nearly fell over. He wished he hadn't drank so much.

'Sorry, dear. I'm feeling a bit tired. I'm saving all my dancing for tomorrow night at our anniversary dinner – ' Irene broke off. 'Do you think you'd be able to handle my husband on the dance floor, Paula?', she asked.

Ben froze. He felt as if someone had swiped him with a cold towel. What was Irene at, setting him up to dance with Paula! Did she suspect something?

'I'd be delighted to dance with Ben,' Paula laughed gaily. 'But you will keep an eye on him to see that he doesn't misbehave, won't you, Irene?' She added roguishly.

'Don't worry, Paula, I'll be watching his every move,' Irene replied, laughing.

Paula rose to her feet. 'Lead the way, Ben…'

He had to admit that Paula was looking exceptionally well tonight. From the moment she had stepped inside the door of Jose's Hacienda he thought she looked gorgeous and the memories had come flooding back. Now, after over twenty years, they were about to dance together….

Just as they reached the dance space the band trio began to play a tango. Paula slid into Ben's arms, her body close to his. 'Our favourite dance, if I remember. Seems like old times, doesn't it, Ben?'

Ben was perspiring – and it wasn't all to do with the heated atmosphere. Paula's dress was backless and his hand was on her bare flesh. There was nothing he could do about it. Not many couples were attempting the tango and there were many pairs of eyes on the dancers. As they twirled and turned Ben tried not to look at where Irene was seated. He didn't fancy making eye contact with her right now!

'I love the way you're holding me close, Ben,' Paula whispered in his ear. 'So romantic…' Ben tried to relax his hold but Paula's arm tightened behind his back. She was enjoying putting him through this agony – although if holding Paula Sheridan was agony he'd go through it anytime! Her face was close to his, her soft hair lay against his cheek. He could smell her perfume…

Doc and Maureen danced past. 'Enjoying yourself Ben, I see', Doc said, winking. Ben reckoned he would be enjoying himself a lot more if only Irene wasn't out there in the shadows watching.

'One of us has had too much wine to drink and it's definitely not me!,' Ben hissed into Paula's ear.

'Benjamin darling, you say the nicest things!', Paula riposted. He heard her tinkling laugh, a memory from the past. What the hell…Ben decided to enjoy himself, go for broke. Together they floated back together in time, lost to the magic of the sensuous tango music.

The music stopped. Some people at the tables applauded. Ben escorted a flushed Paula back to the table, his arm around her slim waist.

'You two dance very well together,' Irene remarked as they sat down. 'Although I have to say, Ben, you looked a bit nervous.' She downed the last of her drink. Ben was pleased, Irene rarely drank to excess but when she did she tended to get into a good mood.

'Yes, I was a bit rusty,' Ben was glad to agree.

'I'm sure he'll be in a more relaxed mood tomorrow night,' Paula said. 'Won't you, Ben?' She flashed him one of her heart-stopping smiles and he realised she was even more attractive now than when they had first met.

It was into the early hours when the gala night revelries ended and Jose began to order taxis as required for his Irish guests. 'You'll share a taxi with Ben and myself, Paula,' Irene said. 'We'll drop you off at your apartment.'

On the drive back through streets still thronged with young people determined to party, Irene asked Paula if she missed Ireland. Ben cocked an ear for Paula's reply.

'I do miss Ireland sometimes, but Vicki and I have a good lifestyle here now and of course I have my friend Edwin to look after me. I've promised Vicki I'll bring her over to Ireland this year – probably for Christmas – to visit her grandparents. They are getting on now and are anxious to see Vicki again. She has only been over to visit them once so far.'

'When you're in Dublin why don't both of you stay with Ben and me for a few days?', Irene said. 'We'd love that, wouldn't we, Benjamin?'

Ben swallowed. 'Why yes, of course. Why not, Paula?' When was this holiday from hell going to end!

'Don't decide right now, Paula. Discuss it with Vicki first, see what she thinks. Our daughter Deirdre is about the same age as Vicki and they could do their Christmas shopping together.'

'What a marvellous idea,' Paula enthused. 'I'm sure Vicki would love that'.

Ben remained silent. In contrast, Irene and Paula were whispering and giggling together like schoolgirls in the taxi. Seated beside the driver he listened to the chitchat from the back seat. His mood was not buoyant. Although it was sweltering right now in Ibiza, he had a feeling that it was going to be a very chilly Christmas back home!

CHAPTER SIXTEEN

Sleep simply would not come to Maureen Duff, no matter how hard she tried to drop off. Was it the lingering excitement of the gala night in Jose's Hacienda, or that fleeting glimpse she had had of Alec Holliday chatting animatedly to that attractive dark-haired lady at the bar that was keeping her awake? No matter how many sheep she counted, or decades of the Rosary she recited, she still could not induce the sleep she needed.

Alec had been strangely quiet during the taxi drive home from Jose's place. Maureen sensed that something was worrying him. He had been in good form earlier until he had met that lady. After that not even Georgia's sparkling Salome dance had lightened his mood. Whatever was worrying Alec he had not discussed it with Maureen before he had bid her goodnight in the foyer.

She glanced at the bedside clock. Almost 4am! Maybe an early morning swim would help, after all she was on holiday. She rose, donned her swimsuit, took down her wrap and slid her feet into a pair of sandals. Minutes later she was making her way along the walkway through the trees. It was beautifully mild with no breeze.

As Maureen neared the pool she heard a splash. Pity, despite the early hour she would have company. Oh well....Suddenly she heard a shout. Someone was in trouble in the pool!

As Maureen broke through the trees she heard splashing sounds. She saw someone flailing about in the deep end. It looked like a man! His head disappeared below the surface, came up briefly, then disappeared again. He was certainly in trouble. Maureen kicked off her sandals, ran to the poolside and dived in.

Recalling her lifesaving course all those years ago she approached the man from behind. He was fully clothed and she reckoned he must have fallen in after returning from a late night out. She put one arm across his chest and with the other made progress towards the ladder at the poolside. Only then did she recognise who it was she rescuing. It was Wayne O'Hanlon!

A few more strokes and she was clinging to the steel ladder. By now her victim was showing signs of life. Maureen was wondering how she would get herself and Wayne out of the water when she heard voices and laughter. Thank God – revellers returning to the hotel! She called out and was relieved when several couples approached. Amid excited talk willing hands grabbed Wayne and pulled him out of the water. Maureen climbed out and was relieved to see Wayne sit up, shaking his head apparently none the worse of his experience.

While the couples gathered around Wayne, Maureen slipped away unnoticed. She collected her wrap and sandals and made her way back to her room. What an ending to a gala night!

Georgia awoke to the sound of rattling delph. She opened her eyes. Her eyelids felt so heavy she was sure she would need props to keep them open. Thoughts of last night came flooding back...her Salome dance in Jose's bar, the thunderous applause, Jose coming into her makeshift dressing-room after the performance flushed with excitement, congratulating her on her stunning performance and hugging and kissing her until she was breathless.

Then the disappointment of hearing that the Contessa and Pilar had left, not waiting to offer their congratulations – or condemnation more likely on the Contessa's part. Georgia had not let it spoil the rest of the night; everyone had partied until three a.m, Jose dispensing champagne at the table where the Irish contingent were seated. When the bar had finally closed Jose had brought Georgia back to his apartment. Georgia closed her eyes again. Yes, it had been a night to remember...

The bedroom door opened and Jose entered. He was already dressed and had showered and shaved. 'Breakfast is ready, madam,' he announced. 'You will eat it in bed, no?'

'Go away, Jose,' Georgia groaned. 'How can you be so bright and breezy after last night. I feel like a heard of elephants has walked all over me.'

He smiled wickedly. 'That was not a herd of elephants, Georgia. That was me!'

Georgia threw one of the pillows at him. 'There, that'll teach you to treat me more delicately in future,'

He disappeared into the kitchen, returning with a tray containing a pot of steaming hot coffee and fresh rolls with pats of butter and marmalade. 'After you have finished breakfast and showered we will go out, Georgia my sweet. I have a surprise for you...'

The word 'surprise' was enough to ignite Georgia into action. She finished the breakfast quickly then dashed into the shower. As the hot water cascaded down, revitalising her, she hummed the tune that was so apt to her present situation – 'If My Friends Could See Me Now...' Yes indeed, if her friends back home in the boutique could see her now they would be envious. This was the stuff that fairy tales were made of. Was all this really happening to her? Georgia still believed that she would make up soon to find it was all a dream.

The only dark spot on her horizon was Jose's mother. Georgia had tried to hide her disappointment of the

Contessa's walk out last night. Jose had been embarrassed trying to find an excuse for his mother's hasty exit.

Georgia put on a pair of shorts and a cotton top, tied her hair back. She looked around; no need to tidy the bedroom, the maid would be in with fresh linen and would see to everything. If she married Jose she would have to get used to having servants about, tending to her every need. Would she be able to adapt? Would a girl like herself from a humble background be able to handle it all? She would have to phone, talk to her Ma…

'Jose, do you mind if I make a phone call to Dublin. I want to talk to my mother.'

'Please, Georgia, wait until I show you something and we return – it's my surprise for you. When we return I promise that you will have something very exciting to tell your mother.'

'Where are we going?', Georgia asked, as she slipped into the car seat beside Jose.

Back to my bar,' he replied. When they arrived there after the short drive Jose opened up, went behind the counter and took down a rather large key. 'Come with me,' he commanded, taking Georgia's hand. He lead her back into the sunshine and inserted the key into the door of a rather dilapidated building adjacent to the bar. Pushing the heavy door open he entered. Georgia followed him inside.

She looked around. The place was obviously used as a storeroom for the bar. There were kegs of beer stacked alongside one wall, crates of wine bottles along another. There were cobwebs and dust everywhere.

She clutched Jose's arm. 'Are there spiders here?' she asked.

He laughed. 'Don't worry, they will not bother us. They like company.'

Georgia shivered, gave a little scream and ran out of the door. 'Jose, why on earth have you brought me here?' she asked crossly.

He followed her outside. 'I am sorry, but I will explain quickly. Georgia, I would like you to set up a boutique here – your own boutique. I will have the place renovated and decorated as you desire and I will provide finance to stock it when it is completed. We will go to Paris, Madrid, New York, wherever you like to buy stock – '

'Dublin also,' Georgia enthused. 'We have some great designers in Ireland!'

'Of course. Then you like my plan? Jose's Hacienda and Georgia's Boutique, side by side – '

'Oh Jose, I think it's great, smashing!', She had always dreamed of owning her own boutique. Georgia threw her arms around his neck, kissed him. When they broke apart she said breathlessly, 'Jose, this would make a wonderful boutique.' Her eyes were shining, her head already spinning with ideas. 'It's a nice location. I'll put in a large window – two large windows maybe! - and make the shop bright and accessible. We'll cater for the holiday market during the summer – and the locals too. Oh, I'm so excited, I really am! – '

'Then Georgia, we are partners. You will marry me?' His eyes were searching her face. Marry him? That brought her back down to earth. Everything was happening so fast. He saw her hesitation. 'What is wrong, Georgia? You say you love me – '

'And I do, I do Jose – '

'Why then not say that you will marry me?'

She paused before replying. She did not want to hurt him, but – 'It's your mother, Jose. I don't think the Contessa likes me. She does not consider me suitable for you – '

Jose took her hands in his. 'Do not worry about the Contessa. I am a grown man. I know what I want. And what I want is to marry you, Georgia. I wanted that from the first time I saw you.' He paused, drew her close. Some passers-by in the street stared, although in Ibiza a cuddling couple was not an unusual sight. 'Tomorrow we will drive out to see my mother. I will tell her I want to get engaged, get married. She will have to give her consent.'

'I don't wish to come between you and your mother, Jose.'

'Do not worry. We will sort this matter out, Georgia. Come, we will lock the spiders in for a while longer. Soon they will have to find a new home.'

He dropped her back to his apartment, drove off saying he had some business to attend to. He promised to return later and take her out to dinner when they would discuss the upcoming visit to his mother.

Georgia entered Jose's apartment and stood for a few moments in the airy living-room. The maid had already been in and everything was in its place. The balcony window was open slightly and a cool breeze drifted in. She looked into the bedroom and was tempted to lie down on the freshly made bed, but she felt an urgent need to phone home. She had to tell her mother what was happening to her.

'Hello?', her mother's voice came over loud and clear.

'Hello Mom. This is Georgia – '

'Ah, so it's Mom now, is it? Anyway, hello pet. How are you?'

'Fine thanks. I'm phoning from Jose's apartment.'

A pause. 'You're in Jose's apartment already? Sure it's only midday. What are you doing there? Did you stay the night?' Her mother was very old fashioned.'

'Yes Mom. I did. So what?, it's no big deal.'

'It is if you get up to things you shouldn't be getting up to, if you know what I mean.'

Time to change the subject, Georgia thought. 'How is Dad?' she asked.

'Your Da is back in work. What's happening to you, Georgia, you're beginning to talk very posh, calling us Mom and Dad? We were Ma and Da before you went to Spain! Anyway your Da's fine, back in his job.'

'Back in work? – but I thought he had an accident, that he was on a stick and couldn't walk?'

'That was before he was caught out. He was down in the bookie shop the other day with his pals when who walked in but his boss from the Corpo. 'Hello Paddy,' the boss says, 'Aren't you supposed to be crippled with pain? Where's your walking stick?'

'Oh my God. What did Da, I mean Dad say?'

'Sure your poor Da was flummoxed. 'I want you back in work tomorrow, Paddy – and you can forget about that compensation claim you have in,' the boss says. Georgia heard her mother sigh. 'Needless to say that was the end of your Da's little holiday. Anyway, tell me about this fellow Jose. Is he serious about you, Georgia?'

'Of course he is. And he's also very rich. He's just given me a boutique!'

'A boutique – one of them fashion shops you work in?'

'That's right. It's beside his pub. It's a storeroom but he's having it converted and when it opens it'll be called Georgia's Boutique. It'll be all mine – well, Jose's and mine.'

'Are you going to marry him then?'

'I would only for his mother. I don't think she likes me.'

'Ah the oul' rip. What's wrong with her?'

'Ma, you can't talk like that. Jose's mother is a Contessa. She's allowed say what she likes.'

'Not about my daughter she isn't. Who does she think she is – the Queen of England! If she ever comes here to Finglas I'll sort her out!'

'Ma, stop it!'

'What's wrong with her, anyway?'

'She was annoyed last night in Jose's bar when I did my dance.'

'Dance? What sort of dance?'

'A thing called The Dance of the Seven Veils. Very sexy. The crowd went wild.'

'It sounds very peculiar to me. You weren't taught that in Billie Barry's School! Did you have to take your clothes off, Georgia?'

'Yes Mom I did. Not all of them. Just the see-through veils – '

'The see-through veils!', Georgia heard her mother screech. 'Georgia, what were you doing wearing see-through veils. Were you wearing anything underneath?'

'Of course Mom.'

'Oh thank God. I thought for a minute – '

'Jose's mother was at the show. She didn't like it – '

'I'm not surprised!'

'She left in a huff immediately after my performance. I've to go out with Jose to see her tomorrow. I'm not looking forward to it, Ma.' Under stress, Georgia was prone to revert to the familiar way of addressing her mother.

'Don't worry, I'll tell you what to do, Georgia pet.'

'What Ma?'

'Play it cute. Get on the good side of that oul' wan.'

'How do I do that Ma?'

'Didn't you tell me before that Jose is her only son? Like any mother she's afraid of losing him to someone else. Now, here's what to do…get friendly with this Contessa one. Show her she had nothing to fear. Ask her advice on things – like how you want her advice on the wedding, that sort of thing. In other words let her see that she won't be losing a son but gaining a daughter.'

Georgia was delighted. Why hadn't she thought of that before! 'Mom, you're a star! I'll do as you say. Anything else?'

'Yes, don't forget to tell the Contessa that me and Paddy were asking for her. We look forward to meeting her.' Georgia heard her mother gasp. 'Bye now pet, I have to go. The dog's barking again, that means the postman is at the gate!'

Georgia's mother replaced the receiver with tears in her eyes. Her youngest girl was moving up in life by the sound of things. She hoped that Georgia would be happy with Jose. Pity about his mother though; Georgia would be better off marrying a nice lad from Finglas.

Georgia left Jose's apartment and made her way back to the Hotel Orlando. Time to meet up with Bernice and Alison and tell them all the latest news. Maybe they too would give her some advice on how she should conduct her meeting with the Contessa tomorrow.

— ☽ —

'Stay still, Mark for just another few minutes,' Caroline urged. 'I've almost finished the basic sketch. It's looking good, even if I say so myself.'

She had asked Mark if he would pose for a portrait. If it turned out well she would present it to him as a token of his being so supportive when she most needed a friend. Last night he had taken her to Jose's Hacienda for Georgia's memorable Dance of the Seven Veils. It had been a great night, despite the fact that Wayne had drunk too much and had ended up nearly drowning in the hotel pool. Lucky for him Maureen Duff had decided on an early morning swim...

'O.K Mark, at ease now. I've finished.'

Mark relaxed, rubbed the tension out of his neck. Posing for a portrait wasn't easy. 'When do I get to see it?'

'I won't show it to you until I've put some colour into it.'

He stretched out on his stomach on the sand with his chin propped in his hands, studied Caroline as she mixed paint on her palette. 'You're all aglow, gleaming. You look beautiful, Caroline.'

'Thank you. It must be the sun and the sea air.'

'If I had my guitar with me I'd sing a song specially for you,' he said dreamily.

'What song is that?'

"It's Just The Sun'…It's a Don McLean song, one of my favourites. Like to hear it?'

He began, humming at first, then breaking into the lyrics. He watched her, sitting on the rock looking out to sea, as he sang. He noted the blush as it crept from her neck up her tanned face to the roots of her dark hair. He longed to go to her, take her in his arms and tell he that he had fallen in love with her, head over heels madly in love. He wanted her to know how much she meant to him already, now and forever. The overwhelming desire for her rose within him in one incredible moment as their eyes locked. He was sure she felt something for him also, even though she had told him that she was already committed to someone else. How do you compete against God?, Mark wondered.

A tear trickled down her cheek. Caroline wiped it away with the back of her hand. Another tear followed, this time falling onto her palette.

'It looks like you're adding a bit of yourself to the portrait,' Mark laughed, making light of the moment.

'You have a wonderful voice, Mark. And the song…it was beautiful.'

'Do you sing, Caroline? I'd guess you have a lovely voice…'

'Yes, I sing a little – and I play the guitar too! You see Mark, we have a lot in common.'

'Will you sing for me now?'

She shook her head. 'Not now – But I will at the last night party tomorrow night, I promise. I will sing something specially for you.'

As the sun got hotter they moved further back from the beach and into the shade of tall, leafy trees under which were dotted several rough wooden picnic tables. They ate a couple of baguettes and drank the orange juice which Caroline had brought. Afterwards they spread their towels and lay down. He held her hand throughout the afternoon and she did not object.

Now it was almost the end of the holiday. In two days time they would fly back to Dublin. Would it be the end of their relationship?, Mark wondered. He had to accept that he was going to lose her. Caroline had told him she wished to become a nun, enter the religious life. He closed his eyes, dwelt on her words again... 'Here in Ibiza I've seen how the other half lives, Mark, and it is not for me. I'll always have you in my heart, but I want to be fulfilled, do something better with my life. You do understand, don't you, Mark?'

He had nodded, not trusting himself to speak. But even now at this late stage he was hoping that Caroline would change her mind.

In the afternoon Maureen decided to call on Wayne to see how he was recovering from his near-drowning ordeal. She liked Wayne; she suspected that underneath the tough guy, macho image which he was fond of portraying there was a shy, sensitive person trying to get out.

When she knocked on the apartment door and got no reply she presumed that Wayne was still asleep. Slightly concerned nevertheless, Maureen turned the handle. She was not too surprised when the door opened at her touch. Obviously neither Wayne nor Mark were the conscientious type on holiday!

Maureen peeped into the bedroom. Wayne was in bed, asleep. She sat down, coughed discreetly. After a few moments his eyes opened. When he saw her he sat bolt upright, rubbing his eyes.

'Hello, er, Maureen. What are you doing here?'

'I dropped in to see how you are. You had an accident, remember?'

He took time to think. 'Oh yeah, now I remember...In the pool, some people pulled me out – ' He broke off. 'How did you know about it? Did you see them pulling me out?'

Maureen smiled, decided not to enlighten him. 'Yes. I just happened to be passing by at the time – ' Informing Mark that he had been rescued by a middle-aged woman would have been bad for his image!

'I must find out who those people were, thank them.'

'How did you end up in the pool in the first place, Wayne? Did you fall in?'

He looked sheepish. 'Yes, I did. I must have had too much to drink. I remember rambling back alone from Jose's place – Mark was with Caroline – and I stopped at a bar. Walking past the pool I must have missed my footing – or maybe I dived in. I can't remember, although I do have a vague memory of somebody holding me up in the water before the crowd came….'

'You're a very lucky young man. Somebody must have been praying for you.'

He pulled the bedclothes up over his bare chest, again looked sheepish. 'Probably my mother. She's always praying for me, trying to get me to reform!'

'Imagine the shock she would have received had you drowned in that pool. You should be more careful, Wayne. Take better care of yourself.'

'I will, Maureen. I will.'

'Are you very close to your mother?'

'Yes I am, especially since my father died. You may not believe this, but I respect my mother a lot. I'd be lost without her.'

'And do you miss your father?'

Wayne sank back on his pillow, paused before replying. 'Yes. A lot. Like all sons you think your father is going to be around forever. He went quickly – a heart attack. Not long after that one of my best mates was killed in a car accident. Two people I looked up to taken away overnight. I began to drink heavily, even tried drugs to give me a boost. You see there was nobody I could turn to, my mother had her own problems – 'Wayne broke off suddenly. 'Hey, why am I telling you all this? I've never discussed it with anyone else.'

'You're telling me because by talking about it you are helping yourself.'

'Yeah?'

'Yes. It's a form of therapy. When we unburden ourselves to someone we release tension, allow the real person to emerge. It's quite simple, really.'

He was looking at her suspiciously. 'Are you a psychiatrist or something, Maureen? I suppose you'll be sending me a bill for all of this advice.'

She laughed. 'I'm not a psychiatrist. I like talking to people, drawing them out of themselves.' A pause. 'I happen to think you're a very nice person, Wayne. That macho image you project is not really you.'

Now it was his turn to last. 'Are you sure it's me you're talking about?'

'As I recall you were very nice and helpful to me at the airport on the way out here. And I like the way you talk about your mother in such a concerned way. It shows that there's definitely another Wayne beneath the surface.'

'Will you give over, Maureen. I can't cope with all those nice things being said about me.'

'I think subconsciously you're still grieving for your father and your friend. Two sudden deaths like those are a big burden for any young man to carry.'

'Okay, so I admit it, I never let anyone know how bad I'm feeling. It's not my style. So what?' He was still on guard, still not sure where all of this was leading.

'Would you like to talk to somebody, Wayne? A professional person, someone who might be able to help?'

He looked uncomfortable. 'You mean someone who would put me lying down on a leather couch. A shrink?'

Despite herself Maureen laughed. 'No, no. Nothing like that I assure you. I'd like you to simply attend a few bereavement session in Dublin, one night a week. You'll meet people there like yourself who have suffered by losing a dear friend, someone close to them. I know the people who run the sessions...'

'How do I know that these sessions will help me?'

'You don't. I can't give you any guarantee. But I think they will. What do you say? In fact by taking part you might even be able to help others...'

That was the selling point. 'Me, helping someone like myself? You're joking...'

'I'm not. It's too serious a subject to joke about. You know that yourself, Wayne.'

'I sure do.' He quickly made up his mind. 'Alright, Maureen. I'll do it. I'll go to these bereavement sessions –'

'Good. I'll jot down the address and telephone number in Dublin. The next session begins in the autumn. Now Wayne,' she smiled at him, 'I'm going to make you a nice cup of tea. You rest, take things easy and get back into shape for the farewell party that's on tomorrow night.' Maureen hoped her advice was not falling on deaf ears. 'Do you take milk and sugar?'

As she was exiting to the kitchen he called after her. She turned, 'Yes?'

'Were you the person who pulled me out of that swimming pool a few hours ago?' When she didn't reply he went on. 'I thought so. Thanks a million!'

Maureen merely smiled and entered the kitchen. There were cups and plates everywhere and it looked like the place hadn't been cleaned for a week. She rolled up her sleeves and prepared to get to work.

When Georgia arrived back at the Orlando Hotel she found Bernice, Brian and Alison soaking up the sun by the pool. As soon as they saw her they waved her over to join them. All of them agreed that she had put on a great show in Jose's last night.

'It was terrific,' Brian enthused. 'Any chance of a repeat performance for the guests here at the pool?'

'No way!', Georgia laughed, pleased at the praise being heaped on her. 'I haven't got my veils with me. Besides, I'm a professional dancer now and Jose is my manager. He wants me to perform one more time in his bar before I go home. I've agreed to dance again tomorrow night.'

'What about the farewell party here by the poolside tomorrow night?', Bernice asked. 'Aren't you coming to that?'

'Of course, wouldn't miss it for the world. I'll have a busy day tomorrow; we're going out to see Jose's mother to sort a few things out, then I'll be back to dance in Jose's. Afterwards we'll come along here for the party.'

'You'll be in plenty of time. The party will be only hotting up around midnight,' Bernice said.

'Sit down and tell us all the news, Georgia', Alison gestured to an empty lounger nearby. 'How are things between yourself and Jose. Have you agreed to marry him yet?'

Georgia thought Alison was being a bit forward asking such a question in front of everyone. 'Nothing is decided between Jose and myself until I see the Contessa tomorrow,' she answered levelly.

'I suppose you know she left immediately after your performance last night?', Alison persisted. 'She didn't look too pleased to say the least. Did Jose tell you?'

'Yes he did, if you must know. Not that it's anybody's business,' Georgia answered, annoyed now. 'By the way Alison, how are you getting on? Have you managed to pick up another fellow yet?'

The implication wasn't lost on Alison. 'If you're implying I'm in the habit of picking up any fellow who comes along, Georgia, I'll have you know I'm particular who I share my favours with,' Alison shot back.

'Share your favours…Is that what you call it now? – '

'Anyone for a cool drink?' Brian cut in, anxious to avoid a girlish spat. His timely intervention cooled the atmosphere while they all decided what to order. Brian noted everyone's choice and headed towards the poolside bar.

Georgia turned to Bernice. 'How are things between yourself and Brian? Have you made any progress?'

'Knowing Bernice you should be asking has Brian made any progress!', Alison sniggered. She seemed to be in one of her waspish moods, probably because of what had happened between herself and Miguel.

Bernice laughed the jibe off. 'Yes, Georgia, we have come to an understanding.' When Brian has fully recovered from his illness he's coming over to Dublin to see me. The firm of accounts he works for have a branch there so all he has to do is put in for a transfer.'

'Isn't that great. Is that all your news?'

Bernice gave a shy smile. 'No. If everything goes well between us we hope to get engaged at Christmas!'

'That's great! Congratulations Bernice.' Georgia was genuinely delighted for her friend. Bernice was always the slowest between them at getting off with fellows.

'Don't tell anyone when we get home,' Bernice cautioned. 'Brian's a lovely fella, very genuine and I like him a lot, but I'm not taking anything for granted.'

'It's all very fine you two talking about men. What about me?', Alison cut in. 'I'm the odd one out. Where am I going to find a fella before we go home?'

'You don't have to. Aren't half the fellas in Finglas mad about you,' Bernice consoled her. 'Don't worry, Alison, there's still time left on the holiday for something to happen.' She turned to Georgia, 'If you get engaged to Jose, will you be bringing your parents over here to meet the Contessa, or will you bring him over to Finglas to meet your parents?'

'I haven't even thought about it,' Georgia told a little white lie. Of course the different backgrounds of herself and Jose was going to be a problem no matter what she did. She didn't tell Alison and Bernice the real purpose of her visit to Jose's mother tomorrow. Better not say anything right now. How the Contessa reacted tomorrow could either set a dream romance in motion or else signal the end of the affair.

When Brian returned with the drinks Georgia gulped hers down quickly. 'Sorry girls, but I have to go now. Jose and I have some important things to discuss. See you sometime. Goodbye!'

Georgia got a taxi to the bar. When she entered she was pleased to see Jose had returned from his earlier business appointment. He came from behind the bar to greet her. 'My beautiful Georgia, how are you?'

'I'm fine, Jose, but we need to talk.'

'As you wish.' He saw the serious look on her face. 'There is something bothering you…?'

'Yes.'

'Come into my office. I tell the staff not to disturb us.' In his office he asked: 'What is the problem, querida?' When she hesitated he sighed. 'If you do not tell me what it is how can I help?'

'Jose, I want things sorted out between us and time is running out,' Georgia began.

'What is it you wanted sorted out? I want you to marry me and all you have to do is say yes. It is very simple, no?'

'No Jose, it is not very simple. You see you and your mother come from a different background to me. I come from what we call a working class family. We are not rich and we don't live on a big hacienda like you do. We live in an ordinary house in a big housing estate on the outskirts of Dublin city. I belong to a big family, I've three sisters who are married – ' actually two of them were living with their boyfriends but Georgia kept quiet about that – 'and I've also got two brothers who have families. There are always lots of children in our house, lots of noise and shouting, and sometimes we fight among ourselves – often loud enough for the neighbours to hear– '

She broke off because Jose had held up his hand. 'Stop! Wait!' He rose from his chair, advanced towards her, took both her hands in his, pulled her to her feet. 'Georgia, I do not want to marry your family, these brothers and sisters – I want to marry you! And I do not care about where you live. That does not matter to me because when we are married we will live here, in Ibiza. You are the girl I want to marry and nothing else matters. Do you understand?'

He was holding her close, gazing earnestly into her eyes. 'Oh Jose, I love you,' Georgia said. And she meant it from the bottom of her heart. She began to cry and she buried her face in his shoulder. They stayed silent for a few moments then Georgia raised her head and looked into his eyes. 'But what about your mother. Supposing she does not want me for your wife?'

Jose laughed. 'I have told you before, leave the Contessa to me. My mother does not want me to marry because she is afraid of losing me. She sees this red-haired Irish girl arriving in Ibiza and taking her only son away. Yes, she would like me to marry a Spanish girl but she must accept that I am in love with you. And you, Georgia, will become part of my family.'

Georgia recalled the advice her own mother had given her earlier. 'I do not want to take anything from your mother. She will remain head of the household, boss of the hacienda. I will be like a daughter to her, helping her, asking her advice – ' She broke off. Now that she was in Spain she should take the bull by the horns!

'Tell you what, Jose,' Georgia said, her voice rising with excitement, 'why don't we drive out now to see your mother. I'll let her know I would like to be married here in Ibiza. I will allow herself and Pilar to arrange the wedding, leave everything in their hands. She will be in complete control –' Georgia broke off, breathless.

Jose hugged her. 'My darling, you are splendid! The Contessa will love your plan. And I love you!' He kissed her passionately then said: 'I will telephone my mother and tell her to include us for dinner.'

'I must go back to the apartments and change,' Georgia said, excited now. 'Pick me up there as soon as possible, Jose.'

An hour later, the breeze was warm and refreshing as Jose and Georgia drove out through the countryside heading for the Contessa's hacienda. Georgia wore a wide brimmed hat to shade her fair skin from the sun. A short while earlier she had left the apartment with the good wishes of Alison and Bernice ringing in her ears. They knew this was a vital visit between Georgia and Jose's rather forbidding-looking mother.

Maria the maid greeted them at the entrance to the villa as they drove up. She wore her usual warm, welcoming smile. 'The Contessa and Pilar are resting on the back veranda in the shade,' she whispered to Jose as they entered. 'They are expecting you.' She then hurried off to prepare dinner which would be served outdoors.

Jose took Georgia's hand, squeezed it encouragingly. He lead her out through the spacious sitting-room and onto the veranda. It was cooler at the back of the house, the well-tended, cultivated land sweeping away towards the mountains, hazy in the distance.

Pilar was busy with her needlework while the Contessa rocked back and forth in a large wicker chair. Pilar looked up and smiled at them; there was no mistaking her pleasure as seeing them again. Georgia felt the gaze of Jose's mother on her. There was a hint of a rare smile on her lips.

'You are both welcome,' the Contessa nodded a formal greeting. 'Please sit down – ' she gestured towards a chair, her eyes still on Georgia. 'Jose, tell Maria to bring some wine.'

Jose exited. Wine wasn't exactly Georgia's favourite drink – it always made her feel drowsy – but no way was she going to refuse the Contessa!

'And to what do I owe the pleasure of this visit of yourself and my son?', the older woman asked. As usual the tone was measured and not very friendly.

Georgia decided to be upfront with her response. 'I wish to tell you, Contessa, that I have accepted your son's proposal of marriage and now I am asking for your help.' Her breathless outpouring of words took both women by surprise. Pilar stopped at her needlework and said something to Jose's mother in Spanish. Georgia held her breath.

'I will discuss the matter with my son when he returns. In the meantime, what is it that you wish me to help you with?' Was it her imagination, Georgia wondered, or had the stern voice softened somewhat?

'In my country it is the custom for the wedding to take place in the bride's church,' Georgia began. 'However, I know you would prefer for Jose and his bride to marry here in Ibiza. I am happy to for the wedding to take place here – ' The two women looked a each other and this time the Contessa did smile. Georgia went on, 'As a stranger I would not know enough about how to organise a Spanish wedding. If you, Contessa and Pilar would help me I would be very grateful so that everything would be done in accordance with the customs of your country. Will you both help me?' Was this really herself speaking! Georgia reckoned if her own mother was here now she would be proud of how her daughter had followed her instructions.

Again the two older woman conversed in their native tongue. It was a brief exchange and then the Contessa turned to her. For the first time ever Georgia saw a warm smile on her face. 'I am pleased that you are marrying my son, and of course Pilar and I will be delighted to offer assistance. We are both very happy that you have decided to hold the ceremony here in Ibiza.'

Jose's mother rose from her chair. Georgia got to her feet also, wondering what was coming next. To her surprise the Contessa embraced her warmly.

'I am so happy to welcome you, Georgia, into our family. My only regret is that Jose's father is not also here to enjoy this occasion.' Jose had come out from the house just in time to witness the scene. He saw the tears in his mother's eyes and also noted that his Aunt Pilar was smiling and crying at the same time. He knew instinctively that all the problems had been solved.

'Madeleina, we never expected to be asked to take responsibility for a wedding!' Pilar said through her tears. Turning to Georgia she asked, 'Have you and Jose set a date yet?'

'No,' Georgia replied. 'We will arrange that when Jose comes to Dublin to meet my parents.' She smiled at Jose who moved close and slid his arm around her waist.

The Contessa spoke up again. 'Before we drink a toast to celebrate this happy occasion I want Jose to accompany me to my bedroom. There is something I must give him...'

As Georgia watched them go Pilar said, 'You must understand how Madeleina feels. It is not easy to give away her only son, for her to share him with another woman. Jose has been a bachelor too long and as for Madeleina – sometimes I think she has forgotten what it is like to be in love!'

'Yes, I understand,' Georgia said. The Contessa and Jose returned a short while later. He was carrying a small black leather case which he opened at his mother's bidding. Lying on a bed of white velvet was the most beautiful emerald ring Georgia had ever seen. Its beauty almost took her breath away.

'Querida mia,' Jose said softly, 'my mother would like for you to have this as your engagement ring. It has been in our family for many centuries and it is her way of showing her approval of our betrothal.' He took the ring out if its case and slipped it on Georgia's finger. It was a perfect fit.

'Jose, what can I say – ' Now it was Georgia's turn to feel emotional. 'Oh, thank you – ' she kissed the Contessa on both cheeks, performed the same ceremony with Pilar. The three of them had tears in their eyes as they embraced.

'Maria, pour the wine,' the Contessa ordered. 'This is one of the happiest moments of my life. And pour a glass of wine for yourself!'

Later, as they sat enjoying the evening sunshine waiting for Maria to serve dinner, Jose announced that he and Georgia would be staying the night and returning to Ibiza first thing in the morning.

'In that case I will tell Maria to prepare two bedrooms – one at each end of the house!' The Contessa noted that the two young lovers were holding hands and were looking longingly into each other's eyes. 'This is my house and here my rules will apply!'

If Ben and Irene thought that their wedding anniversary was of no interest to anyone but themselves they were mistaken. Throughout the day congratulatory cards and telegrams arrived from Dublin from friends and neighbours. The staff in Ben's second-hand car sales had not forgotten him either.

Irene's excitement grew as evening approached. She dressed early; a delicate green ensemble with contrasting trailing scarf highlighting her fair complexion. She had had her hair done in the hotel specially, swept up in a bouffant style off her face, which she thought took several years off her age.

Before they left the apartment Ben clasped an emerald pendant on a gold chain around her neck. 'Thanks for twenty five wonderful years, 'my darling Irene,' he said as he slid his arms around her waist and kissed her tenderly.

'Oh Ben, don't make me cry I'll spoil my make-up,' Irene said, fighting back tears of happiness.

As if all that wasn't enough there was another big surprise when they stepped out of the elevator into the foyer. Their entry was greeted by a round of applause and cheering. Ben and Irene looked around in surprise; all the holiday gang they had made friends with were there – Alo and Mamie, Des and Evelyn, Maureen Duff with Alec Holliday, and the girls Caroline, Alison and Bernice with Mark and Wayne in close attendance.

Paula Sheridan ushered them all into a room off the foyer where a table with several bottles of champagne and glasses were laid out. Paula made a brief speech on behalf of herself and the other guests and the festivities began as toasts were drunk and Ben and Irene were swamped under deluge of hugs, handshakes and kisses. As the applause rang out Paula's daughter Vicki came forward with a large bouqet of flowers which she presented to Irene.

Ben made a short speech thanking everybody, especially Paula Sheridan and the Orlando Hotel for hosting the surprise reception. Half-an-hour later himself and Irene made their exit to the waiting limousine – another surprise from Paula. Ben held Irene's hand during the short drive to the Hotel Tropicana. As they approached they could see the building in all its splendour looming out of the evening mist.

When their chauffeur opened the limo door Irene found herself stepping out onto a red carpet which stretched up the steps of the hotel and into the foyer. At the top of the steps Henri the manager waited to greet them.

'Oh God, Benjamin, this is too much – I feel like royalty!,' Irene gasped as a lone violinist, dressed in traditional costume, led them into the vast dining-room and across to their table, isolated from the other diners on a small dais beside a vast bay window. 'How are we ever going to repay Paula Sheridan for all this?' Ben was wondering the same thing!

'I hope everything is to your liking, senor, senora?', Henri smiled and bowed. Irene felt dizzy. She was overcome with emotion and the splendour of it all. Henri snapped his fingers and a waiter appeared to pour their champagne. The eyes of everyone in the dining-room was on them; speculation was rife as to whom the couple being honoured so splendidly might be.

Then the sumptuous meal began, course after course of superbly-prepared food. Half of the time Ben wasn't sure what exactly it was he was eating, but there was no denying its excellence. Then after coffee, to everyone's surprise, the lights in the dining-room were dimmed and a spotlight focused on the entrance to the kitchen. Head Chef Xavier emerged, flanked by two waitresses. He was a carrying a magnificently decorated 25th anniversary cake, which Henri informed Irene and Ben later had been ordered by their family in Dublin. With due pomp and ceremony it was placed on their table. Irene could no longer hold back the tears and Ben held her hand as, at every table in the room, diners rose to their feet and drank a toast to the happy couple from Ireland.

The evening was far from over. On the bandstand the trio of musicians had played romantic tunes all evening. Now Henri stepped up to the microphone and announced:

'Ladies and gentlemen, your attention please...' All eyes turned towards him. 'As you know we have a couple, Ben and Irene from Dublin, celebrating their silver wedding anniversary with us tonight. For them we will play a beautiful, romantic tune which has been specially requested for them from someone who is very close but who wishes to remain anonymous. Now if the happy couple will make their way to the dance floor....'

Amid a round of applause Ben and Irene made their way through the tables. Just as they reached the polished surface of the dance floor the strains of 'Strangers In The Night' floated out. They began to dance. Irene rested her head on her husband's shoulder, her eyes closed. She could not have been happier.

Ben fought hard to keep his emotions in check. It wasn't easy....Paula had not forgotten; the Sinatra classic had been their song. They had danced to it so often in those heady days when they were lovers. Ben's eyes misted over as he danced.

He remembered a beautiful young girl who had loved him all those years ago with out restraint. Passionately, adoringly, opening up vistas of a future which he had never imagined possible. But it was not to be. Everything that had happened tonight was Paula's way of reminding him what might have been.

'Wasn't that a lovely reception for Ben and Irene? It was very thoughtful of Paula Sheridan to organise it as a surprise for them before their anniversary dinner.'

Maureen Duff sipped her champagne and whispered the aside to Alec Holliday. A beaming Irene and Ben had just departed and everyone was now standing around chatting and finishing off their drinks.

Alec didn't reply immediately until he noticed Maureen looking at him. 'Oh er, yes indeed. Very nice of Paula,' he replied, almost mechanically.

She sensed that his thoughts were elsewhere. Maureen noted that he had hardly touched his champagne; even allowing for him being a pint of Guinness man that was unusual. What on earth was bothering him?, she wondered. Ever since she had seen him talking to that dark-haired lady last night in Jose's Hacienda he had assumed a preoccupied look which was at variance to his hitherto cheerful manner. Right now she sensed that

Alec's thoughts were miles away from the reception in the hotel.

Had it anything to do with herself?, Maureen pondered. Now that the holiday was nearing its end was he worried about how he would handle the situation between them when they landed back at Dublin Airport? She had always been careful not to assume that anything serious was happening between them. She was too independent for that. As far as she was concerned Alec had no cause to be ill at ease; they were dancing partners who had met up and enjoyed each other's company on the holiday…end of story. Maureen Duff had her own plans for the future.

She decided to try once more. 'Anything wrong, Alec?'

'Wrong? No, 'course not. Why do you ask?'

'Oh, just that you seemed preoccupied with something…'

He glanced at his watch, put his glass down on the table. 'Well, now that you mention it, Maureen, there is a little bit of business I have to attend to tonight – right now in fact. I've got to go and meet somebody. Mind if I nip off?'

'Of course not. It's obviously someone very important.'

'It is. Very.'

'Anything to do with that lady I saw you speaking to at the bar last night?', Maureen couldn't resist it. She made sure to smile when she asked the question.

He paused, thinking. 'Yes actually, it does have something to do with that lady. But I can't explain anything right now. Maybe when I come back we can have a chat over a late night drink…'

'If you wish. Now you'd better keep your appointment. Goodbye Alec – and take care.' She didn't know why she added that last bit. She must sense an element of danger in whatever it was he was involved.

Take care – that's exactly what he intended to do, Doc thought to himself as he left the hotel. He wasn't looking forward to keeping his appointment in the park with Donie Crawford. Every since Yolanda had approached him in the bar last night and told him that his former drug-pushing teammate suspected something was not right between them Doc had been worried. All day he had a feeling that something dangerous was about to happen.

Even the assurance by Yolanda that there would be an adequate number of Spanish policemen in disguise ready to pounce at the first sign of danger didn't assuage Doc's fear. He hoped that Yolanda would keep her promise. How on earth had he got himself into this mess!

He decided to walk rather than take a taxi to the park at the end of the harbour. A walk would clear his head, help him to relax. He knew the park well from his early morning jogs along the Figueretas promenade; several times he had jogged through the area, skirting the children's playground before making the return journey to the hotel.

The nearer he got to the park the more apprehensive Doc became, vivid images of those unfortunates who had crossed Dublin drug barons being blasted into eternity torturing his mind. A couple of days ago, giving Ben O'Rourke advice on how to handle his affair with Paula Sheridan and the daughter who had suddenly come into his life, Doc had thought Ben had problems. They were nothing compared to what he was facing right now!

Strolling in the park, now that the heat of the sun had waned, was a popular pastime with Spanish families and young couples. Doc walked into the playground, crowded with young children watched over by fathers and mothers and doting grannies. He glanced around. There was no sign of Donie Crawford, and no sign of Yolanda Segguria either. Everything appeared very ordinary.

Doc glanced at his watch. Two minutes to eight p.m. He was spot on time. He decided to stroll around, keep on the move. Standing alone in a children's playground would draw attention to himself. He hoped Donie would be on time; Doc wanted to get this thing over with and get back to the safety of the hotel.

Three leisurely circuits of the playground and his quarry still had not showed up. Doc looked at his watch again – 8.10p.m Maybe Donie wasn't keeping the appointment, taking no chances? Doc felt a wave of relief wash over him. He could go back to the hotel, have that drink with Maureen. At least he had tried. It wasn't his fault that Donie had gotten cold feet…

Then he saw him. Donie was walking quickly towards him, hands stuffed deep in the bomber jacket he was wearing. Doc watched him approach, his stomach churning.

'Howareya – ' Doc sensed that Donie was nervous also. His eyes were flitting everywhere.

'You're late. What the hell kept you?'

'None of your business.'

'I was about to leave. Thought you got cold fee.'

'Did you now. If you must know I've watching you since you arrived.'

'Why? Don't you trust your old teammate?'

'I don't trust nobody. Now let's get down to business. I want to get the hell out of here - '

Doc was getting even more nervous. Like Donie he was looking around frantically. Where the hell were all the police officers Yolanda had said would be around? All he could see were Mums and Dads playing with their kids in the sandpit, others pushing children on swings. Nobody seemed to be giving him and Donie Crawford a second glance.

'You got the heroin?' Doc asked.

'Yeah.' He heard Donie swear under his breath.

'And the money?'

'Right here.' Donie tapped a bulging pocket in his jacket.

'Right then. Pass them over.' Doc could feel the sweat breaking out on his forehead – and it had nothing to do with the mugginess of the evening. His mouth felt dry and he was finding it hard to swallow. He watched as Donie glanced around once more before reaching into his pocket. He pulled out a flat packet wrapped in plastic, handed it to Doc.

All of a sudden all hell broke loose. Three men in sport shirts who had been tending their offspring on the swings turned and began running towards where Doc and Donie were standing. Several other figures in police uniforms appeared from nowhere, also heading in their direction. Yolanda Segguria was among them.

Donie Crawford swore again. He tried to grab the packet back from Doc who pushed him off. Donie turned, began to run, reaching into his leather jacket. Suddenly a gun appeared in his hand. As Doc watched frozen in horror Donie pointed the gun skywards and fired over the advancing policemen's heads. They stopped in their tracks, also the trio advancing from the other side. The evening air was filled with screams of frightened women and children and everyone was running for cover.

'You squealer, I'll get you for this!', Donie shouted as he brushed past Doc and ran towards the playground exit. He stopped, turned, and to Doc's horror pointed the gun at him. Doc saw Donie's finger tighten on the trigger. He dived desperately behind a nearby tree. Just in time! – he heard a shot ring out, saw a splinter of bark fly through the air as the bullet hit. Another shot rang out. Another splinter of bark flew through the air. Doc made himself as small a target as possible behind the tree and prayed.

Thankfully, Donie was too busy making his escape to take aim at Doc again. Instead he sped off, firing shots into the air at random as he went. Doc heard Yolanda screaming something in Spanish and guessed she was instructing her colleagues not to fire for fear of hitting a child or a parent. He peeped out from behind the tree just in time to see Donie on the pillion seat of a powerful motorbike been driven along the seafront at speed.

'Alec, are you alright?' Yolanda was at his side, looking anxious.

'Sure, I'm fine,' Doc replied easily. It was a lie, his heart was pounding and when he took out a handkerchief to wipe the perspiration from his face his hand shook. No wonder – it wasn't every day in the week he was shot at! He had some story to tell them back in Ringsend!

'I'm sorry. I should not have asked you to do this. It was too dangerous.'

He waved her protest aside, shrugged. 'Yeah, it was pretty scary, but not to worry Yolanda.' He forced a laugh. 'I rather enjoyed it.'

'You are so brave – ' She looked up at him, her eyes shining. Suddenly there was a flash. Doc's heart missed a beat until he saw the man with the camera. There was a young girl standing beside him. By now everything had quietened down somewhat, with adults gathered in groups excitedly discussing the recent events.

'Excuse me,' the girl said in English to Doc. 'My name is Debbie and I'm a journalist working for the Ibiza News, an English language newspaper published fortnightly on the island. Do you mind my asking you some questions? What's your name, are you English, and how come you were helping the police catch that drug pusher?'

Hey man, he was being interviewed – a celebrity! Doc beamed, decided to make the most of his new-found fame. 'My name is Alec Holliday. I'm Irish, staying at the Hotel Orlando – '

Before he could get any further Yolanda, looking annoyed, said something sharply in Spanish to the girl, who answered back equally sharply in Spanish. They seemed about to have an argument. Suddenly Yolanda said something to two of her colleagues who were listening.

They grabbed both the girl and the camerman and began ushering them roughly through the watching crowd towards the park exit. One of the policemen had confiscated the man's camera.

'What was that all about?', Doc asked.

'Those journalists – they had no right to ask questions or take photographs without my permission. It puts lives in danger.'

Doc shrugged. 'I wasn't worried. I'm only sorry you didn't catch Donie.'

'I'm sorry also. As you saw he had an accomplice waiting on a motocicleta.'

'Can't you arrest him later?'

Now it was Yolanda's turn to shrug. 'We will have to find him first. That will be difficult, he has friends in the drugs business who will look after him. Maybe we get him next time…' They had walked out of the playground and into the park. 'I want to offer you a drive back to your hotel – '

'It's okay, Yolanda, I'll walk if you don't mind.' He didn't fancy arriving back at the hotel in a police car. People might think he had been arrested instead of him having risked his life helping to apprehend drug barons.

'Be very alert, Alec.' She touched his arm. 'Your friend Donie is still on the loose and he is dangerous.' She looked into his eyes. 'I do not want anything to happen to you. I will be in touch.'

'Don't worry, I can look after myself.' Doc watched as she got into the car with the flashing policia sign and was driven off.

Despite his bravado he was still shaking inside from the night's ordeal. Yolanda's warning about Donie seeking revenge was worrying. Doc had to admit that he was no James Bond; he was glad that two days from now the holiday would be over and he would be back home, safely sipping a pint at the bar in The Oarsman's in Ringsend.

CHAPTER SEVENTEEN

Doc Holliday pounded along the promenade on his early morning run., the events of last night looming large in his mind. As he approached the park which contained the children's playground he steeled himself to pass through the area where twelve hours ago he had come within a few inches of possible death.

No, he wasn't being too dramatic, he told himself. He really had had a narrow escape; had he not made it behind that tree in time he might now be lying in a hospital morgue with the bullet from Donie Crawford's gun embedded in his skull. Hard to believe that an old teammate would stoop to such a foul deed as shooting to kill.

Yolanda Segguria had warned him that drug pushing was big-time in Ibiza and that the men behind the business were ruthless. Last night's episode had certainly proved that!

The park was practically deserted at that hour of the morning. Doc jogged along the tarmacadamed path, taking the long way around towards the playground. When he reached it he cut in toward the tree, saw the clean area where the bullet had hit and knocked off a small area of the bark. He stood in the exact spot where he had hidden last night; Donie was a good shot – the spot on the tree where the bark was missing was exactly head high.

Doc continued his early morning jog, happy to leave the playground behind. He was happy too that this was his last full day in Ibiza. Tomorrow night he'd be at his usual place at the bar in The Oarsman's in Ringsend, knocking back pints of Guinness and regaling his pals with tales of how he had met an attractive Spanish policewoman and how they had joined forces to trap an Irish drug pusher in Ibiza. A lot of his contemporaries would remember Donie Crawford.

And Yolanda…Doc reckoned there was a mutual attraction there. He liked her style – and he also liked the way she had been very concerned for him last night when Donie had begun shooting. He hoped she would not be too angry after what had happened later…

Having decided to walk back to the hotel to steady his nerves, he had been about to enter the Orlando when a man whom he had noticed lounging near the entrance turned suddenly. There was a flash and when he had recovered from the shock Doc realised he had been photographed. As the man hurried away Doc had recognised him as the photographer who had scuffled with the police in the park last night.

The Ibiza News had obviously been determined to get a picture of him. Doc had thought of telephoning Yolanda and alerting her to what had happened but had decided against it. They had had enough excitement for one night!

Now, as he walked across the hotel foyer in his jogging outfit he saw his favourite receptionist gesticulating to him from behind the desk. 'Congratulations, Mister Holliday,' she said, smiling. 'You are famous. Look…'

She slid a copy of the Ibiza News from the pile placed on the reception desk whence the guests helped themselves to their free copies. Doc saw his photograph prominently displayed on the front page under the banner headline:

IRISHMAN HELPS IBIZA POLICE
IN DRUG BUST.

Underneath was a smaller headline:

Terror as shots fired in children's playground.

Doc stared, aghast. The Ibiza News had given the story a right good spread. Not since his days as a Shelbourne soccer player had his picture appeared in a newspaper. Looking at it now he couldn't help feeling pleased. By tonight Maureen and everyone going to the party by the poolside would have read or heard about his exploits. They would be all anxious to hear about his brush with death – and he would take great pleasure in telling them!

'It is true that the drug pusher shot at you?' The receptionist's eyes were aglow with admiration. Other people at the desk were listening in, then picking up their free copy.

'Yes, he had a go. I hid behind a tree.'

'But weren't you afraid?', the girl persisted.

'Sure I was. Scared out of my wits. I was lucky I guess..'

'You deserve an award for what you did last night,' a lady who had been listening said. 'You could have been killed. But imagine the exciting story you'll have to tell your friends when you go home...'

Doc decided it was time for him to escape to his apartment. He was anxious to read what the girl reporter had written about his part in last night's drama.

'Oh, Mister Holliday – ' the receptionist called out. 'Before you go, a telephone message for you...' She handed him a piece of paper. 'From a lady...' she smiled.

Doc read the message. 'Telephone me immediately.' It was signed Yolanda.

In his apartment he dialled the number. 'Hello, Yolanda. Alec here – '

'Alec! Have you seen the Ibiza News. What happened? That photograph – '

He explained his encounter with the photographer last night as he entered the hotel. 'It all happened so fast. He took it before I could stop him. I was going to phone you, Yolanda–'

'You should have, Alec.' She was annoyed, he could tell by her tone. 'I might have been able to prevent this story.'

She paused, then said. 'You are lucky you are leaving Ibiza tomorrow, that your holiday is over.'

'You mean Donie might come looking for revenge?'

'Yes. That packet of heroin he lost because of you had a street value of maybe one hundred thousand pounds sterling. He will not have liked losing it. Now he sees your photograph on the front page of a newspaper....' her voice trailed off. 'Be careful today, Alec. Don't leave the hotel. That is an official warning from the police.'

He swallowed. All his earlier bravado had vanished and his mouth felt dry again. 'Right Yolanda. I'll do as you say.' He wanted to change the subject, it was too scary for his liking. 'I hope you're coming to our last night party by the poolside tonight? It'll be good fun, just what we need.'

'Yes, I will be there.'

'Good. I want you to meet Maureen Duff. I'll introduce you, I think you'll like her.' A short time later their conversation ended and he put down the telephone.

Doc went downstairs again and joined Maureen at breakfast. He noted she had helped herself to several copies of the Ibiza News. 'You've read the story then?', he asked.

'Yes. So that's what you were up to last night. You could have been killed, Alec. I'm bringing home these newspapers to show to my friends.'

During breakfast several people stopped by their table to offer him their congratulations on taking on one of the island's notorious drug dealers. He answered all their questions politely. 'I'm glad I'm going home tomorrow. I don't think I could handle much more of this.' He told Maureen about Yolanda's phone call and her advice to stay by the pool today.

'Do as Yolanda says, Alec,' Maureen councelled. 'She knows what she is talking about. No point in taking any unnecessary risks now that the holiday is nearly over.'

Maureen planned on spending the morning in town doing some last minute shopping with Caroline. 'She is anxious to sit beside me on the flight home tomorrow. Would you like to join us?' Doc nodded, although right now his mind was on more pressing matters.

He took Yolanda's advice and stayed by the pool all afternoon in the company of Maureen, Alo and Mamie Riordan. He was surprised how on edge he was. He kept a wary out for Donie Crawford or any suspicious looking character who entered the pool area. Nothing unusual happened and when the sun began to wane they all retired to their apartments to do some packing for the departure home tomorrow.

'Well, I suppose you could say, apart from the party tonight, that this is well and truly the end of the holiday,' Alo opined, standing up from his sun lounger and stretching.

'Thank God for that!', his wife replied, eyeing him up and down. 'At least I won't have to stand the sight of you in those dreadful shorts until next year!'

Doc and Maureen joined in the laughter. He was more relaxed now, confident that despite Yolanda's warning, he had probably heard the last of Donie Crawford. He was looking forward to the party tonight.

'Benjamin, wake up! Have you been having a bad dream?' Irene planted a kiss on her husband's forehead and ruffled his hair. You drank too much champagne last night!'

Ben struggled through the haze of sleep to focus on Irene. She was already dressed and looked so alive and happy this morning. She must not suspect anything….he had been dreaming that he was in Paula's arms. They were dancing in a dreamworld and she was telling how much she loved him, needed him, and that nothing else mattered –

'Get up, Benjamin! This is our last full day of the holiday and we don't want to waste a minute of it.' Irene was all business. 'Mamie Riordan and I are going to do some shopping. Get yourself dressed and see if you can bump into Paula around the hotel. Thank her for that wonderful anniversary dinner. Up now quickly!'

Ben got gingerly out of bed. Oh!, how his head ached. Mention of Paula brought it all back...the beautiful dinner, the band striking up as he and Irene approached the dance floor...the strains of 'Strangers In The Night' wafting forth. Irene instead of Paula in his arms...!

He was glad in a way that the holiday was near its end. The strain was beginning to tell on him. Every day he was finding it more difficult to tread the delicate path between two women who were such a big part of his life. He needed a couple of strong cups of coffee to settle his nerves, followed by a stiff drink while Irene wasn't around. And of course a chat with Paula.....

Mamie called for Irene and the two went off like teenagers to shop for presents to bring home. 'Don't get back into bed, Benjamin, when I'm gone,' Irene warned. 'Get dressed and make it your business to see Paula.'

Ben needed no second bidding. Bumping into Paula wasn't very difficult; she suddenly appeared when he exited from the dining-room after breakfast. He got the distinct impression that she had been waiting for him. As usual she was looking smart and extremely attractive, dressed in her figure-hugging supervisor's outfit.

'Good morning, Ben,' she greeted him. 'Did you and Irene enjoy your anniversary dinner last night.' She stared. 'Don't mind my saying so, but you look a little hung-over.'

'Morning Paula,' he responded. 'Irene and I had a lovely time – thanks to you.'

'I'm so glad. Did the band play our favourite tune?'

'Yes. It brought back memories. Nice of you to have thought of it.'

'You're not angry with me, are you Ben?'

'Of course not. How could I? Like I said it brought back memories...' They stood staring, each conscious of the physical attraction of the other. When Paula had first discovered that Ben O'Rourke was staying in the hotel she had been angry. Since then, however, the anger had disappeared, given way to another emotion. Every time she saw him now she felt her breath catch in her throat. What was happening to her?, Paula wondered – she was worse than any gauche teenager! She would have to be very careful with Ben. After all, there was Irene to consider…

'We can't talk here,' Ben said. 'How about a coffee at the bar. It'll be deserted at this hour…'

They sat in a leafy corner, hidden from passers-by behind an overflowing plant, recalling their first meeting and its implications on their lives. And they discussed Vicki, their daughter, the young woman who was a bond from the past, destined to be a part of their future. Occasionally Ben took Paula's hand in his. She was content to leave it there, despite the danger of the intimacy being seen by a passer-by, excited at his touch.

It seemed no time had passed when Paula glanced at her watch. 'I must be going shortly,' she said, 'I've got work to do. Her tone was reluctant.

'I understand. I enjoyed our little chat, Paula.'

'I did too.'

'You'll be at the party at the poolside tonight, I hope. I'd like you to sit with Irene and me.'

'Yes, I'll be there to say goodbye to everyone. I'll be too busy tomorrow to see you all off on the coach. Saturday is an extremely busy day for me.'

'Then you must bring Vicki along tonight,' Ben said. 'I'd like to see her again before I go.'

'You'll see her again when we both accept Irene's invitation and stay in your house at Christmas. Are you looking forward to that, Ben?'

'Er, yes – ' Was he?

'You don't seem very sure - .' She paused, said softly. 'What are you thinking about, Ben?'

'I'm thinking about last night, Paula. And us – and what might have been. If only things had worked out differently...'

'Unfortunately they didn't – and it's too late now.' She fiddled nervously with her cup, spilled some coffee. She seemed nervous, on edge. 'Before I go there's something I want to give you, Ben – '

He watched as she searched in her handbag, extracted a plain envelope. 'I've been carrying this around with me for the last few days. It's for you – and I want you to promise that you won't open it until you are on the aeroplane home tomorrow. Remember, it's for your eyes only...'

'What is it?', Ben took the white envelope.

'Please, don't ask any questions. I can't answer them right now. Just do as I say, Ben. Promise?'

'I promise.'

Paula looked past him. 'Put the envelope away quickly, Ben! Irene and Mamie are arriving back. And they've seen us – ' Ben stuffed the envelope into his trouser pocket.

'Hello, Paula,' Irene put some parcels in front of Ben. 'Take those upstairs, Benjamin. We're back earlier than we thought. We got tired walking, didn't we, Mamie?'

'I'm off to find Alo,' Mamie said. 'Then I'll rest at the pool in the afternoon so I'll be fresh for the party tonight–'

'I must go also,' Paula slung her bag over her shoulder. 'I'm afraid Ben and I have spent too much time chatting –'

'I hope Benjamin thanked you for all you did for us last night, Paula,' Irene said. 'You did us proud. The champagne reception was a marvellous surprise – and the dinner was just superb – '

'I'm glad both yourself and Ben enjoyed it – ' She was anxious to get away.

' – and that tune they played specially for us towards the end of the night. What was it again, Benjamin? You sang every word as we danced – '

'Strangers In The Night,', Ben answered softly, his eyes meeting Paula's briefly.

'It was so romantic – ' Irene gushed. 'Just perfect.'

'I'll see you both at the party tonight. 'Bye.' Paula rushed off. They watched as she walked rapidly towards the exit.

'Oh Benjamin, did you remind Paula to bring Vicki along tonight?' Irene asked.

'Yes, Vicki will be there,' he replied. The envelope that Paula had given him was burning a hole in his pocket. But he would stick faithfully to his promise.

It was approaching midnight when the final night poolside party really took off and turned into a good old-fashioned Irish hooley. The transformation occurred when the ballad group Dubs' Angels and their entourage arrived back from Ibiza Town where they had been performing, and replaced the regular Spanish trio which entertained the guests nightly in the Orlando Hotel.

It took nearly half-an-hour for the quartet of Dubliners to set up their equipment. But when the music started with Kev and Collie on fiddle and tin whistle, the aptly named Hammer on bodhran and the long-haired and multi-talented Pez on banjo, the night really came alive. So much so that the international gathering of guests who were about to retire for the night changed their minds and decided to join their Irish friends at the hooley in the moonlight.

Alo Riordan was the star turn who filled in while the Dubs' Angels were setting up. Doc Holliday, who was sitting with Maureen and Yolanda Segguria at a table near the stage, had appointed himself interim Master of Ceremonies and over the microphone asked who would sing a song or two while the ballad group were getting ready.

Des Murtagh, who was sharing a table with his wife and Alo and Mamie Riordan, immediately jumped to his feet. 'How about a couple of Percy French ballads,' he shouted to Doc. ''lo here is just rarin' to go!'

The man from Co. Clare needed no further encouragement. He climbed onstage and without more ado took the microphone from Doc.

'If my husband makes a holy show of himself I'll murder him when we get back home!', Mamie muttered, although from past performances she knew Alo could entertain an audience. And she was proved right...Alo started off with a rousing rendition of 'Slattery's Mounted Foot' which got everyone foot-stomping and clapping in tune, slowed the tempo down with a beautiful version of the haunting 'Gortnamona', and finished his Percy French set on a high with the saga of the West Clare Railway, better known as 'Are You Right There, Michael?'.....A beaming Alo left the stage to huge applause.

Doc Holliday was in fine singing voice also. Accustomed to taking the stage at the social club in his native Ringsend, he entertained with two of Pete St. John's best-known ballads 'The Fields of Athenry' and 'The Rare Oul' Times.' He too was applauded off the stage.

By this the Dubs' Angels were ready to perform. And perform they certainly did. Not only were Kev, Collie, Hammer and Pez talented musicians, each of them were also excellent singers. In between downing pints of Guinness and lager, over the next hour they came up with a non-stop succession of ballads, jigs, reels and modern dances that had everyone – and not only the Irish – on their feet enjoying the fun.

Despite his traumatic encounter with Donie Crawford twenty-fours earlier, Doc Holliday was really letting himself go on his last night in Ibiza. Now into his fourth pint, sitting between two very attractive ladies in Maureen Duff and Yolanda, and basking in the glory of being featured on page one of the Ibiza News, he was feeling nice and relaxed. He had enjoyed a couple of dances with Maureen already and soon it would be Yolanda's turn. He thought she looked very elegant and cool in that cream trouser suit, her dark hair shining in the moonlight. She was chatting away to Maureen; Doc thanked his lucky stars that the two of them were getting on so well together.

'Hey Yolanda,' Doc exclaimed, 'how about if I ask the Dubs' Angels to play something Spanish, will you get up and strut your stuff. Perform a fandango, like...'

Yolanda laughed. 'I am sorry, Alec, but I am not dressed for dancing fandangos. Maybe when I visit you in Dublin you will bring me to a party and you and I will attempt a fandango together. Yes?'

'I'll hold you to that! We'll put out posters in Ringsend like the way we did for Georgia and her dance!'

Maureen laughed with them. So Alec had invited Yolanda to Dublin...Despite herself she felt a pang of envy. Oh well, it really didn't matter; wasn't she planning to return to Africa to continue the work with underprivileged there, work that she and Donal had devoted themselves to all those years ago...

The excitement and enjoyment at the poolside party reached new heights when the young people, including Bernice, Brian and Alison, also Caroline, Mark and Wayne, arrived to join in the fun. They had been partying in town but wanted to spend the last few hours of the holiday at the Irish hooley. Georgia had yet to put in an appearance; the girls had not seen her since yesterday when she had left with Jose to visit his mother. Alison and Bernice were just dying to know how she had coped with the Contessa. Was Georgia's romance with Jose on or off and was there a wedding in the offing? Surely Georgia and Jose would show up before the party ended?

When a request came from the stage for someone from the audience to come up and perform, everyone in the

Irish party was surprised when Caroline rose and volunteered.

'I didn't know Caroline was a singer,' Bernice said, 'did you, Mark?'.

'Yes she does – and plays the guitar too.'

'I think there's more to our friend Caroline than meets the eye,' Alison volunteered. 'You mark my words…'

Wayne thought about what Alison had said. There was something about Caroline he could never figure out. Why hadn't he been able to score with her the way he had with other girls? She was always so remote, unattainable. He had discussed it with Mark only yesterday but his friend had gone all vague on the subject of Caroline. Had Mark been taken into her confidence? What was her secret?

They watched amazed as Caroline borrowed Collie's fiddle, tucked it under chin in a very professional manner and began to play. Slowly a silence decended over the party-goers as the first haunting notes of the traditional Irish tune 'The Cuilin' wafted softly into the night air. Conversation at the tables died away and all eyes were turned on the young woman on stage. Caroline's dark hair fell over her face and her eyes were closed in concentration as the music worked its magic. The audience sat entranced, spellbound. When the final note faded into the night there was a moment's silence followed by the biggest round of applause of the evening.

Even before the clapping had died down Caroline was back seated at the table with Mark and the others, smiling shyly as they showered her with compliments.

'That was superb, Caroline,' Mark enthused. 'You play like an angel.'

'It was brillo,' Bernice said. There were tears in her eyes.

'Absolutely fantastic,' Alison agreed. 'Eat your heart out Yehudi what's-his-name!'

Even Wayne was impressed. 'Where did you learn to play like that?', he asked.

Caroline hesitated before replying. When she did so she sprung the second surprise of the night on them. 'In the convent,' she said. 'One of the Sisters there is an excellent violinist. She taught me. We often play together.'

Bernice and Alison looked at each other, puzzled. 'The convent …you mean you visit the nuns there…'

'No. I live there with the other members of our community. You see – ' Caroline paused, 'I'm a nun!'

There was a stunned silence, broken by Alison shrieking 'A nun! Did I hear you right, Caroline?'

'Yes you did. I am a nun.' They all stared at her, disbelief in every face. Wayne was so surprised he let out an expression nuns were not supposed to hear.

'You sure you're not joking us, Caroline, having us on like?' Bernice persisted. Although now that she thought about it things began to make sense, fall into place…

'Caroline's serious,' Mark spoke up. 'She really is a nun. She told me a few days ago.'

'Holy God – and I tried to get her drunk the first night we went out,' Wayne said, almost to himself.

'Wait a minute, Caroline,' Bernice still wasn't satisfied. 'If you're a nun what on earth are you doing here, in Ibiza of all places? All by yourself, too.'

'Looking for a fella – like the rest of us!' Alison exclaimed.

They all shrieked with laughter, even Caroline. 'No, nothing like that,' she said. 'It's a long story, and I'd rather not go into it if you don't mind. I'm sorry for not confiding it to all of you before this, but I did want to let you know before the holiday ended.'

'You know I thought of becoming a nun once,' Alison said dreamily, 'but my vocation didn't last. You see there was this fella I fancied – '

'Spare us the gory details!', Bernice cut in.

'You may not believe this,' Wayne spoke up. 'I considered being a priest once. On the missions. I saw myself out in a jungle somewhere converting thousands of black people....Then I discovered pubs and discoes!'

They all laughed, none louder than Caroline. 'Wait till Georgia hears the news,' Bernice said. I hope she and Jose show up before the party ends...'

As the music of the Dubs' Angels blared out into the night air, Paula Sheridan waited for an opportune moment for herself and Vicki to slip away and say goodbye to Ben. Herself and Vicki were seated at a large table with Ben and Irene, Alo and Mamie Riordan and Evelyn and Des Murtagh. Every one was having a good time and the waiters were being kept extremely busy attending the tables.

Paula and Vicki had been the last to join the party. She was very proud of how beautiful her teenage daughter looked, Tall, slim and blonde, wearing a sheath-like dress slit provocatively to the thigh and looking grown up beyond her years, Vicki had been the object of some admiring glances from young males at other tables since she had arrived. Several of them had already been over to ask her up to dance.

Paula noted that Ben's eyes followed Vicki's every movement. He too was obviously very proud of his daughter. Paula could well imagine the emotions that Ben was experiencing right now. Occasionally their eyes met across the table and when they did Paula felt her heart beat just that little bit faster.

The moment she was waiting for arrived when Irene, Mamie and Evelyn decided to go en masse to visit the ladies. Ben's eye caught Paula's and when he excused himself from the table she waited a full minute before excusing herself and motioned Vicki to follow.

They walked in the direction of the hotel entrance. 'Paula! Vicki!' They heard their names being called. Ben was standing in the shadow of a palm tree, out of sight of the revellers by the pool. His eyes ranged over them. 'My two beautiful ladies. What did I do to deserve such good fortune...'

'We haven't much time, Ben,' Paula cut in. 'The others will be back shortly.'

Ben looked at his daughter. 'I want you to know, Vicki, that coming to Ibiza was one of the best things that ever happened to me. I've discovered a beautiful daughter I never knew I had – '

Vicki smiled at her father for a moment, her eyes misty. 'I'm glad also that you came to Ibiza, that we finally met –'

'I have something for you – ' Ben reached into his pocket, took out a slim dark case, gave it to Vicki. 'My first present to my daughter. I'm so happy.'

'Thank you.'

Vicki opened the case, took out a slim gold chain with her name engraved. 'Oh,' she exclaimed, eyes shining. 'It's beautiful. Look Mom, isn't it exquisite…' Her mother nodded.

Ben gave his daughter a hug. 'This is one of the happiest moments of my life.'

'And mine also,' Vicki said. 'We are a family at last.' She hugged Ben warmly as Paula looked on, tears in her eyes.

'Promise me one thing, Vicki,' Ben whispered.

'Of course. What is it?'

'Promise me you'll take care of your mother. Remember I love you both and I look forward to seeing the two of you again soon.'

'I promise.'

Father and daughter stared into each other's eyes before embracing once again. When they broke apart Ben, his voice husky with emotion, said, 'Now you'd better go back to the party, my sweet. There are several handsome young men wondering where you've got to. And be careful, I don't want anything to happen to you – '

'Goodbye, Ben. I love you!' With that Vicki disappeared through the trees. Ben watched her until she was out of sight. He turned to Paula. 'She's so pretty – just like you, Paula.'

Paula smiled. 'Thank you, Ben. She loved your present. It was a good idea.'

'I have something for you also, Paula.' He reached into his pocket again, took out a slim case similar to the one he had given to Vicki. 'To celebrate our coming together again,' he said softly.

'Thank you. He watched her open it, saw her eyes gleam with pleasure. It was a gold chair with a single pearl attached. 'Thank you, Ben. It's lovely.'

The branches rustled as he moved close. 'I'm so happy that this isn't the end for us, Paula. I look forward to seeing you in Dublin.' He knew he was courting danger having Paula visit, but the thought of seeing her again far outweighed that.

Why on earth had she accepted Irene's invitation to visit at Christmas? she wondered. There could be only one reason. She was still in love with Ben O'Rourke and wanted to see him again. Despite what had happened between them, and the anger she had harboured over the years, the attraction was still there – for both of them. He was a married man and she did not want to hurt Irene, but she could not bear the thought of him just walking out of her life.

When she had first discovered that Ben O'Rourke and his wife were staying in the hotel she had set out to ruin his holiday, extract some form of revenge for what had happened in the past. But her feelings had changed. Up to a short while ago she had been happy with her close relationship with Edwin, her German tutor. He wanted to marry her, move in with her and become a father to Vicki. Now things were not so simple...

She felt Ben's arms around her, drawing her close. His lips moved towards hers –

'Please Ben, don't!' She broke away. 'Don't you see, we're only making problems for ourselves – ' He was staring at her wordlessly. 'I must go back, they'll be wondering what's keeping me. I hope you and Irene have a safe journey back to Dublin tomorrow – '

'Paula! Wait! – ' He watched as she moved through the trees back towards the brightness. He did not see the tears in her eyes.

Meanwhile, back at the poolside, a beaming Jose had just arrived with a radiant Georgia on his arm. The two of them strolled onto the terrace, gazing into each other's eyes, obviously very much in love.

'Will you look – here come the lovebirds,' Alison said. 'I have a feeling Georgia has done the business!' She felt a pang of envy. Why couldn't it be her and Miguel!

Georgia smiled and waved to all – making sure to use her left hand! – as herself and Jose moved through the tables. She was dressed in a simple black cocktail dressed and looked very pleased with herself as she sat down.

'Well Georgia, are you coming home with us tomorrow or have you other plans?', Alison was unable to contain her curiosity.

All eyes turned on Georgia. 'The answer to the first part of your question, Alison, is yes, I am flying home with yourself and Bernice tomorrow. But I don't expect to be back in Finglas for long…' She paused for dramatic effect. 'And here's the reason why.' She held out her left hand. The emerald ring on her third finger caught the light and sparkled.

Bernice jumped to her feet. 'Georgia, so you and Jose are engaged! Congratulations!'

Alison put her envy aside and also jumped to her feet. 'Congratulations from me too.' She hugged the happy couple. The excitement at the table was attracting the attention of others and soon they were joined by Alo and Mamie, Des and Evelyn, Ben and Irene and Paula and her daughter. All the ladies seemed to be talking at once, each eager to inspect Georgia's engagement ring.

'To celebrate we will have champagne for all!', Jose shouted above the din. He gestured to a waiter. 'Bring a bottle for every table – '

Everyone gasped, then cheered. 'Careful Jose,' Georgia said, half in earnest. 'You'll bankrupt yourself before we even have the wedding!'

Jose spread his arms wide. 'I don't care. I have just become engaged to the prettiest girl in Ibiza. I could not be happier!'

'Where did you get that lovely engagement ring, Georgia?' Caroline asked.

'From Jose's mother. It's a family heirloom.'

'An heirloom! That means it's worth a fortune...' Alison could envisage the excitement in the Cappagh House when Georgia's Ma and Da insisted she show it off to their drinking friends there.

Pez of the Dubs' Angels called Jose and Georgia up on stage where they kissed passionately and Georgia again displayed her engagement ring in the spotlight. Alison was afraid she would turn as green as the engagement ring with envy. She would go to bed and cry her eyes out only it would look bad on her part. Anyway, there was champagne on the way...

Jose stepped forward on stage. 'I would like to make a short speech,' he announced. 'The past two weeks have been the happiest of my life. I met my lovely Georgia and we fell in love. We will have a romantic wedding on this island in a few months time and I thank you all most sincerely for your good wishes. After we are married Georgia and I will live here in Ibiza; I will be in charge of Jose's Hacienda while Georgia will run her own boutique. Anytime over the years when you return to Ibiza you are invited to call in and say hello to us – and the children!' When the laughter and applause died down Jose concluded. 'Finally I wish all my Irish friends a safe journey home tomorrow. Gracias and buenos noches!'

Pez and the band started up a rousing Irish number and Georgia and Jose lead the couples on the terrace up to dance. In the midst of the celebrations Doc Holliday felt a tap on the shoulder. He turned, saw it was the young man from reception.

'Excuse me, Mr. Holliday, there is a telephone call for you – in the foyer.'

Doc rose from the table. He looked at his watch. It showed one fifteen a.m. Who the hell would be calling him at this hour he wondered? Maureen and Yolanda were busy congratulating Georgia and Jose and admiring the engagement ring; he left them to it and entered the reception area. The young man gestured towards one of the public telephones.

'Hello, hello. Alec Holliday here...'

The voice sounded slurred. 'Well, if it isn't my old pal Doc, the dancing master...'

Alec froze. He recognised the Dublin voice. Donie Crawford! His head cleared and he was suddenly sober. 'Who is this?'

'Don't be playacting. You know who it is.'

'What do you want, Donie?,' Doc said after a pause.

'You know what I want. I want that packet back.'

'I haven't got it. The police took it.'

'Did they now. That's bad news – for you.' Doc's mouth had gone dry. He swallowed, said nothing. 'Are you still there, dancing master?' he heard Donie say.

'Yes.'

'You set a trap for me last night with the police. Cost me a lot of money. That wasn't very nice. Now, me oul' pal, it's payback time – '

'I've just told you, I haven't got your heroin!,' Doc shouted. The receptionist looked up in surprise at the raised tone.

'You're a big hero now, Mister Holiday. Picture in the papers, even got yourself featured on local tv....' Donie's tone changed, became harsher. 'In our business we don't like informers – '

Yolanda's words about the drug barons being ruthless raced through Doc's mind. Back home people had been beaten or stabbed to death, sometimes shot and their bodies dumped in lonely woods, found in the canal. Houses had been set on fire while their occupants slept, every week, it seems, a gruesome death. Doc began to sweat.

'Are you threatening me, Donie?'.

'Course not old pal. Let's just say I'm warning you what could happen if you're not careful...' A pause. 'You still living in Ringsend, Doc? ' When he didn't reply Donie went on. 'Not being very co-operative, are yeh? No problem, I have friends back home who will find out and call around to see you sometime. It might be during the night, when you're asleep. Something shoved in through the letter-box, or thrown through your window – ' Donie laughed. It wasn't a nice sound.

'Get lost, Donie. You don't frighten me, you scumbag!' He knew he didn't sound convincing.

'You'll be hearing from me, dancing master. Now go back to your friends and don't ever show up here again. You've just had your last tango in Ibiza!'

The line went dead. Doc put down the receiver, stared at it for a few moments. He could hear the music and laughter coming from the pool area. It seemed a world away from what he had experienced moments ago. He turned, walked slowly out onto the terrace, rejoined Yolanda and Maureen at the table.

He saw the two women staring anxiously at him. 'Alec, what is wrong? Has something happened?', Yolanda asked.

In a dull voice he began to tell them about the telephone call.

CHAPTER EIGHTEEN

Des Murtagh struggled to get his breath as mounds of pills showered down on him. There were brown ones, green ones, red ones and even multicoloured ones. He covered his face with his hands. Petrified he peeped through his fingers. The pills rained down on him like confetti, except they were sharp and hard. He felt some of them hit the back of his neck. He jumped up and tried to hide…

'Des!, Des, what is it? Wake up for God's sake!', Evelyn screamed, snapping on the bedside light.

He lay back on the pillows, perspiration pouring from him. 'I'm okay, love,' he answered shakily. 'Must have been having a nightmare. He'd had a couple too many of those cheap Spanish brandies at the party last night.

Des tossed and turned, tried to get back to sleep. Thoughts raced through his brain. The party last night with the Dubs' Angels had been great fun. Evelyn had been in top form, joining in all the singalongs. She wouldn't be caught dead doing that at home!

He thought of Alo Riordan and the new job awaiting back home. What if when they got back to Dublin things didn't work out? Being on holiday was a false life, the sun is shining, drink is flowing, chat it cheap. You get on well with someone for a fortnight but if you meet them back home things are different. You look at their holiday snaps, they look at yours, and that's it. End of relationship.

What if Alo is already having second thoughts about employing me?, Des thought as he twisted and turned.

If I'm such a top salesman he's probably asking himself why I was let go from my old job.

The nightmare had left him exhausted. His head ached. Thank heavens there were some Panadol still left in his case. He'd have to buy his own from now on, say goodbye to free samples. Des turned out the bathroom light, went back to bed. Evelyn was already sound asleep.

The sun was streaming into the room when Des opened his eyes. The remains of the headache was still there. He could hear the water running in the bathroom where Evelyn was showering. She had done the packing before they went out last night; he saw their going home clothes handing on the wardrobe door. No sense asking Evelyn to go to the beach for a swim, a last stroll around Figueretas. Going home was all she was thinking about at this stage. Des pulled on a pair of shorts over his swimming togs, called out to Evelyn and headed for the beach.

There's something special about the last day of a holiday, Des reckoned. The sun always seemed warmer, the sky bluer, the sea more inviting. Only now you couldn't enjoy it because it was the last day and there was that empty feeling of leaving it all behind. Still, the coach wasn't due at the hotel until midday so he had a couple of hours yet…

At the beachside cafes waiters were already serving 'full Monty' breakfasts – bacon, two eggs, tomato, beans and sausage. Des was deciding he might indulge himself after his swim when he spotted Alo and Mamie Riordan ahead. He smiled and watched them stop to study a kerbside menu; they obviously fancied a 'full Monty!'

Suddenly Des froze, felt apprehensive. Two Spanish youths in white t-shirts caught his attention. They were sitting astride a motor scooter and were eyeing Alo and Mamie. The more Des looked the more he was convinced the two were up to no good. The courier and the guide books warned of scooter thieves who had bag-snatching down to a fine art.

Des broke into a run. Just as he did so the two youths drove their scooter towards their prey. Alo and Mamie, engrossed in studying the menu, were oblivious to the danger. Des shouted a warning but his voice was lost in the traffic. He saw the pillion passenger reach out and grab Mamie's handbag, wrenching it cleanly off her shoulder. Des grabbed a plastic chair from a nearby table and jumped into the middle of the road, into the path of the scooter which had done a u-turn and was heading in his direction.

The scooter driver was so surprised he didn't even try to swerve. Instead the windscreen took the full impact, the driver lost control and he and his companion sprawled onto the road. Des grabbed Mamie's handbag, turned, and saw that the two robbers had scrambled to their feet. They jumped back onto the scooter, shouted an obscenity at Des, and disappeared at speed while onlookers stood in amazement.

The owner of the café came out onto the road. 'I will call the police, senor. You are a brave man, you stood like a toreador facing the bull. And you used the chair with the skill of a matador. Congratulations!'

People on the pavement and the café's customers burst into applause. A shocked Alo and Mamie came over to reclaim the handbag. 'Fair play to you, Des, that was quick thinking on your part. Let's sit down and have something to drink. We could all do with something after that.'

'With pleasure, senor,' the owner replied. 'And it will be on the house!'

When they were seated a shaken Mamie said, 'Des, you saved our lives. Everything was in that bag, passports, tickets and a lot of the jewellery I bought.' When the police arrived the café owner gave them a graphic account of the incident, with much waving of his arms. He even picked up a chair and re-enacted Des's part, much to the amusement of his customers.

'I was a lucky man to meet you on this holiday, Des,' Alo said as they sipped their drinks. Suddenly the apprehension that Des had felt about his new job melted away. His future was secure. He was looking forward to getting home.

'Did you enjoy your swim, Des?', Evelyn asked later when he arrived back at the apartment. Her suitcase was on the floor and she had one knee firmly pressing it down as she attempted to zip it up.

'I didn't have a swim, dear,' Des replied as he went to her aid. 'I had a brandy with Alo and Mamie instead.'

Not long afterwards Evelyn and Des were climbing onto the coach which would take them and their fellow-guests to the airport. Evelyn saw Mamie waving her into the seat beside her.

As Evelyn made her way up the aisle of the coach Mamie had noted how stylishly her friend was dressed for the journey home. She had to admit Evelyn looked really smart in her pale green linen suit and cream slingbacks. But then Evelyn knew how to dress. Mamie was travelling in a track suit, the elasticated waist was a godsend – it covered a multitude! - while her open-toed sandals allowed her feet to breathe. Mamie never wore socks on aeroplanes; she had read somewhere that twiddling one's bare toes helped circulation and prevented blood clots.

Still, Mamie thought, you couldn't beat a bit of style. If she was going to change her image who better to advise her than Evelyn Murtagh. The lady oozed style. Mamie squeezed up in her seat, caught a whiff of expensive perfume as Evelyn sat down.

After they had waved goodbye to the Hotel Orlando, and the coach was headed out of Figueretas towards the airport, Mamie said, 'Evelyn, I'm thinking of changing my image when I get back.'

Evelyn looked surprised. 'Changing your image? In what way?'

'You know, getting one of them things – what do you call them – a makeover!'

Evelyn smiled. 'Mamie dear, are you serious?'

'I am. Very serious.'

'But why? What has brought all this about?'

'You did Evelyn, if you must know – '

'Me!' Evelyn laughed. 'How on earth – '

'Look at you, the essence of style. I admired the way you dressed the first time I saw you at the airport. Even now you look like you're all set for a night out. Me – I look like something out of a jumble sale!'

'But we are on the way home, for heaven's sake – '

'I know, but it's nice to look well – and you certainly do know how to dress, Evelyn.'

'Thank you, Mamie dear.' Secretly Evelyn was pleased. Karl had complimented her on her dress sense also on several occasions.

'When we go back you and I will have to meet for lunch,' Mamie was speaking again. 'We'll go up Grafton Street, into one of those places that give makeovers. I'm determined to revamp my image, Evelyn, inside and out...'

Evelyn felt a bit guilty. She recalled how initially on the holiday she had looked down on Mamie and Alo Riordan, cautioning Des to avoid them. They just weren't her type, too chatty, unsophisticated. Mamie had even brought over a fridge-full of rashers, sausages and black and white pudding, for God's sake! How could one get acquainted with people like that! She had gone out of her way instead to make friends with people like Karl and Maria – and look how that episode with the German couple had ended. It was too painful to think about.

Alo and Mamie Riordan had known even before herself that Des had been made redundant. Typical of Alo, he had come to the rescue and offered a complete stranger like Des a job. Amazing how one can misjudge people sometimes....

Evelyn felt a surge of affection – an emotion quite foreign to her – as she looked at Mamie Riordan's open, kind face. 'Mamie dear,' she replied, 'you don't need a makeover, inside or out.' She squeezed her friend's hand. 'For God's sake do as the song says –'

'And what's that?,' Mamie asked, looking puzzled.

'Stay as sweet as you are,' Evelyn replied sincerely.

— ☽ —

It was with a mixture of relief tinged with regret that Alec Holliday settled himself into the seat beside Maureen Duff on the coach. After the luggage had been loaded on he watched as the vehicle moved off and the Orlando Hotel faded into the distance.

They were on their way to the airport and his holiday in Figueretas was almost at an end. He should be feeling sad, but he wasn't. That telephone call from Donie Crawford in the early hours had been scary. Very disturbing. Yes, he was glad to be leaving Ibiza behind.

'Well, Alec, a few hours from now and we'll be back in Dublin.' Maureen's voice cut across his thoughts. 'I suppose you're looking forward to getting back to your friends in Ringsend?'

Too right I am!, he thought to himself. His friends who had left him to the airport would be there to pick him up when he arrived back. By then the events of the last couple of days would seem like a bad dream. Aloud he said, 'Ah, I don't know, Maureen. 'I'll miss all the crowd and the carry-on. Wasn't it amazing the way something unusual seemed to happen to everyone on our trip during the two weeks?' He laughed despite himself. 'You know if you sat down and wrote a book about all that happened on the holiday nobody would believe it!'

'You were very unfortunate to bump into that former teammate of yours during the holiday,' Maureen commiserated. 'That dreadful man, threatening you like that – '

'Yeah, just my luck to meet up with Donie again,' Doc agreed ruefully.

'Still, I suppose you could say that if you hadn't met up with him you wouldn't have become involved with Yolanda,' Maureen always tried to look on the bright side. 'She's a lovely lady, and you have her visit to Dublin to look forward to. I'm so glad that you two hit it off, Alec. I hope everything works out for both of you.'

'Thanks, Maureen. I'll keep you posted.'

After the hooley had ended in the early hours and they had bid goodnight to Maureen, Doc had insisted on taking Yolanda home by taxi. The threatening phone call from Donie earlier was still occupying both their thoughts.

'I do not want to frighten you, Alec, but you must be very careful when you return to Dublin. Donie may be only bluffing, trying to scare you, but we cannot take a chance – '

They were standing in the darkened street outside her apartment. She had told him to keep the taxi waiting. 'I'll be careful,' he had promised.

'First thing I will do is to alert your police to what has happened here. I will request them to get in touch with your local police station in Dublin for them to keep a special watch on your house. For yourself, you must be alert when you go out jogging alone in the mornings...'

Doc's mind was in a whirl – and it wasn't all to do with the mixture of beer and champagne that he had consumed during the party. His life was really in danger – and he sensed a deeper meaning behind Yolanda's concern for him.

'You really are worried about me, aren't you, Yolanda?'

Now they were standing close, whispering, staring into each other's eyes. He realised just how beautiful she really was. Perhaps it was the moonlight playing tricks, or was it the magic of the moment? Whatever it was they ever so slowly embraced, kissed tenderly. When they broke apart they remained silent, communicating only with their eyes.

Finally Yolanda said. 'You had better go, Alec. We will meet again when I come to Dublin.'

'I look forward to that, Yolanda. Counting the days...' He kissed her again, lightly this time. 'Take care.'

He got into the taxi, waved goodbye. She had stayed on the pavement until the vehicle was out of sight. Back at the apartment he had retired to bed but had not slept too well. And when he did drop off he had a nightmare in which he and Yolanda were being chased down the dark alleyways of Ibiza by a crazed Donie Crawford...

Doc was pleased that there was no delay at check-in and that the flight take-off would be on time. Just before that happened the three girls from Dublin, Georgia, Alison and Bernice provided the passengers with a memorable send-off when, on the tarmac as they were boarding, they unveiled a banner with a message written on it for Jose, Georgia's fiancé, who was looking on from the balcony of the terminal building.

'What's that that's written on the banner?', Doc asked.

"Te amo'. I think that means I love you in Spanish,' Caroline, who was standing with Maureen, said.

'Looks like we'll all be returning to Ibiza in a few weeks time for the wedding!', Maureen remarked, laughing. People on the crowded balcony were cheering and waving.

Georgia was the last to board the aeroplane. At the top of the steps she turned and, as the breeze caught her mane of red hair she gave one last wave and blew a kiss towards Jose. The passengers on board gave her a rousing cheer as the smiling air hostess ushered her inside the aircraft.

Half-an-hour earlier Mark and Wayne had been waiting in the check-in queue, lamenting the fact that they didn't have another week to spend in Figueretas. 'It seems like only yesterday since we were queuing at Dublin

Airport on the way out,' Wayne lamented. 'Two weeks is not enough. Those last few days flew in…'

Yes, another week in Ibiza might have made all the difference, Mark thought to himself. Given more time he might have been able to persuade Caroline not to return to the convent. Still, it was what she wanted. She was happy with her decision and it would have been wrong for him to try to get her to change her mind. Now it was too late.

He had spotted her a short distance ahead on the queue and had been able to have a few words alone with her in the cafeteria before they had boarded. He knew her mother and father were meeting her at Dublin Airport so this would be his last opportunity to get her alone.

'Caroline told me last night that when she returns to her convent she'll talk to her Superior about working in Africa for a couple of years,' Mark had informed Wayne. 'After seeing the carry-on here in Ibiza she figures she would like to work caring for the poor and the underprivileged.'

'Is that the effect I had on her!', Wayne had laughed.

Now, sipping coffee waiting for their flight to be called, Mark reached down into his duffle bag and took our a parcel wrapped in blue paper. 'I have a present for you, Caroline,' he said rather sheepishly.

'What is it?', she asked. It looked a bit big. She hoped she would be able to get it into the overhead compartment on the aeroplane.

'It's a fold-up easel. Every time you use it think of me.'

'Thank you, Mark, I will.'

'And thanks for the portrait,' he said. 'It's a masterpiece – I hardly recognised myself.' She had given him the finished portrait last night after the poolside party. He reckoned it was the best gift he had ever received.

They talked in whispers for a while. All too soon the flight was called. They lingered for several minutes, until the large queue had filtered through. They rose from their seats. This was the end, almost. Mark could sense it. He reached out, took her in his arms. He held her tenderly oblivious of the stares of passers-by. He knew this was the moment to tell her the truth, that he loved her, wanted her. But was he being fair?

Instead he murmured. 'Caroline, you know how I feel about you. If ever you need a good friend, I'll always be there for you. Will you promise to keep in touch?'

She paused and his heart missed a beat. 'Of course, Mark. I'll never forget you.' She stood on her toes, kissed him lightly on the cheek. Then they both made their way downstairs to the waiting aircraft.

The Aer Lingus flight took off on time. Wayne sat back in his seat, relaxed, closed his eyes. Beside him Mark was silent. Wayne didn't try to start up a conversation, he knew Mark wasn't in the mood for talking right now. The guy had Caroline on his mind. He was torturing himself striving for the unattainable. He'll soon get over her, Wayne reckoned.

He thought about tonight. He would meet Mark down at their local, have a few pints. He could almost taste the froth of that cool beer. Afterwards they would hit a nightclub, pick up a couple of girls. Yes, Mark would soon forget Caroline. But what about her friend Maureen? Was she right about himself, Wayne wondered…a nice guy trying to get out. And that bereavement conselling course she had talked about. He had promised her he would go. What the hell, maybe he'd give it a try….

Caroline had said she preferred the window seat, so Maureen sat in the middle with Alec on her left. Maureen felt very relaxed and happy after her two weeks in the sun, but now it was time to go home and make some decisions about her future.

Not long after take-off she got a surprise when Alec, who had been silent up to then, turned to her and said. 'I suppose, Maureen, a maintenance man like myself would be very welcome in one of those centres for the poor in Africa...'

Maureen looked quizzically at him. Alec had obviously something in mind. On the other side of her Caroline was already dozing. 'Why do you ask, Alec? Are you thinking of volunteering your services?'

'Yes I am.'

He had never mentioned anything about doing voluntary work for an aid agency before. But then Alec Holliday's life had taken some unexpected turns since this holiday had begun. 'I've no doubt that someone like yourself, Alec, with your skills, would be a real asset to any agency.'

'That's what I was hoping to hear. I feel a break from Ringsend is called for right now..' He smiled, a grim smile.

'Would I be right in thinking that the threatening phone call you got last night from that dreadful man might have something to do with your wanting to spend some time in Africa?' Maureen asked.

'Absolutely. Yolanda warned me to take it seriously. She's convinced that Donie means business.'

'And what about Yolanda? How can you go to Africa if you've invited her to visit you in Dublin?'

'I'll telephone her in a few days, tell her what I have in mind. Yolanda will understand. We can organise the visit when we both think it's safe.'

'I don't think you'll have any problem being snapped up by one of the aid agencies,' Maureen said. 'I'm considering going back myself, and Caroline is also interested.'

'Well, well, that's a nice coincidence. Maybe we can all work together out there. Tell me more about the work, Maureen...'

Seated across the aisle, Irene O'Rourke was a bit restive. She wished she was home. For the fourth time since they had boarded she asked Ben to check the overhead locker to make sure the hand luggage was secure.

It would be just her luck to have something tumble out and crash down on her head and ruin the holiday.

'Everything's fine, Irene. The air hostess locked it and I checked it myself a few minutes ago. Relax, close your eyes and have a rest. I'll call you when they start serving lunch.'

'Don't bother, Benjamin,' she replied irritably. 'I'm not having any of that plastic food they serve on these holiday flights. And you don't take anything either. I'll upset your stomach!'

Ben sighed. Irene was on edge again. Travelling always made her nervous. He glanced past her, out through the window. Down below he could make out an expanse of blue sea. The holiday was fading fast, well and truly over. And what a holiday it had turned out to be! He had mixed feelings about leaving Ibiza. True to her word Paula had not shown up to say goodbye this morning before they left. He had looked around the pool area briefly but had not sighted her. He would love to have seen her again, just one more time. But it wasn't to be. Had she come back into his life briefly just to exit again? Of course he would see her again when she came to Dublin with Vicki. What would be the outcome of that?, he wondered.

And Vicki…what a lovely young lady. He was so proud to have her as a daughter. What a pity that their past would have to remain a secret.

They were well into the flight now. In less than an hour they would be landing at Dublin Airport. Irene's eyes were closed and she appeared to have fallen asleep. Ben reached into his pocket; maybe not the best time to open Paula's letter, but it was burning a hole in his pocket…

He couldn't believe how nervous he was. Ben glanced around to make sure nobody was taking an interest him. Some passengers were already struggling with food trays. The palms of his hands were moist with sweat as he opened the envelope carefully and extracted the single sheet of paper it contained. Ben caught his breath as he read the printed words:

Birth Certificate of Victoria Maria Sheridan-O'Rourke

The rest of the words on the page swam before his eyes. There was a note clipped to the birth certificate. Ben read the handwriting: 'One day I knew I would give this to you. That time is now.' It was signed Paula.

This document is dynamite, Ben thought. Everything in front of him was a blur. He could feel his heart pounding. What he wouldn't give now for a stiff whiskey!

Beside him Irene opened her eyes. She was staring at him. 'You look like you've seen a ghost, Benjamin! What is that document you have there?'.

A light lunch had been served on board and most of the passengers had availed of the duty free and the drinks trolley. Now eyes were closed, heads were resting as people were lulled into an uneasy sleep by the drone of the jet engines. The sky at thirty three thousand feet was azure blue and reminded those who were still awake of the hazy days of the vacation they had just enjoyed. Memories were fading fast the nearer they got to Dublin Airport.

Seated between Georgia and Alison, Bernice thought about herself and Brian. It was the first ever time on holiday that she had fallen in love with someone and returned with bright prospects for the future. She could hardly wait to arrive home and tell her mother, she had not mentioned Brian in any of the phone calls she had made during the holiday. And the check-out girls she worked with in the Spar Supermarket – they would have something to gossip about during their tea break. Of course behind her back they would laugh and say it was only a holiday romance, but Bernice knew different. This was the real deal – as far as she was concerned, anyway!

What if Brian didn't get in touch, didn't telephone or write? It was too horrible to think about. Of course he would. Deep down she knew he would. She prayed that he would...

In the seat next to Bernice her friend Alison was not feeling too happy. She hoped they wouldn't meet that chatty taxi driver they had hired on the way to the airport when they were leaving. He'd be anxious to know which of them had won that bet they had made in his taxi. It all seemed so long ago now...

Alison was a little depressed – and it wasn't only to do with the fact that they were on the way home. This was the first time ever she had come home from a sun holiday without a man on her mind. Miguel? – that two-timing creep, he wasn't worth thinking about. Although she had to admit he did know how to make a girl happy! Those few nights they had spent together....But that was over and now there wasn't a man on her horizon.

Alison glanced across the aisle at Wayne. She had enjoyed their night out in Amnesia together. He's nice when he's not showing off, which is always. She would prefer someone foreign, more exotic, someone who might look like Pierce Brosnan but didn't think he really was James Bond – like Wayne.

How she envied Georgia! There she was, with a father and mother who would have a hard time finding out where Spain was on a map, and yet their daughter ends up with a wealthy Spanish fella – a count no less! – who is madly in love with her! Talk about luck, Alison thought, some girls have it in spades – and Georgia Fitzgerald was one of them! Trust Georgia to perform her passable imitation of Salome in front of a handsome hunk, desperately looking for someone to fill his run-down pub in Ibiza!

But wait a minute...Alison sat bolt upright in her seat. Why hadn't she thought of it before...Georgia was marrying Jose – that meant she would be looking for a bridesmaid or two – and herself and Bernice must be favourites for the job. After all hadn't she been with Georgia the day they had walked into his bar. I practically introduced them to each other, for God's sake, Alison almost shouted aloud.

And being an aristocratic Spaniard, wouldn't Jose surely have lots of male friends at the wedding in Ibiza? An eligible best man – that's all she was asking for – and he didn't have to belong to the aristocracy or be rich like Jose – although she would have no objection to either! All she was looking for was someone tall, dark and handsome who would make her heart beat extra fast. If she found him she would have the biggest wedding Finglas had ever seen – that would be one in the eye for Georgia!

Alison suddenly reached sideways and squeezed Georgia's hand. 'Don't forget your friends on the big day!', she said. Georgia, lost in her own thoughts, smiled. She hadn't a clue what Alison was on about. Besides, she was thinking of the future…

Was this a dream or was it all really happening? Two weeks ago she had flown out to Ibiza as plain Georgia Fitzgerald from Finglas, now here she was returning with an outsize emerald ring on her finger and a proposal of marriage!

But what was she letting herself in for? Was she getting out of her depth? Jose was a gentleman with fine breeding, he had accepted her for what she was, but what would he think when he came to Dublin, arrived in Finglas and met her Ma and Da? Worst still, what would happen before the wedding when she had to introduce them to the Contessa? Her mother had a bit of style and would get by – but all her Da could talk about was Manchester United and backing horses! Georgia doubted the Contessa would approve. And not in her wildest dreams could she see the grand old lady joining in the fun and sipping a glass of her favourite wine in the Cappagh House!

'Look girls, the fasten-your-seat-belt sign is on,' Bernice voice raised excitedly brought Georgia back to reality. 'We must be approaching Dublin!'

Another few minutes and the familiar disembodied voice of the air hostess announced: 'Ladies and gentlemen, we are now approaching Dublin Airport where we are scheduled to land fifteen minutes from now. Please make sure your seat belts are fastened and that your seat is in the upright position….'

Georgia sat upright and let the rest of the announcement drift over her head. She smiled to herself, a determined look in her eye. That Aer Lingus hostess didn't know it, but she and her colleagues would be seeing a lot of her in the future. By then she wouldn't be travelling as plain Georgia Fitzgerald from Finglas. No way! She would have a handsome husband on her arm and she would be welcomed on board as the Contessa Georgia Simon of Figueretas.

As far as she was concerned - this was as good as it gets!